NEW HISTORICAL VOICE CONTEST FINALIST!

A WELCOME RETURN

Ghostlike, the man and his horse slipped through the snow-clogged dusk, a red line of wool drawing itself on the wind. Dena recognized the too-thin white duster and the red scarf; the pale horse she guessed to be Whisper.

"Thomas? Thomas Howard?" Her shriek of hope hung on the winter wind like an early spring.

The call of his name sliced through the ice of the wind. He rode hard to her side on the surefooted horse, dismounting in disbelief at the dream suddenly true.

"Thomas Howard!" She moved to him as if on angel's wings while he tore the red scarf from his face. "I knew you'd come back to me!"

Her exuberant greeting and his long hours in the saddle weakened his stalwart stance. He hadn't intended to, but when she bounded toward him, he leaned into her and clasped her close. His shoulder protested, but she felt too good for him to mind.

The unrepentant wind warmed for a second as he spun them around in it, the long tails of his coat flapping like a windmill.

"You've been gone so long," she said.

He kissed her face then, mostly to melt the frozen tears on it. It wasn't a real kiss, of course. She was a new widow, after all.

"Oh, Thomas Howard! You've come home!"

THE
OUTLAW'S WOMAN
Tanya Hanson

LEISURE BOOKS NEW YORK CITY

A LEISURE BOOK®

September 2002

Published by

Dorchester Publishing Co., Inc.
276 Fifth Avenue
New York, NY 10001

ISBN 0-8439-5106-0

Printed in the United States of America.

Visit us on the web at www.dorchesterpub.com.

To my husband, T. L.,
for always believing in me
(and for the laptop!);

To our amazing kids, Matt and Christi,
for tolerating my Rocky Mountain locust trivia,
even on our family vacation;

To author Charlene Sands,
for helping me start this story in the right place;

And above all,
to my dear friend Nancy Mohlman Berkeland,
for telling me about an ancestor who met his Maker at
the horns of an angry bull—the inspiration for this tale.

THE
OUTLAW'S WOMAN

Prologue

Late November 1876
Staircase Creek, Nebraska

He was downright bad at gambling. He would have bet his soul that the widow would be remaining in town, soaking up the comfort of kith and kin, not returning to the empty house where her husband had died a gruesome death.

Her potbelly stove still gave off some warmth, although the coals no longer glowed. He sat as close to it as he could and still be able to watch outside from the slit between her curtains. Even though he was cold clear through, he hadn't lit a fire. Not yet at least; he was waiting until night could hide the smoke.

All he wanted was one night in a warm bed in an empty house. He was just passing through, after all.

In disbelief, he heard the wagon's creaking wheels and the mules' plodding feet long before he saw anything. Night was falling fast. Maybe the wagon was headed for the next farm down the road. Maybe the wagon wasn't bringing the widow home. Maybe his luck wouldn't run out.

Maybe.

A washpan blew off the porch in the wind. His heart hammered. He tried to think of something else. Anything. It was a decent place, he decided. He wished he could stay longer. Although most folk hereabouts lived in sod houses, many covered with lime and whitewash, this one was of wood. The house wasn't fancy, just a big room with three small ones shooting off from it, but the furnishings were fine ones, finer than the house deserved. The widow kept a clean house and obviously insisted on fresh paint outside.

The outbuildings, too, were well-tended, tight and secure against the relentless winds of the plains for the livestock and feed stores within. Looked like the farmer used the old soddy as a chicken coop.

Now that he thought for a minute, maybe he ought to find cover in one of those outbuildings.

He waited too long thinking about it. The buckboard bearing passengers was pulling up the drive, not heading down the road to the next farm. He'd gambled and lost.

He couldn't see much, just shadows, as he pulled his revolver from his belt. Sitting back, taut and tense, he waited, not at all sure what he waited for.

A hearty voice broke through the gloom. He could hear clearly through the closed doors and windows but could not determine if the sound came from the throat of a large blustery woman or of a higher-pitched man.

"Now, Dena, I best leave off Georg to help you with chores."

"No, no. Thank you, Olga, thanks to all of you. I'll be fine. I . . . need some time alone. I can check the animals. I love them. It's really no trouble and will give me something to do. . . ."

That must be the widow talking, and damned if he didn't like the sound, trilling like a bird, lilting like stream water.

"But that dreadful bull . . ." The booming voice again.

"No, Olga, I'll be fine, truly. He's not a house pet, but he has never threatened me."

The booming voice—Olga, apparently a woman—muttered loudly.

That dreadful bull. Vague saloon gossip about her husband's horrible death started crowding his thoughts. Of course she would be grief-stricken, confused, unable to cope. He'd never taken a hostage, but . . .

The pretty voice persisted. "Honestly, Olga, Wilhelm, children. You are all much too good to me. I truly will be fine. Now, it's powerfully cold out. You all hurry home. It's freezing."

"We're likely to get snow 'afore morning," said a man; Wilhelm probably, Olga's husband. "We'd best set up Willie and Georg to sleep in your barn. They can get a start on chores first thing."

"Fine idea! We just don't feel right about leaving you all alone." Olga's words clattered in the wind like the washpan. "Ida's thirteen now. She can stay over and help . . ."

Fingers tightening on his gun, he tensed. That's all he needed, a passel of kids and no place to hide.

But he listened gratefully as the widow refused, emphatic. Indeed, he liked the voice more than ever.

"All right, then"—Olga finally succumbed to defeat with a near-shout—"but I'll send the boys over first thing, snowing or not."

First thing. That'd suit him fine. He'd be back out on the trail by then, snowing or not. All he needed was this one night.

The cart clattered away after several more minutes of effusive good-byes.

In spite of the cold, hot sweat collected under his arms. His brain empty of ideas, his breath became short hard gasps. He couldn't ever remember his heart beating this hard. What on earth should he do? Jesse disavowed violence on women.

But she didn't come right in, this widow, this . . . Dena? He realized she must have gone directly to the barn and chicken coop to tend the livestock. What else had she said, that she

3

loved them? A downright odd notion, that. Farm folk either sold their animals or slaughtered them; they didn't love them.

He moved to the kitchen window and watched her walk across the farmyard in the last of the daylight. Her black clothes whipped about her like angry Jolly Roger sails on a pirate ship. And she undulated just as a ship might over the thrust of waves.

Indeed, he liked what he saw, even in the silly clothes. In fact, he'd liked what he'd seen this morning from the trees along the creek past the graveyard, her golden curls dancing in the wind, her lovely face properly downcast as the coffin was lowered into the ground. Her hands at the back of her neck as she looked around, as if she knew someone was watching her. His light-colored garments and his buckskin horse had blended with both the gray day and the bland bark of the trees. He knew she hadn't seen him.

The image of her performing farm chores dressed in the foolish black widow's weeds amused him. He needn't be afraid of that little mite of a thing. He relaxed. Moving from the window, he sat back down in the ladder-back chair near the stove.

Unsuspecting, she walked in, carrying a lantern.

He had no choice. He pointed the gun at her, poised to stomp out the lantern in case she dropped it. He'd seen places like this go up in flames in mere seconds.

The trigger cocked.

"Good evenin', widow lady," was all he said.

Dena dropped the lantern. Then, as if panicked to set it upright, she bent down and did so, lifting her long black skirts away from the flame.

Standing up slowly, she held out her hand.

For a second, he almost reached for it. In the lantern light, her fingers looked small and very white.

"Evenin', intruder," she drawled. She stood taller than he'd expected, confident, meeting his gaze straight on.

"Oh, this little old thing? I wear it on my leg. For moments just like this," she told him calmly, cocking the trigger of her .32-caliber pistol right back at him.

4

Chapter One

Early April 1877

"Gottlieb, it appears I am not barren after all."

Dena Clayter spoke softly to her husband's new headstone, a fancy piece of masonry his brother had ordered from St. Louis. The picture of a dutiful widow, she wiped away a smudge of mud and laid a crocus from her own garden against the marble.

Loving husband. She touched the carved words and snorted.

She hadn't heard any footsteps so the voice startled her. Hurriedly, she pretended the snort had been a sneeze.

"A pleasant sight, you honoring my brother now that the snow has melted. I don't think you have visited his grave since the funeral," Reverend Jonah Clayter chided her gently.

"It's been a long, hard winter, Jonah." She turned to face him, not taking offense. Gottlieb's death had caused his younger brother much pain.

"A crocus is a much more appropriate decoration than that

thing you laid on his coffin." Jonah's voice hardened with criticism.

She bristled, remembering his disapproval of the bunch of winter kale she'd used as a funeral bouquet. "Jonah, flowers don't grow in the winter."

"But tied with a *red* ribbon?"

Closing her eyes for a second, she tried hard to choose careful words. She liked Jonah, she really did, always had. However, in these past months, he had taken his role as her only male relative far too seriously. She was not a child, and he was only six or seven years her senior. Gottlieb had been vastly older than either of them.

"Aaah, Jonah." She couldn't help the sigh. "I did what I could at a very difficult time."

"Well, there are consequences to another inappropriate decision you made. The Pinkerton agent is back, wanting to talk to you again, no doubt, about that fugitive you harbored after Gottlieb's funeral."

Dena felt a chill of fear ripple down her back in spite of the warm sun, but she kept the secret safe behind her eyelids. Just like she kept the tiny mound of her belly covered by a careful arrangement of her skirts.

She'd be showing big soon, though. Songbird, the Oglala medicine woman, had told her practically the exact date she would burst through her skirts, and it wasn't far off.

"He's already been out to your place, but not finding you home figured you might be in town." Always a gentleman, Jonah reached for her hand to lead her to her buggy. "I don't think he figured you to be honoring your late husband. Come to think of it, neither did I." His eyes narrowed in thought, but he remained polite. "I saw you from the parsonage window and walked up here to the graveyard. The agent's waiting. My housekeeper has prepared refreshments."

There was only one thing to say, the same thing she had said for months.

"I did not harbor a fugitive, Jonah. And I've told the Pinkerton the same thing each time he's come by to harass me, about twice a month I should think. I simply showed him the same hospitality that Gottlieb always did to passersby. I let a stranger sleep in my barn on a freezing winter night, just as Gottlieb would have done." Except if the stranger had been a Reb, a redskin, or a darky. She had long despised Gottlieb's attitude of superiority.

"Gottlieb was never a young beautiful widow," Jonah reproved her, "all alone on the prairie."

"I can protect myself. I have a gun." She remembered pointing it at the stranger, remembered how terror had both chilled and heated her skin.

Remembered the look he had given her, like no other man had looked at her before.

She could still see his face.

"I'll talk to this Pinkerton, but after that, let the matter rest, Jonah," she advised him in a rush, both eager and frightened to relive the memories.

The reverend assisted her into the buggy, something she could do by herself perfectly well. He assumed the reins, clucking the horse into a trot toward town, a half-mile away. Shrugging, she accepted that he would never allow a woman to drive him.

She took one last look at the graveyard. The crocus sparkled like starlight against the dark marble. Around her, spring tried hard to come to life. The sky was blue, although the wind was brisk with leftover winter. Slush still caught at the buggy wheels.

Across the rolling knolls, she saw the stand of cottonwoods along Staircase Creek, where the stranger had said he'd stood, watching her pull the silly widow's veil from her head after the burial. She remembered the biting cold, the townsfolks' grief. Their hidden gratitude that the man gored to death hadn't been one of their own.

Her own hidden gratitude that now she was free.

Today, all around her, the patchwork of neighbors' places hugged the earth as it warmed back to life. Even so, she shivered. All these months, she had tried to keep her lies simple

7

so as to recall them without confusion later. Right now she had a few minutes during the ride to the parsonage to recollect her stories for the waiting Pinkerton.

It was also time to reanimate the grieving widow. She knew she wouldn't look pale; the breeze added blush to her face all on its own. But tears—she could manage those.

She couldn't remember his name, but she had never forgotten his cold, hard eyes. He sat at the dining room table where Jonah's housekeeper, Mira Wuebke, hovered eagerly, almost as if she were in truth the lady of the house.

"Mrs. Clayter." The agent rose with a nod, then pointed to a chair. "Join me."

Dena sat, pulling Jonah down on the chair next to hers whether or not the Pinkerton's invitation had included him.

Mira brought more coffee, pausing near Jonah longer than necessary. A comely widow in her mid-thirties, she could not easily disguise her interest in the handsome young reverend. However, Dena knew that Jonah would never develop an interest in a woman older than himself. Of course, no one had imagined it unusual that Gottlieb had been nearly as old as Dena's father. She felt some pity for Mira, who would never have the man she wanted.

Just as Dena felt pity for herself. For the same reason.

"Once again I offer condolences." The Pinkerton's sly perusal acknowledged the impropriety of the sprigged muslin dress she wore, and he did nothing to soften the insult of his tone. Jonah, too, appeared horrified at her lack of widow's garments. Indeed, purple was an acceptable color for a widow to wear, but not a cheerful gown covered with lilacs.

"Yes, Mr. Pinkerton?" she responded dutifully.

He colored. "I am not Allen Pinkerton. I am Gordon Bruce. Agent Bruce."

"Well then, Agent Bruce, I don't have any more information for you today than I've had before, the last time you made opportunity to disbelieve me."

"Ah, Mrs. Clayter, you misunderstand the reason for my

visit." His voice and face were smug. "It is I who have information for you. The wounded outlaw you befriended has been apprehended and awaits trial in a jail in the small town of Colbyville. In Clay County, Missouri, of course. I figure he'll spend twenty-five years in prison." He looked at her with a smirk. "Same as the Youngers. This time it didn't pay to ride with Jesse James." His voice, granitelike, grated into her soul. "He won't be around to threaten you for a very long time. You'll be an old, old woman by the time he's paroled."

She nearly spilled the hot coffee as she raised the cup to her lips. Straining to maintain her composure, she nodded, as if to agree that the world would now be a safer place.

Placing the cup back down on the table, she laid her hand on her belly as surreptitiously as possible.

The baby moved, deep inside her, for the first time.

Twenty-five years in prison! It couldn't be true. She couldn't believe it. She willed herself to keep her face impassive as the Pinkerton nodded curtly at her.

As Jonah led the agent to the door, Dena rose from the table and sank, shocked and weak, into the overstuffed Queen Anne armchair in the parlor. Gottlieb's body had been laid out in this very room those months past. That didn't matter now; it hadn't mattered then. But twenty-five years in prison! That mattered.

Her breath started to gush out in gasps.

"Dena, are you all right?" Mira came to stand beside her, bearing a tea tray. The two men finally left the house, remaining in deep conversation on the street as the agent mounted his horse.

She fought for self-control. "Oh, yes, Mira. I'm fine. It . . ." She looked around the room, inspired. "It is just difficult at times to be in this house, remembering Gottlieb . . ."

Mira nodded as if she understood. Being a widow herself, maybe she did. Dena had always felt some affinity for the housekeeper, since both had been married to sour, much-older men. And most times Mira was more a friend than a servant, but Dena had never considered her a confidante before and certainly wouldn't now.

"Well, here's some chamomile tea for you. It'll calm you right down."

"No thank you, Mira. I must be on my way. There never seems to be an end to the chores." She tried to speak of normal daily things, although a knot tied itself tightly inside her stomach.

"Come now. You can make time for one little cup. It'll do you a world of good." She handed Dena a dainty china cup.

Dena smiled her thanks, realizing the truth of Mira's words. The tea, in fact, did comfort her somewhat. The warmth of the cup stilled her shaking hand, and the liquid soothed her tight throat.

"How right you are about the endlessness of chores," Mira chatted leisurely, although she remained standing, holding the tray. Then she continued, with more authority than she had right to. "Jonah insists that you hire real farmhands for spring planting. Those little Pott boys can't know much about plowing and sowing."

"Yes, I know his feelings." Dena sighed, having heard them endlessly for months. "And I have been making arrangements." In a halfhearted way, she honestly had been. But in the last few moments, a new network of lies had begun to weave through her thoughts. She had to get to Missouri. She'd perfected the art of untruth quite well these past months. Surely her next batch of lies would be believed. It would serve her well to have Mira as an ally, so she'd try them out on the housekeeper first. She had no other choice; she had to get to Missouri.

"My . . . cash reserves are a bit low, Mira, as anyone can expect. In fact, I've considered taking a trip to Missouri. My late father advised Gottlieb in some investments. I need to meet with my father's colleagues as to income I may be able to access for improvements and hiring help." Her voice shook, both with the residual shock and the disharmony of falsehood.

Mira didn't act like Dena's behavior was at all odd. "That

sounds like a reasonable way to establish funding for your needs. I doubt that Reverend Clayter will have time to leave the congregation, but I'm certain he will give me a few days' holiday."

"What on earth do you mean?"

Mira's blue eyes blinked in disbelief. "Well, Dena, you certainly can't travel without a companion!"

Dena hadn't had time to consider the popular notion that a lone woman wasn't deemed fit to travel unchaperoned. None of it mattered; she had to get to Missouri.

"Nonsense," she declared. "I am a respectable widow perfectly capable of traveling a few hundred miles. I've been to Boston many times. I've even been to London and Paris."

"Not by yourself."

"No, but I am an able grown-up woman. I wouldn't allow either of you to be taken away from your responsibilities on my account. In fact, I will tell Jonah of my decision as soon as he comes back in."

Mira shrugged and strode back to the kitchen.

Dena's brother-in-law was in no hurry to join her. His conversation with the Pinkerton had gotten so involved that the agent swung back off his horse. By now, she could see from the window that Sheriff Eilert and a large group of other townsmen had joined them. The Pinkerton was gesticulating vigorously as he talked. Obviously the capture of a notorious James gang member was news of grave import.

She waited restlessly for Jonah. For a brief second, she considered hurrying him along by joining the male group outside. Already she could see the outrage in his eyes. But she needed him as an ally, too, so she dared not annoy him.

A shaft of April sunlight shot silver and copper through her gold hair. She touched the sun's warmth on her cheek as Jonah finally entered the parsonage and came to her side. Obviously the convocation with the Pinkerton and the town's male population had concluded.

"Come, Dena, you are exhausted. Let me drive you home."

"No, Jonah, there's no need." But she *was* tired. Songbird

had already warned her that these early months would tire her more than the later ones, even though the load she now carried inside was small. At least she had never been sick upon waking. "No, Jonah, I feel fine. The sunlight is warm, and . . ."

The time for small talk was over. She needed to get to Missouri. She needed to tell Jonah now.

After she was finished, his words did not surprise her. The loudness did. Jonah was the type of preacher who made his best points in tones no louder than a stage whisper.

"I forbid it. You will not travel to Missouri alone. Surely the bank in town can make any financial arrangements by wire. And certainly Gottlieb would have let me know of any accounts still in Missouri."

For once, Dena was tired of his overbearing masculinity.

"Jonah, the matter is settled. I am not a helpless child. Gottlieb was a married man. He certainly did not confide everything to you. I'll be making travel arrangements in the morning. You can assist me if you choose. But forbid me . . . that is neither your responsibility nor your right."

In an angry huff, she left him and boarded her buggy without his help. Then she settled down and slowed the horses. Didn't shock and bad news make babies lose their moorings in the womb?

She patted her belly for safekeeping.

The cell was damp and cramped, but at least he didn't share it with anybody. And at least it'd all be over soon. There'd be a trial, and then he'd be on his way to the gallows. A scapegoat for Northfield's body count, certainly, but mostly for the old Swede found murdered in his shanty.

Chapter Two

Six days later, Dena hugged Olga Pott and boarded the Burlington–Missouri River line bound for St. Joseph. Olga had brought her through the freezing dawn. April's fine weather had temporarily turned back to winter.

At first, Jonah had refused to take her to the depot in Seward, but he'd relented enough to arrive in time to see her off. He held out a basket lunch that Mira had lovingly prepared. His face was so grim and stern that Dena hugged him, too, and gave him a merry smile.

He blushed at the contact but managed a half-smile.

"You'll wire me as soon as you arrive."

It was an order, pure and simple, but she decided not to be defiant. His request was reasonable.

"Yes, Jonah, I will telegraph you as soon as I'm settled." Before he could nag her further or ask when she intended to return, she ran to the conductor, who helped her onboard. Olga followed quickly, hauling Dena's luggage.

The locomotive hooted its departure signal, and the steam

hissed as it fused with the icy air. Dena saw Jonah's mouth moving but ignored him, shaking her head and pointing to her ears to show that she couldn't hear him over the din.

She was traveling lightly. Her wearing the unattractive widow's garments had pleased her brother-in-law—he'd nodded in approval when he'd arrived at the depot—but it was a precautionary measure rather than for propriety's sake. Only the most heartless cretins would bother a grieving widow. And she could hide behind the heavy fall of black bugle lace if she arranged it right; then she wouldn't have to talk to anyone.

The ungainly gown had barely closed around her midsection, though, even after she'd let the seams out as much as the fabric would allow. Grimacing a little, she already realized the impending discomfort of sitting still for hours so tightly trussed.

Settling in the coach at a window, she found the worn red velvet seat amazingly comfortable. She waved to Jonah and Olga and placed the large food basket on the aisle seat next to her. The train had started to move, and passengers scrambled for places. If possible, she'd prefer no one next to her.

She had plans to make and memories to recall, memories of the day that had changed her forever. The touch of cold clods of dirt that she smacked against Gottlieb's coffin. The smell of the outlaw's blood dripping on the floor of her house.

The sound of his trigger cocking, and hers replying in kind.

She would never forget the sound. The metallic clicks had bounced around the room like bullets, and now they bounced around her brain. That November day came alive in her mind.

Her gun never moved. She held her arm straight and true. The intruder never moved either. His eyes had widened so large that she could see white all around both pupils.

"I can't even begin to imagine what you think you're doing uninvited in my home." In spite of the terror racking her nerves, she tightened the shaking in her voice and hardened her tone. "A sensible woman by herself on the wide prairie simply can't be too careful."

She remained standing, although she suspected that the last of her strength would leak from her knees any second.

"Learning to shoot was one of the first things my late, lamented husband taught me. Perhaps you've heard of such great generals as Red Cloud and Crazy Horse? For some reason, they always made my husband nervous, although I admire them tremendously." She almost sounded conversational, but in the lantern light, she knew her face was pale with panic.

The intruder's mouth gaped open like a fish caught on a line. She pretended a nonchalance she didn't feel while she swallowed gasps of fright. Truth was, she'd never been this scared before, not even during Gottlieb's rantings.

Her voice shook, although her words tried to be brave. Now was the time for the lessons her husband had taught her. But all she'd ever shot were pumpkins and overripe melons that had splattered like fireworks. She couldn't imagine doing that to a man's brains. But she knew she could do anything she had to.

She remembered once again the pumpkins and ripe melons. Splattering the contents of a man's skull around her well-kept room seemed a nightmare she couldn't make real. Life certainly hadn't prepared her for moments like this. Although Gottlieb had. For a quick moment, she was grateful to him.

She bent her knees carefully and picked up the lantern, keeping her weapon trained on him. Quite surprised, she watched him drop his own gun.

"Kick it over to me," she ordered. He did so, his eyes now a normal shape, his mouth closed.

"What are you doing here?" Her voice had grown incredibly calm, but fear had dimmed it to a whisper.

"I don't mean you any harm." He almost sounded abashed. She waved her gun at him in disbelief.

"It's true." His words were soft in return, sounding almost regretful. "I overreacted, is all."

"Overreacted? You held a Colt forty-five on me. That's attempted murder where I come from. You've broken into my home. I don't normally enter my own house expecting to be shot."

Dena could feel droplets of sweat crown her upper lip like

a mustache. Hearing his labored breathing, she watched his right arm begin to shake. She could almost think that he had never had to look into the barrel of a gun before, but he was probably just exhausted after a long ride. A sweat-stained hat rested by his feet. His boots had tracked slush across her floor.

"Sorry, ma'am. Truly sorry about your husband."

While maintaining her true aim, Dena shook her head in wonderment. What was this, a polite intruder? Her spine was strained with her stiff stance, and her breath became gasps again. She longed for control but didn't dare close her eyes to try to gain composure. Finally she found some words.

"You should have come to the wake to offer proper condolences." Her voice was dry and hard, the gun still true and straight. "Just answer me: What are you doing in my home?"

It frightened her, not that he was in her home, but that she was starting not to mind. He'd put down his Peacemaker without hesitation, and he was looking at her in the lamplight with frank admiration.

She hadn't gotten a look like that in a long time.

For a second, she looked back. His black hair hadn't been properly trimmed for months and lay tousled across his wide shoulders. Somehow its raggedness endeared him to her. Under dark brows, his cheeks were pale. But then, the lantern light was poor.

"I just want a place to sleep tonight." His lips moved over fine, well-shaped teeth. "And a warm place for my horse."

Dena was no great judge of age, but he seemed younger than Jonah. And Gottlieb could have been the intruder's father. He seemed strong and weak at the same time. Maybe he was harmless after all. Then again . . .

She was the one with a weapon.

"Mrs. Rausch runs a boardinghouse in town; nothing fancy but it's clean and warm." Then the realization hit. "Aaah, you're an outlaw!"

Holding a gun, she hadn't been afraid to say the words at first, but horror smacked against her heart again as soon as the syllables left her tongue.

"You're an outlaw!" She repeated the words without a sound. Quickly her mind raced through every room of the house. What could she use to tie him up until Sheriff Eilert got here? Gottlieb kept rope and tack in the barn.

The intruder moved suddenly, but it wasn't a lunge toward her. She really didn't want to kill him. She had managed to disarm him; maybe she could disable him now—shoot him in the knee perhaps—then tie him up. But all he did was sag. In the lantern light, she could see his eyes dull with defeat. With pain.

Moving the lantern, she could see the blood staining the sleeve of the thin white linen duster he wore.

She watched as his blood seeped onto the floor.

Dena didn't normally trust her instincts. They had failed her in the past. Although she had never loved Gottlieb, she had had no qualms about marrying him, for his manner had been kindly and proper at the surface. Not until after the vows were spoken had he given her a glimpse of his brutish nature.

However, on this cold, dark night, compassion reared its noble head. And she, she who could defend a killer bull, tried to trust once again.

"A wounded outlaw," she amended, hanging the lantern and her black cloak on hooks and rushing over to him. The gun, however, remained trained on him.

Stretching a little, he seemed to regain some strength. "I apologize for the mess on your carpet. I'm wounded, but not helpless; not yet anyway." He settled back on the chair.

"I just need food and a bed. And a stall for my horse, just for one night. I can pay. I can clean up after myself, help with chores before I leave in the morning. Done that aplenty."

"I don't need the money. Too bad you didn't offer condolences for real—you just missed a great funeral feast. Stand in the light. Let me look at you." Finally she tucked the gun in one of her skirt pockets. His she kicked across the floor into the shadows of her bedroom.

He obeyed her as she continued, "Enough food to feed five thousand."

"You don't seem too . . . mournful," he chided, as though she were the one caught in wrongdoing.

"Stand still," she ordered. "What kind of injury is this? What did you do?" She helped him shrug out of the long, blood-stained coat. "I should be ashamed, I suppose, but I just don't miss him. Truth to tell, I don't think I ever will. He was . . . he was . . ." She fought for ladylike words, totally chagrined that she was speaking to a stranger what had never been told to anyone else.

He helped her out. "A mean son of a bitch?"

"Watch your mouth, but yes, I guess you'd be right." Leaving him for a minute, she pumped some water into the sink. She swished a rag around in the water and brought it to him in a bowl.

"This will be cold. If you'd rather, I can light the stove first." Her breath misted around her words in the night air.

He shook his head.

"Let's get this shirt off." She tugged gently. "Now, what kind of wound is it? What happened?"

"Gunshot."

Dena wasn't really surprised, him being an outlaw who couldn't show his face in a respectable boardinghouse. If she was stupid to no longer feel fear, then she'd be a fool. She'd just spent three years being afraid.

He was hurt and weak; she had his gun. Why not try to do a good deed? Even her mean son-of-a-bitch husband had been known for being hospitable.

"It's been a couple months, more like three, I guess," the intruder explained. "It just never healed right, got putrid. Had to be opened up to drain out the corruption a number of times. I'd dislocated the other shoulder just the day before, so I guess I took turns babying one, then the other, and I never had a real chance to heal. Finally I started mending right, but I've been riding hard these last days, too hard I reckon. . . ." At that, he turned silent, and she didn't ask him further.

Feeling safe enough to leave him for a while, she lit the Pennsylvania fireplace and put the teakettle to heat on the cookstove. Compassion had won out. "I've no need to add to your torment with cold water. This will heat up in no time. Go on, sit down. I'll be with you directly." Then she wandered about the big room, lighting lamps.

In better light, her first true look at him had her biting her lips together to keep from gasping. Even though he was pale from the cold and his wound, and no doubt thinner than when he was in full health, she wondered how he'd feel warming her on a cold night. He didn't note her scrutiny, busy as he was unbuttoning his shirt. Expertly.

"Why, you're left-handed!" she said aloud, inanely. Thinking it through, that had been his gun hand, not the injured right.

He looked at her, uncertain. "Yeah. But I can shoot either way." The tattered shirt stuck to the bleeding shoulder, and he flinched.

Dena came over to him with a warm wet cloth, steeling herself for the first sight of the bare wound. She wiped the blood from it gently, stomach ready to churn. However, after Gottlieb's harrowing injuries, this young man's gore, while bleeding afresh, was nothing more than a slim entry that had broken open on his ride. The exit wound, far meaner and still raw, seemed to be piecing together well, flesh firmly entwining, corruption gone.

She tended him, liking it. Not his pain, but the touch, the quiet relief on his face. She ran her fingers, warm from the hot water, across his well-carved shoulders. Without thinking, her fingers traveled to the back of his neck, where she kneaded away the tense tautness. His dark hair was too long, and none too clean, but she touched a curl, almost with longing.

"Oh, that's so good," he moaned, "so good. I think you are my angel of mercy. I think . . . God led me here."

She liked the sounds he made. Maybe when his shoulder healed, she could rest her head on it. Sometime he might be well enough to hold her close. However, Dena Clayter was far too practical and proper for such thoughts to continue. The God-talk comforted her a little, though she didn't let him know.

"Nonsense." She was back to the business at hand. "You give the Lord far too much credit. You came here because you thought I wouldn't be here. Now, let me get some binding for your wound and a shirt of my husband's. If"—she suddenly wondered if he would find it macabre—"if you wouldn't mind. It's not been worn since I last laundered it . . ."

He smiled at her, and in the smile she saw rainbows, the gentle glare of dawn. Instinct told her she had nothing to fear.

"I'm Dena Clayter."

"Pleased to make your acquaintance, Miz Clayter."

"Dena."

He did look pleased at that but said nothing else for a full minute. Then, "Thomas Howard."

"Pleased to make your acquaintance, Mr. Thomas Howard—I think."

They both laughed, somewhat nervously, but she sensed from the hollow way he swallowed the sound that he badly needed food and rest.

"Well, Mr. Thomas Howard, I am not able to compromise my reputation as a proper widow woman by having you as a guest, but you're welcome to the barn. The animals keep it warm, and I'll send along a bottle of Gottlieb's whiskey. He was pretty particular; he never bought the cheap stuff."

Dena watched him watch her. The arrangement was as much to protect him from her than the other way around. She felt stirrings deep in her woman's parts that she had not experienced before.

"There's no hot food," she told him hurriedly, moving to the kitchen area as blood rushed to her legs, her feet, and other parts. "I spent most of the day at my brother-in-law's."

Thomas Howard looked blankly at her. Of course he wouldn't know.

"The reverend."

He nodded. "I did see the funeral procession. He seems quite proprietary of you."

Dena never considered that outlaws spoke properly or used big words. He surprised her. "Yes, he is that. He already takes

20

his position as my only male relative far too seriously."

"And that woman in purple who hung on his other arm—his wife? He has a family?"

"That's his housekeeper, who's never more than three feet from his side. I suspect she fancies herself in love with him. But no family. No one but Gottlieb. And now me, I suppose."

Thomas Howard's face darkened.

"But, wait, people have been bringing me foodstuffs ever since . . . the accident." Dena set out heating up some schnitzel. She found a noodle casserole, and laid out a lovely display of Olga's strudel and fresh bread. "And I've got a clutch of fresh eggs I'll scramble up with some rosemary. . . . Fresh coffee, a pot of Olga's plum jam . . ."

Handing him a towel, she pointed to one of the small rooms. "There's a washstand in there, and here's the rest of the hot water. If you want to wash up."

She fussed over him almost as if they kept house together for real. She sensed that he liked it. From a cupboard she brought him a clean shirt and some of her own lavender soap. It had never pleased her to cook for Gottlieb; he had criticized nearly everything she prepared even though he knew well that she had been raised in a household with servants. She simply tried her best; most of the time she was downright successful. Tonight, of course, with the neighbors' bounty, she doubted she would fail.

Suddenly Dena recalled the repast at the wake, and that she hadn't eaten much of anything. Her stomach roiled in anticipation as the scents filled the room.

Dena put a candle in the center of the table and brought out two plates of her mother's fine china.

Thomas Howard ate rapturously, as though the meal would be his last. Dena couldn't help herself, scraping her chair closer to him than she should. Was she a faithless tramp of a widow, an inappropriately randy whore? This outlaw was most certainly a thief and a murderer.

No. She was just a woman, wanting the gentle touch of a

21

man whose eyes told her he admired her. And if he were a murderer, she'd have been dead before now.

She tried to make polite conversation. "So where are you bound, Thomas Howard? Or would you rather I not know?"

"I'll never tell you anything you don't need to know."

"Fair enough."

"Zee's Place." He took a big bite of creamy noodles, and ate with both energy and manners.

"Well, you don't have far to go—eleven miles on a good horse—but it's not much of a place." She laughed. "A feed store and a 'hotel' no decent lady would step foot in, and a saloon that Gottlieb used to say was nothing more than a spittoon full of bad homemade moonshine not good enough to swallow. Although I promise you he swallowed his share."

"Got kin there." His closed voice told her all she needed to know.

Outside, the wind screamed. Both of them shivered at the sound. Remembering, Dena spoke. "Where's your horse? You didn't put him in the barn."

"No. I tethered him in the stand of trees behind the soddy. He . . . he and I both have spent nights like this under the stars."

"Are you strong enough to stable him, or shall I do it? No animal spends nights like this outside if I can help it."

The hot coffee and hearty meal had obviously strengthened him. He stood up at once.

"Gottlieb's"—she pointed at a hook by the door—"Gottlieb's coat. Take it. Yours ought to be burned."

As soon as Thomas opened the door, her famed farm hounds bounded in. She knew of her neighbors' amusement that she allowed them to sleep indoors and, since Gottlieb's death, on her bed.

"Edgar! Allan!" The dogs licked her effusively, and then dashed off to the small room she and Gottlieb had shared. They would sleep with her and keep her warm, and he wouldn't be around to yell about it. After watching them affectionately, she turned to Thomas, suspicion in her voice.

"How in the world did you get inside my house? The dogs don't cotton to strangers in the best of times, and this week has been among the worst. They've even snarled at Willie and Georg Pott, my neighbors, who helped raise them."

"That is a terrible-sounding name."

"Watch your mouth. It is the German way for George. We are most of us German around here. I notice you didn't complain about Olga's strudel, nor her schnitzel, nor the jam."

"I meant no criticism." Thomas Howard hurriedly changed the subject. "The dogs truly snarled and showed nice large teeth. I made friends with them with jerky from my saddlebags."

Dena had to laugh. "Now they will be your slaves for life."

The wind wound itself around their ankles, tight like a noose. Thomas shut the door. "What did you call them?"

"Edgar and Allan."

"After Mr. Poe? He's just about my favorite."

"Yes." Dena was both surprised and pleased. "A long time ago, in another life, I studied literature for a little while. At Missouri State College."

His eyes grew as big as the frying pans hanging on the wall behind the cookstove, although this time she didn't see white outlines. Dena wished she hadn't said it; he was probably like Jonah and Gottlieb, who both considered tuition money spent on a woman the worst form of wastefulness. Jonah himself had never minded teaching girls to read at the one-room parochial school, but only so they could learn the catechism and read the Scriptures. Once they were thirteen or so, they simply prepared to run a household and farm. Reading literature—now, that would be a true waste of time.

Whatever he started to say turned into, "If you could get me a blanket or two, I'll just settle in the barn after I stable Whisper."

"Whisper," Dena breathed. "What a lovely name."

Thomas seemed a bit embarrassed by it. "He's light-colored and light on his feet, got a quiet disposition."

By then, she had made up her mind. Maybe this time the Lord would allow her instinct to be correct.

"No, Thomas Howard." No man who appreciated Mr. Edgar Allan Poe and who gave a manly horse a gentle name would freeze this night in her barn. "You bed down Whisper, then take a place in the sickroom." Pointing to another of the small rooms, she got up to clear the dishes. She saw no need to explain that the room had been the place where Gottlieb had finally died. The little cavelike chamber was the warmest room in the house.

Thomas Howard went outside.

Tossing the horrible black clothes in a heap on the floor, Dena washed her body and teeth and brushed out her hair. Even the huge dogs hadn't warmed the sheets enough by the time she crawled in. She shivered, almost missing Gottlieb. There was, of course, going to be another warm male in her house this night. She had nurtured him, fed him.

She wanted him. It was as simple and as shameful as that. Even in the dark, she blushed as if someone could see her thoughts.

The candle on the table was sputtering its last before she heard him come back inside. She knew he stood in the doorway. She could smell him; not just the lavender soap and the rusty blood smell of the wound, but the man that was all of him.

He came to the bed and leaned over her. Edgar and Allan didn't even stir.

"My thanks to you, Dena. Good night."

Her arms opened to him like unfolding flower petals, but all he did was touch her, whisper like, on her cheek.

"Thank you," was all he said, again.

He left the room and pulled shut the calico drapes that closed it off from the main room.

Once during the night she heard him call out in his sleep. She thought he said Jesse but was too dream-befuddled herself to know for sure. She didn't go to him. Not only was she too snug and comfortable in her own bed, but she was also too afraid of what she might do when finding him in his.

Chapter Three

Dena knew it was morning and that snow had fallen during the night. Her three winters on the prairie had taught her to sense the hushed moist crush of the first snowfall.

Her little room was quiet and very cold.

She did not know that Thomas Howard had already left. Hearing noises outside, Edgar and Allan began to whine, bounding toward the front door. Dena climbed into her clothes, running a careless brush through her hair, undecided whether to feel frantic or not.

Emerging into the warmth of the big room, she saw that the Pennsylvania fireplace had been lit. A hot pot of coffee sat on it. She knew from the sounds—and the sight from the window—that only trouble lay ahead.

Where was Thomas?

Sheriff Eilert had ridden his horse with vigor through the cold morning. The animal's breath rose like smoke from a flue hole. And accompanying the lawman was a group that could only be described as a posse. Little excitement occurred in Staircase Creek. She could see friends and neighbors, flushed with enthusiasm, trying to tame their shying mounts.

Gottlieb himself would have been thrilled at such a scene, eager to join. But today's news she was sure she already knew, and she wondered what lies to tell.

Leading the pack, however, was a well-dressed stranger, not the sheriff. Eilert in fact even allowed the stranger to call out loud orders on his behalf.

She opened the front door and let the dogs out, knowing that they would nip and circle the jittery horses, adding to the men's tension. Chiding her dogs would give her something to do if she needed time to think.

Then she saw them, the hoofprints in the fresh snow, leading in the opposite direction from Zee. Maybe Thomas Howard had lies of his own to tell, but at least he had gotten away. More important, however, was what she saw in her memories, the eyes as clear as rainwater that looked at her as no other man ever had.

"Good morning, gentlemen," she called out. The cold slapped her in the face, but she felt opportunity, not discomfort.

Sheriff Eilert had the courtesy to dismount and come to her, but the stranger stayed astride, looking down at her briefly, then surveying her place. The other six men of the posse directed their horses in the dance around her dogs.

" 'Morning, Mrs. Clayter. This here is Mr. Gordon Bruce from the Pinkerton Agency."

The back of her neck felt as if a hundred new hairs had just started to sprout. Mr. Pinkerton and his agents did not waste their time with unimportant criminals. She understood now why the townsfolk were discomposed.

The agent merely nodded at her. She tipped her head, mumbling politely.

"Mrs. Clayter, we've reason to believe that a member of the James gang may be in the area." The agent spoke in a cultured, unfriendly way. "A stranger was seen briefly in your—in town yesterday who matches a description. He could not have gotten far." He looked pointedly at the hoofprints in the snow.

The imaginary hairs grew longer and started to itch. In her nose, the air turned to ice as it tried to move to her lungs. The shivers across her body, however, had nothing to do with the fact that she wore no outer garment on a frigid morning.

She shooed off Edgar and Allan—the situation was serious—and planned her attack.

"The James gang? Aren't they all accounted for, dead, captured after that massacre in Minnesota?"

The agent shook his head. "The Youngers, yes, are currently in prison at Stillwater and are likely not to see the light of day for twenty-five years. Mr. Jesse James and Mr. Frank James are thought to be either in Illinois or Kentucky. The rest are dead or caught. But it seems that one member of their . . . entourage who was a lookout or an informant or some such is still at large."

One member of the James gang still at large? The situation was more serious than she could have dreamed.

She might as well confess. On a dry day blowing with dust Thomas Howard might have a chance. He would even have a chance to hide if he were still asleep in her sickroom with Whisper stabled in the barn. The Pinkerton wouldn't know that the horse wasn't hers.

But those hoofprints might as well be leading to hell itself.

"Well, gentlemen, sir?" She said the last word with little respect. She read newspapers; Pinkertons were known to do damage to the innocent in their search for truth. "May I invite you in for coffee? The morning is a cold one. I have some of Mrs. Pott's *stollen.*"

Most of the townsmen had dismounted by now; two were playing with Edgar and Allan, whom they knew well. All were decent men, friends who had mourned with her. Was that just yesterday? These men would enjoy the excitement of a posse and could certainly use the largesse of a reward to improve their places, to hoard up coal for the winter, to buy unexpected treats for their wives and little ones. Christmas was not far off.

27

Yes, there were many uses for reward money. However, Thomas Howard would not be the reason for it, not if she could help it.

She had to explain the hoofprints. "Well, I don't know anything about the James 'entourage.' I did let a stranger sleep in my barn last night. It was a grievous night. Gottlieb and I often set up passersby in the barn. It's plenty warm in there, and my husband was always a welcoming man."

This was essentially true; the men nodded.

Sheriff Eilert threw in a quick explanation, as if to dispel any suggestion that the hoofprints belonged to a surreptitious night visitor. "Miz Clayter was widda-ed just t'other day."

"I wouldn't leave an animal out in the snow," Dena continued. The posse still looked hopeful about hot coffee and pastry, but the Pinkerton stayed firm atop his horse, pulling angrily at the reins to keep the animal still. It whickered in dismay at his rough touch.

Dena sensed that the man inspired no love from the horse. His actions reminded her of Gottlieb, who had wasted no sentiment on animals, never finding reason to even name them.

"What is your horse called, sir?" She had to ask.

He looked at her strangely. "Nothing," he replied, as rough in voice as in touch. "Nothing at all. Now about this stranger; what was *his* name? Describe him for me."

No please. Just more orders.

"I'd like to get out of the cold," she mentioned, delaying, wondering what to say. She had a fertile imagination but wanted to mislead while keeping close to the truth. It would prevent her tripping over lies in the future.

The Pinkerton ignored her discomfort.

"He showed up after dark, cold and tired," she told him, defeated. "Saw my light. Said something about having been to Zee, but couldn't find what he was looking for."

Pinkerton nodded in satisfaction. "That'd be kin. All dead, long ago, though he likely didn't find that out until he showed up there." He turned to Sheriff Eilert, who had remounted his horse. The sheriff patted the animal gently, and Dena warmed to him. She had always liked the kindly lawman, who respected the ways of his German forebears but loved the new American state of Nebraska.

By now, the posse had gathered, their hopes for a hot meal dashed by the supercilious stranger.

"Zee's Place," Pinkerton started to explain to them all, "was the refuge of the James boys' mother Zerelda during the War Between the States. With her decided Southern sympathies, she took much harassment in Clay County for having produced two notorious Quantrille raiders."

The posse moaned as one, almost with approval. Notorious or not, Quantrilles had led some exciting lives.

"Yes," the agent continued, "Zee housed some kin of their stepfather Reuben Samuel—they named the place for his wife. All those kinfolk are long dead these days." Something caught his eye and the Pinkerton quickly dismounted. Tethering his horse to the post, he strode along the side of her house.

"Gentlemen, go inside if you want. I'll be along directly," Dena ordered in the gentle way she had, the way that charmed most men to obedience, Gottlieb and Jonah excepted.

Unsure what the Pinkerton had seen, she followed the agent, who turned to her. He was very tall, thin, and humorless. She knew he suffered in the cold and was glad for it. And, she told him silently, I did offer you hospitality. You refused it.

"Tell me again, Mrs. Clayter, what he looked like."

She picked up her skirts so as not to dampen them in the snow. She had not told him at all.

"Just a man. It was dark; I didn't let him in or entertain him. He was likely younger than Gottlieb, but I have no clear idea of his age other than that. My husband just turned forty-three. And the man was swathed in warm clothes. I didn't get a real look or a name. And I think he said something about the Rockies."

Her description was greeted with a snort. Then she saw it, the same time the Pinkerton did.

A snow angel. Outside the barn door but away from the trail of hoofprints.

A snow angel for his angel of mercy. Before he left, Thomas Howard had lain in the fresh snow and waved his arms and legs. The motions must have hurt his sore shoulders.

It was the most beautiful thing she had ever seen.

Dena met the agent's suspicious eyes. "I made it," she told him, defiant. "To honor my husband's soul. He was laid in God's great earth just yesterday."

The Pinkerton bowed to her, polite, his eyes sly and unconvinced. "I'll check out the barn before I ride off. Then I'm off to Zee."

"Please, be my guest. But you'd best be bound for Zee in a hurry." She surveyed the thick gray sky in a pointed manner. "We're in for a mighty blizzard by early afternoon."

Dena had been prepared to weep and wail because Thomas Howard had left her, but perhaps it was for the best. Maybe the storm would delay the Pinkerton's journey to Zee. Maybe Thomas Howard would have left long before the Pinkerton. If he went there at all; she remembered the hoofprints in the snow heading in the wrong direction.

Maybe he would come back to her.

Outside the window, she looked past a windbreak of walnut trees, standing tall and stark against the winter sky.

The coffee Thomas Howard had made was still fresh and hot. She drank some from the cup he'd left on the table, hoping her lips touched the same place his mouth had been. He hadn't taken Gottlieb's coat after all; it still hung on its regular hook. Placing her nose to it, she mourned a little anew; it smelled only of Gottlieb. She worried like the mother of a schoolboy; his linen duster wasn't warm enough.

Noticing that Gottlieb's scarf was gone, she smiled.

The sickroom itself looked no different than always, the bed freshly straightened, the washbasin empty and dry. Lonely. Just like her.

Laying her hand on the bed, she heard Willie and Georg Pott arrive on their trusty mule. Amazingly, though, they found the animals fed and the stalls mucked clean.

"You've been a busy lady, Miz Bernhardena, too busy," the older boy admonished, using her full first name rather than just Dena, as most folks did. "Ma and Pa told you last night that we'd be by first thing, snow or no."

"I know, Willie, and I thank you for your help. But . . . I haven't been sleeping well. It gave me something to do. I've been up forever. You get along now before the storm hits. I'll pay you for the entire day."

"Pa would never approve," Willie told her. "A dollar is as a dollar earned."

She hugged both boys, moved by unfamiliar but not unpleasant maternal stirrings. "Nonetheless, you'll be paid for the entire day. That will be cheaper than feeding you for three days if you get snowed in."

All three laughed.

"Maybe we oughta stay on," Willie reasoned worriedly as he headed for the mule. "Pa says there's a James gang member on the loose."

Dena wanted her words to comfort herself as well as the boys. "Posse's already been here. I'll be just fine. I'm perfectly safe."

"You need to hide a gun in your clothes like Ma does," Georg intoned solemnly.

She didn't let him know she already did just that. The boys playfully shoved each other until Georg fell into the snow. Before Willie could think about it, Georg smashed a handful of snow into his brother's face. They wrestled joyfully for a few minutes.

Dena watched in wonder. How could life go on so . . . normal for everyone else when her world would never be the same? All of a sudden, Thomas Howard's absence hit her, as real as a fist in the gullet. She could hardly breathe.

I can't believe I met him just yesterday.

"Lord almighty, I miss him." Without thinking, she spoke the words out loud.

Busy with brushing snow off his clothes, little Georg heard her.

"Mr. Gottlieb, ma'am, isn't at all far away. When our baby sister Elsie died, Ma cried something awful. Pa said her little soul was just a little way above our heads, and that God, He lets her peek down sometimes to see how we're doing."

She knew the child meant well, and she loved him for it. Tussling the snowflakes out of his hair, she shuddered at the thought of Gottlieb watching her.

The boys rode off, and she waved to them for a while. The morning chill finally seeped all the way into her flesh, and she went back inside.

For the first time in years, she had only herself to please. She could cook or not, clean or not. Sleep all day or stay up all night. Gottlieb wouldn't be around to prate at her in his harsh way.

She decided to get ready for Christmas.

Olga had shown her, her first Christmas on the prairie, how to take a limb from one of the naked winter trees along the creek and cover it and its smaller branches with cotton batting. Then the two women had stuck the limb upright in a bucket stuffed with pebbles, made pretty decorations—nuts tied with calico ribbons, chains of popcorn, ginger cookies in storybook shapes—and decorated the thing for a Christmas tree.

"You'll find no pine forests around here," Olga had laughed, "and you can use it again and again each year."

Most families adhered to the German tradition of no decorating until Christmas Eve, but Dena would put up her tree today. She deserved some joy. Decorating so early would have appalled Gottlieb, and she took great satisfaction in this small act of defiance.

Dena sighed in the sweet haze of memory about Thomas Howard, wishing she were decorating the house for him. Their house. She tried to keep the sweetness alive with the spice of *pfeffernusse,* now cooling on the sink.

She suspected that Jonah would chide her about celebrating Christmas when she should be mourning, but she didn't think too much about her brother-in-law. Thomas Howard was a much more pleasant distraction. She couldn't help considering how aghast Jonah would be at the thought of her entertaining an outlaw with her husband barely cold. Even though he was a preacher, he'd call the outlaw out. It was fun thinking of Jonah defending her honor with a shoot-out in the street, and she almost laughed out loud.

Gray clouds gathered like clumps of dirty snow, and the wind screamed around the walls. For a horrific moment, she remembered Gottlieb, trying to sleep in the frozen ground. They had laid him next to his first wife and the lost baby son.

Maybe they could be warm together. Maybe in the hereafter they could all be happy. After all, Gottlieb had let them die. Songbird had told her all about it.

She laid sprigs of rosemary around the candles on the table and surveyed her domain. Gottlieb had thought the Christmas branch silly, but he had indulged her nonetheless.

Each Christmas he'd ordered her gift from Chicago, always an expensive but practical wool garment. One year Olga had suggested Edgar and Allan, born to the Pott bitch six weeks prior. Gottlieb had agreed with reasonable enthusiasm, but it was Olga who had tied the jaunty red bows around the puppies' necks.

Dena remembered her own shout of joy. For once, Gottlieb had even seemed to smile without reluctance.

At her laughter, the dogs looked up, tails whirling. Then she sobered. Why on earth was she decorating a house that no one would see? She would spend the holidays at the parsonage; Jonah would make certain of that. Olga might stop by for a moment to make sure she wasn't prostrate with grief, but the Potts' eight children kept their mother dizzy. Even by today, just the day after the funeral, the other neighbors would have gotten on with their lives, now that Gottlieb was safely buried, his blood cleaned.

Blood. She looked over at the carpet where Thomas Howard had sat. It was spotless now, and she hadn't cleaned it.

His thoughtfulness amazed her.

Of course she was waiting for him. She could admit it to

herself, to God. As stupid as it all was. The corner where she had thrown his fouled linen duster was empty.

Her heart was empty, too, nearly bereft of life.

He would be cold today, riding off into a blizzard in the thin duster.

She wished he had taken Gottlieb's coat. As she watched from the window, snow began to fall, hard, killing her snow angel.

"Ah, Whisper, we got no place else to go. And she's sheltered us once."

He never felt foolish talking to his horse. The two of them had been through some tough times together. However, this one was among the worst. Loneliness was clearly the cruelest wound of all, although his shoulder had never hurt this bad.

The sound of his voice slapped back against his ears in the wind. He slowed. He'd ridden Whisper hard before the blizzard began to spit. Those cottonwoods ahead in the blowing mist—he remembered them outlining the creek. Sticking by it like a path, he could find his way back to her farm.

Dreams dashed, Zee empty of any kin, all he could think of was the comely widow asleep with two foul farm hounds instead of a man. The only person for five hundred miles who could call him by name.

Even if it wasn't his real name.

"Maybe I should have got captured with Cole and the boys. Leastways we'd all be together. And I'd never have got shot riding the other way. Or should I have stayed with Frank and Jesse? Those two will never get caught; luck and life are always good to them. What did that newspaper headline say, someone saw them in Rock Island at nine A.M. and by ten they were invisible?"

The blowing snow turned to icy needles that stabbed the back of his neck and every dot of skin where he had no whiskers. By now, the cold was freezing the rioting pain in his shoulder, which was a good thing.

"We got to make tracks while we can still see, old boy. At

least I've got a good sense of direction and you've got steady feet." Around his head and mouth, he tightened the old red scarf he'd taken from Gottlieb Clayter's coatrack. Though ragged, it was clean, but to his sorrow smelled not at all like Dena.

For some reason, he started to recite that poem of Mr. Poe's, that one to Helen, to that beautiful statuelike woman. Of their own volition the words turned to music, and he sang aloud to an opera tune, changing the name to Dena.

"Dena, 'thy beauty is to me Like those Nicean barks of yore . . . That gently, o'er a perfumed sea, The weary, way-worn wanderer bore To his own native shore . . .' "

No sane person would be out and about this day to hear his foolishness or to capture him.

The scarf stole the sounds, but Whisper nickered, kicking up his heels.

Her bright green cloak was his beacon. He could see her looking his way through the falling whiteness.

Ghostlike, the man and his horse slipped through the snow-clogged dusk, a red line of wool drawing itself on the wind. Dena recognized the too-thin white duster and the red scarf; the pale horse she guessed to be Whisper.

"Thomas? Thomas Howard?" Her shriek of hope hung on the winter wind like early spring.

At first she stumbled through the drifts, the ice needles stitching pain across her face. She didn't mind; pain meant that she still had feelings left to feel.

The call of his name sliced through the ice of the wind. He rode hard to her side on the surefooted horse, dismounting in disbelief at the dream suddenly true. He barely felt his shoulder scream.

"Thomas Howard!" She moved to him as if on angel's wings while he tore the red scarf from his face.

"My angel," he said foolishly.

"I knew you'd come back to me!"

Her exuberant greeting and his long hours in the saddle weakened his stalwart stance. He hadn't intended to, certainly, but when she bounded toward him he leaned into her and clasped her close. His shoulder protested, but she felt too good for him to mind.

The unrepentant wind warmed for a second as he spun them around in it, the long tails of his coat flapping like a windmill.

"Oh, Thomas Howard, you've been gone so long," she told him.

He kissed her face then, mostly to melt the frozen tears there. It wasn't a real kiss, of course. She was a new widow, after all.

The red scarf blew away in the wind.

"Oh, Thomas Howard! You've come home!"

Chapter Four

As Thomas Howard tended to Whisper in the barn, Dena shuddered for two reasons.

First, the wind keened a terrible sound around the window frames. She had always felt unease when the north winds assaulted the plains. Despite the secure windows from Montgomery Ward and Company that Gottlieb had installed in their steadfast wooden house, and the windbreaks of trees, she couldn't help missing her sturdy St. Louis mansion with its dozen fireplaces and the elegant plantation-style house of her mother's kin in Cape Girardeau.

Second, the wind seemed to chide her, chastise her. For her wanton behavior.

Gottlieb barely asleep in the earth and her dancing through a blizzard with another man, letting him kiss her. Wanting him to do more.

I'm a licentious hussy, nothing more than an adulteress.

She was blushing bright when he came through the door. Hanging up his disreputable duster on the coatrack, he behaved as though he belonged. Just watching him made something stir deep inside her. Even the weariness that draped around him like a cloak couldn't hide the power he seemed to have over her.

His own face was reddened by the wind. She held her hands at her sides to keep them from rubbing his cheeks to warm them.

To caress.

Dena shook her head a little in a way he wouldn't notice. Being a woman confused her. Before her death, her mother had often told her that desire was just as natural in a woman as in a man, but that women weren't as free to act upon it because of the likelihood of bearing babies. However, society told Dena that it was wrong, certainly to act upon it, as well as just to feel it.

Since she liked tending Thomas Howard, liked watching him, hoped he would remain . . . she couldn't determine what her mother's relationship to her father had been. They'd only had one child, after all. Did it mean they had only been together as man and wife one time? Maybe her father had had a taste for lightskirts. However, nothing of her past life mattered anymore. Dena sighed again. Busying herself with the coffeepot, she shook all lustful, confusing notions from her mind.

All around her place, the storm gathered the night into itself, bringing an early darkness.

Once more she sighed. As if he heard, he looked right at her and smiled.

Smiling back a little, suddenly shy and unsure of herself, she made for the room where he had slept, both to ready it for him and to hide.

Home. The word warmed him through.

"You weren't really out in that weather waiting for me, now, were you?" He smiled at her, holding a china cup of steaming coffee between both hands to warm them.

She hadn't needed to do much in the little room and had no excuse for remaining inside it too long. Besides, she had good manners and knew all about being a good host to a guest in her home.

Even if the guest took her breath away and made her imagine unimaginable things.

Even if the guest was a notorious outlaw.

While he'd stabled Whisper, she'd set out some food and moved a soft, overstuffed chair close to the cookstove. He sat in it. She pulled off his boots and brought him a tray, padding his soreness with pillows.

Dena smiled back. The snow he'd brushed from himself, his hair and clothes, already made a silver puddle at the door. She could smell the damp wool as her own cloak dried in front of the Pennsylvania fireplace.

As for the disreputable linen duster, she took it, rolled it into a ball, and threw it in the corner as she had once before.

"I'm going to burn it when I have a chance," she explained, unsure what else to say. He watched her with obvious curiosity. "Gottlieb's coat is finer and much warmer. Neither he nor I"—she gave a little laugh—"have any further use for it." She didn't say any more right then, but she thought it. The linen dusters of the James gang were already legend, and there was a Pinkerton on the prowl.

"I wish I could flatter you, but I can't." She sat in a ladder-back chair near him and answered his question. "I knew the storm was coming on, and I wanted to string a rope between the house and the barn so I will have a way to get to the animals, even in the blizzard."

She watched him from beneath her eyelashes, hoping he wasn't like Gottlieb and Jonah and the rest of the local menfolk, who considered her soft in the head for thinking animals had feelings.

"You might've mentioned it before I went outside," he chided with a grin. "Nearly hanged myself. No, no—just fooling with you. The animals would be all right on their own for a few days, you know." His thoughtful glance reminded her of how well he had tended them that morning.

She remembered it, too. "I know. And I must thank you

for . . . all your help this morning." Later she would ask him why he had left without saying good-bye. The completed chores and the fresh coffee and the snow angel, well, those had been thanks enough, but leaving with no farewell had hurt. "I just like them to know I'm nearby, that's all."

"You need some young'uns."

She knew he meant the remark as harmless, but she reddened once more. Hiding her face, she turned to put more coal in the stove.

"The Lord did not see fit . . ." She spoke tonelessly into the fire.

When she turned to see Thomas Howard's sympathetic eyes on her, she read their question clearly. *Barren?* She nodded back at him, almost in anger. He and everyone else for a hundred miles blamed Gottlieb's childlessness on her.

As if to ease the awkward moment, he snuggled further into the comfortable chair and complimented her on it. "You have some fine things in this house."

She knew what he meant, of course. Many of the things were worthy of a St. Louis mansion, not a humble farmhouse on the prairie. Like him, she would reveal only what he needed to know.

"My mother would be pleased; most of our—my furnishings once belonged to her." She stopped for a moment, deciding just what he needed to know. "My late father's estate had to be auctioned. He had met . . . with some financial difficulties before he . . . before his death.

"Gottlieb and I had just been married, and he loaded up our wagon the night before the proceedings and stashed away as much as he could."

Her heart nearly warmed at the recollection but hardened immediately. Gottlieb had not done so to please her or to give her the comfort of family heirlooms. He had intended to sell the French antiques and fine china himself and pocket the cash.

"Well, I am grateful to him."

"It did not fare well for you in Zee, then," Dena stated flatly, changing the subject. Gratitude toward Gottlieb was not an emotion she liked to feel.

He looked shrewdly at her, as if wondering how she knew.

She smiled again. "You would not travel back here in a blizzard had you found what you sought."

"Would you believe that I wanted to see you again?"

Her heart warmed now and stayed so. "Yes, I would believe that." She remembered his fingers flitting across her cheek, the smell of him on the pillow. Something deep in her woman's part clenched. Wriggling her bottom for a second against the hardness of the ladder-back chair seemed to give a second of relief. "But not that you would ride back here so soon. I *am* newly widowed, you know." She didn't care at all about the propriety of it, not with Thomas Howard, although it would be a worthwhile weapon to toss at other men.

He met her eyes square on, as if to see how much widowhood meant to her. She had once agreed that Gottlieb was a mean . . . well, man.

Golden light from the lantern glistened in the room.

Her look told him what he wanted to know. Gottlieb's death had been a relief. Her gaze was direct, sweet, saying that she was glad he was under her roof for another night, even though she was a proper woman.

"You have no kin left in Zee, do you?"

"No." He washed the tonelessness of his voice down his throat with a long drink of the coffee. "Not in Zee, anyhow."

"Why was it so important to go to them?" She wasn't sure how much to press, but it would be interesting to see what he deemed necessary knowledge for her. Gottlieb had never considered that she needed to know anything.

Thomas Howard's brow tightened in decision; then his lips tightened in silence.

Her disappointment was profound. "Thomas, it may be important for you to know that a Pinkerton agent came by here this morning, asking about a member of the James gang."

Thomas Howard's face paled, and he started to rise from the chair. The hot coffee spilled on his knee, but he didn't act like he noticed. She motioned him back down as though she could offer succor.

"My God, what did you tell him?" His voice was almost soundless.

"Pretty much the truth. That a stranger spent the night here. In the barn, though. Gottlieb was known to offer the same to riders passing by, even in good weather. Everybody around here knows that."

"Did you tell him my name, or anything else?" His panic was real. His troubled eyes closed, and wrinkles of worry etched around them as he waited for her to answer. The wrinkles enhanced his handsomeness, the tension making his carved cheekbones even more lean and taut.

"I told him we didn't talk or make introductions, and that I didn't get a close look at you in the dark but figured you were a bit younger than my husband's age. That you were bound for the Rockies." Dena turned from him, heartsick at his lack of trust; then she faced him again. "I'm not a very good liar, but I think he believed me. He's the one that said Zerelda Samuel's kin had long since left Zee."

Thomas Howard grimaced anew at the sorry situation. "Now I can't stay here. He'll be back."

"No, he won't. He looked the place over plenty and left satisfied. It was a good trick, your hoofprints leading the opposite way."

Thomas almost smiled. "Yeah. I rode that way to the creek, then doubled back through the water."

"That freezing creek? How dreadful for Whisper!" she chided.

"He's a tough one. Once we weathered a blizzard together, in a stand of Northwoods pine. I covered him up with a horse blanket, head to tail, which made a tent for me to sleep under."

Dena considered. Obviously the man knew the wilderness and ways to survive in it. She found it ironic that he should think he needed her now.

The wind howled around the house, and Dena shivered even though she was plenty warm within. It would be different by morning, though, when the coal in the stove had died down and the small rooms were nearly as cold as the outside.

"Well, I'm glad you and Whisper are safe and warm now."

Was she? Well, for Whisper anyway, unless this man trusted her some more after all the lies she told. She pushed on.

"Therefore, Zerelda Samuel *is* your kin."

Thomas Howard stretched among the pillows. He acted like his shoulder was feeling better. She supposed it was the warmth, the nourishing food. Maybe the nurturing of a woman . . . Dena tried to hide her blush. Maybe he would trust her. After all, she hadn't turned him in.

He nodded. "Well, her husband, anyway, the man Frank and Jesse love as dear as any true pa. It was mostly family legend when I was a kid, that Reuben Samuel and I were cousins a dozen times removed or some such. I was grown by the time we all figured it out, and Frank and Jesse welcomed me as though we shared blood."

He looked around the festive room, his eyes landing once again on Dena's face.

"They have an enlightened sense of kinship and take it very seriously. In fact, they'll consider themselves bound to you for taking me in. I'm sure of it." He pointed to the Christmas branch. "I pray they'll be home for Christmas. Each has a wife, Jesse a baby boy." His face creased in lost thought for a moment. Dena considered the oddness of outlaws having wives and kids.

"Why didn't you betray me?" he asked suddenly.

Dena blushed a little. Her earlier actions had to be based on more than just a gentle touch on her cheek and the blazing way he looked at her, she thought.

"Instinct, I guess. The fact that you could have shot me on sight and didn't. Your gentleness with Whisper," she confided almost childishly. "No one that gentle with his horse is a killer."

He disputed her instantly. "Even the cruelest outlaw is good to his horse. The animal means his survival. But in truth, I'm no killer, nor did I ever steal anything. Jesse would have my ass if I ever harmed a woman." Then he stopped, as if unsure how to continue.

"Well, I confess I was with them in Northfield last September. That's a fact," he admitted finally. "But I injured myself—tore out my shoulder when a horse threw me—and Jesse wouldn't let me ride out with them the next day. I was to stay and recover and be part of the next raid."

The raid that never was.

"Whisper threw you?" Dena asked, aghast, almost as if she regretted her trust.

"No, not Whisper," Thomas Howard told her with a smile.

"One of the gang, Clel Miller, had a mean son-of-a-bitch horse—I beg your pardon—that couldn't stand no rider but him. Bet me a bundle that I couldn't last eight seconds."

"How big a bundle?" she couldn't help asking.

Thomas was silent for a long time. "Well, it was to have been my share of the robbery. Jesse has a righteous sense of fairness. He dictated to one and all that I'd get a share of the loot, regardless that I was too injured to join in the raid." Thomas Howard didn't speak for a while.

"Relax," he finally said with a smile. "I won. I lasted fifteen."

"Well, I should think you'd be glad to have escaped the carnage," she announced like a schoolmarm. "But why . . ." At that word, she saw his face shutter like a window against the storm. He pretended interest in his empty coffee cup, and she got up to bring him more. Obviously the confidences were over.

She rose from the chair and busied herself heating up something in a pot on the stove.

Darkness had dropped heavily, like the snow. Thomas's head bobbed against his chest.

"I'm glad to be here, with you." He looked up at her disarmingly, and those strange woman's parts tightened. "But I am so goddamned tired—beg pardon—that I don't think I can get to my room."

She warmed. *My room.*

"You need rest and healing," she announced, again in the

schoolmarm voice, while she took something from the pot, "and believe me, during this storm you won't get a chance to do much else. I put some laudanum in your coffee. Dr. Burkhardt left some for me for the nights I couldn't sleep, but I never took any. You go to bed now. You'll sleep like a baby. I put a nightshirt out for you. Take this."

He took the calico pillow she held out to him.

"My God, it's warm!" he exclaimed simply.

Dena gave more orders, but smiled as she did so. "Keep it at your feet, or your shoulder if it needs comfort, or wherever you're coldest. It's a little bag filled with feed corn. I heat it up for a little while on the stove or in the oven, and the warmth lasts for hours.

"Now I know my homestead surely is a better place than using Whisper as a tent, but I warn you, come morning, it'll be nearly as cold inside as out. I'll let you borrow Edgar and Allan."

"I'd rather borrow you." He laughed lightly, but his eyes were glazed with sleep, his mind obviously fuzzy with the drug. As soon as he realized the indelicacy of his words, he turned red.

Not only was Dena pleased with the color against his pale skin, but she was also secretly pleased with the obscene remark. She pretended otherwise. "Now, Mr. Howard, and me a new widow. For shame!"

As he stumbled off to his room, he asked about the preacher. "So now the town knows I was here. What about your brother-in-law? D'you think he'd be one to turn me in?"

"Goodness, yes," she exclaimed. "But he'd never venture out in a storm."

The next morning, Thomas Howard made his way along the rope she had tied between the house and the barn. From the side window, she watched his every move, simple moves that were somehow music and magic combined.

Dena considered that she would never tire of watching Thomas Howard. She remembered admiring Becker Blanchard, but she'd been just a girl, and Becker not much more than a boy. His breaking their betrothal had had a great deal to do with that.

Now she was all grown up. Yes, at twenty-three she was a downright woman. Even if Gottlieb had never been able . . .

The snow had stopped sometime during the night, but the fierce wind still blew, piling up ice along the buildings, stirring snowflakes into white tornadoes. Drifts across the land would be deep and impassable; the Pott boys would not be showing up this day.

A whole day alone with Thomas Howard.

In anticipation, she wrapped her red shawl tighter around her shoulders, even though the room was warm enough. The dogs still slept on her tussled bed.

As she watched Thomas, breath from her lungs caught in her throat like cold air, although the thought of him made her warm. He was beautiful, even wrapped as he was in Gottlieb's own coat. The past night of longing, hearing his gentle snores from the room beyond, had been even worse than the night of shock following Gottlieb's death. He had been dead. Thomas Howard was gloriously alive, and she'd let nothing but two huge dogs warm her.

Wind whistled after him as he opened the door. She was at his side in an instant, brushing snow from him.

"Good morning," was all she could think to say, even after her year of studying great literature. "Sit down. Get warm. Here's the corn bag to warm you."

She held out the little calico pillow. His fingers touched hers as he reached for it, and a jolt shot from her toes to her brain in less time than a fire started in straw.

"This is a fine little gadget," he remarked, sitting down, as though the touch hadn't happened. Her face fell.

Looking up at her, he saw, and smiled then, a smile that warmed her as no summer sun ever could. "Yes, this is a fine idea."

She smiled back, almost content. "I cannot take credit. I have a friend . . . who told me about it." She thought of Songbird and her wise healing ways. Gottlieb had shunned the older woman's wisdom, and many others considered her a heathen, but Dena felt some kinship with her. The last of a tribe wiped out by smallpox—the same epidemic that had taken Mira Wuebke's two babies—Songbird was as outcast as Dena often felt. Dena, a society belle from St. Louis, sometimes deplored wasting her youthful beauty as a farm wife. However, that had been Becker Blanchard's decision, not hers, and truth to tell, she most often appreciated the anonymity.

Now she found herself single again in a cozy house on a cold winter day with a handsome man.

Smiling still, Thomas Howard sounded almost coy. "Yes, this handy little item kept me mighty warm last night. Although I was still lonely."

She melted but said simply, "Yes," turning her back, unsure what else to say. The blush was automatic. She brought him a cup of hot coffee and couldn't help herself. Snowflakes sparkled atop his hair and she touched them, twining a curl around her finger for just an instant.

"Edgar and Allan helped me out some in the warmth regard." She turned to him, trying to act proper. She was a widow lady, after all. She remembered her mother's dicta about natural urges, but she had been an unusually enlightened woman. Society continued to tell Dena that her baser instincts were evil, even for one's own husband. It was hard to know who was right. Although she hoped her mother was, she had had no such feelings for Gottlieb.

"You're doing all right this morning?" she asked him, somewhat inanely. It was time to bustle about preparing food, to correct her wild thoughts.

"Yes, ma'am. A whole night of good sleep in a warm bed did me wonders." He smiled a little then. "And I suppose that dose of laudanum helped some." His next words sounded tight, as though his throat closed around them trying to hold them in. "I . . . sometimes get bad dreams, about Northfield, you know, but last night I didn't have one."

"I've got some fresh eggs." Dena turned away quickly, again

not knowing what to say, not really, nor how to feel. She remembered the cry from his bedroom, that first night. "Let me scramble up some." Cooking was a safe topic. Her cheeks had grown hot. "And I'll fry up some griddle cakes." She tossed in some raisins for good measure, and poured into a little pitcher the syrup she made from the sap of box elder trees.

"I must say, you have a decent place around here," Thomas Howard remarked with relaxed words and a different smile. She might as well have been a waitress at a hotel dining room, or even his mother.

Dena's spirits couldn't help falling. "Yes, Gottlieb did manage to create a fine homestead."

"Will you stay on?"

She shrugged as she broke the eggs; he leaned his elbows on the table. "Certainly. This is my home now. I've no other place to go."

When Thomas spoke, she heard the curiosity in his voice. "Where'd you start out from?"

"Cape Girardeau, my mother's ancestral home. But my father ran his business in St. Louis, so we had a second house there. After my mother's death, we spent most of our time in the city."

"Know both well. I'm a Missourian myself."

"Clay County?" Dena asked him, knowing about James country.

"No, not at first. I was raised in a little place on the border with Arkansas. My pa was a preacherman who died young." He didn't say anything else.

"Ah, a preacher's kid." Her voice filled the quiet before the eggs crackled in the melted butter in the frying pan.

"Yeah. The boys started off calling me that, but it settled down to just 'kid' after a while."

"The boys?"

Thomas seemed lost in fond memories. "Frank and Jesse. It was a joke between us all; their own pa was a preacher who died young, too. And then . . . well, I wasn't really the youngest of the group, the gang, you know"—he was clearly embarrassed—"but I had the, well, the least experience, so the name stuck."

Frank and Jesse. He said it as calmly as she said Edgar and Allan. Two murderous outlaws who got others killed as well, or captured, or shot. She couldn't help the little hairs crawling at the back of her neck again; the memory of the grim Pinkerton crashed back.

"How'd you end up homesteading?" Thomas asked her, but she knew what he really meant, what everyone always meant. Why had she married an old farmer twice her age when she belonged with her elegant china and fancy furniture in a big city mansion with a rich young husband? A husband like Becker Blanchard.

"It's a bit hard to explain." She laid a plate of eggs in front of him, along with Olga's plum jam and feather-soft rolls now slightly stale, and the griddle cakes.

"Long ago," she started dramatically as she sat down beside him, "well, in the thirties," she amended with a smile, "our families became acquainted on the journey from Potsdam and settled near St. Louis. Gottlieb's people became farmers in Red Bud, Illinois, mine went into banking in the city. The families kept in touch from time to time.

"I remember Gottlieb coming for dinner sometimes when I was very small. He seemed kind. He was always gentle with his little brother." Her voice grew almost nostalgic.

"The preacher?"

"Yes, Jonah."

"Too many preachers in this tale," Thomas said with a laugh. She joined in for a moment, but the joy wasn't real.

She knew Thomas watched her face in between bites. Pain rather than grief wrinkled her forehead. Dena tried to eat anyway.

She spoke again, pulling the red shawl tight around her out of habit; the room was warm enough. "He helped on his own father's place but got the wanderlust and sold it when his parents died. There was enough money to send Jonah to boarding school back East. Gottlieb couldn't resist President Lincoln's

Homestead Act." She waved her arms around the room, although she meant the whole farm.

"My mother had died, and things went bad for my father." For me, too, she cried silently, not saying aloud that her father had been charged with embezzlement, or that Becker Blanchard had broken off their betrothal when he couldn't share her shame. But memories that would not be drowned surfaced nonetheless. "Papa lost all his money, even our home. By then, Gottlieb had been widowed and was ready for another wife. It seemed to all make sense. I needed someone. He needed a wife. Then."

The wind started to moan across the land, and even Thomas shivered at the sound, although the room was plenty warm. For a second, she wondered how life would have been had they met during a springtime with its sweet mild fragrances and breezes gentle to the touch. A springtime before Gottlieb Clayter and Northfield, Minnesota. She wanted to touch his cheek.

As if reading her mind, his fingers reached out to her cheek for a moment. Even with the corn bag, his hand was still cold from the outside.

She liked his fingers on her. It didn't matter that they were cold. But he snatched his hand away quickly, far too quickly, as if he regretted the action. In spite of his hurry, she wanted to take his hand between hers, to warm it. Instead, she got up and cleared the table.

As if he'd done so a thousand times, he got up from the table and settled into the armchair near the Pennsylvania fireplace. Feet propped on the ottoman, he shifted comfortably. Over the sounds of the water pump, Dena heard his light snores. She smiled.

They were just like a real couple already.

Chapter Five

Thomas Howard indeed dozed for a few minutes but woke up soon after. His sleep hadn't been peaceful. Relief at his whereabouts covered him soft and downy, like the pillow on the chair. The corn bag made him warm, but the sight of Dena bustling about the house brought on a heat that had nothing to do with the coal-burning stove.

Hell, he wanted to do more than just touch her cheek.

The red shawl couldn't hide the glories of her form; shamefully, he considered how her nipples would taste, and that special place lower down. He hadn't been with many women, but he'd learned what to do, learned how to do it with gentleness and respect. Actually shaking his head, he tried to train his thoughts on more savory matters. He was a guest in her house, after all. In a way, she was his savior.

However, he couldn't help his thoughts. At least they were more pleasant than the blood-drenched memories of Northfield. He concluded that she must surely be experienced enough to pleasure him in return. Unless, of course, with a mean bastard of a mate, she knew only how to lie like a stiff board underneath a man's ministrations, counting the seconds until he was done. The possibility saddened him.

Even still, she was beautiful, and under the right circumstances he was sure he could teach her a thing or two.

He blushed, ashamed. She had only been widowed for a week. He stirred uncomfortably in the chair, hoping she couldn't read his thoughts or see the bulge in his pants.

At that precise moment, however, she looked at him, her whole heart in her eyes. Her lids slipped slowly down, like butterfly wings, a blush dewlike on her cheeks. Hope stirred his groin even more.

"Are you awake? Are you still hungry?" Her simple dress of blush silk belonged to a summer day, but he knew why she wore it. Her new life was beginning. "Let me get you some ham. Gottlieb smokes a good ham."

It wasn't what Thomas wanted, but he agreed to be polite. He noticed her use of the present tense and wondered if it was important. She came to stand next to him. The wash water had warmed her hands. As if with a life of its own, her hand fluttered away from her body to touch his cheek.

He laid his own hand on top of hers, and for a second, his heart stopped.

Before she pulled her hand away, Dena felt that odd clenching down below around a void that longed to be filled. The hole in her heart started to heal.

"You look good in red," Thomas Howard told her later.

New snow had begun to fall, not the sharp shards of a blizzard but the clean, gentle layer of a goose-down comforter.

A snowfall that could hide his trail. He'd have to leave soon. The reality grieved him. It seemed near as painful to leave her after a day than parting from his own kin.

Settling in front of the Pennsylvania fireplace, he propped up his stockinged feet. His boots dried before the coals; he'd been outside checking the chickens, ensuring that Edgar and

Allan did their duty before coming back inside, and filling the coal buckets from the cellar.

Dena smiled, brushing snow from Gottlieb's coat. "I certainly prefer it to black."

He mentioned the red scarf. "Sorry I lost it."

"No matter." She smiled at him. "I'll make you your own." She got out a lump of bread dough that had risen enough to knead.

"I crocheted it for Gottlieb one Christmas, and made this shawl for myself, too. He actually complimented me; he didn't like impractical gifts. One thing about this society girl—I learned my needlecraft." Her smile was secret, and Thomas Howard noticed.

"What's that smile for?"

"Gottlieb never realized that I made it to spite him. In his own hard way, I think he tried to please me by wearing it, and he never knew."

"Knew what?"

"A red shawl is Susan B.'s trademark." Dena giggled as if she couldn't help it.

"Susan B.?"

"Susan B. Anthony." She watched him out of the corner of her eye. This was dangerous territory. Whenever she displeased Gottlieb, he threatened to burn her collection of *Revolution* newsletters. Jonah had more than once interrupted her discussions with Mira Wuebke on the subject of voting rights for women, and their proclamations that Wyoming must be an enlightened place because it actually allowed women to participate in the political process.

"You're a suffragette? 'Susan B.' got arrested for voting, you know."

Dena spoke proudly. "She is a wonderfully brave woman! You certainly recall Henry David Thoreau's call to civil disobedience. I absolutely stand for the rights of every American, no matter what sex or color."

"You were an abolitionist?" He frowned.

"I was a mere child in those days, but yes, I suppose you

could say I was." Thoughtful for a moment, she made a design in the dough. "My mother was an ardent supporter, and she demanded rights for women as well. Were she with us now, I know she could consider the needs of the Indians, too."

"Redskins and savages? I don't know about them even being Americans. It's been a hard thing to accept, this voting of Negro men."

"What? What do you mean?"

"You forget; I'm a Southerner." He fought to keep his voice low.

"Missouri never left the Union!" She pounded the bread dough with extra force. Then she raised her downcast eyes to him as much as she dared.

"I'm from Arkansas." His voice hit a sour note.

Dena was embarrassed. "Please forgive me for getting political with you. It was a battle of words I had sometimes with Gottlieb, just to add a spark of intellect to the routine of everyday living here on the plains. Truth to tell, I don't think he or Jonah believe that women even have souls."

Thomas Howard was far too comfortable to leave his perch. She sure looked pretty with anger painting her face and flour dusting her nose. Jesse and Frank had taught him a thing or two about diplomacy.

"Well, that would be their mistake," he soothed. "I'm in agreement about the importance of strong women. My Aunt Zerelda could outlast any army march."

Dena relaxed, still somewhat embarrassed. In an odd way, Thomas Howard was a guest in her home. Both Gottlieb and Jonah had often warned her to hold her tongue on the subjects of the Indians and former slaves, and depending on the company she either followed their advice or sermonized aplenty. Gottlieb's opinion had rarely mattered to her, but Jonah was an educated man with manners, so sometimes she complied. This seemed such a time.

"My mother, too. At least until she lost her only brother on Sherman's march to the sea." Dena sighed loud and long. "Her heart seemed to die then. The physicians said she suffered from melancholia. But she was with Mrs. Stanton and Mrs. Mott at Seneca Falls in 'forty-eight."

Dena's face glowed with the memory. "Yes, there was a time when Mama had real fire in her eyes. She had set up some of her own fortune in a college trust fund for me and weaned me on Margaret Fuller's book."

"No wonder, then, that you think women are equal." He spoke seriously and with no condescension at all.

"You know Miss Fuller's writings?"

"Perhaps more than other men."

"Why is that?" Dena was amazed. It had never occurred to her that an outlaw would care about such things.

"I want to college for a while myself," he explained in such a soft voice that she couldn't determine whether he was sad or embarrassed. "It was my mother's wish. While there, I made a good friend, Anna Ralston. We felt highly intellectual about a great many things."

"Why did you quit?"

"The money ran out."

She wanted to inquire whether that was when he took up the notion of robbing banks, and if he and this Anna Ralston had been lovers, but the afternoon was starting to be perfect. She decided against ruining the daydream that they were a real couple in their own true house.

A dream that could perhaps become real.

Almost with a life of their own, the words burbled from her lips. "Thomas, stay with me. Stay here at Clayter's place. I'll lose the farm if I don't continue to make improvements—that's the rule of homesteading—and I'll never be able to handle the spring planting, just myself and two young boys. You said once you could earn your keep."

He got up to stand in front of her.

"Dena." He put his hands on her shoulders and spoke, his words sensible and soft. "I can't stay. Dena, I've got to leave you soon. Surely you realize that."

Even at the look of shocked disappointment on her face, he

continued, "Dena, I have to leave now. Right now. While the snowfall can hide my tracks."

"No!" Her own voice was almost a shriek. "You can't. Not now. Not yet. You're safe here. No one knows you. You could be my hired man. It'll be perfect!"

"Dena." Again his words were gentle, almost as if he were breaking bad news to a heartbroken child. "I am a fugitive. The Pinkerton Agency is after me. It doesn't matter to them that I never robbed a bank or killed anyone. They *think* I did."

"But he's been here already, that Gordon . . . something," she protested, shrill. "I am sure he believed my lies that you'd been and gone. Why on earth would he think you'd come back?"

"The Pinkerton will go to Zee—if he's not there already—and realize that you lied, Dena, that I hadn't been there before coming to Staircase Creek. At any rate, he will be back with more questions."

"Well, then, you can hide!"

"Where? The coal cellar? Listen, Dena, the Pinkertons are ruthless. There are few boundaries they won't cross. Trust me. Not two years ago, they hounded and hounded Aunt Zerelda. They were convinced she was helping Jesse hide out at her place. A smoke bomb they tossed into the house was supposed to drive Jesse outside, but it exploded instead."

Dena's face paled. The kneading had lost all effort.

"Aunt Zerelda lost her right arm," Thomas said in a strangled voice that grew only more horrible. "And her youngest son, a simpleminded little boy only eight years old, was killed."

His voice was hoarse with grief. Dena's eyes filled with hot, bright tears.

"I am so sorry, Thomas," she managed finally.

"Jesse wasn't even there, Dena. Be sorry all you want, but be smart, too. I cannot put you in danger. Dena, I'm telling you, the Pinkerton will stop at nothing. He is not gone from your life. You'll be questioned, spied on, harassed. I've got to leave now. You've got to pretend that none of this ever happened when the Pinkerton comes back. You need to pretend that you haven't seen me since that first night."

"Oh, Thomas, I can't pretend that. And you can't leave, not just yet!" For a second, her voice sounded too loud, for the wind had quieted.

"Not just yet." Her voice sweetened, and he stared at her. She was right. Thomas moved to see out the window.

"I won't leave, Dena. Not just yet." He reached out a hand.

The snow outside stopped, almost with a thud.

They looked at each other, awed at the silence. She put her hand in his.

He amazed her. He helped cook up supper, even stooped so low as to wash up afterward.

"Done all this plenty of times," he explained to her silent, chagrined face twice, once while chopping onions and the last of the summer squash from the root cellar for the stew of leftover prairie chicken, the second when grabbing a linen towel to dry dishes. Once again, she had used her mother's finest ware.

Now he continued, "Told you I could take care of myself. Did all this for old Sweyn before I came here."

"Old Sweyn?"

Thomas grimaced a little as he took his now usual armchair in front of the Pennsylvania fireplace, almost as if he had spoken without thinking.

"An old . . . friend who helped me out somewhat after Northfield. I had to earn my keep." He smiled then, and Dena relaxed.

She stashed the last crystal flute, then sat in the ladder-back chair near him. Her mother's fainting couch and settee had been too large for Gottlieb to manage. No matter, then; she and her husband had never longed to sit close and cuddle. Now, she regretted not having a larger piece of upholstered furniture so she could have a reason to sit close to Thomas.

"How about Northfield? Can you talk about it?"

He smiled a little, but it wasn't a true smile. Pain glazed his eyes. "A pretty girl like you with delicate sensibilities shouldn't be bothered."

"This pretty girl with delicate sensibilities helped clean up her father's brains that were splattered all over a wall and slipped in her husband's entrails after a bull ripped him open. I think I can handle anything you can tell me."

She spoke emotionlessly, not having intended to outdo his horrors. Thomas looked at her aghast.

"I had no idea . . . Dena. I am so—sorry. Why, sure. Northfield . . . changed my life, I guess as much as—your events—changed yours."

His face had whitened so much that she got up to bring him a glass and Gottlieb's whiskey.

"Get yourself a glass, too. You might need one," Thomas advised.

"It was last September, the seventh to be exact. I think I told you I'd injured my shoulder the day before. I ripped the bandages off and used them to staunch the blood pouring from Jim's nose and mouth. Jim Younger. Well, where Jim's nose and mouth had been, anyway." His voice became little more than a whisper. "A bullet had taken away half his upper jaw."

Disbelief hung in his words now, as they had hung in the air that day, along with the sweet wind of leftover summer.

"Then Cole rode up—Cole Younger—holding little brother Bob. He told me it was an army and to be glad I missed the massacre.

"I hear his flat, dead voice every night in my dreams, Dena. Sometimes I even find myself answering him back. Bobby had taken gunshots in the wrist and thigh." His words slowed. "Cole got off his horse and held his brother like a baby before putting him down in the dust of our camp.

"I can still smell the blood." He stopped speaking for a while, looking out the window as if lost in thought. "The horses all pawed nervously at the smell, too. Frank and Jesse talked together in a stand of trees about thirty feet away. It was windy; I couldn't hear 'em, but Frank was gesturing pretty wildly."

Thomas's hands started to claw the air, maybe like his cousin's had done.

"Cole started to talk to me again, telling me that those Northfielders sure weren't the scairdy-cat potato farmers Chad told us to expect. I still remember swallowing down my heaving stomach when I saw Jim's wounds. I thought I'd lose every meal I'd eaten for about the last year." He laid his right hand on his belly.

"Then Charlie Pitts, barely conscious, came up behind Bob, hanging on to his horse. I had to ask about Chad, even though I was scared what I'd learn.

"That was when Cole turned to me for a split second before he ran back to Bob, telling me to pray that Chad—Bill Chadwell—was dead. They left him screaming in the street begging God for mercy, his eyes shot out."

Thomas Howard sat still, obviously wounded, obviously all alone with miserable specters that wouldn't rest. His mouth worked hard to find the right words.

"Cole sat on the ground with his brothers like a mother dog with her pups. He was shot up pretty bad, but the bleeding stopped quick." His fists clenched against his thighs. "I'm no doctor, but I knew just looking at Charlie's grievous wounds that he wouldn't last a day." His voice slowed to a stop.

"I was right," he almost snapped before he went on. "Cole had always told me how he'd ridden with Frank and Jesse for ten years and never been harmed, not a scratch."

Thomas was silent then for a long time, taking a long swig of whiskey. He nodded in quiet satisfaction, as if the painful words had been killed off. Dena did not understand the satisfaction obtained from the manly drink, but Thomas seemed to appreciate it just as much as Gottlieb had.

"I might understand, just a little." Her voice was quiet. "Gottlieb had a . . . heavy hand as well as a cruel tongue. He could rant at me plenty, but he never lifted his hand against me. Our livestock took the brunt. For years and years. Each day was more of the same. Finally one day Bruno had had enough, and our lives changed forever."

The wind kicked its white heels outside, making more of a dancing song this afternoon than yesterday's mournful dirge.

"Yeah. I think I know how life can turn on you. . . . That's one thing I learned riding with the boys. We didn't leave each other. We didn't snitch or turn on each other. So I never expected Frank and Jesse coming over, advising us to split up and head out of there quick.

"Mind you," he assured her in a defensive tone, "they were genuinely concerned, convinced it was the best way. A posse was already hot on our trail.

"Cole told them flat out that he might manage an escape, but his brothers couldn't. He refused to leave them to the mercy of the mob. They'd find a quiet place to rest until they were found, and they offered to keep Charlie. He was already unconscious."

Thomas's beautiful face twisted in an unlovely irony.

"The good folk of Northfield would help 'em and heal 'em before they hanged 'em.

"Jesse said he and Frank were thinking about heading southwest to Dakota country for a while. Posse would think them bound for Clay County.

"He advised me flat out to steer clear of him and Frank. He said that no one was looking for me. They'd be expecting the usual eight. I was the ninth; no one knew I was with 'em."

Thomas got up to walk restlessly about the room. He paused at the Christmas branch. Dena had already considered knitting him a neck scarf for Christmas.

He turned to face her again. The desolation in his eyes was almost palpable.

"Frank made sure I remembered I was family. He even told me I belonged with them, and they wouldn't stop me if I wanted to stay with 'em. In fact, he said they'd welcome me. But both he and Jesse insisted I'd be safer away from 'em. We'd meet up again someday. They gave me their word."

Family. The words were the dearest Thomas had ever heard, and even today they warmed him through. The unity of the beleaguered Younger brothers still touched his heart. He wished he could remember that in the night instead of the blood. Yet talking to Dena, he realized anew that Frank and Jesse had been right; he'd be safer alone—if he had a place to go.

"That's when Frank told me about the kin supposedly in southeast Nebraska that gave refuge to his folks during the War of Northern Aggression.

"I left them all then, riding as hard as I could. I tried to ignore the pain from my separated shoulder. All I had to do was see Jim's ruined face, Charlie's slow death, to know I didn't have it near so bad.

"Of course I knew it was hundreds of miles to Nebraska. But it was early fall, late summer really. The cold weather would be weeks off. I knew how to track and hunt. I could be safe, do it on my own. Whenever I felt fear, I knew that somewhere ahead there was that refuge at Zee's Place. After all, Frank was right; nobody knew about me.

"Then, maybe seven miles outside of Northfield, a gunshot I never expected rammed into my good shoulder. I managed to stay astride for another few miles."

Dena had blistering memories of her own, and had felt pain that she was certain no other human had. But seeing Thomas's tortured face, she wondered if perhaps she had a kindred spirit in this man who had ridden up in a pale coat on a ghostlike horse who made no sound. Would he mind her coming over to him with an embrace? Or were these painful words something he must endure alone?

He looked over at her. His fingers touched the soft batting of the Christmas branch as lightly as they had her hair.

Fingers that she wanted on her.

Running to him, she threw her arms about him as she had yesterday in the blizzard. Twice now; something she had never done before. In their fervid embrace, no words seemed to need saying.

He picked her up and carried her back to the armchair, where he sat down still holding her. She liked it. No one had held her like that since Papa, when he had recited fairy tales and nursery rhymes. Some of the rhymes had made sense. Mistress Mary quite contrary had been the traitorous Mary Queen of Scots. Oh, Papa had known so many wonderful things.

When Thomas ran his hand up her leg under her skirt, she couldn't decide whether to be outraged or randy. He stopped, though, at the gun she slid into her garter every morning.

She wondered if he thought she was still afraid of him. He took the gun from its perch and considered it carefully.

"I don't mean anything by it, Thomas. I'm not afraid of you. It's just force of habit . . ."

He smiled. "A good habit. Could save your life. Would have"—his smile was wry—"if I'd been a real killer."

"I'm glad you're here. I can't explain it more than that. Without Northfield, you wouldn't be. I'm almost glad it happened."

He nodded but wasn't at all romantic at the moment. She decided to be miffed. He studied her gun with inordinate care.

"This is an interesting firearm, Dena. Where did you get it?"

"My papa. Just before I married Gottlieb and moved to the prairie. I think they had talked about ways to keep me safe. It's small, you know, so I can conceal it, but powerful enough to . . . be effective."

She decided to confess. "I've never shot anything but melons and pumpkins."

He finally looked at her. "Well, your aim was true. You scared the hell out of me."

"Just because you didn't expect it."

"Maybe. But this here is a very interesting gun."

She shrugged. Firearms were another of the manly things that had never held any great interest for her. Always expecting the worst, Gottlieb had kept a loaded shotgun under their bed. She supposed it was still there.

"I'm serious, Dena. This is a rare piece." His eyes never wavered.

For a moment, Dena was impatient with men's obsessions with horses, whiskey, and guns. It was more annoying than the debutantes at the Cape whose sole reasons for living were new ball gowns and the handsomest rich Republicans.

"Well, you can have it and sell it if you want. I can probably find something else." She had the loaded shotgun for now.

"No, Dena. This is a thirty-two-caliber Baby Le Mat. The South requisitioned this design from a British gunmaker during the War of Northern Aggression so the Confederate foot soldiers could have concealed weapons in addition to their muskets. But the deal soured. There were only a few hundred of these made, even less in circulation. It's . . . interesting to find a Northerner with one."

Dena bristled, tensing against him. "So you join the gossips who think that my father smuggled with the blockade runners?"

"Dena, I don't think any less of your father no matter what he did. No one should judge the choices other folk make without knowin' the true story behind it. But it sure looks likely. People often have understandable reasons for doing things that aren't quite moral, if not downright illegal. Like me riding with Jesse and Frank, or your dad smuggling."

"My marrying Gottlieb?"

"Maybe. The point is, all that is in the past. I think we ought to look ahead."

"It hasn't started to snow yet."

His face took on a little leer, a nice leer. "Exactly. I won't be leaving for a while."

Chapter Six

She sat before the Pennsylvania fireplace drying her hair. The night around the little wooden house was clear and cold. Thomas wished they could talk a stroll in it. Her wet hair and a footprint trail made it impossible.

He wondered how she could be so important to him already. Three days ago he hadn't even known she existed. Watching her during the burial from the stand of gnarled cottonwood trees had given him no sense that he would ever even meet her, much less . . . fall in love with her.

Love? Impossible. Those things happened over time. Jesse and his wife, a first cousin named for his own mother, had courted for nine years. Anna had agonized over her love for Frank James.

Desire, now . . . perhaps that was all it was. Frank and Jesse insisted on honorable treatment of women, but that never prevented the Youngers from visiting brothels on the ride. Thomas had tried once but had been too drunk to perform. Nor did overdrinking hold much allure for him.

Maybe a plow and a hearth of his own were all he needed. Wanting to think, he reached for Gottlieb's warm coat.

"Going out to roll a smoke," he told her, and her eyes widened in disgust.

"A smoke? Men think it is a sophisticated habit, but it is merely a smelly one. I loathe it." Her voice was prim.

Nonetheless, he went outdoors, feeling like a naughty schoolboy. He never lit up. From outside looking in, he watched her by candle glow.

She was an enigma. A debutante thoroughly at home on the prairie, a rich girl making do in a humble four-room house. Her widows weeds and today's silk dress had been of the finest kind, but he doubted they were the latest fashion. Her hands, while still young, were work-worn, certainly not the sacred vessels of a society girl accustomed to a cadre of servants. This woman worked hard.

How could she be so important to him already? Maybe the womanless months with Sweyn had made him susceptible to the first woman he saw.

The candle light bathed her with flecks of gold. As it dried, her hair turned as bright as it was during the day. She had Gottlieb's old flannel wrapper over her nightdress, and the red shawl tight around her shoulders. For the first time, he saw tiny pearl earrings in each lobe.

She was not at all a half-dressed trollop who would instantaneously incite a man's lust. But he had never wanted anyone more.

He waited long enough for her to think he had indulged in a smoke. Edgar and Allan, who had come out with him to do their nightly duty, gamboled around him, gnawing playfully at each other's throats. Then he went back inside.

She was already in her room, the curtains drawn. In his, a sprig of rosemary lay on the pillow.

Rosemary, for remembrance. He remembered his Shakespeare. He held it to his nose, sighing in the fragrance. Yes, this was definitely an odor of which Dena would approve.

The corn bag was already between the linens, warming the bed for him.

Dena lay wakeful. She heard him come in but didn't smell the acrid odor that had hung on Gottlieb whenever he returned from the barn after rolling a smoke. She had lived in terror that her husband's ashes would go awry and set the place ablaze, but at least he hadn't corrupted the atmosphere inside their house.

Gottlieb. She pushed the thought of him away, pondering instead whether she had been indecent in reaching inside Thomas's bed with the corn bag. The gesture had been terribly intimate somehow; the sheets had smelled of him. She had loved the scent so much that she had almost resisted laying the fragrant rosemary on his pillow.

Rosemary. For remembrance. Indeed, she wanted him to think of her while he slept instead of the blood-soaked Youngers. But maybe he would misread her gesture as a wanton invitation.

In the dark, she waited both in anticipation and indecision. What would she do if he came to her bedside?

What would she do if he didn't?

For a while, she could hear him washing himself, tidying up for the night. Maybe he was readying himself for her. He hummed a toneless little tune, which surprised her when she remembered his *Aida* that had blown in the blizzard wind.

After a while, she lay in complete darkness. Thomas had blown out the last candle. She listened as well as she could—his footsteps stopped in his little room. She could only imagine his next reaction, either his horror at her blatant invitation or his sigh at her thoughtfulness in making his bedclothes sweet and warm.

She heard a bit of soft movement, as though he lay down and settled the covers around his form. Olga stuffed the many mattresses at her house with cornhusks and dried reeds from the creek, and they rustled aplenty whenever Dena visited during the children's naptime. However, Gottlieb had been able to afford goose-down bedding for his household; the softness swallowed any sounds of Thomas Howard.

Feeling both insulted and grateful that he had ignored her wantonness, she curled herself up in her own cold sheets. She would have to make another corn bag for herself if Thomas Howard stayed long enough. She was freezing. Maybe he truly meant it that he wouldn't leave unless new snow fell to cover his tracks. Maybe it wouldn't snow for the rest of the winter.

In the darkness, she heard one of the dogs snuffle in a sleepy way. She felt abandoned even by her own dogs, who were no doubt warming the bed of their new jerky-feeding hero.

She turned over with a huff, knocking into the tiny Louis XVI table by her bed. Something bounced to the floor. She reached for it—her pistol.

For a while she pondered Thomas Howard's words about the "Baby Le Mat." She had no reason to disbelieve him about the origins of the rare gun. What if Thomas was right? What if her father's misadventures had included blockade running? Would it have been so wrong to help Southerners in their need for medicines and supplies and receive this uncommon gun in return? How could friends and neighbors become enemies so suddenly? Shouldn't they still care about each other?

But wouldn't that have been the final misery in her mother's life when her only brother had sacrificed all for the North?

Dena had too much thinking to do. Life had been far simpler just a few days ago. Then she had fallen into the routine of farm life, not the only woman she knew whose days revolved around making a home for a gruff, unloved husband. Gottlieb kept her fed and clothed and never struck her. She'd gotten to believe that was all there was. Couples like the Potts who clearly adored each other were more rare than a white bull. And at least Dena hadn't been aged beyond her years by constant childbearing.

Something bore into her sleepless brain, something that wasn't Thomas Howard's light snores. She wanted that adoration. She wanted children. Her life hadn't been enough in the past, and a continuation of it would never be enough in the future.

She didn't know how she could be so certain already, but Thomas Howard was her future. If he'd passed through Staircase Creek a week ago, she would still have been a married woman. Most likely Gottlieb never would have allowed her to see or speak to the stranger using the barn for one night.

Everything had happened according to a divine plan. It made the marriage to Gottlieb worth it.

She tensed in delicious anticipation, wondering what the future would bring her. The fingers of her right hand touched her mouth as lightly as his lips had when he kissed away her frozen tears. A kiss. Their first real kiss. She could still taste it.

When she heard the crinkle of the curtains in the doorway, her heart pounded, then stopped completely still, before starting up all over again.

"Thomas?" She spoke the name with no sound at all.

Instead, Edgar and Allan parted the curtains and jumped on her bed.

At least she was warmed up by the time she fell asleep.

The next morning, Dena woke up more grateful than disappointed. At least she didn't have anything to be ashamed about, having slept by herself all night. She could look her guest in the eye without a blush.

"Thomas? Thomas!"

He was nowhere around, but she knew he hadn't left. Edgar and Allan wouldn't have been able to resist following his horse for a while with their friendly but frenzied barking. As before, coffee perked on the cookstove. She peeked into his bedroom. Well, the sickroom, anyway. The bed was made; her sprig of rosemary sat on the chest of drawers in a water-filled Mason jar.

She started a strudel baking, then headed out to the barn to help him with the chores. He had taken Gottlieb's coat again. Tying the shawl around her shoulders, she wondered if he would like the dress she wore, a pretty yellow tea gown with lace around the elbows and bare arms thereafter, a made-for-her dress from her debutante days. She had refused to discard it, although it was long out of fashion and certainly nothing a married woman would wear.

Stopping by the soddy first, she fed the chickens. The weather was still clear and cold, although the wind was as ungentle as always, rushing down from Canada and the North Pole. Or so Gottlieb had said. Looking north, she saw clouds piling up like dirty laundry, but she figured the wind would blow them away. Thomas had assured her, after all, that he couldn't leave until a snowfall.

She knew Thomas liked her hair down, especially as it was today, freshly cleaned and shiny. Today, with the yellow dress and the weak but sparkling sun, her hair seemed spun from gold.

The barn door was open to freshen the noisome air a bit for the animals and for the benefit of human noses. She remembered when the folk of Staircase Creek had gathered for the raising of Gottlieb's new barn, a task that had taken just a day. The expensive lumber had been milled and sent from the woods along the Blue River. The structure was humble compared to the outbuildings Gottlieb had been used to in Illinois, but it was sturdy, built with pride and love, and certainly kept their stock and supplies safe. She'd fed all the workers and their families, cooking up plenty of sauerkraut and a pork haunch slathered with a spicy sauce she remembered from barbeques on the Cape. The German neighbors had praised her, and for once, Gottlieb seemed proud.

Thomas had climbed the ladder to the little hayloft, where he stacked the fodder into piles neater than Gottlieb ever had.

She laughed in silent delight, wondering if he simply wanted to outdo her husband or if he truly had a better system.

Or, she frowned darkly, was he avoiding her by performing a needless task? The mangers and troughs were all freshly filled, the stalls mucked. He really didn't have much else to do but join her in the kitchen.

Whatever his reason, she couldn't help standing stock still, watching him. It amazed her anew that just a few days could make such a difference in his physique. He looked as strong and hale, as healthy-colored as any man who hadn't survived a raid, been gunshot and on the run from a Pinkerton. As Jonah. As Max Bauer, her neighbor.

But his beauty made those men and all others pale into insignificance. Maybe she ought to suggest trimming his hair—she had done so for Gottlieb—but she liked the locks resting too long on his shoulders, bouncing when he moved. She remembered his pain of just a few nights ago. Was he harming himself by his actions? She hoped not, because she didn't want the motions of his muscles to stop.

He noticed her, then, and called out with a voice and gestures that even a deaf person would know held delight at seeing her.

"Hello, yourself!" she called up, smiling. "I'm thinking you ought to take it easy for your shoulder's sake."

He did stop then, leaning on the rake, looking down at her. "I'm stiff and sore, I don't deny it, but I can only improve my strength and movement by actually moving. Rest during the night is good, but too much in the daytime makes me hardly able to move. I need to keep the hinges greased so I don't rust up.

"Come on up. I'll hold the ladder."

She was almost insulted. "I've climbed that ladder hundreds of times. What do you take me for, a helpless ninny?"

"No." He hung his head like a little boy but looked at her sideways in a way that made her hot. "I just want . . . to help you up."

The way he said it let her know he was as eager to touch her as she was to have him do so.

"Well, I've got something in the oven. Breakfast will be ready soon."

He almost looked disappointed. "No, come on up. I've got something to show you." True to his word, he climbed down, took her hand, and followed her up. The idea of her rump in his face excited rather than mortified her.

"Here." He pointed, and she realized why he had been re-arranging the straw. He had been carving a safe haven for a barn cat and her new litter.

"Fraulein Katze. Katie!" Dena squealed softly, kneeling down to pet the pretty calico cat. "I've considered that I haven't seen you around lately, but I must confess I have had other things on my mind, and you always seem to take care of yourself." She looked up at Thomas. "Katie is a great favorite of Edgar's. They are rarely apart when she is . . . up and around."

She busied herself with the kittens. "Now, we'll need to bring up some freshly scrambled eggs for the little mother, perhaps a pat of butter or two. This is a rare event, however," she added.

"No daddy cat nearby?"

"Oh, yes, Homer is somewhere about. I named him that—"

"Let me guess," Thomas interjected. "Because he is always on an odyssey somewhere with a long-suffering wife left to wait at home."

"Why, yes," Dena replied, delighted, remembering that he had once studied literature also, "but no, it's that kittens aren't often born in the winter."

"Well, new life is always a thing to rejoice, isn't it?"

She rose at Thomas's words, knowing just what it was he meant. Both of them were starting new lives. When he opened his arms, she went into them gladly, without hesitation. Remembering his first night in her house, when she had opened to him like a flag unfurling. Remembering how he'd touched her gently and how ever since she had longed for more.

His lips landed on hers, tentative at first, like a moth testing the blaze of a wick. As if realizing there was no pain, no fear, Thomas explored her mouth with a determination as urgent as he dared. Yet he was gentle, so gentle that the newborn kittens would not have been harmed.

Dena's mouth opened under his as though she needed air

71

and was dying. Was it possible she had lived her whole life and never felt this way? Was it possible that she had been made just for Thomas Howard?

Somewhere in the breathless depths of her was a need that was almost agony, a wasteland that needed life. Her lower body grew tight, unfilled, moist, as it had never been for any man.

Against the pleating of her skirts, she felt his hardness, and she knew full well what it was. Never had Gottlieb been able. And Becker Blanchard had obviously been an undersized boy.

But Thomas was a man, all man, her man. Here with her now in the sanctity of a place full of new life. Acres away from any living thing other than animals whose comforting snuffles and shuffles down below reminded her of the continuity of life.

He maneuvered both of them to their knees. With one hand, he took her shawl and laid it across the straw, laying her against its softness, cuddling at her side. Then his mouth sought hers again. Acutely aware that she was wearing far too many clothes, Dena was unsure what to do next. Gottlieb had tried to bed her, he had tried many times, but only by fumbling beneath her nightgown, himself fully nightshirted, all candle-light doused.

What did one do in the daylight, fully dressed? She wanted to spread her legs wide around him. Shamefully, she felt her nipples tighten against her chemise. What in the world did that mean? Were all these tight places meant for Thomas?

Calling his name, she ran her fingers through his hair as she had longed to do for days.

Was it possible that she had never been kissed, really kissed? Her lips had blossomed under his like the sun warming a crocus frozen from the snow.

He bent to her again as she rose up slightly to tighten her arms around his neck. This time her mouth opened willing, less surprised, and her moan was real. His groin tightened; he moaned back. Although her head barely reached his shoulder, their bodies fit perfectly. She was soft where he wasn't; he was flat where she was curved.

"It's . . . like a breath of heaven," she whispered, awed, as if she had been there. Heat curled around them both, then spiraled between his legs. He wondered if it was the same for her.

"No, just the breath of a man," he told her. He could hear her smile, although she kept her face buried at his chest.

She didn't look at him, she a widow of barely a week. What must he think? His arms held her body against the hot hardness where his legs joined.

She spoke at last. "I don't know what to do next. Gottlieb . . . never kissed me quite like that."

"I can't imagine how he could restrain himself," Thomas Howard told her, bemused. "I've been wanting to do that since the first time you stood in that doorway." No. Before that, he reminded himself, when he watched her from the trees. "But you told me once he was a mean bastard—beg pardon. I don't suppose men like that take time to . . . appreciate a beautiful woman."

"Do you think I'm beautiful?"

"Beyond beautiful. I don't think I could have made you any better if I'd been the Almighty Creator with Adam's rib in my hand."

Dena moaned again. "My gratitude, Thomas. I was once a society belle known for my pulchritude, but those days are long gone. Out here on the prairie"—she relaxed against him—"one finds beauty in a newly born calf or the first green sprouts of wheat."

Tears slid down her cheeks.

"Oh, my God, Dena, I am ashamed of myself!" He pulled away, aghast. "I have overstepped my bounds and insulted you. I beg your forbearance." Shyly, he turned from her, then told the truth slowly. "You overwhelm me."

At first she gasped, then looked at him straight on.

"No, Thomas Howard." Tears in her eyes made them almost green, as when rain brought life to a drought-struck field. "Do not trouble yourself. You have done nothing untoward. I am

73

grateful. I have not felt this wonderful for a very long time."

His own eyes were bright. Taking her hand, he pressed it to his lips, trying to ignore his raging manhood.

Suddenly he pulled away, breathing hard, watching her with bright eyes. "Ah, Dena, kissing you is like a garden of a million flowers that no one but us can go into. But . . ." He looked away for a second. "As for the rest of it, I don't think we should. It's . . ."

All of a sudden he could see she was mortified. Of course he was right. They shouldn't. They couldn't. The reasons were legion.

"I'm sorry, Thomas, I don't know what came over me. What you must think of me."

"What I think is that you are a beautiful, desirable woman who has saved me. But I think . . . I do think this truly, Dena, I do . . . that we will have a time for—this. Just not now."

Dena saw the regret in his eyes. She was a new widow, after all. He had ridden with hardened outlaws who had taught him to respect women, who themselves were faithful husbands to devoted wives. Right now, he couldn't stay, regardless of faithfulness and devotion.

She had indeed saved him. Anything now would be taking advantage, not repaying in kind. Yes, she knew all about honor.

She pulled him back down with her on the shawl. The straw scratched her skin where her sleeves bared her arms at the elbow.

"Beautiful gown. Better suited for a summer day than the first of December! Are you cold?"

Even before she answered, he ran his hands up and down her arms, her body.

"I know it's for summer"—she was almost too breathless to talk—"but I wanted to feel joy." To be pretty for you. "To remind us that maybe there are better times ahead."

As if trying to calm down, he stretched out on his stomach and picked up a piece of straw, sticking it into his mouth like a cheroot.

Dena had to laugh. "Gottlieb did that whenever he got the urge for tobacco and none was available."

Thomas Howard didn't seem to flinch at the mention of her husband, but Dena felt rude mentioning Gottlieb nonetheless.

"Too bad this isn't any other time," she remarked, snuggling close again. "A time when we could picnic along the creek, maybe even be normal people together. Go to church, go to town. Mrs. Rausch runs a tasty little dining room some evenings."

"Court proper, you mean?" His eyes were intense.

Dena flushed. "Well, yes."

"I say again I think those times will come. But if this weren't the time it is, we would never have met. That's a fact."

Dena wanted to reach for him again, but she remembered and cried out, "My sweet *himmel*, the strudel's going to burn and I'll set the house afire!"

She could hear Thomas's understanding laughter as she scrambled down the ladder. The man could cook, after all.

Chapter Seven

Thomas sat as sure of himself as the lord of the manor in the armchair in front of the Pennsylvania fireplace. The noonday meal had obviously set well with him.

Dena watched as surreptitiously as she could over a basket of mending. First on the agenda was adding lost buttons to a Scots plaid woolen shirt that should fit Thomas with room for plenty of warm underwear beneath. Gottlieb wouldn't need it anymore; he had been buried in his Sunday best. His wool trousers . . . well, they were far too ample in girth for the well-constructed Thomas, but Dena had remodeled them as best she could. Then Thomas's vile denim pants could be burned along with his wretched duster.

Time seemed to have stopped. The tableau was as frozen in Dena's mind as the prettiest portrait of homelife she might have seen hanging in a museum.

She sipped tea from time to time, still full from the noon meal. However, Thomas, being a man, might be hungry already. Gottlieb had never seemed to fill up.

"Thomas, supper's not due for a while. Would you like a little something now?"

"Time for high tea, is it, ma'am?" he teased in a hoity-toity voice. She laughed, although she blushed a little; teatime had been a sacred ritual in Cape Girardeau.

"Well, maybe some coffee, some bread and cheese? I can reheat the strudel?"

"No, I am fully content." He looked it. In fact, he looked as confident and comfortable as her father used to, sucking on his meerschaum pipe from the confines of his hand-tanned leather wing-backed chair in his well-appointed study.

Dena laughed silently for a moment, comparing the elegant room of her memory with the spare, utilitarian room that was now her home.

"But I have my doubts about the faithfulness of the good folk of Staircase Creek."

"Why's that?" Dena asked. It seemed a peculiar thing to say. She hadn't thought about her neighbors for days.

"Well, here it is, past midday. There've been no concerned neighbors clamoring to see how the Widow Clayter fares even after being visited by an *outlaw*. Even those little boys didn't show. It isn't snowing now."

For a moment, Dena considered his remark. She had been glad in her heart for the lack of intrusion from the outside world, but Thomas's words made her think.

"Well, I suppose there could be drifts preventing the boys. I confess"—she looked at him shyly—"no, I'm *ashamed* to admit that I have so much enjoyed my time with you that in my heart I'm glad there's no one else about. Especially the Pinkerton. But the boys do have a sure-footed mule. . . . I sure hope nothing's wrong."

"How about that brother-in-law of yours, the preacher? Surely he's a likely one to pay a call."

Suddenly Dena felt a sense of panic that her world once again was about to tumble. "Jonah does not like to be out in bad weather, but he lives in Staircase Creek, after all. He could easily stop by today if anyone has managed to drive a wagon down the road and give him a trail. Gottlieb made certain his brother had a Portland cutter nearly as nice as our own. Then again, Jonah is devoted to his parishioners. Perhaps there are others in greater need.

"Now Max Bauer, my neighbor to the north . . . I suspect he'll stop by on Sunday after services. He'll want to be dressed proper. He'll probably even hint as to buying my farm, since I'm likely incapable of caring for it myself."

Thomas looked chagrined. "Seriously?"

"Yes. He mentioned it in a general way at Gottlieb's wake. In any event, he has some cousins who I may hire for spring planting."

Once again she looked around the cozy place that was her home. "I just guess everyone else has gone on with their lives, Thomas. I think they know from my . . . remarks and some of my habits that I am not a helpless infant, and that I want things a certain way. Most likely they expect me to show up for church on Sunday and have fellowship then. Besides, I am convinced that many of them are a bit frightened of Bruno. They all know I refuse to get rid of him."

"He's not exactly on the loose."

"No." Dena had spoken gently to the animal that day while feeding and watering him. "But I suspect the specter of evil, of murder, hangs on him. Poor dear."

"Poor dear!" Thomas laughed out loud, a quick, joyful bark that woke up the dogs. "I wish I could earn some of the devotion you lavish on those animals."

She giggled a little in return. "They deserve it. They have no one else." *Just like I hadn't, until you.* And who had Thomas Howard had, until Frank and Jesse?

She asked him.

He remained relaxed, although she could see tension wrinkle the little place between his eyes.

"Had a step-pa I liked well enough, but he left to make his fortune and never came back. A buggy accident took Ma a few years later. I guess I was about twelve. A neighboring farm family took me in, and my sisters. For a time they were kind to us, gave us a sense of kin. Ma had put a bit of money aside for me for college in a Doniphan bank. I grew up strong and smart and went to college just as she wished."

For a few seconds, he stretched as if his shoulders were suddenly stiff. His face tightened around the mouth. She guessed rightly that the next portion of his memories were not happy ones.

"Well, when the farmer found out about the college fund, he sued me in a court of law for reimbursement for the upkeep of us kids all those years. The girls, my two sisters, were married by then."

"Where are your sisters?" Dena had never had any, and the concept of siblings was a novel one. Why weren't these women helping their brother now?

Pain seemed to tweak even the end of his nose. "They . . . they don't know about me . . . riding with Jesse. I don't know that I want them to; not yet, anyway."

"You're the one always harping about kinship. Do you really think they would turn their backs on you now?"

It took a while for him to answer. "Yes, I do. After they turn me in, of course."

"That's a brutal thing to say."

"I believe my instincts about them to be correct." His voice was suddenly cold. "You see, Dena, all Ma left them was a couple of pieces of pretty jewelry. She wasn't being mean. She figured they'd marry, be taken care of. When they found out about my college money, they told Darcy—the farmer—about it. He sued me with their full support and permission, gave them each a little share of what he won." He looked at her again with a bitter smile. "So you see, our ideas of kinship are pretty different. And I am certain somewhere there's a reward out for my head that they would love to claim."

He got up then and walked to the armoire where she kept Gottlieb's whiskey. Taking a quick swig from a new bottle, he turned to her once more, his face nearly as pale as it had been the night she had wiped up his blood.

"I don't much like talking about these things. But now you know."

"Oh, Thomas." She left her mending and ran to him, holding him close as a mother would an injured child. He allowed it, but just for a moment.

"I'll go tend to Whisper." He broke from her gently and climbed into Gottlieb's coat. "I'll be back in a while to help you with supper."

"I thought you weren't hungry."

"You thought wrong." He leered at her in his nice way, and she felt at peace.

"Wait a minute. I'll go with you. Let me scramble up an egg for Katie first."

For a second, he looked at her blankly.

"Fraulein Katze, my cat."

Smiling with a nod, he rocked on his boot heels while she cooked, then took her hand as they walked to the barn.

Thomas stood in the doorway watching her sleep. It was bound to snow tomorrow; the clouds had piled up like his dirty linen duster on the floor. He hated the thought, but he was going to have to leave her.

At least they had had this day. Not only the kiss in the hayloft and the unspoken vows for a future, some confidences, and a new litter of kittens. But a day like any other couple on the plains.

Devotion and nurturing were something Thomas Howard was not used to. And here he found it with a woman he had known less than a week.

"Good night, Thomas." She had touched his hand as she said the words with an invitation that she both offered and rescinded. And now he watched her curl up with a corn bag. She had made a second one while they sat quietly by the Pennsylvania fireplace after the evening meal.

Ah, devotion and nurturing. He had witnessed a little of it between others. It was a sight to see whenever Jesse could spend time with the lovely Zee, named for her aunt. And

Anna . . . she had found her soul mate in Frank James, although until Dena, Thomas had fancied himself half in love with her.

He wondered how Dena had become so important to him so quickly. While she shifted in her sleep, her left hand landed lightly on her cheek. How he wanted to be that hand.

Something stirred deep inside him; his manhood, surely, at seeing a beautiful woman in bed, but also something deeper, more elemental. The something that had broken his mother's spirit when his stepfather had gone off to the goldfields, never to be heard from again. Losing her first mate had been bad enough, but she had believed enough in the power of love to try again.

Would it be worth it to have such a love even if just for a short time? Watching Dena, he believed it to be so.

Tonight he couldn't help wondering if he could have changed any of his life along the way. At Darcy's he'd learned how to work the land and perform honest labor. It shamed him sometimes to think that he had joined Frank and Jesse for an easy ride to wealth. And yet he loved and forgave them. Maybe he should have used the college money to buy a little place for himself and his sisters instead of spending it on himself. Maybe he should understand their jealousy and forgive them, too.

Dena moved once again in her sleep, an almost-smile curving her pink mouth. Thomas wished he could have such peace when he slept. But then he remembered that Dena had demons of her own to keep at bay. She hadn't loved Gottlieb, but he had died tragically, well before his time.

Thomas didn't feel much guilt about that, however. Maybe he needed a good deal more forgiveness, too.

Dena woke up once in the night to use the chamber pot. She felt slightly embarrassed, wondering if Thomas Howard could hear. She considered her thoughts; she had been eager to make love with him in the hayloft, for their bodies to join in the most private way imaginable. Surely bodily eliminations were no more intimate than that.

She lit a candle and padded through the cold house to pump some water for a drink. In her heart she knew why; she wanted Thomas Howard to see the candlelight, to hear her. To wake up. To invite her to be with him.

It didn't have to be in bed. She simply wanted to be with him, to do the normal things with him that they had done all day. Perhaps it was like this with real couples. Perhaps even her own parents had enjoyed each other at one time, doing everyday things. Then she decided against that; her parents had always been surrounded by a contingent of servants.

She sat in the soft armchair Thomas favored, close to the leftover heat in the Pennsylvania fireplace. The room was cold, making the idea of sharing of a warm bed with a warm body all the more inviting. Allan had followed her out, curling into a huge ball on the rug at her feet. She stuck her toes beneath him to warm them. She could hear snoring; it was either Edgar, still on her bed, or Thomas snug in his.

Thomas's words about the lack of friends visiting her haunted her. The seclusion with Thomas had been so delicious that she hadn't had time to realize that her friends had neglected her. Even Jonah. Right after the accident she hadn't been left alone for a split second. Now, deep in the darkness of a cold night, she felt a powerful sadness. It seemed impossible that Jonah hadn't continued his obsessive protection, particularly with a notorious criminal at large.

In fact, Jonah had nearly refused to let her return home with the Potts after the funeral feast, insisting in his righteous way that she remain in the parsonage guest room with Mira Wuebke as chaperone. Dena fairly sighed with sudden contentment; if she hadn't thrown a fit to come home, she would never have met Thomas. He'd have been long gone before she finally got home again.

Nonetheless, she decided to be miffed at her brother-in-law.

Suddenly she heard soft screams above the sounds, so it wasn't Thomas snoring. Thomas was having one of his nightmares. Obviously telling her about Northfield had helped to make that evil day live once more in his mind.

She ran to his bedside. He needed the sanctity of sleep; the torment of nightmares would only weaken the health he had made strides to regain.

"Jesse. Alone? Alone? Charlie . . . Char*lee.*" He thrashed, his skin heated even in the cold room.

She could think of only one thing to do, the same thing she had done with Gottlieb in this very room as he lay dying. She climbed into bed and held him.

How could she have ever thought a winter night to be cold? The hot body of Thomas Howard seemed to fuse into hers even through their nightclothes. At first she held him from behind, her body around his. Her arms, far stronger from farm chores than any prissy-faced society girl's from lifting a teacup to her lips, held him still. Into his ears she crooned the baby songs she remembered from her mother's bedtime stories.

Along his shoulders, his too-long dark hair lay damp, and he seemed to want to shrug out of the nightshirt. His hair started to curl around the collar.

"Thomas, hush, love, it's Dena. You've had a bad dream. Everything's all right. Hush, now, you'll see."

He turned in her embrace to face her. In the blackness of the winter night, the candle glow from the main room seemed to light up the place like a meteor. For the first time, Dena was close to him without the confines of corset and binding undergarments between them. For the first time, Thomas, too, was free of trousers. From behind Gottlieb's nightshirt, his manhood raged against her belly.

Against all reason, she wanted it elsewhere. Inside her.

His eyes were open, startlingly bright in the candlelight.

She could see his torment. Tears tracked from the corners of his eyes.

"Dena, how do you do it? How do you hold the beasts still? At night, when you're the most vulnerable?"

She hadn't been needed very often. Even Gottlieb, when he had needed her most, had been too far gone to realize it.

"Thomas, hush." She stroked the damp hair. It started to dry against her hot hands. "Sometimes I pray. Other times I remember wonderful things that I've known." Her voice took on a singsong lilt to try to lull him. "The first time I saw the ocean. The hill of Montmarte in Paris. Queen Victoria's guards at Buckingham Palace. Tasting champagne at Eperne that was like swallowing stars."

Then she realized her childhood of privilege might make no sense to him. Her mind moved on to things she'd grown to love that he might appreciate. "A newborn calf, its mama licking it clean. The townsfolk singing with their whole hearts on Christmas Day. Crocuses peeking out from the snow."

He hadn't really moved, but she could feel the tension drain from him.

"And then I try to realize that other people, many other people, have it so much worse than I. I remember Mira telling me about a baby in her hometown born without a face. Just a hole with a membrane across it. And some of the war veterans . . . One man in Cape Girardeau had no limbs left at all. And hope, Thomas. Hope is the greatest thing of all."

"Hope." He nuzzled against her chest, not as a lover but as a lost soul.

They fell asleep together.

Chapter Eight

"Oh, Lordy, someone's coming up the road!"

At Dena's shriek, Edgar opened one eye before curling back against Allan on her bed. No human had heard her yell, though. The man called Thomas Howard was busy outside, shoveling a path to the barn not long after their noontime dinner.

She paused once before screaming again, just to remember. Remember wrapping her arms about him in the dark, his own arms holding her close while he slept. Did he remember? He'd eaten her fine home-cooked breakfast with appreciation, but never did she sense him awash with romantic inclinations.

She ran out to him, hoping he would remember but planning on being embarrassed if he did.

"Thomas, someone's riding this way!" Her voice reached an unhappy pitch, startling him. It had snowed a little during the night, but the day had warmed somewhat. Still, the cold pimpled her skin.

Thomas had hung Gottlieb's coat on the barn-door latch.

She'd been admiring him from the window while she finished rinsing socks, his and the pairs that Gottlieb had dirtied before he died. The hot water soothed her cold hands.

She marveled anew that Thomas could work so peacefully now when he had come to her in such pain. How relaxed he was in the daylight after the torment of his nightmares. Would she ever tire of watching him?

"Thomas!" She ran closer. "Somebody's coming!"

He smiled at her, a smile that started small then glared across his face, like the sun coming slowly up at dawn, busting all of a sudden into day.

"Well, I should think you would be happy. Yesterday you were more than a little miffed that no one had come a'calling."

"I was not!" But she was; how had he known? "Anyway, maybe it's the Pinkerton! *Maybe it's the Pinkerton!* Let's get you hidden!"

He stopped shoveling, squinting surreptitiously through the barren branches of the windbreak. Then he smiled. "No Pinkerton would ride a mule, that's for sure."

Dena's blush was bright as she remembered their night. His smile was gentle; surely he didn't think her a shameless hussy. Then she settled to the task at hand.

"A mule? What's wrong with mules? They're a great deal smarter than horses."

He nodded. "That I know. But in spite of my personal admiration for the beasts, I do not believe the visitor to be the Pinkerton."

"Then it's Olga! Thomas, you must hide nonetheless! She notices everything and, God love her, is Staircase Creek's biggest gossip."

"In size or in scope?" He continued to smile, and furious now, she fought an urge to slap the nonchalance off his face.

"Both! Now get in the barn!" Dena grabbed Gottlieb's coat and unlatched the door. "In fact, Bruno . . . I'll lead him from his lean-to and tether him out here, near the barn door. She won't dare go inside."

"Lead him? A man-killer?"

"Gottlieb, God rest his soul, got only what he deserved. He was going after Bruno with a pitchfork, and not for the first time. I'm sorry to have to say it, but gentleness was not a word he equated with manliness. I remember the children showing their bulls at the county fair when I was young, and they minded like pussycats. A kind touch, a gentle word. That's all it takes with any living thing."

He looked carefully at her. "All right, I'll take care of the bull. Why, you're trembling. What's got you so shaken?"

"I can't help it. Olga's bound to notice something I just can't see, something that's not the usual."

"Then let's really give her something to talk about." The mischief in his eyes caught the glare of the morning sun, then softened into a look that reflected her dreams. "It was real nice last night," he whispered softly, pulling her close.

She wanted to resist, to hide, to prepare for Olga's visit, but she was helpless for this little while. His lips warmed hers, then parted, nibbling at her own.

Then his tongue touched the cleft in her lips, gently forcing her mouth open. Briefly, she wondered, awhirl with sensation, how it was Becker Blanchard had never stirred her so. In her other life, Becker might be her husband now. The thought made her grateful for the present. Thomas's kisses only got better and better. She was more than ever convinced that Thomas Howard was meant for her, that his finding sanctuary in her home that night for whatever reason was more than co-incidence. Fate . . . God . . . had led him to her.

For a few seconds longer she indulged herself, worrying that he might find her wanting. When she drew back and sought his eyes, she didn't think so. He was as breathless as she.

But Olga would be here soon.

"Hurry on, now!" She gave one of the orders that only she could give and still sound delicate.

Thomas hugged her once more, then let her go. He laughed. "I have survived dangers far greater than a farm wife. I'll be fine. We'll be fine." He reached out to touch her hair; she wore it loose, long and golden across her back. Then his fingers lingered just a second too long on her neck. Her eyelashes lowered like butterfly wings. He reached down to her again.

Olga was so close that the moment had to end. The winter air chilled him as soon as he stopped shoveling, and he shrugged into the old coat. "All right," he relented, "I'll go in the barn, but why move Bruno? Why would Olga go in the barn?"

Nervously, Dena stretched her red shawl around her shoulders and scraped her hair into a knot. She was still shaken from the kiss, embarrassed about last night, and hardly able to speak coherently. "I don't know. But she has the propensity to do and say just what I hope she won't. And if we don't take precautions, she'll notice Whisper, sure as morning comes."

"All right. I'll get Bruno. And start relaxing. Go inside and set the teakettle to boil." He smiled, as if to say everything would be all right.

Olga reached the front door in no time at all, and Dena was far from calm.

"Olga!" She tried to smile brightly after the woman's energetic hug. Would the experienced married woman be able to sense that Dena was freshly kissed? Her words were shaky at first but ended up sounding fine. "Please come on in! I'm making tea. Let's get you warmed up. Why on God's good earth are you out and about on such a winter's day?"

"It's a fine day to breathe good clean prairie air, but I came out to see how you fare." Olga followed Dena into the main room, pausing to wipe her feet on a doormat she had braided herself as a gift.

"Olga, come on in. Let's get you warmed up before it starts to snow again."

Olga laughed, a deep-chested sound. "Snow! Dena, I've lived here long enough to know it won't snow again afore mid-morning tomorrow!"

"How on earth can you know that?" Dena asked, honestly interested, and grateful, too. It meant she had another whole night and then some with Thomas Howard.

"I can just feel it. I know that sounds foolish, but I just know.

It's the wetness or lack of it in the air. I just know the snow is done for this day." Olga stretched suddenly and took off her coat. Well, Wilhelm's coat, underneath which she wore a pair of his overalls. She noticed Dena's wide eyes. "I cannot ride astride in a skirt, foolish garment. Now, Dena, you know I came to check on you, hoping you weren't sick. I brought my chicken broth just in case." She held out a thick pottery crock wrapped in an old towel and set it on the table.

"I am so sorry we Potts missed yesterday. All the boys—including my Wilhelm—are down with an ague that also causes griping in the belly and bowels. It afflicted Willie and Georg evening afore last. The *kleine jungen* seem unaffected.

"Wilhelm took the wagon into town yesterday afternoon to get a barrel of molasses and was stricken about a half mile down the road on his way home. Soiled himself like an infant. He had thought to stop by and check on you but wasn't presentable in that state. With so many down sick, this is my first chance to see what you need. And God's fresh, clean air, I needed that, too." For a second, Olga's plump cheeks wrinkled as she alluded to sickroom smells, then grew radiant again at the mention of her husband, soiled or not. They were perfectly attuned to each other both emotionally and physically, and over the two decades of their marriage had even grown to look a little alike, barrel-shaped with plump arms and legs, and hair turning to pewter gray.

I want that look on my face when I think about my man. My Thomas, Dena amended.

And if it doesn't snow again until tomorrow, I have another whole night with him.

She blushed. Of course Olga noticed.

"My goodness, Dena, you taking on the fever? You're as red as a beet! Thing is, Reverend Clayter has taken down with it, too, says Wilhelm, and a bunch of townsfolk as well. Frau Wuebke is delighted to nurse our pastor into health and call on other sick ones in his stead. As a pastor's wife might." For a moment, Olga's eyes met Dena's knowingly. Mira's crush on the pastor was no secret. "Well, you know Mira worked as a nurse during the war. She is convinced that those folk that took sick all ate from a potluck dish at Gottlieb's feast that had gone bad while still tasting good. They should be up and about in a few days, after some broth and strong tea."

Olga put out her hand to touch Dena's forehead. The cold hand felt good against the heat, but Olga apologized for her thoughtlessness.

"Fool mittens. Don't warm me worth a wooden nickel."

"I am feeling fine," Dena began, then noticed Olga's eyes scrunch together in puzzled shock. Widows weren't supposed to feel fine. "I mean, I didn't really eat anything at the . . . funeral feast. And I am grateful that Gottlieb was such a good provider that I hardly miss him."

Olga's eyes narrowed even more.

"No, no, Olga!" Dena rushed on, horrified. "That came out poorly. What I mean is, all the stores are in order for winter. I haven't needed to come running to my neighbors for help."

"Well, never you mind about that. That's what we all are here for." Olga wandered comfortably around the room, and Dena tensed. What did Thomas's room look like? Had he shut the drapes? Made the bed?

Horrified, she forgot the man's stockings she'd been rinsing. Maybe Olga wouldn't realize what lay wet and crumpled. She actually held her breath.

Apparently Olga noticed nothing amiss. The big woman found a chair and plopped down, waiting for tea. "Max Bauer too, Dena. We discussed you at the wake. He's most eager to assist you in any way. I'm on my way to his place next, making sure he isn't under the weather. Got another crock of broth in m' saddlebag just in case."

At the name, Dena's stomach turned, but she busied herself making the tea. She wasn't sure why the mention of Mr. Bauer made her nervous. All the man had done was offer to help her hire some field hands. Yet he had sometimes had a look in his eye, even before Gottlieb died, that was a little off from proper.

Somewhere she might have some ground ginger that should help settle her belly.

Suddenly Olga began to laugh, pointing to the corner.

"I'm seeing your Christmas branch! Sure looks pretty. But aren't you celebrating a mite early, considering?"

"Considering that I'm in mourning, you mean?"

Olga ate two of Dena's cinnamon cookies before nodding.

"I don't stand much on formality and ceremony, not here on the prairie, Olga," Dena announced firmly, sounding not at all like the debutante she had once been. "I want to cheer up my home after so much sadness. I don't hold it disrespectful to Gottlieb to celebrate the Lord's birth."

"Ah, Dena, no disrespect intended. I know these are unkind days for you." Olga got up and ambled around the room to stretch her legs after her ride. For a moment, Dena's mind danced around memories of her house: Had Thomas left anything about that would give him away? Would Olga notice the stockings now?

Peering in Dena's room, Olga merely laughed at Edgar and Allan, and Dena started the farewells. Olga didn't appear to be too worried about the sick folk, so Dena wouldn't either. With her nursing experience, Mira Wuebke surely would have recognized dire symptoms of such evils as cholera or diphtheria. This wasn't the first time a little tainted food had soured some stomachs after a big gathering.

Then Dena pulled her friend away from the sickroom that Thomas had used, just in case.

"Olga, I am glad to have your company, but I fear you should start to Bauer's before the afternoon cools down. You don't want ice on the road."

"*Ja,* I guess you're right," Olga agreed with a hearty smile, "although my foolish old mule is so surefooted he could climb the Rockies while he sleeps. But I best be getting along, see about Max and my own menfolk. Although Ida's a handy little woman now."

As Olga mounted her mule, she took a careful look around the yard, with the shoveled pathway, the cleared porch. "My heavens, Dena, you truly have been busy! That looks as good as a man's job. And you don't seem tired at all. The place looks near as tended as Gottlieb used to leave it. You haven't missed my boys' help at all!" For a second, her lips pursed into a little pout.

Her eyes held a second's worth of suspicion that quickly turned to curiosity. Surely she would never imagine the ever-proper Dena Clayter entertaining a mysterious stranger, an outlaw yet. Dena could hardly believe it herself.

Nor could she believe her shameful thoughts of wanting to kiss him again. Perhaps share another night with him. A real night.

"The busier I am, the less apt I am to think about . . . what might have been." Dena forced the prim words from her mouth. "And Gottlieb taught me well. I know what to do and how to keep up a place."

"Well, my dear, I am sure Willie and Georg will be up and around in no time."

"I do hope so. Give them all my good wishes." Dena waved as the woman plodded off.

She knew that Thomas would be watching somehow from the barn, waiting for Olga Pott to leave. Indeed, he stood in the barn doorway, and she ran down the little path he had dug and tossed herself into his arms.

Dena thought she heard him say *I'll never leave* into her hair but figured she'd just imagined it. The cold air was real, however, and didn't matter; she felt hot.

His lips met hers lightly, like a butterfly, then hers opened beneath his like a blooming rose.

"Dena." Thomas drew her hard against him, tightening his arms at her waist. Her own crept up to his shoulders, her body snug against his manly form.

He kissed her again.

Never had she been kissed like Thomas Howard kissed her. Becker Blanchard's lips had been childlike and closed. Gottlieb had offered a perfunctory peck once in a while. He'd never attempted kissing her during his blunders at bedding her.

Shaking away the bad memory, she reminded herself that it

wasn't the time to think of someone else. Yet she remembered a name Thomas Howard'd mentioned and couldn't help herself.

She snuggled against him first as wantonly as she dared, then looked at him shyly. "So who's this Anna Ralston? Was she your . . . What I mean is, were you two in love?"

He laughed in honest delight. His long dark hair shook along with his shoulders. "Not on your life. She was secretly in love with someone else. Had to elope, it was so scandalous." They walked back into the house. His cheeks were winter-reddened, and he bore the faint animal smell of the barn.

Dena had had enough of scandal in Cape Girardeau, but Thomas looked so joyful that she didn't think she had to fear his response.

"Why?"

"Her intended was Alexander Franklin James." He had mirth in his eyes, but some caution, too.

The name meant nothing to Dena at first.

"Frank. Frank James," Thomas amended. He hung up Gottlieb's coat and settled himself in the upholstered chair.

Her smile was halfhearted as she was unsure how to react. She decided to grind up some Arbuckle's coffee beans and brew a fresh pot.

Thomas continued to smile. He'd told her once that the Jameses would probably consider her kin as well, and the notion confused her. She couldn't imagine anyone who robbed and killed being nice people, but Thomas seemed to carry great affection for them. And this Anna; she was an educated woman who had gone to college. Dena was troubled.

"That's how I hooked up with Frank and Jesse, through Anna. Before I even knew about her and Frank, I mentioned to her once in college that I had heard family lore for years that I was somehow related to Reuben Samuel. She took the tale to Frank later on. The rest is history." He stoked the Pennsylvania fireplace with more coal and held his stockinged feet in front of it.

"Well, I can understand the need for finding family, especially after those awful sisters," Dena admitted, "but why on earth did you decide to rob a bank? Couldn't you just have borrowed some money for college?"

"I wanted to avenge the wrongs of the North against my new folk," he stated flatly, not looking at her. His words sounded like those repeated from someone else.

Dena remembered how irked Gottlieb and Jonah became when politics were discussed; she wasn't sure how controversial to get right now. She was a patriot, after all, and they had already discussed some touchy subjects. In all fairness, she decided to let him speak his mind and respect his opinions, something she herself had rarely been allowed to do after leaving life with her parents.

"The North was unkind to my folks, Dena. Arrested Aunt Zerelda as a Southern spy. They hanged Uncle Reuben to try to get him to confess. By that, I mean they hanged him by his neck just long enough not to kill him. But his voicebox was crushed, his brain hurt when no air could get to it."

A gulp of true horror rose in her throat just as the coffee boiled.

"Now, Northfield, it was all a mistake," Thomas told her, his regret clear, "I know it now. I never intended anyone to die."

He got up for a while and looked out the window. Dena couldn't decide if it was regretful memories or cabin fever. She too felt the smallness of the rooms, smelled the staleness of the air.

It must grate on a man used to riding long miles and living great adventure to be cooped up in a farmhouse in the middle of nowhere, doing endless chores for stock and a farm not even his own. If it was another season, if snow wasn't covering the ground to leave the proof of footprints, they might even have got to walk along pretty Staircase Creek, to have supper under the tangle of cottonwood trees along the banks. To kiss with just God watching.

She cut up a pie some neighbor had made from dried wild plums, wondering why she wasn't afraid, with an outlaw in her house. Much less wanting him to be man to her woman. His last words told her why. She and he, they had a connection.

"Neither did I," she replied softly, thinking about Gottlieb.

Thomas looked back at her, apparently lost in his own thoughts.

"Did what?"

"I never wanted anyone to die. I knew practically from the first that I was making a mistake in marrying him, but I never wanted him to die."

"Pie looks good."

She smiled a little, agreeing silently that the subject didn't need to be discussed.

"Why did you let me stay?" Thomas asked, maybe feeling the same. "Here in the house, I mean? And welcome me back a second time?"

Having been raised to be coy, Dena had to think for a while before responding. She walked over to him and took his hand, leading him to the table.

"You didn't shoot me. You could have, but you didn't. You could have . . . ravished me, but you didn't. You . . . looked at me like you thought I was beautiful." She couldn't say the other reason, that he was beautiful, too.

"You were hurt. I wanted to help heal you, something I couldn't do for Gottlieb."

His fingers tightened around hers. "Have you ever been in love before?"

She didn't mind him knowing. It seemed the right time to tell him of Becker Blanchard, of her father. Maybe even all the rest.

"I thought so. But I was just a girl. Then my father had some bad times, and my young man left."

"Because of the bad times?" He sat down and played with a fork.

"Yes, indeed. My father embezzled a great deal of money and got caught and convicted. I guess maybe Becker—my betrothed—realized that I was no longer an heiress and got cold feet. Or perhaps he felt I was too great an embarrassment."

Dena sat down at the table next to him. By then, he had eaten more than half his slice.

"My father and I were close. He spoiled me, and I always took his advice on important matters. In fact, he was Bernhard. My mother called me 'Bernhardena' after him. He devised 'Dena' for short." She smiled for just a moment.

"My father suggested that I marry one of the Clayter brothers." It didn't seem strange to be telling him these things that even Olga didn't know. "They wouldn't consider that I had some sort of stigma. I could live far away in a new place where no one knew me.

"Jonah is more my age, but he was still in seminary and said that he couldn't afford to take on a wife. I, too, was attending college, but that fact didn't seem important to anyone but me." Her voice turned rueful, and Thomas paused in his joyful eating.

"Gottlieb was eager to wed, but of course I refused him. He was old enough to be my father. But then the gossip got worse."

The words caused pain as they left her mouth, the pain in her soul that she had thought long stilled. But like Thomas's wound, the infection was taking a long time to heal.

"It had been humiliating enough to have Becker publicly disavow our engagement. But then . . ." Her voice stalled into a silent whisper. "Lies started spreading that my father had made a lot of his money helping Southern blockade-runners during the war.

"Folks even started to say that my mother knew about it years before, and her heart broke, having already lost her brother. I had always thought her the world's strongest woman, but I almost believed the gossip myself. Something desperate had to have killed her. She just went into a decline, wouldn't eat, and died in her sleep. Now, if what you say about the Baby Le Mat is true, maybe all of that was true."

Outside, the sunlight split the clouds so that blue shone through. Rays in turn streaked across the gloom of the room.

"I just wanted to leave St. Louis, and the Cape was worse.

My mama had grown up there, and folk were rife with talk that they all knew she married unwisely to a hard-nosed German Lutheran."

Dena stopped suddenly. Meeting Thomas's eyes, she smiled with honest apology. "I am truly sorry, burdening you with all of this. You have troubles enough of your own."

He poured them each more coffee, then touched her hand. "I have in truth burdened you with my troubles. No apology is needed a'tall."

Since he seemed agreeable, she decided to finish her saga. "I had no place left to go and no money to start over. College was a lost opportunity. Staircase Creek seemed a whole world away, where nobody would know anything about me. And at that time, Gottlieb gave every indication of being a gentleman."

Edgar emerged just then from his hibernation in the bedroom, coming to Dena to lay his head on her knee. For a few seconds, she buried her face in his back, her arms about his neck.

"So I agreed. We had a tiny wedding in the pastor's study. No new gown, no diamond ring. The pastor's wife did bake us a little cake, and she served us some wine. Both Gottlieb and my father seemed happy enough, and I felt relief.

"And that," she declared solemnly, "that was my wedding day. That night, with me all taken care of, my father . . . went to his study and stuck a pistol in his mouth."

Jonah was too considerate to mention these terrible events even when they were alone. But Dena had no qualms about sharing the story with Thomas Howard. Now she spoke with no vocal inflection at all.

"Jonah insisted that he be buried in consecrated ground." She almost smiled. "For being so dignified and well-behaved, a man who follows all the rules, he made so much noise that the church agreed. But he rests in St. Louis, not with my mother in her family's vault. There was one cousin left at the time, and he refused to allow it."

The smile left her face just as fast. "Then I came here."

Her voice took a lighter note. There was no sense in allowing the man before her to believe her to be maudlin or a malcontent. Having him think well of her was a priority. "It is a nice house, for the prairie. Not what I had in the Cape, with the Japanese lanterns around the pergola, and garden parties. Certainly not the mansion in St. Louis, where I had a fur-lined cloak to wear in the winter and a driver for my buggy. But nice in its own way. And so different, each inch, each minute, that nothing reminds me of my old life." The buggy and the expensive cloak had gone in the auction. Gottlieb hadn't for a minute considered that she might want the garment.

"I know all about that," Thomas agreed. "Life can change in a split second, and folk you think you know can do what you never imagined."

Still holding her hand, he brought it to his lips, causing her to breathe fast. Then she nodded.

"Gottlieb took care that no one else knew . . . all the rest. Everyone just assumed he'd somehow charmed a foolish society girl whose father had once been his friend. He could be handsome when he tried. And I was young enough to bend to life on the prairie. Kept so busy that I had no time to recollect." For a few minutes she remembered the transition. Church attendance on Sunday was Staircase Creek's social event of the week, and her first quilting bee in the dead of winter had rivaled the governor's gala in Jefferson City. Most different of all, she found herself making friends with animals when the nearest folk lived acres away and her unpleasant husband rarely sought her conversation.

Finally she sighed and spoke again. "Indeed, Papa had helped Gottlieb invest some money when he was younger. Ill-gotten gains? Who's to know?"

"No one needs to remind me of the perils of ill-gotten gains." Thomas sniffed at his own memories, and their gazes met both with wonder and regret.

Dena shrugged. "Gottlieb had always thought himself too good for the soddy, and he was able to afford lumber from the mill at Milford along the Blue River. No mere whitewash for him."

From some dark corner, Edgar brought an old stick to Thomas to throw. Both of them chided the dog; then Dena's eyes grew dreamy and sad. "Gottlieb wanted to build a wooden house for his first wife. I never met her, although I think Papa had. She's been gone ten years or more. Poor dear. She died in that soddy while Gottlieb stood by and did nothing."

Memories of Gottlieb that had softened somewhat since his death hardened again. Thomas Howard stiffened, aghast. "What on earth do you mean?"

"She bled and bled after birthing a dead baby. Songbird was right outside. Olga had gone to get her. Songbird had poultices and herbal cures that could have staunched the blood and saved her, but Gottlieb refused."

"Who's Songbird? Why?"

" 'A heathen redskin.' " Dena could almost hear Gottlieb's voice.

Her tale certainly did nothing to add holiday cheer to the homestead, nor romance to the atmosphere. In fact, Thomas slung his arm around her for comfort, not sparkin'.

She found she liked his touch anyway.

Suddenly Thomas Howard came to life as he pulled back from the curtain. "Someone's coming."

"Who'd be out when it's threatening to snow again?"

"You know better than me. Mrs. Pott didn't seem to mind the weather. Any other neighbors wanting to check up on you? Maybe your brother-in-law? My guess would be the Pinkerton."

"Thomas, would he really be harassing me again? I told him everything I knew."

They shared a secret look.

"I guess it could be Jonah, or Max Bauer, my neighbor on the north one-sixty," she continued. "Maybe he has some news about the York cousins who want to get hired for spring planting. I'm certainly going to need help." Life was practical on the prairie. No one stood much on ceremony. Dena had not been offended when Max mentioned the possibility to her at Gottlieb's wake.

"I don't think the Pinkerton will leave you alone, leastwise not until I'm captured. Or killed."

"Don't say that!" Dena slapped at his words as she did summer flies.

"Well, it's true. *You* have actually *seen* me."

"I told him I didn't see you clearly. Why wouldn't he believe that?"

"Probably because it's not true. I doubt you're very experienced at lying." He smiled tenderly at her. Dena reflected on the remark. She certainly had not been able to hold her tongue and say proper words during Olga's visit.

"Dena, the Pinkerton Agency's motto is 'We Never Sleep.' You better believe it."

"Well, no matter who it is, get on out to the barn," she ordered him.

"Can't," Thomas replied. "I'm not going to leave footprints in the fresh snow."

"What fresh snow? Olga said it wouldn't fall until tomorrow."

"Look for yourself. Frau Pott was obviously wrong." Thomas held the curtains apart. Off in the distance, she could see a horse trotting through a light snowfall.

She persisted. "Well, why would anyone think I wouldn't walk out to my own barn?"

"No one will think that, but my feet are a sight bigger than yours. Besides, I just don't want to take any chances. I'll hide under a bed or something."

"Oh, God, it *is* the Pinkerton! I'm sure of it!" Dena's voice rose to a frantic shriek as the figure came closer. "I remember his horse, that pretty paint."

"Hold on! I can hide good. Hid from the law for months," he reminded her with a laugh probably meant to relax her since he didn't sound nervous. She only glared at him.

"You weren't here when he questioned me, Thomas. He was sly and mean, waiting for me to trip over my own words. He must be coming back because he doesn't believe me. Maybe someone saw you on the road. Maybe . . ."

"Hold on," Thomas repeated. "Just get busy in the kitchen. Act normal."

She froze in panic once again. *"Whisper!"*

Thomas put his arms around her, as confident as one who had done so a hundred times. "Bruno's still tethered in front of the barn. Because of Mrs. Pott. I truly doubt that the Pinkerton will confront your bull. I'll just bet that his reputation in town has grown to insurmountable proportions."

As Dena rushed to examine the room, dispassionately trying to discern whether proof of Thomas lingered anywhere, he hid under the bed in her room. She'd kicked his gun in there that first night, but he'd obviously retrieved the Peacemaker before leaving that next morning, for she heard the trigger click.

This time she remembered the stockings. Would any intelligent person think she still washed up after a dead husband? Wrapping them in a square of oilcloth, she tossed the bundle into her butter churn. She saw Gottlieb's woolen coat hanging on its hook and remembered the noisome linen garment that Thomas preferred. She'd never gotten around to burning it but couldn't see it anywhere now.

She wouldn't worry about the ragged coat now. But what would prevent the Pinkerton from investigating her room? A full chamber pot, that's what.

"Sorry, Thomas." Her embarrassment was acute. He murmured something from beneath the bed.

The bed skirt touched the floor, but she didn't feel confident even then. Taking some of her unlaundered delicates, she tossed them around the floor, as if she had untidy personal habits. She doubted that any man would want to finger a woman's undergarments. For good measure, she found some particularly noxious drawers that hadn't rinsed well from the last time she'd had her monthly flow two weeks earlier.

She had a cup of hot coffee waiting for the Pinkerton when he knocked on the door.

"Saw you coming down the road," she said as she ushered

him in politely. "Have some coffee to warm yourself." She tried to keep the conversation light and friendly. She motioned him to sit, but he did not. "Now, sir, why in the world are you out and about on such a day?"

"A little snowfall never harmed anyone." He looked down his nose at her. "Besides, it has stopped. And I think you know why I am here."

"Well, I do not. I hope you do not think I am sheltering a notorious criminal." She figured if she spoke the truth he wouldn't think it.

"No, Mrs. Clayter, that I do not think. But I do know he was here and that you saw him. I also know you lied."

Stunned, she stopped the coffee cup just short of spilling down her front. She tried to sound insulted. "What do you mean? I told you everything I know."

"Except that he *had not* been to Zee yet when we talked the first time. No harmless passerby in a barn would give you reason to confuse that detail. You and that outlaw are up to something."

"I have no idea what you mean. I told you everything I know. Whether you believe me or not does not matter to me."

"It should matter, Mrs. Clayter. The James gang boys are charming, but they are also killers."

She wanted to scream that he was wrong but tried instead to appear bored with him and eager to return to her chores.

"I am starting to prepare my evening meal, which under the circumstances I do not think I will invite you to share. You had better leave now Mr. Pinkerton, so that you can get to the boardinghouse before it snows again."

He nodded at her, polite, but she saw the insolence in his eyes. He pulled something from an inner pocket of his thick coat.

"I did not see the significance of this until just this moment." He held it out, an unmistakable match to the shawl she was wearing.

Gottlieb's red scarf.

Her face took on the color of the scarf, but she found it easier this time to weave words into a lie.

"I made it for my husband." This of course was true. "It must have blown off his grave. I put it there to warm him."

Perhaps the Pinkerton had heard town gossip that theirs had not been a sentimental marriage. Pure disgust twisted his lips as he spoke, and she heard him sniff a puff of air from his nose. Without invitation, he strode farther into the house, and, with contempt, hung the scarf back on the coatrack. He fingered Gottlieb's woolen coat and turned to face her.

"This would have kept your husband far warmer, Mrs. Clayter. A fine garment. Much more fitting for winter than a linen duster."

Her face crumpled with confusion. She had no idea as to the Pinkerton's train of thought.

"Yes, it is a fine garment. Gottlieb had it sent for from Chicago. And I have no idea what you mean about linen. Olga grows flax and spins it once in a while, but that activity has never held any attraction for me. Linsey-woolsey is a far more practical fabric for our way of life. I can buy it off the bolt at the mercantile or order it from the Montgomery Ward catalogue." She forced her eyes to focus on his.

He made no more comment about either coat, but his eyes narrowed in a disquieting way.

"I will be watching you, Mrs. Clayter. Every move you make. Something is not right. You just are not a heartsick widow. There's lovelight in your eyes."

Since he spoke the truth, she found herself marveling at his perception. Had she been a James hater, she would have been grateful that the Pinkerton Agency had found this man. But now, his insults sent anger pricking around her nerve endings.

He began to walk around her house without permission, peering into the rooms. To distract him, she began to rant.

"You think that I am somehow behaving like a trollop with some outlaw because I am not tearing out my hair with grief over Gottlieb? Your inability to find this fugitive has nothing to do with me, *sir*. I take no responsibility for your failure. Take your frustration out on someone else. Good day."

Chapter Nine

"My Lord, that was close." Dena's heart rate had finally slowed down to near normal. She snuggled in his lap as they warmed up together near the stove, as they had that night he had found her gun. He ran his hands up and down her trembling arms. The shakes from her body vibrated into Thomas, then stilled. It was nearly over, her time with Thomas. She sensed it now.

"Close? You mean Frau Pott noticing you have managed to shovel snow as good as a man? Or that a Pinkerton agent accuses you of having lovelights in your eyes?" Thomas's words dropped like starlight in her hair.

She blushed.

Dena wanted to giggle but couldn't, not yet. She wanted to enjoy him but couldn't, not yet. "Olga . . . she'll just remember everything, that's all. Sometime soon she'll realize that something, one little thing, was just not as it should have been. And as for the Pinkerton, well, he's dead-on right. And right usually wins out."

"And as for the lovelights, Dena . . ." He lightly touched her hair with his lips. "Things are different now. Your husband is dead."

And you're not. Still. "Somehow, someday, this moment will come back to haunt me." Us.

"What do you think he meant about Gottlieb's coat? And talking about yours?"

He took his left index finger and smoothed the furrow that grew between her eyebrows. "I believe he said it just to discompose you and see your reaction. You did just fine, by the way. Maybe he wanted you to think that he knows I'm here because the coat is still hanging there. Meaning just what has gone on—I wear it because it's warmer than my old one. But as I say, you did just fine. Now stop messin' up this pretty face."

Dena smiled again. "All right, outlaw. You have faced dangers far more grim than a farm wife and a nosy Pinkerton!" Her smile stopped. Now her heart was beating normally again. And while neither spoke the words, he had, after all, outrun the law for months.

Maybe the time was now.

"Thomas."

He stared into the steaming coals of the stove, almost as though he didn't hear her. "Thomas?"

Finally he looked at her. Whoever Becker Blanchard had been, she suddenly couldn't recall. She was stunned anew at Thomas Howard's beauty. It terrified her that he was in danger and that someone could destroy or even end his life.

"Thomas, tell me about . . . who it was that hurt you. Where you've been all these months."

He pulled her close, his words landing on her hair.

"I was on my way out of Northfield, on my way to Zee, just like Jesse advised me, when a bullet came out of nowhere. I don't know who shot me. It probably was a farmer panicked by the news of the raid. I managed to hang on to Whisper and put a half-dozen miles between us. The pain was . . . well, intense."

"I know some of this. You told me already. But that was when, September? It's been three months. What happened until now? Or is this one of those things that I don't need to know?" She remembered his dictum, the first day they met.

"It's pretty," he said, inanely. She realized he was admiring her Christmas branch again. "A bit early."

She smiled sadly, her disappointment acute. Obviously she hadn't earned his trust. "Olga made it with me, my first winter here. I put it up to make me feel a little more cheerful. About everything. About you leaving." She met his eyes firmly then, happy at the warmth she found in them. "I make a new decoration or two each Christmas. This year I'll make some sort of angel."

He must have remembered his snow angel because he smiled. "And I'll make a heart-shaped basket. I learned how from the old Swede who saved me and took Whisper in."

"What? Where?"

"Outside of Northfield. After I got shot. When I came to, it was in a smelly hovel with a demented, wild-eyed old man swearing over my injuries in a foreign language.

"Whisper was already comfortable in the shed; a shed, by the way, that was nicer than the man's house. Sweyn." For a moment, Thomas Howard's mind apparently went back to visit the odd old man who had saved him.

Then his voice turned rueful. "Long ago, he brought his wife and young'uns to the north woods and set up a little homestead along the Cannon River. They drowned in a terrible accident— he never explained just how he was responsible, but he quite lost his mind because of it. White folks leave him alone thinking he's dangerous, and Indians leave him alone thinking his affliction grants him great medicine. So it was a safe haven for me."

"Were you there all this time?"

Thomas nodded. "I don't know if it was Sweyn's herbs and ointments or just nature being cantankerous, but my gunshot healed poorly. Maybe because my body was already busy mending the other shoulder, too. Several times Sweyn tied me up with a stick between my teeth and cut into my wound with a vengeance to drain peculiar fluids. But he never treated me as an invalid. He kept me busy helping out around his little place, kept my bones strong and my muscles moving." As if to demonstrate, he tried to stretch his beleaguered shoulders, grimacing in discomfort.

"And finally I was ready to find Zee," he continued. "I wanted to get there before winter."

"Pinkertons didn't find you in all that time?"

"Guess I'm lucky. Everyone else is shot up or dead."

"Except for Frank and Jesse."

"Yeah, but no one really knows. Maybe they'll get home to their wives for Christmas. How the Pinkerton Agency found out about me, I can't really say. Maybe from one of the Youngers."

"But . . ." She remembered all his yammering about kinship and loyalty.

He held her hand gently. "They wouldn't have turned on me. Maybe one of them let loose words slip because of sickness and pain. It happens."

She knew what he meant. She had heard him call out names in the night herself.

Her fingers interlocked with his like her yarns did when she knitted. For a second, he twisted her wedding band around and around without thinking.

Purposefully she moved her hand in such a way that the ring slid off.

The Pinkerton agent had ridden off more than an hour past, clearly headed for town. The snow had stopped, but Dena knew the storm was holding its breath.

Just as she knew she would not have a whole night with Thomas Howard. Just as she knew he would have to leave.

"Sorry about the chamber pot. I . . . didn't want to take chances." She was busy making their supper. Thomas had drawn and plucked a chicken that morning, and Dena knew all about preparing it with fixin's. Even being a society girl, her gravy was already legendary in Staircase Creek.

"It's all right." Thomas laughed without embarrassment. He

washed up the cup the Pinkerton had used. "Use them myself. And believe me, no air's as poisonous as Sweyn's cabin."

"And also . . . my delicates . . ."

"Had sisters of my own, remember."

The time for any jocularity had gone. She faced him.

"Thomas, I know you must leave. I know you must leave as soon as the snow falls again. Before the wind kicks up. You don't want to wait until the drifts are too difficult for Whisper. Songbird . . . she will help you if you tell her you are my friend. She has a little dugout about five miles downcreek. Not everybody around here considers her a pagan; she lives on the Kraft homestead. Many of the women in Staircase Creek seek her cures for—well, female complaints. She'll have friends who can hide you out all along the way to . . . wherever you need to end up." Songbird had told her this, just in case she had ever felt the need to run away.

She left him for a moment, feeling under the mattress in the room she had shared with Gottlieb. Back at the kitchen area, he was busy at the stove peeling potatoes and chopping up some of the rosemary from her winter garden. For a moment, she admired the picture of a man doing woman's work. Then again, she had mucked her share of stalls, cleaned fish, and pounded nails. She almost laughed out loud at the incongruity of the lady she had been raised to be performing such menial chores, and well, too.

"Here." She held out her hand to him in much the same way she had pointed the pistol.

"What's this?"

"Some five-dollar half eagles. Gottlieb hid them in case of an emergency. I think this is one."

When he started to protest, she shut him up quick.

"You can consider it a loan," she insisted, impatient. "I mean, I hope after you leave that you plan on coming back somehow. Or at least keeping in touch with me some way."

His eyes were sad. "I can't be in touch, Dena. Not with the Pinkerton watching. Please understand. It may be months and months. He'll be watching your place, checking out what post you get, if you receive any telegrams. Whom you wire; where your letters are sent. I got no one at Zee to shelter me. I don't even know where I'll end up. I'll find you somehow, someday. But it won't be for a while."

He added carefully, "Most like a *long* while."

His words both chilled her bones and fired her wrath. But he was right. Of course he was right.

"Listen." She hadn't felt so disconsolate since her father died. "Leave that food. I'm not hungry after all. I am about to go stir crazy locked in this house. Can't we go walking by the creek? Just for a little while, like regular folk? The Pinkerton's been and gone, and it'll snow again before nightfall to hide our tracks."

Thomas seemed wary, but he consented. Dena recognized by the look in his eyes that he was not about to refuse her anything. Gottlieb's had never borne such a look.

"Dena, I meant it when I said it earlier. I do think there is a future for us. It just is not going to be now."

"I think I do miss him a little," she confessed, not looking at Thomas. His arm lay across her shoulders without any effort at all, just at the right level. She leaned against him as they walked to the tree-straggled stream.

"At least I knew then what the next day would likely bring."

Ahead of them, the current of Staircase Creek burbled happily as it chased the snowdrifts on its way to the Blue. Although the sky was thick and gray, a stripe of blue lay across the horizon. As Dena watched, clouds quickly scudded across it as easily as the watercolors painted across pebbled paper when she had studied art.

She shivered. The snow would start soon.

Thomas's arm tightened. "Did you ever love him?" he asked carefully.

"No. Not ever. It was, in truth, a marriage of convenience. I knew such things happened even among sophisticated people. I guess I was young enough not to feel desperation." She gave a rueful little chuckle. "Of course, getting stood up practically at the altar wasn't good for my sensibilities. I was truly ready for a change!"

Her voice grew serious again. "Gottlieb knew his manners and was wise with his money. So it seemed the proper resolution to . . . many predicaments."

She looked up at Thomas. His face wore the color of cold, but it wasn't an ugly redness, nor did his eyes water. He knew how to live in winter, after all, and obviously how to look good in it. She pulled the glove from her hand and touched his face.

The heat from his flesh warmed her fingers, and she tucked her glove in her pocket, unwilling to remove any aspect of Thomas from her.

They reached the creek bank and walked down it as well as they could among the cottonwoods and snowdrifts.

"This must be a beautiful place in the fine months," Thomas remarked.

"Oh, it is." She sneezed a little as the frozen air skipped up her nose. "Sometimes Jonah baptizes folk here, if they want to do it like John the Baptist. And I've always thought 'twould be a lovely setting for a wedding." The words had rolled out of her mouth without conscious thought. She gasped as silently as she could, hoping Thomas Howard didn't think she was . . . suggesting such a thing between them.

Instead, he took her bare hand and squeezed it gently, then kept her fingers enclosed in his warm fist.

"You need mittens."

She nodded, unwilling to admit that she had bared her hands on purpose, hoping to have him take her fingers into her own.

"Yes," Dena said, surging into safe territory, "the Germans who first settled here named it Rolltreppe—moving staircase. If you look upcreek"—she turned with him and pointed—"doesn't it look like the water is flowing down stair steps, all the little hills and mounds?"

Thomas nodded. "Funny. One always thinks of the Great Plains as vast flat plates of hairy grass. Beautiful country, this."

Dena nodded back. "I've even had some happiness here. And of course I met you." That was a shamefully forward thing to say, but she didn't mind. He would leave soon. As soon as the snow started.

She checked out the sky and moaned sadly.

Thomas turned her to face him and pulled her close. He said nothing. The tightening of his arms said it all.

He rested his chin on the top of her head. She could feel her hair wiggle as the air from his nostrils took in its scent.

As if to steer them from sad thoughts, Thomas began to speak of inconsequential things. They walked again.

"How come no one uses the German name for the creek anymore?"

Dena relaxed a little, then stumbled as her boot met an unstable pile of snow. Landing against Thomas's amazing chest, they both laughed. She wanted to lean against him forever, waited for his kiss.

He didn't kiss her, though, and she felt fretful. She couldn't believe that the history of Staircase Creek was so all-fired interesting.

She pulled away but caught the tenderness in his eyes, realizing she'd be kissed good and proper before too long.

"Lots of folk enjoy the old ways and speak the language almost better than English. But Gottlieb and many others wanted to Americanize. In fact, Gottlieb was among the first to legally change the spelling of his name. It's C-l-a-y-t-e-r now, just like it sounds, but the old way used an *O* with the German umlaut."

"Don't speak German. Picked up a bit of Spanish just in case . . ."

He didn't finish the sentence, but she remembered he was an outlaw. In case he needed to escape to Mexico.

She changed subjects, too, realizing it might be impolitic to go further. They might not share the exact same feelings about Americanizing, him being from the South and all. Gottlieb hadn't fought in the War Between the States and had regretted it ever after.

And as if to prove that all was well, Thomas bent to her

then, touching her lips with his as gently as the first dew on a rose.

Then he took off his hat and reached beneath her shawl. The edges of it fell across them both like red wings.

Then their tongues tasted both innocence and tragedy.

Olga Pott's mule had thrown a shoe.

Before that, she had been accosted by the Pinkerton on her way home from Max Bauer's. At least Max hadn't picked up the ague. She guessed the agent was going to go harass Max next.

She had tried to be polite, insisting that she hadn't seen any strangers hereabouts and had given safe harbor to no fugitives, but the Pinkerton had been mighty talkative, almost as if he didn't believe her. Finally she was downright rude, exclaiming that she was needed at home, where she had sick folks.

Now she walked the creature gently along the road back to her farm, and the journey was tedious. At least her Ida was home, capable of tending to necessary tasks and caring for the menfolk. Fortunately the girl had grown up without a squeamish stomach and could handle slop pots and upchucking like a matriarch. Olga breathed easier.

When she saw the couple walking together, way off in the distance by the creek, she recognized Dena right off. Hard to miss that red shawl, the cascading golden hair. She'd be chilled soon. The wool shawl was thick, but the afternoon was turning fast to a cold winter night.

As for a dark-haired man, why, it could only be Jonah. Tall, dark-haired. He usually wore a prim derby, not a soft felt California hat with a big brim, but maybe he expected snow to fall afore long. He must be up and about already, recovered from his ague. It was certainly foolish to be out in the cold, but then again, Olga herself liked feeling refreshed after being cooped up indoors. And she'd be spared her trip into town tomorrow with her chicken broth.

She smiled a little. Jonah was more Dena's age, her temperament, her training and intellect than had been his dour older brother.

Of course it was far too soon for any such pairing in public. And certainly many of the snoops in the congregation would harp about the inappropriateness of a brother-in-law hooking up with a widow. Nonetheless, Olga liked them both and enjoyed being part of their little secret.

She waved, but they didn't see her.

Back at the barn, Dena couldn't help sobbing in his arms. The snow fell steadily, although the wind had yet to blow.

She had to let him go. Once the winds started, he would be lost in the tumult of another Nebraska winter.

Yet right now the snowflakes almost felt warm, like a lacy crocheted shawl against bare arms. Soon though the lace would turn to knives of ice that could cut through even the thickest coat, not to mention horseflesh.

"Thomas, I'm sorry. I'm not usually a weepy woman. It's just . . . been a week beyond imagining. Gottlieb lying there torn asunder. His entrails like . . . like a herd of snakes swimming in blood. Do snakes even come in herds?"

Turning her face from its refuge where his arm met his shoulder, she gazed up at him. He almost seemed to be smiling at her silly question. Gently his right hand moved underneath the waves of her hair to knead her scalp. It relaxed her some; she closed her eyes, squeezing back tears, moving her head against his fingers in the same rhythm.

Whisper whickered gently behind them.

Then her voice hardened, and her eyes opened in fury. "I should definitely not rebuke a dead man, but Thomas, it was his own fault! He was chasing Bruno with a pitchfork just for being a bull. And not for the first time."

Through the curtain of snow, daylight flickered beyond the barn door and the tiny window in the loft. That was the tragedy of it all. They would not have even one more long winter night together.

Nor even one last day.

He had to leave while he had light to see. Before the wind sliced his skin. While snow fell to cover his tracks.

Nonetheless, she tried, one last time. "Oh, Thomas, how can I let you leave me when you just found me? Can't you remain . . ."

Her gaze turned shy. The dictates of her girlhood had strongly discouraged forwardness in a woman, but what did it matter now? Folks on the prairie were responsible for sculpting the shape of their own destinies.

He placed his hands on both sides of her face as if indeed he wanted to mold her image against his palms. "Oh, Dena, I . . ." Tilting her chin upward, he bent to her mouth.

"Dena . . ." He breathed her name once more as his lips touched hers, the sound tasting as sweet as his mouth.

Her lips parted like she was drawing life from him. Shivers that had nothing to do with the cold quivered against her skin. How could something as simple as a kiss be so staggering?

Her tiptoed feet stumbled a little in the straw.

Shuddering somewhat himself, Thomas dropped his hands from her face to her waist, clasping her close to him. His voice shook as much as her body.

"Dena, it must be this way," he spoke into her hair. "Somehow when it's safe, I will find you."

Dena tried to stop shaking, but that statement almost made her feel afraid. Could he? More than that, would he? The James gang was charming. Even the Pinkerton said so. Wouldn't he find another compliant woman somewhere else, somewhere where no Pinkerton hovered?

But then she saw his eyes, sparkling gray and honest, so clear she could see another world in them.

"I will, Dena, I will. I promise. You have my word. Now, I hate to say it . . ." He left the words unsaid but she heard them anyway. He had to leave.

"Help me with Whisper," he invited, obviously remembering that the surest way into her heart was through an animal. Like a preacher blessing a believer, he held out his hands, one towards her, the other at the horse.

114

Shaking her head, she twirled away from him, still on her tiptoes, just like a ballerina, so he couldn't see her fresh tears. She turned from the solace in Whisper's eyes. Instead of tending to either Thomas or his horse, she busied her hands and emptied her mind by leading Bruno back to his lean-to.

She closed the gate to his little corral, considering that she might have seen a flash of compassion in the bull's eyes. The snow landed on her red shawl like stars, like stars against the moon that Revelations said would turn to blood when the end of the world was near.

Dena shuddered at the prophecy. She couldn't even bear to look back at Thomas, so she ran along the rope between the house and the barn, stomped off the snow, and busied herself inside the house.

The house where he should spend the winter safe and warm with her. Sitting in the armchair that already bore the imprint of his form, warming his feet at the Pennsylvania fireplace.

Sleeping in his bed, calling out her name in the darkness of a heavenly dream.

Sleeping in her bed, making the dream real.

She couldn't help blushing even though there was no one about to see. Unless—she looked upward uneasily—Gottlieb did get to peek down once in a while.

At least the house was still theirs, hers and Thomas's, at least for this little while. And it was up to her to care for her man.

For a moment from the little kitchen window, she watched him, making a memory for later. He stood in the doorway of the barn, shaking out a saddle blanket. Even through the web of snow, Thomas's muscles ebbed and flowed like rippling waves against the blue woolen twill of Gottlieb's old shirt. Then he went back inside.

It occurred to her just then with a true shooting pain in her heart, that this might be all she would ever have. A phantom man riding through the twilight of her years on a horse too quiet to hear, too pale to see.

Sighing, she hurriedly examined the array of food the neighbors had left her. She wouldn't be fixing chicken now. Instead, she considered what would travel well and packed it neatly in oilcloth. Squares of noodle pudding wouldn't crumble, and a chub of ham should last for days in the cold. Dried apple slices wouldn't bruise, and he could roast potatoes in a campfire. And a flask of Gottlieb's favorite whiskey would provide medicinal qualities as well as fire in his veins.

She opened the back door. Even with the snow, the temperature was not at all what Dena knew to be cold. The air was completely still. Understanding what had to be done, she could not make it more difficult. He deserved this chance at freedom.

For a split second, she peered inside the barn, making another memory. Thomas easily saddled Whisper, petting the horse's flank often as he did so, carrying on a real-life conversation.

"A man who talks to horses, now, what about that?" She tried to keep her voice lighter than air, but the rest of the words were heavy with doom.

"You'd best get along now." They were the hardest words she had ever had to say.

She hoped they were the hardest words he had ever had to hear.

Whisper stood quietly now, ready to go. He nodded at her as if he understood. Maybe he did; Thomas conversed with him human-like after all.

Thomas smiled at her, almost shy. "Yep. But he never talks back."

Dena handed him the package of supplies, and he loaded Whisper's saddlebags. He wore Gottlieb's coat. It looked good on him. An inane prayer formed in her brain, thanking her husband for his good taste and the fine quality of his warm gear.

But it was Thomas, real and now, who captured all her attention. Dena saw every dream he had ever dreamed in his eyes. Then his shyness changed. He was urgent, incautious.

"Dena, God help us."

She melted into his arms like wax to a flame.

As if it were a breath from heaven, the silent air brushed against her heated body. Instead of just her imagination filling the empty years, she wanted ripe memories of something that had been real even for just a brief space of time.

"Thomas I know you must leave," she cried recklessly, "but please don't leave me unsatisfied."

The pampered girlhood no longer mattered. A lifetime of emptiness did. She was a woman full grown, a woman who had never been fulfilled.

Hands dropping in surprise to his sides, he hesitated, but just for a second.

"Dena?" His brow knotted up in doubt.

"Thomas, I am certain." She stood resolute before him in the fragrant straw. He had tended the barn, her entire place, as if it were his own. Whisper stood silent, but Dena could hear the shuffling of her own animals in their stalls.

"Dena, are you asking what I think?" Caution returned to his well-carved face.

"I'm asking. If you think we have time."

At her heartfelt invitation, Thomas took her hand, looking around for a potential spot, away from chance dung or restless hooves. Watching her carefully, he breathed out in awe. "I'll make time."

He pulled her tight against his side as they walked to the other side of the barn. "Well, I can't argue that this will be an amazing memory to take with me." Stooping, he bent down to her.

"An amazing memory for me to keep with me," she murmured against his mouth.

"But Dena, maybe we shouldn't, not here, not on the ground," he protested almost like a prim frightened maiden.

"Nonsense," she persisted, tightening her arms about his neck in a loop of love that would make him hers forever. "Adam and Eve made love—" the words came out slowly as if she tasted them on her tongue first, "on the ground, after all. We're in fine company."

He lifted her in his arms, laying her gently on a little tussock of freshly raked fodder near her parked buggy and far from animal scents.

"Ah, my Dena, how could I have lived my life . . ."

For just a brief moment, his weight upon her brought her heart churning like a mill wheel. He tried to shuck out of the cumbersome coat while keeping their lips together.

Suddenly the daylight dimmed. Right then the clouds started to dump their load with more energy.

He rose from her so fast she felt wind from the flapping of his coattails.

"No, Dena, I must leave. Now. This might be my only chance. It'll be getting dark soon. We may get a blizzard. Dena, goodbye, just for a while."

"No, no, not just yet!" Her voice deepened with sorrow, but she lay where he had placed her, willing herself to be strong, not wanting his last sight of her to be a weak simpering wreck.

She might as well weep, she decided, for he led Whisper out into the snow and mounted him without even looking back. What kind of man was that?

But what kind of woman let her man ride off without watching, without waving?

Without teardrops freezing like pearls on her face?

She stood in the doorway, seeing that the snow had already covered most of his hoofprints.

Just then the snowfall lightened to nothing but a gentle sifting of sugar across a cake.

"Thomas! Thomas!" She ran after Whisper. "Not just yet, please."

Her voice carried sweet and dreamy through the flaky mist. Thomas heard and promptly halted Whisper.

As he shook his head in gentle defeat, flakes tumbled across his shoulders. Turning the horse back, he wore a resolute little smile. By the time they met in the middle of her barnyard, she began to grab for Thomas's hand as he dismounted.

"We have no time to spare." Breathless, she pulled at the coat he wore. "But we do have time enough."

Smile gone, Thomas nodded urgently, shrugging out of the

coat. Laying it down on the snow, he reached for her. She struggled against her clothes. Why did women wear so many of them?

"I don't know about this, Dena. I do need to go." He brushed snow from her face.

She brushed away second thoughts from his.

"I'm no romantic, Thomas. I was for a while, until real life got in the way. I no longer look at the good in everything. You are right." She hated to admit it; she hated to think it, much less speak it. "You may get captured, or killed. Now may be all we have."

She had always wondered how it would be to make love and where it would happen. Never had she imagined joining with her man in a barnyard kissed with winter.

He lifted her skirts before he laid her down on the coat, using them to pillow her head. For a moment, she blushed bright. Was this permitted in broad daylight, under God's watchful eye? Remembering once again little Georg telling her dead folk watched down from heaven, she tossed that unhappy conversation into a mental drawer. That meant even her parents.

At least her bloomers were clean.

Thomas tussled with the buttons of his denim trousers, his eyes somehow apologetic. "Dena, this should be better. Our first time. There's so much I won't be able to do for you."

"It's time, Thomas. I hope there are others. But if not . . ."

"I vow it to you, Dena. Just wait here for me. You're my woman. You're my home. I will be coming back home someday."

"Come home now, Thomas." She shivered both from cold air and virile heat on those sections of her body that had never seen daylight or a man.

Of course she had some sort of an idea about what was about to happen. She had often seen Bruno's masculinity as he performed—much to the scandalized horror of the town's women—but she had never seen a real man. Unable to help herself, she watched Thomas's body, lower down.

When he had bared his manparts, she gasped. Songbird had

119

told her somewhat of the act that happens between a man and a woman, but Dena had never been able to conjure up anything like this.

But then she realized she must behave worldly and experienced. She had been a married woman, after all, and she doubted that Thomas would take advantage of an untouched maid.

Thomas smiled. The snowflakes spotted his dark hair like white dots. "Normally I would take my time, but we're going to stick together like a tongue on a pole if I don't hurry. Speaking of tongues . . ."

Never taking his eyes from her face, he knelt between her legs.

"Thomas?" she whispered in shock, laying her hands on his hair. The snowflakes sizzled at the heat in her fingertips. He nodded, as if he knew a strict German husband, no matter how Americanized, had never attempted such a feat.

Her fingers tightened, tugging at his hair as though she were dying. Dena had never imagined any man's fingers, much less tongue, at her secret places. Dena died deep down, both from the sensation and from the worry. Would he know that she was untouched? Would her inexperience disappoint him? After all, a normal widow woman would know a trick or two, wouldn't she?

"I've got to take the time to do this. I can live on this memory forever," he spoke to her, but the sounds entered her woman's body along with his kisses. Then he began to massage a special part of her that even Songbird had failed to mention in any specific way.

The moisture and motion of his tongue was magic, swirling into a spiral of rainbows that melted the snow underneath them. She felt her body tense with a sensation she could never describe in human terms; she grasped the top of his head as if she were drowning.

Fortunately Edgar and Allan had been left in the house, or they would have whined inconsolably at the primal sounds coming from her throat.

"Thomas, Thomas." Her knees all but choked him.

"Now!" was all he could manage as he raised himself above her.

And then they were one. The falling snow covered them like a bridal veil.

Chapter Ten

Snow had fallen steadily but lightly most of the night, and Dena was positive that Thomas had made it down the creek to Songbird's. Despite her words to him the afternoon before, she was starting to believe that there might be a good ending. How could she wake up feeling so wonderful otherwise?

She stood on her front stoop enjoying the morning while Edgar and Allan romped in the snow like toddling youngsters, each pausing to take aim at her bare-root rosebush. There weren't any hoofprints anywhere, although the realization saddened her somehow. Peeking back toward the barnyard, she saw only a desert of snow. Snow that had once again killed Thomas's snow angel.

Across the snow-drenched fields the cottonwoods and willows wore a mantle of white, as did the windbreaks of walnuts. So would Gottlieb's grave.

"Be happy for me, husband," she advised him over the white silence. "I was always faithful to you in life. And you did save me, just like I've just saved someone else."

The Outlaw's Woman

At the sound of her voice, Edgar ran to her, slavering from his exertions. His tongue flopped from his mouth like a veteran's armless sleeve.

Dena had never minded being alone on the prairie. In fact, she had rather enjoyed Gottlieb's long days in the fields, when he had not been around to probe her every move. But today, with Thomas Howard's presence still warming the ice in the air, she wanted to hear her voice, hoping the sound would carry across the way. He had sung to her across the blizzard, after all.

But Edgar's eyes were wise; his head was cocked as though he were really listening. With Gottlieb's name still on her own tongue, she had to deliberate for a while with her conscience.

"Edgar, help me. Have I been unfaithful now? Truth to tell, I am a widow, but . . . was our lovemaking wrong?" She stood, stretching a body still fragrant with Thomas's loving. Edgar pawed at her toes. "Jonah's sermons say so. But if it were, how could I feel so alive?"

So full. So complete.

Like a child, she ran to the barn, Edgar and Allan tugging at her heels. Following Olga's lead, she had restructured a pair of Gottlieb's enormous coveralls to fit her womanly frame. The project had kept her hands company all the evening past while her mind relived every moment she had spent with Thomas Howard. He'd managed somehow to stock up the coal buckets before he left, even emptied the pestilential chamber pot, ground up coffee beans for this morning's brew, and tidied his room. He even washed the fish skin she used to filter coffee grounds, knowing she would need it again.

She almost wished that he had smoked. At least the acrid smell, as much as she loathed it, would have kept him nearby.

She felt like a child missing her family, but she wasn't a child anymore, she reminded herself. She was a woman full-grown.

A woman in every way.

She smiled, remembering how he'd looked at her, during and after. All that girlhood talk about feeling sore the next day . . . well, that hadn't happened. Thomas Howard had gone just where he belonged, and all was well.

The cow was eager to be milked, a chore Dena could do in her sleep. She petted the creature gently. At one point she had named the animal Grace; for being a great lumbering beast she was amazingly swift on her feet. However, true to form, Gottlieb had only called her rude, mean terms. Today Dena said the name four times and smiled at the large soulful eyes looking back at her, almost with comprehension.

The mangers still contained satisfactory amounts of hay and water. Therefore, she left the rest of the routine tasks until later. Jonah being sick . . . well, it would do her good to take a drive into town and check on him. He had certainly been there for her during all her times of need.

After making sure that Katie and her brood were cozy, she checked out the stall where Whisper had lodged. In a way, she was happy to muck out his droppings. It reminded her that Thomas Howard hadn't been a dream after all. In the cold still air, she could almost hear the horse nicker.

Then she drew away a tarpaulin from a corner in the barn. If she were to visit Jonah today, she would do it in style.

Gottlieb had bought the Portland cutter just a year ago, selling their older model—cheap—to Jonah. Looking close, she saw that the runners had been freshly sanded of summer dust and rust, and oiled, the dark blue upholstery freshly wiped. Surely Gottlieb hadn't been that full of forethought, particularly as he hadn't expected to die on an autumn Saturday.

Aaaah. Thomas Howard. She preened. Always one step ahead of her. How had she managed to find the world's only perfect man?

She hitched up her own fine Morgan to the sleigh.

Back in the house, she walked by the coatrack, which stood empty save for her green cloak. Thomas had taken Gottlieb's coat. It reminded her of something, and she wandered about the rooms, looking for the decrepit linen duster. Shrugging, she realized that Thomas must have cleaned it away, too.

She washed and readied herself for her trip to town. If she

tried hard enough, she could smell that quiet essence of Thomas Howard. Her lavender soap mixed with the skin smell of his healing wound. The coffee on his breath. The gentle vegetable scent of the corn bag that had lain across his shoulders, the rosemary that she had placed on his pillow.

Peeking into his room, she saw the Mason jar, empty now, still sitting on the dresser.

Allan pushed against her, eager for a stroke across his back. "So you think I'm giving Thomas too much attention, do you?" She scratched him behind the ears. "I think you'd be correct." She laughed out loud. "I guess I better hold all of it close to my heart. I will relive it all again, another time, when I'm all alone with no other tasks.

"Right now, I must see to Jonah. If he truly is sick, I need to be there, Mira or not. He has indeed always been there for me."

Saying the words, whether aloud or in her mind, brought back Gottlieb's death, and she quickly stuck the memories in another mental drawer, shutting it tight. She had other worries today.

Would Jonah know? Did she look different? A glance into her looking glass didn't tell her a thing. Her face was already bright from the cold air outside. There was a little spot, though, where Thomas's stubble had rubbed her cheek. Jonah was certain to comment.

Prudently, she donned the mourning garments that she had relented enough to rescue from her floor and iron properly. The ensemble had no doubt remained packaged for years in the back room of Staircase Mercantile and Dry Goods, for it was slightly out of fashion. Local women had neither the inclination nor the money for impractical clothes, no matter how bereaved they felt.

Nonetheless, Jonah had insisted that Dena look the part, and she had been too distressed by Gottlieb's death to refuse. Considering all the proper mannerisms Jonah had developed during the years of his Eastern schooling, she wondered how he survived the plain, simple life of Staircase Creek. Unlike her, he had never needed a place to retrench. She had had to survive.

She rolled the back of her hair into a proper chignon, arranging the top into a bird's nest. Plopping on the mourning bonnet, she screwed her facial muscles into a childish mask of ridicule. The thing was beautifully made of black crape draped with a profusion of black silk violets and jet ornaments hanging at the ends of the ribbons down her back, but it made her look sixty years old. She'd pulled the heavy fall of bugle lace from it at the burial, however, tired of it dangling in her face.

The dress itself was too long, but she hadn't cared at the time, despite both Mira and Olga's willingness to hem it. She refused to wear the cage under her petticoats that Mira had suggested to help raise the hem. Dena had long considered that the most pretentious nonsense devised by man. And surely it had been a man.

Now she could laugh at how she must have looked, traipsing and tripping to the barn as Thomas Howard sat in her house, watching her from the window, waiting to point his Peacemaker at her, that first night. The night it all began.

Before she left for Jonah's, she draped her green cloak about her person, drawing the string of the hood around her chin. Although the air was cold, it was not brutal, and she didn't feel like redoing the handiwork to her hat and hair upon arrival, nor enduring Jonah's pursed lips should she not look her best. Tucking lap robes about her, she took off with a shout of laughter on what should still be a day of mourning, visiting a sick relative no less.

All during the drive to town, she longed for sleigh bells. Maybe she would buy some, just to scandalize the neighbors. It was a fairly mild infamy compared to adultery. She laughed again, wishing Thomas could hear her joy. Her horse danced through the snow and the runners of her sled slid like quicksilver. She saw neighbors' places, smoke curling up from their chimneys, and she marveled that their normal lives had gone unchanged while her world had exploded into a rainbow of a million hues.

The Outlaw's Woman

She composed her face into a dutiful mask before she knocked on the door of the parsonage, her breath tumbling about her face in a white fog. It was a simple dwelling no fancier than her own, but Gottlieb had at one time treated his brother to a brick fireplace. A pile of coals glowed in it today.

Jonah was as patriarchal as she had suspected.

"Dena, you drove yourself! At least you could have waited for me to help you from your cutter. I heard you arrive."

Once more she marveled at his manners, almost pretentious here on the prairie, and certainly out of place.

"Jonah, I was not about to sit in the cold. And driving myself is something to which I simply have to become accustomed. Besides, you shouldn't expose yourself to the elements."

She was shocked at how formal she sounded. Did her choice of words change depending on whom she was with? Why was she so much more comfortable with Thomas Howard when she had known Jonah for years?

It was hard to continue to chide her brother-in-law, however. Weak and pale, he limped back to the great armchair where she had sat during the funeral feast, noting the townsfolk's relief that it hadn't been their loved one gored to death by a bull.

Even in his satin dressing gown, Jonah still managed to look handsome and important. She remembered the gown; her parents had given it to him one Christmas during better times.

As usual, Mira Wuebke took it upon herself to act exactly as the lady of the house should. She wore the same deep violet gown she had to Gottlieb's funeral, a subtly patterned brocade with a watteau back and updated gigot sleeves. With her auburn hair highlighted by her matron's headgear, a muslin cap with lavender ruche and ribbons, she appeared even more a suitable mate for the reverend.

"Dena, please join us," Mira, the perfect hostess, invited.

All pretense at propriety was lost on Dena, although Mira's affectation amused her. The housekeeper always strove to meet Jonah's high standards for polite conduct.

"Jonah, Mrs. Pott drove by yesterday with the news that you

had taken ill. I wanted to be positive that you are on the mend."

Mira brought Jonah a tray, but he waved her off, instead rising and walking as steadily as he could to the table in the dining room.

"No, please do not fuss over me," he ordered Mira. "And please bring Dena some refreshment." Mira's face fell; her role had once again been clearly established.

"How are you feeling? Has Mira been staying here at the parsonage with you? I would have come if I had known." A lie, but he would never know.

Jonah's eyes snapped. They seemed as black as obsidian chips, but with fire behind them. "Absolutely not! Mrs. Wuebke has returned to Mrs. Rausch's boardinghouse every night!"

Dena almost smiled. He was as testy as a man in a lover's quarrel, assuring her of Mira's proper place.

He seemed to remember his role as well. "It is I who must apologize for not calling upon you. You have obviously heard that I have been ill. Please do not assume that I am neglecting you. And please do not feel that it is your duty to nurse me."

How was Dena to respond? That she was glad he had stayed away? That she'd had uninterrupted time with . . . her lover?

"And then I hear that an escaped fugitive is on the loose and has stayed in your barn!" His eyes flashed brighter, and his fists pounded on the table.

"Jonah, relax yourself!" Dena expostulated. "There is nothing amiss. I gave a stranger a place to sleep in the barn, then he left. Enough said. Gottlieb did the same a hundred times."

Fortunately, just then Mira returned with a tray. For Dena, it included hot tea and some splendid homemade madeleines. For Jonah, a soft-boiled egg and dry toast.

Dena watched his throat work to control a heave as he spooned the dripping orange fluid toward his mouth. Being a nurse, Mira certainly must know best, but Dena could imagine little else so unpalatable as slimy half-cooked egg for one whose stomach had rejected everything it had contained for days.

Jonah gagged, then gave up.

Dena stepped up in support. "Mira, please heat up this chicken soup." She held out the crock Olga had left for her. "And put a little butter on the toast."

Jonah looked at her gratefully, a little color back in his cheeks. He was indeed an alarmingly handsome man, but compared to Thomas would have to come in second.

"You look remarkably spry," he commented, "different somehow." She busied herself with the cookies for a while, trying to hide her face behind her teacup.

"It is the weather, Jonah. Exhilarating. You know I always like to be out and about on a winter's day."

That was true. She had even brought her ice skates with her from St. Louis, but Staircase Creek hadn't any ponds large enough for skating.

"Well, I am glad that you apparently didn't eat whatever tainted food caused this misery."

Mira returned from the kitchen with a bowl of warm soup. She acted almost as though she wanted to feed it to him like a baby, but he waved her away.

As if needing to regain a little respect, she stood tall and proud and announced, "I have consulted with all those who took sick after the funeral. The conclusion is that the tainted food was Emil Chrismon's wild turkey. It is a capricious creature to prepare. If left too long in a warm room before cooking, or if not cooked inside quite long enough—although the breast and legs are deceptively browned—it can cause havoc to those who dine upon it."

"I am spared, then." Dena smiled, meaning it, although Mira and Jonah would never know why. She had not needed these past days to be vomiting all over Thomas Howard and making even more horrid use of the chamber pot.

For a moment, she couldn't remember what day it was. They had all melted together, dream like, since Thomas Howard had lived them with her. Gottlieb seemed another life. For a moment guilt assailed her, but she cut it off at the flow.

She deserved some happiness. Looking up for a quick moment, she saw the heartfelt devotion in Mira Wuebke's eyes as she slathered butter on Jonah's toasted bread. What would be so wrong to wish the same for her friend, for her brother-in-law who had remained celibate for far too long? What would be wrong in wishing everyone could feel as she did, well loved and hopeful?

She finally figured it out. Tomorrow was Sunday. "Jonah, certainly you will not be up and about for services tomorrow? Perhaps Mira and I can arrange a hymn-sing. I've never forgotten how to play the piano."

Jonah was clearly aghast. "I will not desert my flock! I will attend them as is my calling. And Dr. Burkhardt is more than adequate on the pump organ." She knew most of his horror resulted from the unconscionable suggestion that women be leaders in church.

As if to prove himself, he stood up from the table, tall and strong. On the way up, his eyes met the wondrous mounds of Mira Wuebke's bosom. For a split second too long, he couldn't seem to take his eyes away.

Dena was pleased.

"Thanks for the tea, Mira. Jonah, I am glad to see you in health again. I needs must visit the mercantile, then I'm bound for home. I am running low on Arbuckle's."

Mira walked Dena to the door of the parlor, again as the lady of the house would.

"You indeed look very merry, Dena." She smiled, and Dena concluded that her smile was an innocent one. After all, Mira herself had known the horror, not grief, of an unloved husband's sudden death.

After the comments that she looked spry and merry, Dena tried to look more dejected, more like an honorable widow, while she did her shopping.

Compared to the affluent stores of St. Louis, the mercantile's merchandise selection was humble, and like today often dusty and sparse, but she usually found what she needed, even widow's clothes. Which proved that the place served its purpose, much like everything else in her life.

The Outlaw's Woman

Later on in the month—how could it be December already?—Mrs. Thostenson, who owned the mercantile with her husband, would try to prettify the place by stringing gold ribbons across the window frame and hanging her collection of gorgeous German handblown ornaments. Dena's mother had had some just as lovely, but other than one or two, most had gone to auction years ago.

Remembering them, it made her sad to think of the store window, although the town's children would stand beneath it, gawking in awe.

She selected the coffee and a few yards of lace, and ordered several lengths of light merino wool, in black and woeful shades of gray. Rather than continue to wear the copious widow's gown, she would create a couple of simpler day dresses to wear in public. It would placate Jonah and keep her respectable. Of course, in her own home she would wear whatever she chose, including the yellow tea gown that Thomas had loved.

From a small collection of hats, she selected a dark gray chip bonnet with deep maroon ties. It would be appropriate for a widow once she attached some of the black ribbons and silk violets from the original mourning bonnet, yet it would look reasonably normal.

She pulled a ten-dollar eagle from her reticule to pay for her purchases. As she made change, Mrs. Thostenson's words of thoughtful condolence made Dena smile gratefully back.

"Louise, I am so profoundly thankful for everyone's love and concern. How is your husband on this bright day?" Dena looked around the little store, where Oskar usually stacked cans and jars, measured up the dry goods, and packaged items in brown paper.

"He is now on his feet, after having taken down with a bit of sickness. We'll both be at church tomorrow."

"I, too," Dena promised, meaning it at the time. Several other women uttered polite condolences, both for Dena and for Mr. Thostenson's sickness, then everyone chatted harmlessly for a while before moving on to choose their wares. They

131

nodded at the appropriateness of Dena's purchases.

A tiny silver bell over the shop's doorjamb tinkled as behind Dena, the Chrismons entered. As his wife ambled over to the yardage shelf, Emil turned to Dena with a polite dip of his hat. Obviously forgetting that his wild turkey was probably just as infamous, he started in on Bruno.

"So, Miz Dena, what you gonna do with that bull?" His voice was coarse, his words thoughtless, but he was a decent enough neighbor. As one, the throng of shoppers snapped alert, although each woman pretended to continue her shopping—one fingering a store-bought shawl, another reading the cover of *Godey's*, the last picking up and putting back a canned good she had no intention of buying.

"Emil!" His wife's fussy voice rebuked him.

Dena nearly choked on the polite neighborly reply she had intended. "Bull? Bruno, my bull?" She swallowed hard.

"You know, that mean old bastard that gored Gottlieb and murdered him."

"Ach, Emil Chrismon!" His wife's outrage was loud and righteous. Her plump arm stopped halfway to her head with the cheap bonnet she was about to try on. "Emil, mind yourself!"

Honestly distressed, Dena made to leave but realized she had to defend the creature. The memory of Gottlieb's last day haunted her mind. She had tried to save Gottlieb, she really had. No one, not even Gottlieb, deserved to die that way.

She gagged. Thomas Howard and the lovely winter's day seemed to vanish. Emil was a clear reminder of what her life had been and, Thomas Howard or not, that the life had to go on.

"Emil!" His wife's anger matched Dena's, but Dena had no right to rebuke the man.

As always, Dena regained quick control. "He remains with me, Emil. He's a champion; he's a famed stud."

Emil's wife, the shopkeeper, and the other women in the store looked at Dena as though she didn't know anything about breeding. She sighed. As a city girl, she would have been chided even for using the term bull; *man cow* was more seemly. Here in Staircase Creek, most folk referred to Bruno as Gottlieb's *boese bah*, bad cow.

Sighing again, Dena guessed the thoughts rampant in their minds. Since Gottlieb had impregnated the wife before her, the fact that Dena had never conceived had been an unspoken fault laid at her feet. After all, his virility had already been established. Never could Dena explain to these fruitful, hardy people that her husband's weak fumblings beneath their dark covers had never prospered enough to bring his seed forth, nor to bring her any kind of pleasure at all.

Silent, she both blushed and paled, particularly now that she had lain with Thomas Howard. In the daylight. In the snow.

"I did all I could," she managed truthfully.

"Of course you did, dear, of course you did," Mrs. Chrismon comforted, coming over to take her hand.

"And Bruno," Dena continued with some desperation, "Bruno was only defending himself. Gottlieb was going after him with a pitchfork. I . . . decry cruelty to any living creature, man or beast."

Everyone relaxed, most managing to smile. Dena's affection for farm animals was well known, since most folk considered livestock only as food or profit. The bull—Bruno—was truly a fine stud.

"*Ja*, well," Emil persisted, "keep him locked up, away from decent folk and defenseless critters."

Dena nodded. What Emil did not know was that Bruno had likely protected Thomas Howard from a Pinkerton. She would speak kindly to him and pet his flank as soon as she got home.

Chapter Eleven

Likely it was the cold weather keeping the sprig of rosemary fresh. Thomas pulled it from an inner pocket and held it to his nose. Amazing how one simple scent could bring back a thousand memories.

Whisper trotted in the snow as surefooted as always. The sun peeked out from the clouds from time to time, and the wind was no more threatening than a breeze in August. But Songbird had warned him that a blizzard was coming, and he believed her.

As Dena had promised, Songbird had welcomed him to her dugout lodge yesterday. He could see smoke blowing from a flue hole in what looked like a mound of grassy snow, just before dusk arrived to hide it. She'd built her little lodge into the side of a small hill.

"Any friend of Golden Heart is my friend," the woman had told him, inviting him into the smoky interior. A fire of cow chips and cornhusks smoldered in the center of the small room.

Her face was marked terribly by scars and pits.

"Golden Heart?" He refused to dishonor her by looking away, but all he could think of was Dena's golden hair.

"Miss Dena has a golden heart," the woman told him. "The white man holds gold the most precious of all things." She paused in her speech, and Thomas recognized pain in her tone.

"The white men now destroy Paha Sapa in search of more yellow rock. I once lived in Paha Sapa," she whispered.

"Paha Sapa?"

"The white generals call it Black Hills. Three Stars now seeks to restore honor to your General Long Hair, who was slaughtered with his men at the Greasy Grass. But enough of those troubles. My friend, our friend, is as beautiful as her hair."

Thomas found himself nodding in agreement with Songbird's description of Dena. He knew about sobriquets from reading Mr. Fenimore Cooper's book and the newspapers. It was the Indian way of bestowing meaningful names. Canada had become known as the Grandmother Country, in honor of Queen Victoria, a gentler land than that of the Great Father's in Washington. General George Crook had come to be known as Three Stars when he avenged last summer's defeat of Long Hair Custer at Little Big Horn.

For a second, he wondered if Jesse was known by any sobriquet—well, other than the usual.

Thomas had no need for Songbird to expound on Dena's goodness, but Songbird went on with a quiet explanation.

"Golden Heart does not despise me or call me a savage because I do not pray to the Christian God. We discussed this sometimes. Her husband did not agree with her opinion. In truth Songbird likes your Jesus very much."

She stopped then, speaking no more. Instead, she gestured to a small iron pot hanging from a tripod of sticks over the fire. The gray liquid, the mysterious meat, and the other unfamiliar lumps did not inspire Thomas's appetite, but once again, he refused to be dishonorable and rude.

His changed attitude startled him. Indians had never before seemed worthy of his respect. But for the dignified woman before him, that was all he could feel.

"The blizzard will not come until tomorrow between the midday and sundown. Tonight will not freeze. You may shelter your horse in the trees. Here." She handed him a buffalo hide. "You may cover him if you choose."

Her English was excellent, with little native inflection. Yet he knew she loved her heritage and missed her roots. Along the walls of the simple sod lodge she had hung deerskin hides. One was pointedly designed with Indian head silhouettes clearly riddled with spots.

"It is the 'hide record' of a bitter year," she said simply, catching his eye. "You see . . ." She pointed to a sketch of a black hat. "This means the white man. And here, here is the day the sun hid the moon. Our winter count." Her voice grew so sad it was nearly silent. "Forty-four braves and twenty mounted warriors. We had twelve rifles, three pistols then. But that was the winter before the smallpox.

"I then had my husband and four children."

The ceiling nearly touched the top of her head, so she hunkered across the dugout, pointing to several small leather cases decorated with turtles and a snake.

"My children's life cords are inside. These are creatures of long life. They were to endow my sons and daughter with long lives. It did not happen."

Her voice was so flat that Thomas figured her grief was spent. But when her fingers lovingly touched each little decorated container, his heart tightened. It had not been a thought he had ever had before, that an Indian would know love and pain.

He remembered Dena's words that all people deserved rights and respect. On his knees, he moved over to the woman and laid his hand on her arm.

She gave him a twist of her ruined lips in what was meant to be a smile. "It has been in many ways a good life. I was medicine woman for my tribe during the Sundance. Do you know of this dance?"

"A little."

She explained, her face aglow even in the smoky room as she recalled her life's proudest moment.

"Because my father had survived a dangerous accident and because I was considered a woman of virtue, I was given the mission to conduct the sacred rite. My relatives collected tongues from bull buffalo, which were buried by a few women while we faced the setting sun and prayed for our loved ones.

"At my direction, the center pole for a medicine lodge was erected. Young men who made vows to the sun would purify themselves inside the lodge."

She moved back to the fire. Joining her cross-legged on the floor, Thomas ate from the clay bowl she handed him, finding the stew tasty and filling. He nodded his thanks, and with a gesture of his hand, invited her to continue. The tale was fascinating.

Songbird's face reprised its wry smile. "It is a story of torture. Rawhide ropes led from the center pole and were tied to sharp sticks skewered into the young men's breasts. Then the strings were tugged and jerked as the men prayed for their wishes to come true.

"Then they danced until the sticks broke loose. The skin torn from the dancing and the jerking was cut from the body, mixed with sagebrush from the young men's head decorations and placed at the bottom of the pole as their offering to the sun."

Thomas felt the muscles in his chest spasm on their own. Remembering how the pain in his shoulders had tested his endurance, he wondered at men purposely mutilating themselves. But he realized his own wounds were just another form of proving his manhood. The two situations really weren't so different after all. He, too, had made vows, vows that for all intents and purposes he planned to keep.

But Songbird had gone on to another subject before he could react to the Sundance.

"Two of us survived the smallpox. We had so few left to begin with. The blankets sent to us from Fort Randall were unclean, but we could not see the disease on them. Mira nursed us as best she could. She did not take ill, but her children died.

The only other to survive was the half-white child of a young squaw taken in lust and violence by soldiers. The child lived here with me until she married a Pawnee. The Pawnee are long the enemy of the Sioux. I hear from her no more. She lives at Fort Robinson now, where her husband takes pay to work for the soldiers as a scout."

She looked at Thomas straight on, her black eyes ageless and wise. Pride and honor mixed with grief and defeat in their dark depths.

"There are others like me, the last of their villages, people who chose to live on their own, or white folk who are outcast for reasons no one tells. Golden Heart tells me that her God allowed me to live so that I could be an instrument of His peace and healing. If Golden Heart says to tell you of another safe place, tell me which direction you follow and I will direct you to someone who will shelter you."

"But I'm a white man."

"There are many white people who are kind. If you are one of them, you will be treated with kindness in return."

Forehead knotting up, he considered her words and believed her. Even though his mind hadn't been bent on kindness when he hid in Dena's house that first night, he was a good person at heart and she had sensed it.

"Somehow this all reminds me of the Underground Railroad the 'bolitionists set up." He watched Songbird warily, hoping she would believe his next words. "Now mind you, I never owned a slave."

Songbird nodded. "Good. I know of that railroad. The redskin and the blackskin have not fared so well against the whites, but there are always good people of any color who help out others in need. Those who treat us well are valued."

A dog shuffled in the shadows of a corner, stretched, walked to the doorway to be let outside. Thomas reached out to pet him, remembering Edgar and Allan. "Hi, pooch," he began.

Songbird silenced him immediately. "Do not speak to him. He is my friend. He obeys me, and he has tasks that he performs well. But do not speak to him. If he speaks back, you will die."

"What? You mean, if he barks?"

Songbird's soft voice sounded dreamy. "No, not a bark. Speak. Long ago, animal spirits ruled the earth, and dogs did converse with man. But when the spirits turned Earth over to man, animals could no longer use speech. It is a grave thing to tempt them."

Thomas looked at the friendly dog, whose tail swished dangerously close to the fire. His tongue lolled out his left jowl while he panted in the hot, smoky room. Thomas couldn't help chuckling into the bright, curious eyes, almost wishing the dog would talk and tell him his point of view. He thought of Edgar and Allan again, cocking their heads in an intelligent way, as though they wished to converse.

And Dena. She could pop into his mind in a heartbeat, with no reason other than that she was beautiful to remember. Would she be warm enough tonight? His manhood clutched at the dream of sharing her bed.

Night fell quickly inside Songbird's dugout, and Thomas grew tired. The journey from Dena's homestead had been only a stone's throw, but he had many miles to go yet and had no clue as to what awaited him. He had to be up and about early the next day to reach his destination before Songbird's blizzard hit.

She handed him a buffalo robe, sadness glistening in her eyes. "So few left. Easterners eat just the tongue and have no need for the skin, with their fancy clothes from far across the oceans. Hunters let the rest of the carcass rot. As for us Sioux, we thanked the Great Spirit when the animal gave its life for us, and used as much of the buffalo as we could. For food and raiment, for tools and jewelry, for medicines and cures."

Her voice was flat, as if she were reciting a simple fact instead of revealing a great tragedy. "It is said there are lakes and oceans so grand that eyes cannot see the end of them. It was like that with the buffalo. A black endless ocean, moving like a tide."

Thoughtful, he bid her good night and curled up in a corner. When the dog came back in, it snuggled up near him. He remembered again Dena and the farm dogs sleeping near her. Of himself sleeping curled up into her.

Deep in the smoke-filled darkness, he heard Songbird moan a tuneless song that he knew was part of some sort of religious ritual. He tried to pray himself, but thoughts of Dena burst behind his eyelids with colors he didn't usually see. His manhood rose in response.

Even though he was warmed by the buffalo robe, he could still feel the cold ground under his knees as he had poised above her. The snowflakes on her lips and cheeks as he kissed her. The cold air that nearly fused their tongues when her mouth opened to his.

And her woman's body . . . the moist heat seemed to cover his manhood even now. The incredible tightness. It was almost as if he had been the first. That was impossible, though. She had known she was barren. She had as much said that Gottlieb had been mean and that they hadn't been very happy. Perhaps they had not shared the marriage act in some time.

He felt almost sorry for Gottlieb if that had been the case, to die unsuspecting after a night without the glories of her body, without one last time.

Surely another day would come when he could do to her— no, *for* her—all that he dreamed. Yet, what if that had been their last time?

He sighed in tune with Songbird's ritual before he fell asleep.

Dawn was still caught in the night, but Songbird woke him with a corn cake and a mug of water.

"I have saddled your horse. I found the firewater in your saddlebag." Her voice was full of reproof. He almost felt like a small boy being confronted by his mother. "It is a poison. You must hurry, before the snow."

So now Thomas Howard headed south, miles from Staircase Creek. He put the rosemary back in his pocket and took a strengthening swig of firewater, regardless of Songbird's opinion.

His fingers still retained the scent of the herb, and he waited as long as he could before putting on his gloves.

Unfortunately, no new snow fell to preclude Dena's attendance at church on Sunday.

Not that she wasn't a worshipful woman. She had suffered too many blows in her life not to need spiritual guidance. And of course Jonah would have been embarrassed had she been absent without cause.

She simply loathed the thought of the multitude of sad eyes upon her, the sweet smiles of condolence, even the gentle hugs of care. Yes, Staircase Creek meant well, but for these folk, life went on as it always did. Nothing had changed. For Dena, one world had collapsed, and another was no more than a fragile soap bubble, beautiful but with little chance to survive.

Yesterday's euphoria had dribbled into reality. She had had other beautiful worlds collapse around her. Yet Thomas had said he would find her, whereas Becker Blanchard and her father had abandoned her. Thomas would keep in touch even if it took the longest while. He would be back.

She had to believe it. She had nothing else.

As her cutter slid on its elegant runners to town, she passed the Pott buckboard, crowded with children.

"Good morning, all!" she called out with sincere cheer. She adored this family, although she could never keep quite straight the five littlest ones, including two sets of twins, so close in age and looks. But she knew the eldest three well, and knew they would love the treat of riding to church with her.

"Willie, Ida, Georg, come on board!"

It was a tight fit, what with the thickness of lap robes and heavy winter outerwear, but the laughter and waves of those left behind gladdened her heart.

At the church, she figured her bright green cloak would raise eyebrows, but underneath, she was perfectly proper. She hadn't had time to redecorate her new gray bonnet, but she had worked most of the night to create and finish a dress of dark gray. Although she'd only had time to hold it together with basting stitches so far, she knew no one would be able to tell. She had a nimble needle and could finish up later. The idea of wearing the mourning gown again so soon had caused her undue agitation.

In truth, life was back to normal in Staircase Creek. Jonah stood tall and impressive in front of his flock.

"Our worship today and my sermon will revolve around the Advent of the Lord and the necessity of the penitential season of the church year." Her brother-in-law looked vastly better than he had the day before, even though the starkness of his black robe enhanced the unnatural pallor of his cheeks. Dena paled, then felt her cheeks grow hot. Surely Jonah would think that she had much penance to obtain.

If he only knew.

Mira sat in the front row, as if to be close enough to catch him if he collapsed. She did look wifely, however, in her dark blue pelisse and muff.

Jonah looked almost proud when Dena's true clear voice soared through the humble church. *Es Ist Ein Ros' Entsprungen.* She loved the old German hymns and could still sing most of them from memory, regardless of Gottlieb's philosophy of Americanization.

By the time the service ended, storm clouds roiled through the black sky like bubbles in a pot of boiling gravy. Jonah stood in the doorway, shaking hands with departing parishioners. Most farm folk left the churchyard immediately, especially those with open wagons. Edna Rausch hurried back to her shabby little boardinghouse to prepare Sunday dinner. Often town families stopped by for a meal whatever the weather, since they didn't have more than a few hundred yards to travel.

Dena wondered if the Pinkerton was staying in town. She supposed so. He had threatened to watch her every move. The thought of seeing him again almost made her protest out loud.

Jonah tried to induce Dena to remain for Sunday dinner.

"It won't be wild turkey, I promise!" He even smiled at his little joke.

"No, Jonah, though I am grateful that you are hale once again and I thank you for the invitation. And yes, I remember"—she nodded at his crestfallen face—"I remember that Gottlieb and I always shared Sunday dinner with you at the parsonage. Next week, certainly, if the weather permits." She pointedly looked at the sky. "But today it's about to blizzard."

Mira looked somewhat relieved as Jonah assisted Dena into the cutter. The Pott children had already left with their parents, but Dena passed them along the way.

An odd thought struck her, an idea she had never really had before. She wanted children of her own.

Because she'd been up before dawn tending to the livestock, Dena had no chores to do upon reaching her place. Katie and her babies now had a cozy nest in a basket near the Pennsylvania fireplace. Allan stayed near the little mother.

After unhitching the Morgan, she parked the cutter in the barn. She remembered how Thomas Howard had gotten it ready for her, how he had tended to everything that was important to her. How he had . . .

She walked back to the house, grateful for the rope she had tied between it and the barn days ago. The wind had begun to thrash through the air and would have carried off her mourning bonnet to kingdom come if she hadn't practically nailed it to her head with a half-dozen hat pins.

What did men do to keep their hats on their heads in the wind? Where was he today, Thomas Howard? Was he safe and warm? And Whisper, Whisper, too, deserved the same. As Dena entered her back door, she turned to look at the spot where she and Thomas had made love.

Even in the miserable chill, she felt warm. How could she have lived so long without feeling so? Would he remember each single second of it as she did? Even in spite of all their clothes, she had been completely one with him. If it was that wonderful all the time, no wonder Gottlieb had been hateful and accusatory when it didn't happen.

A single thought struck her: Would Thomas Howard know that had been her very first time? Could a man tell such a thing? Just thinking of it turned her womanhood tight and wet. How long would it be before she could love him again? Be completely naked with him, all of their parts touching and fusing?

Just before she closed the door tight, waiting as she was for Edgar and Allan to relieve themselves, she saw a rider coming up through the wind.

For a moment, her heart stopped. It might be Thomas . . . but no, it couldn't be. He had said he wouldn't be back for a long, long time. He had made that very clear.

The Pinkerton? No, she knew his horse by now.

Her heart sank to her feet when she realized it was Max Bauer.

Her neighbor had no reason to be paying a call, not with a blizzard starting. On a normal Sunday, yes, and she would properly invite him in for a piece of pie. But not today. Even if he had good news about his cousins coming to work for her, that information was not essential on a foul winter's day.

Then she remembered the way he looked at her sometimes, not quite unclean, but not a way that caused her to feel complimented. She couldn't remember seeing him in church, although he was coming from the direction of town. What if he was stopping by hoping to get snowbound with her? That would be a way to get her farm, insisting she was a compromised woman who now needed to wed.

She shook her head as she went through the house to the front porch to greet him. No, Max wasn't that devious or that clever. He was probably being kind. No need to think the worst, as Gottlieb had always done.

As he prepared to dismount, she shooed him back on.

"No, Mr. Bauer, don't you dare get off your horse. There's a blizzard starting to rage, can't you tell? You get home and warm yourself up."

"Ah, Miz Bernhardena, I been through weather far worse. I thought we could set a spell, talk neighborly." Ignoring her lack of welcome, he dismounted, hitching his horse to the post by her porch.

The Outlaw's Woman

Since he gave her a friendly smile while he did so, she considered inviting him in. Conversing with a real person instead of a dog had its attractions, particularly with a blizzard coming. She wouldn't be seeing Olga for days and days.

But it was the change of his friendly smile to a smirk rather than the coming blizzard that decided for her.

"Any other time, Mr. Bauer," she responded with a stare as cold as the wind, "and you know I'd welcome you. But I think not today. You may rest assured I'll hire your cousins for my planting if that's what you're wanting to discuss."

The lips beneath the pale mustache parted, but she anticipated what he wanted to say next, his offer to buy her farm. Since he had little money, it might be interesting, if not amusing, to hear his strategy for such an acquisition.

The wind shrieked again. Suddenly the only image in her mind was that of Thomas and Whisper freezing beneath a blanket in a stand of trees. Even underneath the warm green cloak, she shivered, unable to restrain the motion.

"Feel that wind, Mr. Bauer? You hurry on home right now. Either that"—she threw him a smirk of her own—"or you head right over to my barn and settle yourself in for a long winter storm. I wouldn't be able to . . . offer you hospitality inside my home overnight, you understand."

Apparently he did understand; he had the grace to blush. The color that splashed across his face actually improved his looks.

Getting snowbound with her might even have been his hope, for he mounted his horse, waved back at her without another word, and headed off again.

Back inside, she warmed up and let herself puzzle over Max Bauer for a while. For, working as hard as he must to have such a successful place, he remained far thinner than one would expect, with white flaccid skin that never seemed to keep the summer sun. And his cornsilk-thin yellow hair never seemed any too clean. Yet certainly at some time Max Bauer would catch the eye of some spinster, or even some giggly schoolgirl growing up too quick, in Staircase town or somewhere else in the county. In his own way he had a great deal to offer. Was she simply doomed to compare any and all men with Thomas Howard?

And then the blizzard came with such fury and madness that Dena prayed out loud. She prayed that Gottlieb was safe and warm, for he had always kept her so. Then she wept, wept because Whisper had once endured a storm such as this, making a tent for Thomas. That they might be doing so now, or worse yet be stranded, frozen stiff, were monstrous thoughts she simply had to thrust from her mind. Keeping herself busy would certainly do that.

She took the yards of lace she had bought in town, using it to fashion angels for her Christmas branch, making heads for the heavenly host from corn kernels. When she had about two dozen of them, she removed all the decorations from her past Christmases except the handblown German angel that had been her mother's. Then she hung the angels along the branch. Olga might wonder, but Thomas would love them. And somehow, sometime, she had to believe that Thomas would see them, and understand.

As she prepared for bed that night, the wind blew harder across the plains than she had ever heard before. Would Songbird be warm enough? What about the birds in the trees? The fish, the fish in Staircase Creek—would they freeze solid, or did streams somehow protect those swimming within?

It somehow made perfect sense to sleep in Thomas's room. It was, after all, called the sickroom because it was the warmest room in the house, closest to the Pennsylvania fireplace as well as the cookstove. The sheets still smelled of him. She heated both corn bags and stuffed them under the covers. It was a bed much smaller than the one she had shared with Gottlieb, although she and Thomas had fit perfectly therein the other night. Edgar and Allan seemed to realize there wasn't room for them next to her, for both plopped down on her own bed.

She left a candle lit; it was wasteful, she knew, but it would burn most of the night, and maybe then she wouldn't feel so alone. Maybe with the shadows it cast, she could imagine his image in the armchair that he had liked, sitting there as if he belonged.

Well, he did belong. She turned on her stomach, her body cold and empty, longing to be heated and filled, stretching her hands under the pillow to warm them.

But Gottlieb had belonged here, too, in this house he had built for her and paid for. Once again swaths of guilt tightened around her heart like winding sheets about a corpse. Would she always feel this confused and doomed when she thought of either man? She had been a good faithful wife, after all, and she had never wanted Gottlieb to die even when she had not cared to have him around.

Under the pillow, she found it. A heart-shaped basket fashioned from parchment from the kitchen and scraps from her stash of brown paper that had wrapped parcels from the mercantile. The paper was cut in strips that he had somehow interlocked.

The way their fingers had interlocked.

Right away she got up, took the candle, and padded through the house to the Christmas branch. She hung the basket right at the top along with the Christmas angel.

Chapter Twelve

By Christmas Eve, she had herself convinced that the miserable weather had prevented Thomas from writing.

True, he had warned her that he wouldn't write or wire—not with the Pinkerton watching, at any rate—but Edna Rausch had told her that the detective had moved out of her boardinghouse weeks ago. And surely Thomas would write somehow; it was Christmas, after all.

She finished knitting a scarf for him, all his own, in a manly blue.

Neighbors' wagons and sleighs and the wind scouring up drifts had kept the road to town passable enough for brave souls. Jonah had made it to her place a few times, inviting her for Christmas on one occasion. Insisting, rather.

"I'll come to services on Christmas Day, Jonah," she promised. "I understand how difficult it will be without Gottlieb."

She meant it. Her husband had not been ungenerous during the season, either with gifts or good humor.

Already last summer she had ordered Jonah's gift. It was a

sophisticated treatise published by the seminary he had attended in St. Louis, on the correspondence between the Tuebingen theologians and the Patriarchs of Constantinople in the sixteenth century. After making her updated mourning dresses, she had knitted him a cardigan sweater out of gray tweed yarns from Chicago. She knew he would never wear it in public, with the proper, more formal image he liked to project, but it would keep him snug and warm when he read in his study or sat in front of the fire.

"But Jonah, I will not be able to attend Christmas Eve candlelight service at midnight."

"Dena! That is a most holy occasion!" Jonah's shock was real.

He opened his mouth for additional protest, so she hurried to continue. "I know I'm your only kin, Jonah, as you are mine, but it will be impossible for me to drive home in the dark, especially if the weather turns drear again."

She held up her hand, almost as though she could physically stop his words.

"Yes, Gottlieb felt comfortable driving at night with carriage lamps, but it is an art I have not yet mastered."

The allusion to his brother seemed both to delight him and hearten his resolve. Suddenly she realized his first Christmas without his older brother gave him far more impetus than normal to want her around.

"All the more reason for you to put up in the parsonage overnight," he nearly echoed her thoughts. "Mrs. Wuebke will remain instead of returning to her room at the boardinghouse. It will be entirely proper.

"For that matter, Dena, come earlier in the day for supper and to trim the trees. You always enjoyed that sort of thing." He had three small *Weinachtsbaumen,* Christmas trees with branches made from goose feathers that sat on the parlor table.

She shook her head. "I thank you, Jonah, but I cannot. I have . . . responsibilities." She knew he wanted to dispute her, to tell her that any of the chores could wait, but he remained silent.

Dena almost blushed shamefully. It was being alone with herself, with the memories of Thomas Howard, with the chance to remind herself of him by looking at the angels flying on the Christmas branch that kept her from church this Christmas Eve. Even though she felt much sympathy for Jonah, she hardened her resolve.

Now, on that holy afternoon, the coffee was hot and fragrant, the gingerbread warm and covered with extra molasses. The *lebkuchen* was ready for the oven. For some reason Dena had been ravenously hungry lately. Fortunately eating alone had never thwarted her.

Nearly content, she sat in the armchair Thomas had favored, remembering how delicious Christmas Eve was for children waiting for the *Christkindl* to arrive.

She would be properly prayerful later on, reading the Christmas scriptures by candlelight. And tomorrow she would probably meet up with the Potts wagon on the way to church, as often happened. This time she'd give the littlest Potts a ride in her cutter.

Smiling, she looked at the gingerbread family she had made for them, each cookie decorated with the proper name.

Utterly at peace, she heard the cacophony of her dogs outside, where they had gone to chase winter creatures in the snow. Even more unexpected was a knock on the door.

She wasn't wearing a widow's gown today; she didn't want to waste them on housework and baking. The woolen day dress of Black Watch plaid kept her warm and matched the season. It was dark enough as fabrics went, deep blue with dark green and black, but the visitor's eyes lighted up with contempt.

"Good afternoon, *Mrs.* Clayter." The Pinkerton bowed over her hand scornfully.

"Edgar, Allan, go to your room," she scolded the dogs as if they were children, totally unable to say anything else. Her heart pounded so dreadfully that she raised her hand to her chest. The dogs shook themselves as though they had been swimming. Dena almost didn't mind. Cleaning up the muddy slush would give her something to do if she survived this awful man's visit.

"Merry Christmas, Mr. Pinkerton." She found her voice.

"Agent Bruce," he advised through stiff lips.

She did not repeat the correct name. "May I offer you a cup of Christmas cheer?" She never drank Gottlieb's whiskey; there was still some in the armoire. It was time to remind herself of Gottlieb's kindness to strangers. It was Christmas, after all. The cold of the afternoon bit easily through human flesh no matter how many woolen layers one wore. Dena knew this full well from her last journey to the barn.

"Yes, as a matter of fact. And I thank you." For a split second, his voice held a modicum of sincerity.

She poured him coffee with a healthy dash of whiskey therein, and brought a plate of gingerbread to where he sat at the table.

"I'm saddened that you won't be with your loved ones this Christmas," she told him politely, realizing that some little particle in the core of her being actually meant it.

"And you also." He drank, but his eyes held their usual sneer.

"Of course I mean your husband," he amended, the sneer remaining.

Even still, Dena refused to be rude to a guest in her home.

"I am surprised to find you still in town," she told him, meaning it.

"Ah, yes. Fine gingerbread. Well, I haven't been in Staircase Creek for some time, as you may already know. I've been to South Dakota, even down to Junction City, Kansas, where there have been sightings of your . . . the outlaw who appeared here several weeks ago.

"Now I am bound for Nashville. It appears that the James brothers have been spotted there with a third gentleman who can only be our . . . hero."

He chewed rapidly and washed down his gingerbread with the whiskey-laced coffee. She actually marveled at him, believing the coffee too hot to swallow in gulps.

"Nonetheless, I thought you would be interested in this. I found it half-buried in the snow, last time I passed by."

She couldn't speak. He held out the contents of the saddlebag he had been carrying. It was what was left of Thomas Howard's linen duster, several bloodstained rags.

"I can tell from the tussle marks that dogs played tug-of-war with this item." He looked pointedly to the room where Edgar and Allan had retreated.

Then he got up and walked purposefully to the coatrack. On it, the only garment hanging was her bright green hooded cloak.

He touched the cloak but said nothing. She knew, though, what he remembered—Gottlieb's warm woolen overcoat and the red scarf she had made. Both were gone.

"I am on my way to Nashville, it seems, Mrs. Clayter. I trust you know that there are laws against aiding and abetting criminals. Oh, blessed New Year to you, too."

Christmas Day proved just as grim. Dena had been testier than ever before in her life with the chattering Pott children riding with her to church.

She was a whore. She had fornicated. She had rescued an outlaw. She was a criminal who had broken the law. She had lied and lied and lied.

During the service, she had broken down and cried during the singing of a particularly majestic hymn, "O Come All Ye Faithful." It had been Gottlieb's favorite, and she hadn't remained faithful to him for even a week.

The townsfolk, however, construed it as a touching measure of her grief. Mira, who had taken to sitting in the front row with Dena during services, placed a comforting arm around her shaking shoulders, as though they truly had family ties.

At dinner, Jonah wore his prissy-lipped glare again, for Dena had removed the gray bonnet she had retrimmed in a semi-mournful way. Not only was her true widow's bonnet left at home, but now she wore nothing at all. Mira Wuebke, prim and proper as usual, looked like the lady of the manor. Dena normally liked the woman, but today she wanted to scratch out her eyes.

Jonah bowed his head and said grace over the meal. In addition to the parlor where Gottlieb's casket had been laid out on trestles, Dena hated the parsonage's dining room. Here she had sat on display during the funeral feast, unable to eat with the entire county watching her every move.

She could still remember the food. She had been eager to eat but forced to play the devastated widow's role. Dollops of freshly whipped cream had sat atop Mrs. Mohlman's pumpkin pies like snow on an orange plateau. And Mrs. Thornburg had lovingly polished a treasured silver porringer in which she had plumped up dried peas in a rich white sauce. Since both old women had sharp tongues that criticized Dena constantly, their thoughtfulness that day had nearly restored her faith in humankind.

That wasn't even a month ago!

After his prayer, wellspoken and meaningful, Jonah smiled at Mira. She had prepared roast duck, not at all Dena's favorite, but if the knowledgeable Mira had fixed it, it probably was not a victim of taint as the wild turkey had been.

"I trust we do not have to worry about the same taint that struck Emil's beloved turkey!"

Dena almost started at her brother-in-law so nearly speaking her own thoughts aloud.

He and Mira shared a tender laugh, and she felt compelled to join in. Mira shook her head bashfully at Jonah's approval of her efforts.

Dena took just a little piece of the duck, drowning it in gravy that was nearly as good as her own, she had to admit. Instead, she bulked up on sliced potatoes drizzled with vinegar and chunks of bacon, and corn canned from the last harvest that Mira had cooked up with stale bread crumbs and rich cream.

Jonah exclaimed once again over the treatise on the patriarchs that Dena had given him and claimed that he would wear his new cardigan that very night.

"And my *Innocents Abroad,* Jonah, I will treasure it," she

told him honestly. "It's pleasing to realize that you remember my fondness for America's writers, as well as the travels of my youth." Her smile emphasized her words. He smiled back.

As for herself, Dena had tried to read the Tuebingen correspondence before wrapping it. She enjoyed the rare occasions when she had time to exercise her brain with intellectual stimulation, but this particular publication had been exceedingly dull.

If Jonah had gotten Mira a gift, no one said. The housekeeper wore a prettier apron than usual when she served, and it looked new. She removed it, however, when she joined them at table. The table had been set with dinnerware before Dena's arrival, so she figured the arrangements had been worked out between Jonah and Mira earlier. Certainly on this celebratory day Mira would be family, not servant.

When Mira brought out her tour de force, a beautiful Bavarian torte, Jonah ruined everything.

"Why, Dena, have you taken to not wearing your wedding ring?"

Mira looked so gleeful with Dena caught in a faux pas that Dena figured she hadn't gotten a Christmas gift from Jonah after all.

To give herself a few seconds to scramble for words, Dena jammed a huge bite of the torte into her mouth. In truth, she had no idea where the thing was. Hadn't Thomas laid it somewhere? But she had certainly kept house since then, dusted and swept. Where on earth was it?

"I . . . I did remove it, Jonah, because I want to . . . cover it with intertwined hairs, both of Gottlieb's and mine." It was a reasonable, most appropriate response. After all, mourning jewelry was quite the fashion, thanks to Queen Victoria.

How had she become such a good liar that people believed everything that sprang so effortlessly from her lips?

Jonah nodded, touched.

Mira looked on approvingly. "Of course, dear. You remember that Mrs. Pott and I cut off a lock of his hair prior to Gottlieb's laying out." She turned her eyes demurely to her lap.

"I can assist you if you wish. I made some lovely pieces when my . . . when Harold passed on."

Dena did remember everything Mira said, also realizing that she had no idea where the lock of hair was. All she could think to do was nod vigorously as she mashed more cake against her teeth.

Maybe the Pinkerton was wrong. Maybe Jesse and Frank had gotten home to their wives for Christmas, just as Thomas had wanted. Maybe they weren't in Nashville at all. Maybe Thomas was on his way to her.

Maybe.

Thomas still marveled at Songbird, how she seemed to know everything and everyone for a hundred miles.

He had almost run out of the contents of the small skin bag of the arnica she had rubbed into his shoulders before he left those long weeks ago. That thought, coupled with this Christmas night spent hidden in a freezing-cold, half-ruined shed near Lawrence brought self-pity prickling his spine like a rash.

Surely if he asked them, the folk befriending him on his journey, like the kindhearted woman outside Fort Riley, would pass messages back to Songbird that she could get to Dena. That he was all right. That he would be back someday. Word of mouth would do, safer than the written word.

Two sheep in a pen strewn with not very clean hay *baa*ed at him. The laughing sound let him know how ridiculous he was. No, he could not cause any more innocent folk peril. After all, he had cautioned Dena before leaving that it would be a long, long while until she heard from him.

After Songbird, he had sheltered near Fairbury with a half-breed Pawnee, or so the odd little man said. Now Thomas was bound for Coffeyville or thereabouts. But as Songbird had decreed before he left, it was now the Moon of the Snowblind, and with the blizzards and freezing rain, his progress was slow.

He was warm at least in the buffalo robe she had given him, although in the darkness of night, he remembered the corn bag. Remembered Dena curling into his body, chasing his evil

Tanya Hanson

dreams away, not realizing he knew she was there.

Each place he went, he left one of her half eagles, always recollecting Songbird's remarks about Golden Heart.

Must have been New Year's Day when he set out for Missouri. Whisper was bearing up just fine, but someday, someday soon, he would love to pay back the faithful animal by giving him his own stall and easy days without endless trekking into the unknown.

It was far too easy to lose track of time when snow and cloud covered the sun. He patted Whisper and spoke kindly above the stiff wind. They had many miles to go today. He reached in the pocket of Gottlieb Clayter's coat for his little talisman, Dena's sprig of rosemary.

Rosemary for remembrance. He remembered every second of it all, every inch of her. Even in the freezing rain, his manhood heated and hardened.

He was embarrassed, but not for that reason. He caressed the other memory of Dena he carried. Somehow, he had never returned it to her but kept it in his pocket, the silver band Gottlieb had put on her hand. It still felt oddly warm whenever he touched it, like it had just left her finger. Even in the icy air.

The sprig of rosemary crumbled into fragrant dust as he lifted it to his nose. He picked up every speck and put it back in his pocket.

Chapter Thirteen

For four days right after New Year's, Willie Pott was snow-bound at Dena's. The winds tore through the night, leaving shards of ice and noise; during the day, the two of them fought like valiant knights at the joust just to reach the barn.

"Do you expect my pa and ma to be worried about me?" He was fifteen and stocky like his father, but suddenly his face wore the expression of a little boy. He pulled off his sodden coat, and Dena could see the snow-wet hems of his trousers, his soaked boots.

Dena squeezed his arm. "They will know you are safe and warm and keeping me company. Now, let's go find you something dry to wear."

"Surely Herr Clayter will not mind me wearing his clothes?"

"Willie, my husband would be honored to have such a manly boy fill his shoes. Truly. And we can't have you freezing to death, now can we? Then we would all miss you forever."

She laid out suitable garments for him and left him to his

privacy in the room she and Gottlieb had shared, just once bringing him hot water and a towel.

"When you're dressed, I will have some cocoa heated up."

In truth, he kept her company. Children, she decided, could certainly liven up a marriage, give a couple something to talk about. Gottlieb's mood had been dismal in the winter, with no fields to plow or seed to plant. She concluded that offspring might well have lightened Gottlieb's spirits. Perhaps in his own harsh way he had still been grieving for the lost baby son just as much as for his inability to produce another.

Indeed, it didn't take much effort at all for Dena to imagine that Willie was Thomas's son, sent to help his mother about the house while his father busied himself in the barn. When she cooked, when she cleaned, when she addressed the boy, she pretended that somehow Thomas could see what a kindly mother she would make.

The midwinter days were very short to begin with, made dark not long past three o'clock by the endless sheets of sleet and blankets of clouds. That was fortunate, for Dena found herself exhausted every day right after supper. Trained well by his mother, Willie felt no insult at washing up after she cooked.

"Miz Dena, I promise not to break anything! Let me help. Ma would blister my hide if I did not help you."

"Well, I guess you can earn your keep. But it's near bedtime, so don't lollygag."

"I like the warm water on my hands. It's right cold in the barn tending to your stock."

"Then you certainly won't complain about a hot bath!" Dena announced, enjoying his look of disappointment just as a real mother might. She retrieved the wooden hip bath.

But in the mornings, her energy was boundless. The house was cleaner these days than even under Gottlieb's strict regimen. In an unexplained frenzy, she sewed and knitted, even cut squares from the scraps of her mourning dresses to make a quilt for Songbird. All she needed was the batting. When the weather cleared she would buy some at the mercantile.

She cooked and baked until she started to run out of supplies. Her appetite keeping pace with the growing boy sharing her roof, she found herself praying the roads would be clear enough soon to drive to town for provisions.

"Ma always says you eat like a bird, Miz Dena," Willie laughed, "I'll happily report to her that she'd be wrong if she saw you now. And may I please have some more brown Betty? It is the best I've tasted."

Delighted, for Gottlieb had never complimented her, she served up another helping of the pudding made from dried apples and bread crumbs.

The boy admired her Christmas branch with the angels, and helped her pack everything up on the sixth of January.

Dena herself touched each angel with reverence.

"Reverend Clayter will be holding Epiphany service to-night," she remarked, "but the weather will preclude our attending."

Willie's brow crinkled a little at the big word, but she was certain he possessed the youthful restlessness that turned into a blessing any event that excused him from church attendance.

When he removed the woven basket, he remarked about it. For a moment, she wished she had been the last one to touch it. It might bring Thomas back to her, like the rub of Aladdin's lamp.

"This is a beauty. I'd like to make Ma one. Can you show me how?"

Dena started to babble. She had tried; the procedure was far more intricate than it looked. "Ah, Willie, let's put that project off until next Christmas. Then we will fill it with marzipan or gingersnaps for her as a special surprise."

Both of them hung on the rope in the daunting wind to tend the animals. Willie gave his dependable old mule a hug, but as always, he remarked about her Morgan.

"This is a fine animal, Miz Dena," he complimented with the innocent envy of youth. "Maybe someday when I'm grown I can get me one."

Dena nodded, thinking about Whisper.

That night, after Willie slept—with the dogs in the bed she

159

and Gottlieb had once shared—she took the paper basket out of the packing box and placed it under Thomas's pillow, where she had once found it. His scent had long since gone away, but she slept in his bed every night.

By the time the weather caught its breath several days later, Willie had become enamored of Katie's five kittens.

"I think since there are five babies, they will make perfect gifts for the littlest ones at our house."

"I suspect that your mama has enough barn cats, Willie, but if you ask her politely and she agrees, the little ones can each have a kitten once they are ready to leave Fraulein Katze." She remembered the day Thomas had pitched hay into a comfortable den for the cats.

Ah, Thomas.

Finally, life returned to normal, as normal as it could be without Thomas Howard there with her. Willie saddled up his mule and headed west toward his parents' place, and Dena waved to him as her sleigh sailed on toward town.

Mrs. Thostenson at the mercantile greeted her with sweet friendliness. "Reverend Clayter was real disappointed that the weather kept so many from Epiphany service." Her husband loaded up bags of flour and cornmeal into the cutter.

Dena laughingly relayed her adventures with Willie to the kindly couple. As casually as she could, she selected copies of all the recent newspapers, no matter how dated.

"I must catch up on what's been happening." She laughed again. "I feel as though I've been holed up in a cave!"

Unwilling to wait until she got home, she parked her cutter in the drifts not far from the cemetery. The skeletons of the walnut and cottonwood trees sheltered her somewhat from the brisk air, but her green cloak had her visible for miles. She pored over the papers for any news of Frank or Jesse.

Or Thomas Howard.

The only item she found was a speculative remark that the pair had been seen in Kentucky for a time shorter than a falling star.

As if on cue, Max Bauer rode up on his horse.

The Outlaw's Woman

"A fine day! Been housebound as I have, Miz Bernhardena?" He was friendly enough. "Not having trouble, are you? Horse cast a shoe? Runners on slick and tight?"

"No, I'm fine, Mr. Bauer. I just wanted to enjoy the air and . . ." She looked pointedly at the graveyard. Max Bauer nodded in sympathy. Gottlieb had no headstone yet and had never bothered to purchase any for his wife and son. In the mounds of snow, no one could discern just where he lay.

"It'll melt soon enough, ma'am," he told her, using a truly thoughtful voice. "Then we'll be able to tell."

"Thank you, Mr. Bauer. You are always so kind." Cold wind blew down her back.

"Well, Miz Bernhardena, seeing you out on the road like this will save me a trip to your place later on." He sounded disappointed. "I have heard from my nephews in York. Their ma and pa suffered great losses after the grasshoppers last summer. My cousins will be happy to hire on for spring planting; harvesting, too."

"I will welcome their help," Dena said, "and I am truly sorry for their tribulation." She spoke a gentle nonsense word to her horse, for he was anxious to continue his brisk trot home.

Max had removed his hat in politeness, and as he nodded, his thin yellowish hair shifted as one piece. He smiled in gratitude, and his cheeks rounded like wild plums as the corners of his mouth pushed them upward. The cold air had brightened his pale skin to the same color as ripening fruit.

She couldn't help but remember Thomas. His shaggy untrimmed hair had lain across his head and neck in a way that enhanced his manliness. Even as they had made love in the snow, the wind had bronzed his skin, not reddened it.

Sudden grief made her shake. She squeezed her eyes shut tight to prevent tears, although Max would probably consider that she wept for Gottlieb. He didn't seem to notice anything, however, intent as he was on a lecture on locusts.

"Such was a plague of biblical proportions. I have done some studying up on the matter, but my brother disbelieves me. The eggs are laid in the autumn but can be destroyed by harrowing

161

the ground and breaking up the nests. Then the cold and rain can destroy them before they hatch. If they hatch in the spring, even more desperate measures must be used."

As Max droned on in a Gottlieb sort of way, Dena made a polite sound of interest, attempting to think about other things, mostly Thomas. However, her response only encouraged him, and Max's conversation grew livelier.

"Yes, ditches must be dug around the fields, a foot deep at least, with deeper holes every rod or two. Then the young locusts crawl into the trenches, falling into the holes, and are buried when they cannot get out."

Dena had had enough.

"I shall remember your advice should the locusts infest Staircase Creek." Dena raised her hand in a gentle but firm farewell. "And I am grateful for all your trouble on my behalf, Mr. Bauer."

"No trouble. I would take it kindly if you were to call me Max." He gave her that look again, nothing totally untoward, but it made her skin flush and prickle nonetheless. If it hadn't, she might have agreed.

"Mr. Bauer, I wish you good day."

She clucked her tongue, and the eager horse pranced through the winter crust. Around her, snow covered the prairie like a featherbed that showed the lumps of the sleeper underneath. Winter here was clean and bright; she wore her bonnet brim low over her eyes. Gottlieb had sometimes worn wooden eye protectors with a thin slit cut in them to protect himself from snow blindness. Maybe she would use them; she could probably find them among his things.

For a moment she recalled the grime and smoke in the city that turned the purity of winter white to unhappy gray slush.

The purity of winter. The season when she had lain in love with Thomas Howard with the snow for their featherbed. Deep inside, her body tensed in remembrance. Would he be remembering it, too?

Maybe he was thinking of her at this same precise moment. Maybe he would be back by spring, when the fields started to sprout the wheat planted last fall, and phlox of many colors scented the land with heaven. Alfalfa would return nutrition to the soil. Bluestem grass would root in the uncultivated ground like hackles of fur on an animal's back, and by late summer goldenrod and sunflowers would outline the road and creek like a necklace of yellow beads on a dowager's neck.

Surely Thomas Howard would return to her by then.

Once at home, she made tea and pored over the papers. It was almost as if she expected that somehow he could speak to her across the pages of newsprint. And when he didn't, she cried until she had no more tears left.

At least, no more that day.

Maybe Aunt Zee wouldn't mind him coming by. Or maybe he could call on her namesake, Jesse's wife, in Kearney.

All he wanted to do was find out how to catch up with Frank and Jesse. Then he'd leave right away.

He rode out of Coffeyville, thanking the farmer again. The old man's eyes were bright, and he gave Thomas his own thanks for the money.

The old man told him of another friend, a comrade at the Missouri border, kin of Red Monkus, another Raider. And that was fine. These folks, taking in a stranger unaware, simply by word of mouth, deserved his undying gratitude. But he needed somewhere to end up. Whisper was finally wearing down in the tough snow, the endless wind, the insufficient rations, and the transient accommodations.

Indeed, they both needed a rest, a home.

He remembered telling Dena that she was his home. But he couldn't bring the Pinkerton down on her. And after thinking on it, he couldn't go to Aunt Zerelda, not after what the Pinkertons had done to her and her littlest boy. And as for Jesse's wife and child, how could he betray their secret identity?

No, somehow he'd have to go on and figure it out by himself.

The road wasn't a good one, even in the best of weather. Today the mix of ice and half-melted mud sucked at Whisper's feet. The wonderful horse was wearying. At least the sun was shining. The wind had slowed, but its brisk touch still warned that the Moon of the Snowblind was far from finished.

The box elder trees around him were scarecrows, bare sticks with branches that reached upward like bony arms. Thomas tried to make himself laugh. Toss on a ragged coat and a hat, and you had a man. No bird would nest in there for a hundred years. The thought reminded him of his old linen duster, of the warm woolen coat he wore now that had saved him.

Just as Dena had.

That night, he slept with the old farmer's kin, right in front of their fireplace in a respectable house outside Coffeyville. Slept like the dead in a real blanket, after stabling Whisper in a halfway decent barn for a change.

In the morning, the wife woke him up with a cup of coffee and a warm beaten biscuit. "Husband's just back from town. He's in the kitchen."

Thomas walked in, expecting to wash up a bit at the pump, to thank the man for his hospitality, to finish the coffee and maybe a second cup before he left. He did not expect a sheriff and a three-man posse.

"It's been a hard year," the wife told him, both sorrow and greed in her eyes. "It was my decision, this one. Don't you go holding it against my man. Your coin was attractive, I don't deny. But we got nine young'uns, and another on the way. The reward money will be a sight more helpful than a half eagle."

The newspapers said nothing about Frank or Jesse James or any part of their entourage. Maybe no one but Dena cared any more. Red Cloud's problems took up much of the copy.

Dena considered for a while what she had told Thomas once before, that other people often had concerns far more grievous than her own. The plight of the Indians brought home to her all her blessings. And it made her remember that she and Songbird had not had Christmas together as was their usual custom. Each year they celebrated it in their own way, and in their own time, just the two of them.

She supposed Songbird knew it was February by now, but

Songbird didn't keep Christmas in the same way Dena did. Oh, they had discussed it endlessly. Songbird agreed that the Great Spirit and the Holy Spirit were likely the same, but she held the earth as her mother, not a father god she couldn't see.

"I admire your Jesus, I tell you true. He came naked and needy as any babe, taking no fame or glory as a grand king. Performing great medicine. Teaching to do unto others as one wishes done to himself." Her voice was wistful. "Seems like few of his followers mind him."

Dena never liked entering the smoky airless little dugout, but she respected her friend who lived within. And as she had known, Songbird exclaimed with joy over the warm patchwork quilt. Unable to help it, Dena wondered if the young Songbird had rejoiced as much for the tainted blankets that had arrived from Fort Randall all those years ago.

Then Dena asked her question, as casually as she could. "Songbird, have any of your . . . friends heard any news from . . . Thomas?"

"Your man? The man you sent to me? No, I do not ask. They do not tell. But you, child, you look ripe."

Dena shrugged. She was rarely sick, and she and Willie had eaten like grand kings.

"Your last moon time?" Songbird persisted.

Dena considered for a while, her mouth twisted into her right cheek. It was hard to remember a time before Thomas Howard, and she knew she hadn't been bothered with the messy process since he left.

"I guess it was . . . well, before Gottlieb's death. Why does it matter?"

"None since?"

Dena shook her head. "No. It has been rather a relief not to be pestered with the muss of it all. Olga mentioned once that a disaster or tragedy can cause the . . . monthly flow to cease. I have given it no real consideration."

"Yet you hunger often and tire easily. You feel hot in the midst of these cold days." Songbird went on to ascertain that Dena felt tenderness in various places.

From the conversation, Songbird's pointed questions, and a few gentle probes, Dena learned that to which she had given no thought.

She carried Thomas Howard's child.

"My God."

"Yes, your Jesus. He was a little babe once. Rejoice."

Rejoice? If Songbird could tell by looking at her, could anyone else?

"Songbird, how can this be? It was only . . . well, I know you suspected that Gottlieb was . . . unable."

"Takes but one time. I say rejoice."

"Songbird."

The wise woman looked intently at Dena. "Your man will return. He is good, and he will love you and the babe. And I will not help you rid yourself of it."

"Oh, no. I am not asking that. I just may not see him for a long while."

"You will manage. He will send word."

Dena nodded. Her heart beat triple time, and a delicious terror rippled over her.

Leaving Songbird's dugout, she laughed with ineffable joy.

Thomas Howard wasn't gone from her, after all.

Chapter Fourteen

Dena wept.

Tears dripped down her face as the train pulled into St. Joseph. The bugle lace of her mourning bonnet lay plastered against her cheeks as she grabbed a handkerchief. She had ripped the lace badly, tearing it off at Gottlieb's burial, but she had reattached it to perfection. One thing about this society girl—she had learned her needlecraft.

A child noticed her tears with concern.

"She weeps for her dead husband, darling," the mother said sagely.

You're wrong, so wrong, Dena told the mother silently. But she busied herself disembarking from the train and hiring a hansom cab to take her where she needed to go. Thinking of Thomas Howard, of making love to him as snow fell like a blessing upon them, could not take up any more of her time.

The baby kicked her, deep inside.

Before she left the depot, she picked up a Northern Missouri Railroad timetable for trains to Colbyville. As far as she could figure, she had almost seventy more miles to go. The speed of the railway amazed her, up to sixty miles an hour. The realization exhausted her, but the reality that she would see Thomas, be his helpmeet, gave her new strength.

Gottlieb in truth had a few decent investments. While his worldly goods had nowhere rivaled her father's—until his downfall at least—Gottlieb was far from the conservative farmer Jonah imagined. In no time at all, the bank arranged a transfer of five hundred dollars from an account administered by one of her father's colleagues in St. Louis. Thomas Howard would no doubt be in need of bail money, and certainly the services of a competent attorney at law.

She hadn't visited St. Joseph in years, and the last time had been with her mother. Thomas Howard's odd aria, to Mr. Poe's Helen, suddenly danced through her mind. How had he known it was her mother's name? She smiled for the first time in days, spoke silently to her mother about her grandchild. For some reason, she found it hard to mention Thomas. She doubted that her mother would approve.

Remembering Jonah's dictum, she wired him of her safe arrival. Of course, he was not to know that this was just one of her stone-skips around the state of Missouri. She kept the duration of her trip vague, and the return date as well.

Before leaving Staircase Creek, she had hinted that she would need at least a week for her business transactions, let alone the days needed for the round trip.

"Colbyville, here we come!" She patted her belly as she boarded the next train. Even the passengers bustling about her with their noise and body smells couldn't halt her reverie. Almost as though Thomas was with her again, she could feel his fingers tighten in her hair. She removed her widow's hat and veil and unloosed the stern bun. How would it be to see him again? Would she blush in a ladylike fashion after what they had done? Or would she claim him boldly and seek his lovemaking again?

She could hardly bear her joy.

* * *

The handcuffs cut deeply into his flesh because he strained so much against them. At least his shoulders had healed enough that he no longer ached constantly.

Much of the journey from Missouri had been by train, but he was on horseback now to Cannon River. He was no different than the convicts of days long past, bound and gagged, being driven to the axman in a tumbrel. Whisper was a memory from another life.

"We're gonna auction him off to help offset your room and board!" the warden of Colbyville jail had guffawed cruelly. "Maybe the glue factory will be the highest bidder."

He couldn't bear thinking of it, his only consolation that anyone who appreciated good horseflesh would find Whisper a bargain. Dena crossed his mind constantly, not just because she had loved Whisper, too. He missed her.

However, he knew full well that he alone had made the decision not to stay in touch with her. By now, as April gilded the world with spring, he would surely be nothing more to her than a memory of snow angels that had melted long ago.

Even if he should survive this, she surely had gone on with her life. Settled comfortably into widowhood with her affectionate friends and her animals around her. Maybe even settled up with that neighbor she always talked about, that Max Bauer. Surely she had more in common with her neighbor than with an outlaw.

Now that would be something, them joining successful farms on the fruitful plains.

No woman before had ever pined for him. Why in the world should he imagine that Dena had? Still, a little corner of his mind called her name.

And sometimes his manly parts tightened at the mere thought of her.

Yes, he had turned into a mighty important criminal. He wondered if he had made the Nebraska papers. Jesse and Frank were still on the run, but his capture had been just about as noteworthy as Appomattox, in western Missouri at least. Right now, a posse of six federal agents surrounded him, most of them with their guns drawn just in case.

"We should make Cannon River by nightfall," one of the feds told him. "You'll soon once again enjoy the comforts of a jail cell."

Most of the group had preened with importance at the opportunity to accompany one of the James gang to his final reward. However, it was the capital charge of murder—not his James connection—that folk were trying to prove.

"I did not ride at Northfield, and I did not kill old Sweyn," he spoke through gritted teeth for the thousandth time. Why did the sun feel so comfortable and warm on his face? Shouldn't he feel cold if death was staring him in the face, or hot if hell was? He decided to enjoy the day; he didn't have that many left on this earth.

"The old man was kind to me," he persisted, "and he was alive and breathing when I left him last November."

"You know the charges." One deputy halted his horse and looked back at him steadily. "The crazy old man suddenly appeared in town spendin' gold pieces. Obviously his mind returned enough to remember where he'd hidden them. You heard about his sudden wealth and lay in wait and killed him. A neighbor seen you ride off."

"The money was mine, you fools. After he took me in, I gave it to him to use to buy medicine and supplies."

"Tell it to the judge." The deputy snorted.

The sun hid behind the clouds.

And Dena . . . well, she was gone from him, too, but that was his own fault.

Dena was tired and hot, more tired and hot than she'd be without a babe in her belly.

Songbird had told her this. The damp wool of her widow's weeds had been beyond bearing, as well as the enduring scent of her travel sweat. She had traveled light, with just a hatbox and Gottlieb's leather satchel, but she'd stuck her two simple everyday gowns inside, the black and the somber gray, to keep up the appearance of widowhood. Today she wore the gray with a black pelisse lined in gray velvet, and the chip bonnet she had trimmed with some of the black silk violets.

Colbyville, although a decent little burg, made her long for Staircase Creek for the very first time in her life. She had traveled extensively in her youth, but unless she connected with Thomas Howard soon, exhaustion and hopelessness would overwhelm her. The bed she had shared with him became the place she most longed to be.

Prim and proper, she stood in front of the town's sheriff, eager to see the man she loved. Disbelief at his words rendered her speechless.

"No Thomas Howard is imprisoned here, ma'am. You can look in the cells yourself. We had a suspected James man here for an odd month or more, sent up from Coffeyville in Kansas, but not by that name. Let's see here, something . . . Woodlake. Woodluke. No, it was Luke. Luke Woodlease."

She found her tongue, even though the name meant nothing. "Well, where is he now? Maybe he knows where Thomas is."

"And Thomas would be . . . ?" He was probably no older than Gottlieb, but his white mustache aged him, as did the scratched spectacles crowning his nose.

Of course she wouldn't say. "Just a family friend."

The sheriff's eyes were kinder than she figured they should be, her being a single woman traveling alone and all. Certainly in his heart he would suspect her of being a mistress or joywoman in spite of her refined appearance. It was a common ruse of harlots to use the disguise of widowhood to gain respectability during their travels.

"Well, there is a Thomas Howard who keeps house over in Kearney. Don't think he's been there for a while, though. That might be worth investigating, mind you." His eyes were suddenly very bright, as though he and she shared a secret.

"But as for this Woodlease—he's been extradited to Minnesota to stand trial for murdering a helpless old Swedish immigrant, a crazy old man who lived like a hermit."

Dena raised her arm in frustration, resting her hand on the

brim of her black and gray bonnet. Something about the last few words were more than a little familiar. But at least it wasn't Thomas on his way to Minnesota. She couldn't bear the strain of more travel.

The disappointment of not finding Thomas as she had thought she would after all these miles suddenly knocked her behind the knees, and she stumbled. The sheriff leaned forward and gave her his arm.

"Maybe you ought to set some, ma'am."

"No, no," Dena protested, although she thanked him. If she sat down, she doubted that she'd ever get up again. "But I am confused. I . . . received word from a reliable source that Thomas was in prison in Colbyville." She avoided mentioning the Pinkerton.

"Well, mebbe you should thank the Good Lord that he's not. Mebbe your . . . source was wrong. Mebbe there's a mistake in identity. Happens." His eyes were still bright and kind. "Livery has a piano-box buggy you can rent cheap. Won't take but a half hour to get to Kearney."

She drove briskly. The sheriff's directions had been good ones, as had been his suggestions. Of course, she was glad Thomas wasn't in prison. Certainly it had been a case of mistaken identity. After all, no one had actually seen Thomas in Northfield. No one except she really knew what he looked like. In fact, the Pinkerton hadn't even given a name.

And maybe someone in Kearney knew where he might be as he waited for a safe time to get in touch with her again.

The house wasn't much more than a cabin and didn't look any fancier than her wooden house on the prairie. In fact, her paint was much fresher. But the garden around it was well designed and neatly tended. Someone lived here. Someone who could tell her . . . something.

Her rented horse trotted happily along the drive. The afternoon breeze blew her skirts away from her legs. The movement of air cooled her skin and lifted the fabric away from her belly. This gray dress, too, was growing far too uncomfortable to wear. Maybe soon, maybe even now, she would find Thomas,

172

so that she could tell him, and the secret wouldn't have to be kept anymore.

It would be nice to have him help her at such moments like this, lifting her in and out of a buggy. She knew how cumbersome her body soon would be.

Late daffodils bobbed their yellow heads around the porch. Some people called them Lent lilies, but Easter was already past. She knocked on the door, holding her breath.

A pretty woman with brown hair answered the door. She held a baby in her arms. A boy, Dena thought, although the white sleep gown gave no clue.

"Yes?"

"I'm sorry to disturb you, ma'am." It was all so strange suddenly. Thomas had mentioned loathing his sisters. Perhaps . . . one of them had turned him in.

Dena forced herself to continue. "I'm looking for Thomas Howard."

The young mother's face wreathed in smiles. "Do you bear news?"

"Why, no." Dena's confusion was real, but she decided to tell the truth. "I haven't seen him for a while. Before Christmas, not far from Lincoln."

"But he was all right?" The woman's voice was anxious. With her free arm, she waved Dena inside. Dark hair wreathed her head like smoke.

Dena remained standing on the porch. "He had been slightly wounded but was healing nicely. I haven't seen him since. I came to Missouri to conduct some family business, and . . ."

"And you thought to let me know! Thanks be to God for all our friends such as you, who give succor blamelessly as needed. He's not here." Her voice grew wistful with longing. "I'm . . . we're packing up to leave to meet him. I'm Mary Howard. This is our little boy, Jesse." She announced both names proudly. Then she whispered, "We're off to Nashville. Please keep our secret."

Dena's baby beat a drumroll underneath her ribs and her heart crashed through her rib cage after stopping completely.

How like Thomas to make her keep more secrets.

The day had grown dark and cold. She couldn't see anything of Thomas in his infant son, but for a brief space of time she wondered if her child and this one would look alike. Neither parent would ever know. The name Jesse even made sense, with Thomas's exalted notion of kinship.

Words failed her as her world collapsed, but she must have looked normal because Mrs. Howard remained friendly and hospitable. "Please join me for coffee. You can tell me his tale."

"No, no," Dena said, her body as stiff as a doll. "No, I need to go." She backed down the porch.

"Who shall I tell him has called?"

Dena said nothing more. Already the baby made her ungainly, but she entered the buggy competently enough. However, she drove the gentle horse recklessly back to town, all the while forgetting about the life deep inside her.

At the livery stable, she saw a horse that looked almost like Whisper. It was then that the tears came, and the sobs that tore from the center of her being.

And now she thought of the baby as well, and wept for it also, poor fatherless babe.

Chapter Fifteen

The first train out of Kearney headed east, but Dena didn't care. Spending the night in this town while waiting for the next one on the Burlington–Missouri River line to St. Joseph was unimaginable.

Just thinking about running into Thomas Howard's kin again made her heart hurt with such an ache that she thought it might stop beating. The station master had told her she could connect with a westbound train in Lexington.

All around her the pretty spring afternoon cast shadows as delicate as lace. And all around her, people young and old walked and ran, hopped and skipped through lives that went on just as they had the day before and would tomorrow.

How was it possible to be jealous of strangers?

The passenger car filled up fast, and the everyday odors of humanity started to turn her stomach. Where were people going? she grumbled to herself. Didn't people work? What on earth was there to do, who on earth to visit, on a Wednesday in April?

"Mind if I sit here?"

In the crowded coach, Dena had no choice but to let another traveler sit next to her. She nodded. However, she stubbornly kept her face pasted to the window, looking outside. For some reason, all she could see were the dancing daffodils around the Howard porch, flowers that would soon die after such a short life. Somehow Dena felt just like that.

The woman in the aisle stood stalwart, impassive, before straightening her skirts to sit down. She possessed a dignity and confidence that Dena liked to see, and she felt a little bit better. Dena supposed that was why she liked Olga Pott so much. Olga never worried that her waist wasn't eighteen inches or squeezed herself into a corset to try, a woman who spoke her mind instead of tittering foolishly behind a fan, batting her eyelashes like feathers in the wind.

Setting a valise on the floor at her feet, the passenger held a small basket on her lap. It probably held a cold dinner, and Dena realized she was ravenous. More than that, Songbird had told her that feeding herself helped feed the baby.

Baby! Poor fatherless mite.

Nonetheless, she refused the woman's offer to share the food basket with her.

"Are you sure, young lady? I have plenty," was all she said, holding out the basket a second time.

"Thanks, but no."

Shaking her head a little, the woman dug inside the basket, clucking her tongue appreciatively. "Now, what's this? Two slices of sweet potato pie. Made it myself." She nodded in invitation once more.

Dena raised her hand to wave away the offering and glanced at the basket once again, startled to notice that the older woman had just one arm. Her shawl was strategically placed so that one could hardly tell, but the movements necessitated by her hospitality had shown Dena the truth. Odd to see a woman so tragically deformed. It was pitiful enough to see the veterans. The woman had probably had an accident of birth and never known differently. It would be far worse to start out a hale, healthy man and then be crippled by bullets. Even with her malformation, the woman sat imperious and resolute.

Nonetheless, Dena looked away quickly in discomfort, unable to think about accidents of birth. It had been a day of many terrible emotions, and besides all that, she was hungry and tired. Maybe, tucked safe inside her womb as it was, her baby wouldn't know any of this.

Ignoring the lunch basket, the woman met Dena's eyes straight on.

"You're far too young for such dead eyes, darlin'. You can bring life back into them by prayin' to the good Lord, and by being strong. Only the strong survive, and tomorrow will bring them more strength than they had yesterday. You will survive to improve the choices that took away your spirit."

"I thank you for your concern. I have recently lost my . . . husband."

"Ah. I've buried three. Miss the last one most of all. Let me assure you that each day does dawn a little brighter." Her eyes were kind.

"Yes, I've been told that. Thank you again for your concern." Dena managed a smile.

Then the woman made small talk about journeying to relations in Jonesboro. Dena was polite, but soon she indicated that she wanted to doze off.

The woman connected to the St. Louis–St. Joseph line before Dena changed in Lexington. Dena never knew whether or not her fellow passenger meant to leave the basket of half-finished supper, but she couldn't resist investigating it after several miles had passed. From the woman's self-confident demeanor, Dena half-expected the train to back up to return the basket to her.

The sweet potato pie was indeed delicious.

For just a second, she considered catching the train to St. Louis along with the woman. She had no desire to relive old memories, nor to meet up with old foes, but so many years had passed since she had visited her father's grave. It would be nice to bring him flowers, to tell them of his grandchild.

In fact, Jonah had ordered Gottlieb's headstone from the same masonry company her late husband had selected to prepare the gravemarker for her father. Gottlieb had shown her a few sketches in a catalog; she had been allowed to select the calligraphy for Bernhard Albert Wegner, born Potsdam, Germany, 1829, died St. Louis, Missouri, 1873. That was it, no pretty poetry, no carved exclamations as to his success as a loving husband and father.

Just like I will, Dena prophesied. Unless Jonah outlives me and doesn't find it unseemly to have a wife on each side of his brother.

And then she thought everything through, all the kinship and connections and the reasons for everything. It was best that Thomas Howard had an honorable wife, for Dena had been nothing more than a lusty trollop throwing herself at him in the snow, with her own husband barely cold.

Right now, in the stuffy train car, exhausted and dispirited, Dena felt shame lave her skin as no hot humid summer sweat ever had.

Of course he wanted nothing to do with her. If he had wanted to be in touch with her, he would have found a way. Songbird's trail of friends would have helped if he had asked. And what man would want her now, having trapped him with an unwanted child? She had, after all, inferred to him that she was barren.

This was absolutely not the first nor only life-altering crisis she had faced. She would figure it all out as it was meant to be.

As the woman on the train had told her, only the strong survived. To fix their mistakes.

She had been strong enough to lie while looking straight into the eyes of a Pinkerton agent. She could lie again. Sometimes it was the only recourse. The righteous Jonah had lied, small half-truths to be sure, to get his brother a proper Christian burial. And she could lie again now, whether big or small, to take care of her child, to make sure the baby always had a home, and land of its own.

Soon the folk of Staircase Creek would believe that Gottlieb Clayter's city wife had not been barren and that he had given her a child before he died.

After switching trains in Lexington, she doubled back to St. Joe, both eager and terrified to be headed home again. The spring rain ran down the windows in sheets. All along the Missouri River, the cottonwoods that had sparkled so on the start of her trip were slick with gray rain, long drops of which looked like pond slime. Nothing pretty about this spring rain. Unless it was all in Dena's mood.

No one met the train at the depot in Seward. Dena hadn't wired any of the folk in Staircase Creek about her arrival time. She planned to spend the night in Seward; she needed time to perfect her next web of deceit. And maybe some garments to accommodate her belly. The constricting mourning dresses had just about strangulated her.

She walked from the depot, deciding to stop at the dry goods store. The rain had stopped, and she looked around the pretty town built on a rolling hill. Westward, fields and prairie loomed toward the blue-skied horizon for hundreds of miles, though they looked like she could walk them in an hour.

The stateliness of the one-armed woman on the train haunted her. She had read the secret pain in the woman's eyes, watched the wrinkles tighten around her lips after her smiles. Whatever grief she carried in addition to her injury she bore with stoicism and hope for the future. Dena nodded in return, wishing the woman could see her agreement. For a moment she regretted not sustaining a meaningful conversation with the woman during their journey.

Something niggled at the back of her mind. She booked a room in a small but tidy hotel and headed for the dry goods shop. A one-armed woman was an unusual thing. And a one-armed woman in Kearney reminded her of something Thomas Howard had told her. The Pinkertons had bombed Zerelda Samuel's homestead, killing her child and destroying her arm.

"Could it possibly be?" she whispered to herself, causing a

man leading his horse nearby to look up curiously. If so, she felt worse than ever before. "Zerelda surely could have helped me! Possibly she even knows where Thomas is! They're kin, and kin keep in touch."

But Thomas Howard had a wife. He didn't need Dena. It was better this way.

She had no tears to spare just then, but her heart felt like it weighed a thousand pounds.

"I've just . . . I'm with child and need suitable garments," she explained to the shopkeeper, obviously a matron herself.

The woman's eyes widened in some disbelief. "Suitable garments? What you have on is perfectly fine."

Dena lowered her eyes, acknowledging her widowhood. "Yes, but I . . . am going to bear . . . my late husband a child. I am about to choke to death."

"Have you no mother or friend to advise you?"

Dena shook her head. Both Mira and Olga had given birth prior to her arrival at Staircase Creek, and she rarely noticed the condition of any town women. Come to think of it, sometimes she was more than surprised when a couple brought a newborn babe to the baptismal font, having not realized the woman was expecting.

"You may continue to wear your day clothes; just let your corset out a half-inch or so. You'll be appropriately attired."

Dena wanted to scream. A corset? Appropriate attire? That nonsense had been left in Cape Girardeau. She wanted comfort and lungs that could take in air.

"Yes," the woman continued, "some fool doctors claim that wearing an invalid gown is preferable when one is in your condition, but no woman can appear in society in such an indecent garment."

Almost laughing, Dena excused herself to look around the store's meager wares. She did not consider the Nebraska prairie a place of perfect society or appropriateness. She discovered a somber dress of wool challis, gray shot through with purple tattersalls in a size larger than she normally wore. She could certainly wear an "invalid gown" at home alone and make a stylish dress or two slightly roomier in spots that she could take in after the birth.

The shopkeeper looked at her with approval. "You've chosen well. And I grieve with you at your loss."

"Yes." But Dena knew she grieved over the loss of Thomas Howard. And she wouldn't consider the torture of wearing a corset at such a time. Why did society dictate that a woman's condition must be hidden while motherhood was glorified as her greatest role? Did people still think infants were found in pumpkin patches?

By the time she sent a quick note to Jonah, paying the young courier from the telegraph office to deliver it, she felt like she supposed someone a hundred years old does. Passing the office of the sheriff of Seward County, she couldn't help noticing the WANTED poster of the James brothers hanging in the window, and for the first time she wished she hadn't met Thomas Howard, wished that he had never hooked up with his kin to commit robberies and hadn't hid out in her home.

Instead of being an abandoned woman, with child and no husband, she would be a respectable widow, doing her chores like always, playing with her dogs and the kittens who were already nearly cats. Going to church under the eagle eye of her brother-in-law, maybe fending off proposals or at least eager looks from neighboring bachelors.

She shook her head, ashamed. Being with Thomas had brought her to life and given her life. The baby stirred. She had made the decisions herself, to let him stay, to allow him to return. To take his love and seed.

Then it caught her eye, a fuzzy sketch of three men torn from a newspaper, pasted on the window glass at the bottom of the WANTED poster. An eight-year-old child could have drawn the crude portraits. Goodness; a thousand dollars. That was an attractive sum, particularly to anyone who had had bad times with the grasshoppers. Who'd been "widda'd" suddenly. Who simply wanted a wooden house instead of a sod one.

She couldn't read the date, but it seemed to be earlier in the month. The caption claimed that the trio was the James brothers and an unidentified dark-haired young man, supposedly seen in Tennessee. She remembered the Pinkerton talking of some such long ago.

It could be Thomas Howard, she determined, although she couldn't tell for certain. The three heads looked more like smudged thumbprints than anything else. At least he had found safety, along with the indestructible Frank and Jesse.

She slid her hand gently along the glass in front of the most likely smudge.

"You're one of them folk who hold those gentlemen in high esteem?"

Dena's hand froze; startled, she looked up to see that the county sheriff had come up behind her. For a moment, she smiled. If she were painting a picture of a storybook lawman, he would look exactly as the man before her did. His black-brimmed hat and well-worn boots were likely left over from his cavalry days. The star of his office gleamed on his dark blue sack coat, unbuttoned so that his Peacemaker was prominently displayed on his right hip.

Then she blushed. She didn't hold the gang in high regard. Or did she? Was she still a God-fearing, law-abiding woman who deplored killers and robbers? Unsure that she was, she glanced away from the man's gaze, feeling heat crawl up her cheeks.

"Not that I'd hold it agin you, ma'am." He tipped his hat. "Compassion is a wonderful thing.

"Fact is, Mr. Jesse James has a heart of gold and a whole lot of disciples in a half-dozen states or more. Got something of a reputation as the Robin Hood of the west. Or south, depending on which direction you think about."

The sheriff paused in his speech, acting like he was ready to spit out a load of snuff. Dena jerked quickly away from the line of fire.

"Yes, ma'am. Jesse feeds hungry families and never refuses loans. Young'uns of the Quantrille raiders often receive envelopes of cash and boxes of vittles. All anonymous. Or so it's said."

Dena nodded, not at all certain how to respond.

"Fact is, we had one of Mr. Jesse's gang hiding hereabouts, before last Christmas it was, over in Staircase Creek."

Hackles danced up and down her back like the flies that pestered Grace the cow in the summer heat.

Then she relaxed. This man was no Pinkerton, after all. And Thomas Howard—surely he'd made it to safety in Tennessee. His wife had hinted so, hadn't she? Wife or not, Dena wanted no harm to come to him.

She nodded conversationally. "Yes, sir. I recall a very nosy, quite nasty Pinkerton interrogating me and my neighbors. But surely"—she tried to laugh as she indicated the smudge—"surely this is our—outlaw. Wasn't everyone else at Northfield captured?"

"All but Frank and Jesse, ma'am. No one knows who this here man is. He didn't ride at Northfield. Our man is in prison in Minnesota for killing an old Swede who took him in after he got shot up outside Northfield."

"But . . ." Dena couldn't think of any words to say. "How . . ."

"Likely on trial up there as we speak. Got caught in Coffeyville, Kansas. A bit of reward money out for him, too."

"But how can you know for sure?" She clearly recalled the sheriff in Colbyville instructing her on mistaken identities. Truth to tell, no one had even named the third smudge. It could be Thomas; she couldn't really tell.

"Well, the law is as sure as can be. He was identified positively"—he spoke all four syllables of the last word with equal emphasis—"by the bartender at the saloon in Zee, who seen him there just before the first big blizzard last winter."

Dena's brain found the words, but she didn't know if her lungs would find the air.

"Would you know his name, by chance?"

The sheriff grinned at her with his apology. "Not off the top of this old noggin. The part of my brain that stores my recollections is not as agile as it used to be. But come to think of it, I may have last week's paper hereabouts. The editor of the *Bee* likes to print all the stories related to the infamous James gang, including want posters and the like." He disappeared inside his office briefly, and then reappeared.

"Yessirree, ma'am, here we go." He held out a front page a few days old. "Fella by the name of Luke Woodlease."

She hadn't moved a muscle, not a twitch of a nerve all during the lawman's conversation. And she couldn't move now.

Thomas Howard's face stared back at her.

The traveling judge, though tough, had a reputation for being thorough and fair, and the man called Thomas Howard prayed that it was so, since he had forgone a jury trial. Prayer was all he had left. But considering the nature of his activities in the recent past, he doubted the Lord was too impressed with him.

His lawyer seemed an impartial sort, too, advising against a jury, doubting that anyone in Minnesota would declare a member of the James gang innocent of anything.

A temporary courtroom had been set up in the saloon, packed today as it had been for the entire six days of the trial. Most trials were started and finished on Saturdays, but not his. At least he hadn't been subjected to a speedy trial and hanged the same day.

Witnesses came out of nowhere from a dozen miles around, like box elder bugs getting dug from the bark of the tree. Old Sweyn had suddenly been elevated to a patriarch of such magnitude that his murderer rivaled John Wilkes Booth in evil and ignominy. Folks who had probably never even spoken a single word to Sweyn now swore under oath and revealed laudatory tales of his excellence.

Idly he wondered how it was that folk could spend so much time away from their planting and chores. Weren't children in school these days?

With much irony, he spoke to his lawyer about Sweyn's heroic deeds.

"Folks hereabouts gave Sweyn little attention during his lifetime. Called him a droolin' half-wit. He was ridiculed on his rare forays into town. Children tossed rocks at his melons, threw his own tomatoes at his front door, hung dead fish from the arms of his scarecrow.

"Now that he's dead, you'd think the inconsolable world has lost a treasured grandfather." Thomas nervously tugged at his shirt collar. The shirt hadn't started out as his, and it fit poorly. Above its faded gray, his face bore nearly the same hue. He hadn't felt the sun on his face in weeks.

The lawyer loosened the cravat at his own neck and nodded.

"Some of what you say does make sense, I'll allow. But folk knew that Sweyn always muttered to anybody who could hear about some gold coins he had hid away. No one believed him, with his mind half gone. But after he showed up with half eagles to buy supplies, then got murdered a short time later, the responsible party had to be the stranger he'd been caring for: you."

"And you believe it's me?"

"Doesn't matter what I believe. I don't even want to know. I'm just here to defend you. Hard job, Mr. Woodlease, with you having been found with half eagles in your pocket, too."

The man Dena called Thomas Howard had no way of responding. He had been found with her money in his pocket. . . . There was no way he could confess that Jesse James had given each of the riders a handful, beforehand, in case they needed to get out of Northfield fast, and that he'd given most of them to Sweyn for his room and board. And that Dena, an innocent, proper widow in Staircase Creek, Nebraska, had given him some, too.

Given him so much more. His groin tightened, but he ignored his manhood. He needed to stay out of her life. He was trouble. The Pinkerton certainly would help find her guilty of something for having helped him, especially now that there was a murder charge on his head.

The lawyer led him to the stand, and he took a solemn oath.

He said all he could say in his own defense. "I never robbed Sweyn. He helped me. I gave him money to buy me medicine and food, and left the rest to thank him for taking me in."

"And how did you get hurt?"

"Got shot by a sniper, somebody shooting carelessly. Somebody made a mistake. I got no truck with anybody."

Packed with bodies, the saloon became a sweat lodge. The painted cats who entertained the drinking men at night lined the stairs to the second-floor rooms, today dressed in modest attire. Even respectable housewives, wearing their Sunday best, had entered the foul halls of the erstwhile drinking establishment, expressions of superiority tensing the muscles of their faces.

Sweat ran in rivulets down his spine. He couldn't help thinking of Songbird and her role in the Sundance. He wanted to smile, but instead his spirits fell because he doubted he would ever see her again to thank her. Far worse, he would never see Dena again, never get the chance to thank *her*.

Most of the faces turned to blurs. He refused to focus on a single one, unwilling to see the identical expressions of righteous condemnation the townsfolk wore. His fingers fidgeted again with the collar of his shirt, which had dampened with the humidity and his own perspiration.

The lawyer had a bag of his personal goods stashed somewhere but had provided a cheap suit of used clothes from a charity box.

"It'll go better for you appearing presentable, instead of wearing your clothes from the road," the attorney had explained.

He pricked to attention. The judge was speaking to him in an almost fatherly tone.

"If you tell us where Frank and Jesse James are hiding out, things will go easier for you, young man." The judge's face was kind.

At the mention of Frank and Jesse, the crowd moaned. This time, the sound wasn't one of secret admiration at their exciting lives. This was, after all, the land that the James gang had bloodied and torn up.

His flesh crawled with hopelessness. The hatred in the gazes of the townsfolk of Cannon River was almost palpable.

His mouth remained sternly closed. Finally, he told the

courtroom, "I didn't ride at Northfield. I don't know where they are. And I didn't kill Sweyn."

At the mention of the old man, the crowd stirred, this time noisily. The judge pounded his gavel.

"Evidence says otherwise, young man. I find I have no choice. I might have been able to show some leniency if you had proved yourself a friend of justice and helped us locate those killers, but I have no choice. I hereby sentence you to death for the murder of Sweyn Willemson, a sentence to be carried out two weeks from this day."

He closed his eyes and nodded. A fitting end to his supposed life of crime. It mattered little that he had done none of the things of which he was accused. That his worst offense was keeping company with the James gang. Two weeks would be sufficient time to construct the gallows and to plan a picniclike atmosphere for the town.

"You will hang by your neck until you are dead."

"I never rode at Northfield, and I never killed anybody," he repeated tonelessly as the deputies led him back to his cell and harshly threw him in.

The lawyer joined him shortly. "I'm no pettifogger, Mr. Woodlease. I have done all I can for you in an honest way. One of the testimonials came from a nephew of my wife, who was pinched once for thieving. I do not believe him to be a man of integrity. I shall attempt to discuss with him the . . . validity of his words and see if he can assist me in discovering the truth. In the meantime . . ." He held something reverently in his hands. "Are you a Catholic?"

Luke Woodlease shook his head.

"Well, this may not work then, but I suggest you try any prayers you got." The lawyer examined the pale green rosary dangling from his fingers for a moment before gently tucking it into a little silk case and placing it in his pocket.

"If nothing else, you can expect efficiency and some respect when your day comes. You will be allowed a last statement, and a clergyman, if you choose."

While the lawyer caught his breath, his eyes downcast and

defeated, Luke Woodlease thought of Jonah Clayter. He shook his head abruptly, shaking Dena Clayter from his reflections.

"I wish I could say I haven't been part of this sort of thing before, but I can't." The lawyer's voice was nearly kind, as the judge's had been, but he rarely met the prisoner's eyes. "Good day."

Luke Woodlease listened to the lawyer's footsteps as he exited the tiny jailhouse. For a second, he remembered the weeks he had spent on the trail, and how he had longed for a roof over his head. He had never imagined four prison walls as his home.

One of the deputies walked up to the bars. His unfriendly face let it be known to anyone with eyes that he had held old Sweyn in high esteem. Luke Woodlease snorted out loud. The lawman probably had never even seen the outcast old lunatic until he examined the corpse.

"Yessir, say them prayers. I been at many of these things myself." The deputy leaned casually against the iron bars. "First your feet and arms will be bound. I might even do that myself, nice and tight. The hangman—a good friend of mine, by the way—will place the noose snug around your neck, with the knot stuck just under your ear. Likely your left one." He reached his hairy arm into the cell, groping for Luke Woodlease's left ear. Luke backed away, wanting to spit on the deputy but knowing he would pay for the disrespect.

The lawman continued his heartless discourse. "When you fall, the impact will break your neck if that knot's placed just right. If not, why, you just might dangle for a while, high-stepping in death's last dance. Seen that aplenty. Takes several minutes that way, unless you got a sharpshooter in the church steeple to end your pain. I wouldn't count on it, though. This crowd wants to watch you dance."

He laughed cruelly; then his voice softened. "But you'll miss the performance. You'll have a black hood over your face. Maybe Timmy Tyler will do a drumroll like he did as a kid during the war when the hangman gives the signal to open the trapdoor. Like I said, if that knot's done right and if you fall

straight and strong, it'll be over in a heartbeat. Your last one."
He scratched his back against the doorjamb and took a pearl-
handled bowie knife from a fancy leather sheath strapped to
his leg. Luke Woodlease watched him use the tip of it to scrape
under his nails in a nonchalant way.

"Now, my goodness, maybe I ought to let you use my dull
little rattlesnake cutter here to end it all before facing such
humiliation." He pretended to hand over the knife. "But my,
oh my, you just might turn the tables on my kindness and use
this fine piece of weaponry to widdy on out of here by picking
the lock. Tsk, tsk."

With great accuracy, he spat a mouthful of chaw into the
far corner of the cell and turned his back. He let loose a loud
string of flatulence before he walked away.

Chapter Sixteen

Thomas or Luke? Who was he? Where was he? Whichever, one was married, the other a murderer. Dreams that had died yesterday now were dashed to eternal damnation. Waiting for Jonah to pick her up at the Seward Hotel, she shuddered even though the late April morning was very fine.

For a few months she had come to life, felt life. But now, even with the glories of April dancing about her, she had never felt so low. Why was it that everyone she loved let her down, changed beyond recognition?

Jonah arrived, helping her into his buggy as politely as always, nodding to himself at her proper attire. She took his good mood as a positive omen. Nonetheless, his first words were not kind.

"You look dreadful, Dena. I advised you not to take such a journey, and alone yet. I cannot imagine any business you needed to conduct that required such travel. I fear your health has been compromised."

From the reflection in the small, mottled hotel mirror, she

knew she looked wan and overcome, though she felt that Jonah was rude to say so. She frowned at him.

"Thank you for the compliment. I missed you, too."

"Oh, Dena, I meant no insult. I merely worry about you."

She relented and tried to improve her mood. The fact that she preferred Thomas Howard to do the worrying and to meet her train was simply not Jonah's fault. Nor was it Jonah's fault that the cad might be married, unless he had performed the ceremony.

"Thank you, Jonah." This time her voice was soft and sincere. "As always, I do appreciate your care and concern. I am awfully tired."

He tossed her bag into the back of the buggy. Apparently he wasn't done chiding her. "Had you wired me of your arrival time, I could have been here yesterday afternoon. You had no real need to hire a hotel room."

She did not bother to reply. He nudged the horse to go, then mentioned, "I hope your venture was fruitful and that you accomplished what you felt you needed to do."

Her lips curved into a forced smile. "Yes, indeed, I found out some information that is very helpful for me to know."

Turning her face away from him, she said no more in spite of the look of blatant curiosity on his face. Instead she pretended great interest in the stately new courthouse in the center of town.

She had stuffed herself into the dark gray merino dress for the last possible time; her hair was neatly pinned into a neat swirl underneath the bonnet covered with maroon and black ribbons. Truly she looked demure and respectable. She wondered what Jonah would do if he knew her dreadful secret, making love in the snow with a fugitive who now was on trial for murder. A man who had lied and tricked her.

And what would he do if he knew that she had lied and tricked people herself? His good opinion of her mattered a great deal, but she had no recourse but to ignore her shame. She had to proceed with caution. He must never suspect that the baby wasn't Gottlieb's.

Still, she felt her heart dance when she thought of Thomas Howard, in spite of his crimes and perfidy. Walking at the creek holding hands. Making snow angels, making love.

Making a baby.

She lifted her hand to hold up her chin. Would it all have been different if he'd arrived in the spring? When the violets dusted the air with their particular fragrance, when the baby lambs gamboled in a dewy field gone fallow for a year? When at least her husband hadn't still been warm underneath the snow?

"Dena, you simply look more . . . unwell than comforts me. I fear the trip took more energy than you had stocked up."

"Well, you'll know the reason soon enough, Jonah. I really am all right. The trip was . . . enlightening but exhausting." She began to chatter, to play the delirious female to the hilt. She needed to start dropping hints about her condition in preparation for the formal announcement.

"Then you must be relieved to be nearly home. To celebrate your return, Mrs. Wuebke suggested that you dine at the parsonage tonight. She will prepare something a little special. Only if you feel rested enough, however."

Dena smiled inside even in her turmoil. This was going along even more smoothly than she had hoped.

"That is a splendid idea, Jonah. And I ask a favor, a boon. Please invite the Potts."

"All of them?" He sounded unnerved. A fastidious bachelor, Jonah normally did not care for swarms of children.

"Why, yes." She had it all planned out. "I know Easter has passed, but can't we celebrate for a while?"

He smiled, but his brow was a checkerboard of puzzlement. "I would be happy to celebrate your return. However, I wonder if that is quite what you meant."

Steering the buggy expertly to the road that led to Staircase Creek, he slowed down as he turned onto Columbia Avenue. For a moment, Dena tried to calm her nerves by concentrating on the view before her, spring's opulence of phlox and violets. The town had taken Arbor Day seriously; a grove of ash sat plump and shady at the junction, elm standing full and green.

She knew she sounded foolish, but she meant it. "I never got to decorate Easter eggs with the little ones. Gottlieb's . . . marker arrived during Holy Week, and I . . . we had a lot on our minds. And Olga didn't have eggs to spare. My pullets . . . well, they are hearty girls. And you know that Willie and Georg have been at my place when time permits, helping Max's cousins with spring planting, and Ida kept house during my absence. This would be a way to say thank you."

Jonah would certainly excuse this whim as a manifestation of her condition once he knew about it. She could certainly cook them a meal on her own at her own place. But he politely said nothing.

Truth was, she needed Olga and Wilhelm near her for the momentous announcement. If there were any questions or suspicions, Olga would support Dena unconditionally, and Wilhelm always agreed with his wife. Mira and Jonah would be outnumbered. And if she was not in her own home, she could run out the front door and escape if necessary.

And the children deserved a special meal. She found herself loving them more and more, even if she couldn't keep the youngest ones' names straight. Olga's cuisine was wholesome but cheap and plain. Ever since the child began to move in her belly, Dena had realized that it was a whole real person, and she remembered that children had wants and plans just like grown-ups.

"Well, I don't know . . ." Jonah began, but he saw her eyes fill with tears, real ones that she hadn't planned. "Of course, since it means so much to you, I will instruct Mrs. Wuebke to arrange to include the Potts, unless time is too short to prepare adequately."

"Don't you worry about that," Dena stressed. "Olga won't arrive without a mess box the size of a railroad car. She never goes anywhere empty-handed."

Jonah nodded in rhythm with the clip-clopping horse, but his voice was still worried. "You'll keep the children entertained . . . and out of my study? And no animals? No dogs, or fish to clean . . . ?"

She wiped away the tears, figuring it was the baby that made her so weepy, and started to laugh. "Agreed."

"Dena," Jonah said suddenly as he swerved to avoid an even deeper rut in the road. His right arm automatically rose from the reins to extend across her midsection, as though to hold her in. She had not expected the bump, and her breath came hard and quick. "Are you certain you are all right? Did all fare well with your business dealings?"

"Ah, yes, dear Jonah." She found her breath and squeezed his arm affectionately rather than embarrass him with a hug. "You'll understand my moods when you know the reason for them."

He watched her expectantly, but she held her finger to her lips. "It's a surprise."

The euphoria that her dinner plans were working out fell flat as unrisen yeast when she was back at home, all alone.

A veil of clouds hung across the sky and the sun dappled her fields. The wheat was already sprouting, and most of the place was well planted now. The orderly rows promised life-giving food by fall but only reminded her of the mess she had made of her life.

Jonah practically carried her to the front door, almost as if he suspected, but she understood that he considered her frail and exhausted. Good heavens, hadn't the man remembered she'd traveled across the ocean? Ida Pott greeted her at the door with a pie she had made all by herself of dried apples and cherries, but Dena had soon scooted her and Georg home on the mule to get ready for the dinner at the parsonage.

"I'll bring this wonderful pie to the parsonage tonight for dessert. The reverend will be most grateful."

Ida's face had glowed. Many country folk hereabout tended to hold a preacherman as nearly a deity, and Dena realized that Ida was one of them.

Ecstatic at seeing her again, Edgar and Allan whined like lost souls seeking God and finding Him.

She unbuttoned the tight dress and took a gasping breath as she sat heavily in the armchair Thomas had liked. Where he had sat looking as if he belonged here. How was it possible that just days ago she had set out with full hopes of rescuing him again, of exonerating him, of bringing him back here to be her man, the father of her child?

The house was the same, but everything in it was different. In her mind, she remembered Thomas, cold and bloody by her stove, wild-eyed with terror at her gun staring him in the face. Beyond, she saw the bed where she had slept ever since he left. It would be worse, of course, going to the barn, seeing the final resting places of the snow angels, and the place where she and Thomas had been one. Or was he really Luke Woodlease? And why had he lied?

She looked Edgar straight in the eye. Exhausted by his earlier excitement at seeing her, he lolled on his haunches, looking at her.

"At least I had good reason to lie, Edgar." The dog's head cocked, as if he could actually understand her. "At the time, I believed myself to be protecting an innocent man. Now I am protecting my babe from growing up without a home.

"Now, since you've been a good dog, let me find a piece of fatback for you." While she bustled around the house like she always did, she marveled again at how quickly life changed.

Certainly her child deserved Clayter's place, and she'd take care of it for him or her. And Gottlieb, no matter how grim and pitiless he had been, was a sight better man to claim as a father than a murderer who had killed a harmless old man.

Suddenly she remembered that the James brothers each had adoring wives. Now she had a bit of a notion of what these women went through.

She needed to rest for a bit before washing up. At least the clothing she had bought in Seward would fit her a little more loosely than her usual.

The Potts would pick her up in their buckboard and bring

her home after the meal. They'd never been able to afford a springboard wagon, and she didn't look forward to the jostling and tumbling over the winter-toughened road to town. It would remind her of the ride home from the funeral, with the bustling children and the air freezing her tongue when she talked, those last few seconds of her life before Thomas Howard changed it forever.

Nevertheless, it was a far superior arrangement to spending the night in the parsonage, facing curiosity and perhaps even suspicion.

The announcement on a Saturday evening was perfection, also; her news would spread throughout the congregation, as Emil's tainted turkey had, before the service even began.

"Now, what's this fine news you've been bursting to reveal?" Jonah greeted her at the door. Dena's stomach was still tumbling a little from the jounces of the wagon ride, and he noticed her pale face at once.

"Please sit down. You are looking no better than earlier today. Perhaps we should have postponed this event. Mrs. Wuebke, bring some water. I have half a mind to send for Dr. Burkhardt."

"No, Jonah, I'm all right. It was just a long ride, with all the children and no springs." They laughed together. While Gottlieb had not at all been a wealthy man, he had managed a few business dealings in St. Louis that had enabled his brother and his wife to experience a few things finer than most folk in Staircase Creek.

Mira Wuebke came to take Dena's coat and scarf while Olga unwrapped her children. Wilhelm walked disconsolately about the parlor, and Dena felt bad about making him have to wear his uncomfortable Sunday best two days in a row. Then she regretted not insisting on more guests, such as the Chrismons, so that Wilhelm would have someone to talk to. She knew he, like his daughter, felt honored to be dining with the pastor.

Mira was almost angelic in her serenity, until she saw Dena's bulge. Dena stood purposefully, holding the fabric tight across her middle. Mira's eyes widened, brightened. Dena could see that she literally held her tongue still with her teeth and lips so as not to ask something impertinent. Dena smiled tranquilly in response.

"I'm going to set the little ones to dye eggs in the kitchen," Dena announced, gathering the children to her side.

"It sounds like an odd activity, since it's nearly May, but Jonah asked me to boil up some eggs, and I did so," Mira told her. "I think you'll find whatever you need. Oh, and would you mind"—her eyes and voice suddenly were anxious—"would you mind if the littlest ones ate in the kitchen?"

Dena could understand Mira's consternation. Five small children would well tax the reverend's resources. "That will be fine. They all exclaimed on the ride to town how exciting this is, dying eggs after Easter. Eating with the pastor, now, that came across a clear second."

While she showed the children what to do, Mira set their places with plain, serviceable stoneware and fare that Dena knew was far simpler than what the adults would eat. She took the leaves she had plucked from her garden and from the cottonwoods and elms and showed the children how to lay them against the side of a clean dry egg along with onion skins, and tie it tight with cheesecloth. Before the children got too involved, she tied large dishcloths around their necks to prevent spills.

"Now, keep these on while you have your supper, too, so that you don't ruin your Sunday best and make more work for your dear mama."

Then the eggs were placed in a pot of boiling water and vinegar. They emerged tinted lovely shades of taupe and brown, with white leaf prints.

Ida came into the kitchen to be Dena's little helper. Too bad she wasn't older, Dena mused. She could marry Max Bauer. Then her heart stopped . . . wait a few years, and the difference in age wouldn't matter, anyway. It would be like her and Gottlieb.

"Here, dear, put on one of Mrs. Wuebke's aprons so you don't spoil your church dress."

"I can watch my brothers and sisters," Ida told her solemnly. After all, that was a task she performed most hours of the day. Dena sighed at Ida's lost childhood, and also at her own lonely one.

"You are old enough to join the grown-ups."

Ida's face, pretty in a plain, scrubbed way, shone like a halo at the compliment. "Well, in a minute. I want to check out their handiwork."

"Look, Miz Dena, at my leaf egg," one of the little ones shrilled.

And so Dena did, then joined the adults after the tinted eggs sat drying on an old towel. Olga settled the little ones in the kitchen, where Willie offered to supervise.

After Jonah led the group in an elegant, poetic grace, the Potts attacked their fancy food with enthusiasm. Dena pondered when to make her incredible announcement, then decided that the end of the meal would be best. At least most of the delicious food would then not go to waste.

"Tell us about your trip, Dena," Mira encouraged politely, although Dena suspected that she was stuffed with curiosity, particularly after seeing Dena's belly. "You went for some of Gottlieb's business dealings?"

"Why, yes. I needed to get some of his affairs in order." Dena dropped her voice a little, hoping everyone would hear her attempt at grief.

Mira rose to bring in a course of potato pudding, an easy and economical dish to make for a crowd. Willie followed her with a golden baked pork loin.

"St. Louis is a long way to go." Jonah sniffed again.

"Oh, I went to St. Joseph."

No one else seemed to care much at the final destination, but Jonah's eyes narrowed. "I thought this was to conduct business with associates of your father."

Dena did not answer right away, giving the others time to

enjoy their food and Jonah to stew. She didn't often have a chance to annoy him.

Ida came through the kitchen door with fresh sliced bread.

"Thor has spilled," was all she said, and Olga's face crumpled at the spoiled Sunday garb.

"Have no fear, Olga," Jonah told the worried woman kindly. "The Lord will not mind. He looks into our hearts, not at our clothes."

Olga relaxed.

Jonah obviously hadn't forgotten Dena's destination. He looked at her with raised eyebrows that made him look old.

"I will explain. Let me first help Mira with dessert."

After serving up Ida's pie and Mira's gingersnaps, Dena poured some Arbuckle's coffee. It would be a real treat for the Potts, who drank mostly rye coffee.

"Mira, please sit down. I have something important to say. I asked the reverend to have you all together tonight because you are my dearest friends, my family. I have suspected this for some time but said nothing to anyone until I knew for certain. I did tend to some financial business in St. Joseph, but I also saw a medical specialist."

Forgive me, Thomas. As I will try to forgive you.

"I am with child." As she spoke, she turned to Jonah for effect. "Before his death, Gottlieb blessed me with a child."

As she had with Mira, she once again moved strategically in her ensemble so that the little protrusion was tastefully obvious.

"What?" Jonah gasped without a sound. He sat as white and still as an alabaster saint in a medieval cathedral.

Only Olga came to life, dragging Wilhelm with her.

"*Ja*, God be praised," she howled, dragging Dena into her ample arms. "This is a blessing from beyond." Releasing Dena, she made Wilhelm do the same.

Jonah was silent for so long that Dena wondered just what Gottlieb had told him about their marriage bed. Did his silence portend disbelief and doubt? Or simply dead dreams suddenly resurrected, like Easter eggs long after the event?

Finally he spoke. "I see the reason for the eggs now, Dena. New life. I am speechless with delight. The congregation . . . too will be delighted."

He was too well mannered to show any physical reaction, but she was certain that his smile was genuine.

"I . . . thank you, Dena," Jonah said simply. "I wish Gottlieb could know."

In from the kitchen to show Dena and his mother the fruits of his labor, Georg spoke next, words that Dena had heard before. "He can peek down from heaven once in a while, Reverend. He knows all about it, I'm sure."

As before, Dena's stomach churned just in case that was true.

Chapter Seventeen

Dena might as well have had a crown on her head, considering the way the townsfolk all but bowed to her after church.

One would think Jonah had announced her pregnancy from the pulpit. But such things weren't discussed, not in a public group, anyway. She knew for certain that the gaggles of farm wives assembled after church were discussing every second of the three years she had spent in Staircase Creek, and how, interestingly enough, the great conception hadn't happened until Gottlieb's last days.

Mira took her hand encouragingly as they walked toward the parsonage.

"Mira, I am terrified." Dena indeed was, but she didn't reveal the actual reason. The lie ate at her soul, but even more destructive was the loss of Thomas Howard. Or Luke Woodlease.

Whatever it was he called himself these days.

"Well, bringing a child into the world is a frightening thing." For a moment, Mira's face took on a shadow of grief. Dena remembered her two little ones, asleep in the graveyard. Then Mira met her eyes, nodding. "You think that once the load has been carried, and the labor ended, you will never have to worry anymore. All the fingers will be there, the heart will beat strong.

"But that is just the start." She tried to smile away her melancholy, but Dena could clearly hear the pain. "Here I go off. It is a glorious time, Dena. And you are blessed not to be ill when the day starts, and truth to tell, you look as beautiful as always. And you know that Olga and I and Songbird will be with you every second."

"Yes, I know," Dena agreed emphatically. "Songbird will attend me, regardless of what Jonah orders."

They both laughed in understanding.

Jonah was receiving silent congratulations from the menfolk as though he had had something to do with her condition. To his credit, he blushed like a schoolgirl after an attempted kiss.

Max Bauer, however, glowered at everyone. She began to understand why. Now she had more reason than ever to work hard to preserve her place. Dena would be less likely to accept defeat, sell it to him, and move on.

She nodded to Max, who reluctantly came to her side. They stood at the edge of the church grounds. The town lay ahead, the parsonage to their left.

"Mr. Bauer, I must compliment your cousins again. The spring planting has been successful. Karl and Erik's work is splendid. Gottlieb would have approved. We'll have oats and corn and alfalfa. In fact, your kin even started to lay down seed in my kitchen garden! I shall have celery and cabbages and all the rest in no time at all."

"I will make sure they know your good feelings." He nervously brushed a strand of his thin hair from the sleeve of his dark suit. His head was slick with macassar oil.

"Oh, I have already told them," she spoke enthusiastically, "and I certainly hope to hire them on during the harvest. The wheat should be ready by the Fourth of July."

"Gottlieb would be pleased. Maybe they work as well as he

did." He was too young to look so defeated. Had he honestly thought she would consider him as a suitor, when the requisite time had passed? She sighed. It likely was a logical thing to have come to pass, until Thomas Howard.

Or Luke Woodlease. Whatever he called himself these days! Mira rescued her. "Dena, let's get you off your feet. Come in for some tea."

Excusing herself from Max, Dena nodded, unable to rid her mind of Thomas now that she had allowed him in. Maybe he was safe in Tennessee, or maybe he was in trouble in Minnesota. She wondered if she owed it to her baby to find out.

"Dena, are you all right?" Mira's cool hand touched her cheek. "These next months will be times of vapors and moodiness, I must warn you."

Her lovely face twisted in concern. "And I must warn you also of this: It will be difficult for you to be living alone with all the changes coming upon you. I . . . can stay with you at your place."

It was a truly generous offer, particularly when Dena knew that Mira loathed being far from Jonah's side. Her situation was as hopeless as Dena's; perhaps they were kindred spirits after all. She didn't want to dash all the woman's hopes.

"Perhaps, later on. Let me think about it."

She followed Mira disconsolately into the parsonage. The interior was dark, almost dank. Mira left the curtains closed most days to keep the temperature cool. Dena realized she preferred sunlight and fresh air, no matter how hot it got.

Life just wasn't kind. She wanted to slam the door. Mira made small talk, but Dena didn't hear her, trying as she was to imagine how lovely it would have been to watch Thomas's eyes light up with joy when she told him that he was to be a father. To lie close enough to him in the night so that he could feel the baby kick. To pick out names and dream of the future.

A future that could never be.

"There's a lady here to see the condemned man," the deputy announced to the town marshal.

Both men had actually started to treat Luke Woodlease with a modicum of dignity, perhaps understanding the terrible situation of facing one's last days on earth. Once the deputy had initiated his participation in a card game; the invitation had not been repeated, however, as the prisoner seemed incapable of losing.

A lady! He rejoiced at the words. Certainly it was Dena. She had occupied his thoughts each waking moment for months, danced with him in his dreams at night. Now it was not snow swirling around them; it was apple blossoms in a springtime of new hope, of life eternal. Certainly Dena had heard of his plight—was he important enough to warrant stories in the newspapers?—and had wangled an appeal or a parole or bail. Or a miracle.

His manhood twitched just at the thought of her. Seeing her for real might be more excitement than he had the strength to handle.

"My boy, our dear boy!" The confident words pealed over the clomping footsteps of the speaker and the two lawmen.

He peered out from between the bars. The jailhouse, or cooler, was flat-roofed and two-celled, with walls of huge, tight logs. Five iron bars two inches thick stabbed the window frames and cast shadows of horizontal stripes across the dirt floor. He was allowed to sweep the floor as often as he wanted, and the blankets on the hard thin cot were well-woven and warm on the cool spring nights. The cell's previous denizens had either consistently missed the chamber pot or decided to ease their boredom by marking their territory. The scents in the small enclosure grew more unpleasant as the weather warmed.

He knew from the voice that the visitor wasn't Dena, but his heart had no reason to fall to his feet in disappointment.

"Aunt Zerelda! What on earth . . ."

The marshal unlocked the door while the deputy stood by with his Winchester pointed vaguely at the group in case the prisoner and his one-armed visitor tried to attack.

The woman gathered him to her as well as her one arm

would allow, her voice crooning to him like he were a colicky baby.

At first he couldn't find words; then his voice was husky with emotion. He was afraid he might humiliate himself with tears.

"Why are you here? Come to watch the hangin'?" he asked her bitterly. "I think the townsfolk are making it a celebration as grand as the Fourth of July. Bringing their little ones and picnic lunches."

"Bah. That is an unconscionable thought. I'm here to bail you out."

The marshal was stunned. "Bail don't work on a condemned murderer, ma'am."

Zerelda Samuel turned on him and silenced him with the same look she gave her sons when they sassed her. She was a formidable woman weighing in at nearly two hundred pounds, and her dark traveling clothes made her seem much larger. So did the tentlike draping of a shawl. The marshal backed away from her.

"The judge is taking bail under advisement," she proclaimed. "I believe these to be trumped up charges with no hard evidence behind them. Now, gentlemen, if you please, I'd like to meet with this young man in private. Feel free to lock me in here with him."

The lawmen followed her orders instantly. She stood upright, as tall as either. "Privacy, please."

Rather like chastened puppies with their tails between their legs, they left the cell.

She wrinkled her nose at the smell, then shook her head at the disheartened shell of the prisoner. "They feedin' you right, darlin' boy?"

He nodded. "I don't have much appetite, especially the closer it gets, but Sheriff Jones's wife is a good cook and sends over a tin plate of vittles three times a day. But like I say, I don't have much appetite. And the smell—that's thanks to my predecessors—doesn't help much. Now what are you doing here?"

He motioned for her to sit on the cot. At least he had straightened the covers that morning.

"You should have written me," she rebuked him as she sat down, the cot sagging dangerously. "I found out about your plight in a roundabout way, or I would have been here with my lawyer long before the mock trial."

"I didn't want to get you involved, nor the boys." He took her hand affectionately. As usual, she had artfully arranged her shawl about her torso so that the missing arm was less noticeable.

"Foolish sentiment. I *am* involved. We're kin." She clucked over him as though he were a misbehaving child. Actually he had heard the sound many times.

"It's just not that easy, Aunt Zee. As it is, the judge tried to trade my freedom for the whereabouts of Frank and Jesse. I don't know where they are, but I wouldn't have betrayed them anyway."

She murmured her approval, before standing up to look out the window. Then she spoke in a near whisper. "No one is a'listening beneath the sill. But the walls often have ears." She sat next to him once again, her voice softening further.

"Well, I do know my boys' whereabouts, and I've been instructed to do all it takes to get you out of here."

Glad as he was to see her, he sighed at the pointlessness of her efforts.

"The judge won't accept James money, Aunt Zee. He'll say it's blood money, or some such."

"It's cash money honorably earned by your uncle Reuben, an esteemed physician, before his untimely death."

He was pleased to hear that last comment, but still had his doubts. "These folks won't let me go, Aunt Zee. I'm one of the James gang. I've already been convicted. I'm due to hang!"

Aunt Zee almost lounged on the flimsy cot, as satisfied as a guest after Thanksgiving dinner.

"Here's the good news, young man. Your lawyer seems to think the real killer of that old man can be identified." And then she explained further. "I took a recent trip to St. Louis to meet up with a fancy lawyer. Told anyone who doesn't know me it was to see kin. Well, this friendly gentleman has been able to obtain authentic affidavits from Jesse James, declaring that you never rode with him into Northfield. As I understand it, that is perfectly true. The documents are notarized and legal."

He was astonished. "You've seen them? Where are they?"

"No, I've not seen my sons. They're hiding out in Tennessee. I hear from them only from time to time. When it's safe, they'll be back home."

He sat back on the cot in disbelief. Her words should have brought him joy, but they didn't; not at all.

His aunt reproved him sharply. "You've got your life back. What's that sour puss for? Our mulatto boy found out about Whisper and bought him back at auction in Colbyville. He's happy and fat at our farm, waiting for you. My lawyer is prepared to discuss your case with the governor himself, and he's got the clout to do it. I'm amazed to see your empty eyes."

She examined him closely. "I've just recently seen eyes as dead as yours, a tragic young woman I met on a train. I wanted to become acquainted with her, but she kept to herself."

He had no need to hear of tragic young women. The only woman he wanted was Dena.

"I may have my life back, but for what? The woman I love . . . well, she hasn't been waiting around for me; I know it. And if there's any chance she's heard that I'm a killer . . ." He got up and grabbed the iron bars, squeezing them as if to draw strength from them.

"The woman you love? Let me in on this secret." Zerelda Samuel made herself comfortable again. He had to smile. This woman could adapt to just about any situation without losing her aplomb and inner strength.

"She helped me out in Nebraska last winter, hid me for a while until a nosy Pinkerton showed up. She had a . . . friend who helped me get started on the trail."

He remembered Songbird, knowing his aunt would approve. He'd save the story for another time.

"Well, go back to her when you are free." Aunt Zee's voice took on the imperious tone that no one dared gainsay.

He nodded obediently.

Then she went on. "I think you should reconcile with your sisters." She looked him straight in the eye, and when he turned away, she grabbed his chin and pulled his gaze back. This was one promise he didn't want to make, but he knew she would never relent.

"They wronged you to be sure," she admitted, "but they are kin, and that means all. You shared a womb. My boys . . . well, they don't always do me proud with some of their antics, but I will always shelter and support them. They lived in me, after all. As for this Nebraska woman, if she means what you say, she'll be worth finding again."

Zerelda made no move to leave, forcing him to reconsider.

"Well, Aunt Zee, I'm always one to trust your judgment. If I ever get out of this place, I'll mind what you say."

At that moment, the sun brightened outside, sending silver streaks across the striped shadows on the floor. As the breeze kicked up, the shadows wiggled. A loud voice from the doorway startled them both.

The circuit judge stood on the other side of the bars, imperious as befitted his station but exuding some of the kindness that Luke Woodlease had been shown on the stand.

"Luck lands on you twice today, Mr. Woodlease. First off, Mrs. Samuel arrives before I leave town and takes it kindly to have your case reviewed, promising to support you with bail money. All that will not be needed, but I admire your generosity and your courage, ma'am." He looked at her somewhat admiringly; Luke Woodlease knew the judge decried her having spawned the James boys but commended her duty to Luke Woodlease to show herself in enemy territory.

"We have found the true killer of Sweyn Willemsen." The judge mentioned a name Luke Woodlease did not know. "His apprehension has been assisted by the lawyer who defended you. The killer suspected that there was more of your money in Sweyn's shanty, so as soon as you departed, he robbed and killed the old man. All charges against you are dismissed."

Zerelda Samuel cheered loudly with Reb war whoops.

The judge waved her silent, his look of disapproval now impossible to hide. The deputy stepped forward with his keys. "Madam, if you will allow us some privacy?"

"I'll be waiting on you outside," Zerelda told Luke as she waved a little good-bye with her good arm.

The judge went on as soon as she left. "Sir, all will go better for you in the afterlife if you let us know where the James boys are."

Luke Woodlease shook his head. "I can't tell you that, your honor. Truth is, I don't know. My aunt didn't say. But I wouldn't tell even if I did."

As always, Dena had no reason to expect that another momentous event in her life was about to take place. If she had, her father would still be alive. Gottlieb would never have been gored to death. Thomas Howard would never . . .

Wednesday was the day she normally did her wash, and with the May sun as warm as it proved, the laundry would take no time at all to dry.

Even with Thomas's lies and perfidy, she still liked the chance to be alone with her thoughts, with the shameful reality that she wanted his lips both soft and urgent upon her own, her body crushed against his powerful chest. She didn't even mind that such thoughts were particularly untoward for a woman with child. She especially liked tasks that took no brain power at all, like boiling up a pot of dirty linen with lye soap, so her mind could go off at full gallop.

The thoughts of Thomas pleased her and helped get her through the reality that he was a liar and a murderer. She almost laughed. If the fancy folk of Cape Girardeau could see her now, hair streaked with moisture hanging across her face, lye tearing up her eyes! The loose invalid gown she'd sewn did no justice at all to a form that was still pretty near girlish. Would Thomas mind seeing her this way? In her soul, she hoped he wouldn't. But she knew real life was a great deal different than one's imaginings. Maybe he would be repelled by her condition, horrified at her whoredom. Then again, she remembered that he was a liar and an outlaw, probably a murderer and perhaps an . . . adulterer as well.

Ready for a good cry, she was annoyed when Max Bauer rode up through the noon sunshine.

In all honesty, he was a decent enough fellow; she had been fairly close to his sister until she married and moved away. And while the grasshopper infestation last fall hadn't ruined anyone this far east, Max had experienced some minor problems and worried incessantly that eggs lay in wait for his next crop.

She didn't need to worry like that. Her father and Gottlieb had made certain of it by providing a little money for her to be able to fall back on. Gottlieb had cursed the few grasshoppers he had seen, but they had been a mere inconvenience. He'd gathered them in a tray of kerosene. The worry she felt now, for her child, was something else. She needed a home for her child. Perhaps she ought to consider grasshoppers, and tornadoes, and wildfire.

Her skin didn't exactly crawl, but she didn't think the visit portended anything good. Max's grief at Gottlieb's passing had been sincere, and she knew he had lost a good friend. Because of his proximity, Max had been one of the first gawkers when the awful news about Gottlieb had spread like wildfire. Yet she knew he had an undue interest in her farm, and his glances at her body had always made her feel uncomfortable.

"Mr. Bauer!" She decided to be a proper and formal widow as she answered the door. Throwing her red shawl across her body in spite of the spring warmth, she scraped her damp hair into a bun at her neck. But none of her attempts at dignity worked.

"Now, Dena, it's Max. Don't get all mannerly on me." He tried to emit a casual laugh.

"Well, come on in for a minute and have some coffee. What brings you out and about? It's a beautiful day. Your planting in good shape?"

Max laughed almost condescendingly. "Now, Dena, I've been living on the prairie far longer than you! I'm real good at planting. And I hope this time around to be good enough to escape them grasshoppers. I was just a kid when Pa homesteaded here. I still live in our soddy, not some fancy-Dan wooden house! My place is in real good shape, or will be if there's no locust eggs hiding around, waiting to hatch. I have plenty of time to . . . discuss our situation and head on home." He pronounced the word "sit-chee-AYE-shun."

"Our situation?" She enunciated the word correctly. Her eyes narrowed. Her good manners ushered him to the eating table. Without asking, she poured one cup of coffee, deciding it wasn't exactly rude but was far from welcoming if she didn't join him. She remained standing.

"Sit a piece, Dena," Max pleaded like he was the host. "Dena, Miss Bernhardena, I highly respected your late husband—a careful, considerate neighbor who would not want his beloved place to fall into disreputable hands. I treasure his place as I treasure my own."

Dena, knees weak, finally sat, watching him as if from another's eyes, as if seeing him for the first time. He was a good dozen years younger than Gottlieb. Probably to some other widow, or some unmarried prairie spinster, he would be thought good-looking, but compared to Thomas Howard, his colorless hair and thin blond mustache made her lonelier than ever. Comfortable apparently with the welcome she gave him, he shrugged out of his overcoat, and she could see he was wearing his Sunday best. But it was a Wednesday, and Dena felt the unseen little hairs on the back of her neck prickle as she tried to discern the reason for his attire.

He sipped his coffee slowly, his lips clinging too long to the edge of the cup. She refused to offer him food, knowing herself rude but unwilling to prolong the meeting.

"Now, Miss Bernhardena." He paused, and her own eyes narrowed. For a man who had just insisted on her calling him Max, his formality was frightening.

"My haste may be unseemly, but if we keep a secret promise

between us, in our hearts, we could wait until a proper time to announce it."

Aghast, Dena's mouth and eyes opened to unusual proportions. "Secret promise? Unseemly haste? Proper time? What on earth are you suggesting, *Mr. Bauer?*"

He actually seemed surprised. "Why, a union of our farms. Of ourselves; a marriage of man and woman. It makes perfect sense."

Dena stood, shaking. "Mr. Bauer, I am beyond insulted at your suggestion."

At her haughty manner, Max stood as well. "Direct your indignation elsewhere, Miss Dena. Gottlieb, in his cups one night, allowed in confidence that you and he had some rough patches. I'll do right by you, and honor your husband by assisting with the preservation of his place, his legacy, and the rearing of his child. I intend to honor my friend by raising his child good and proper.

"Furthermore, I am a lusty man, and a considerate one. Should you and I be blessed with children of our own—and I am convinced that we shall be—their legacy would be the combination of the two finest places in Staircase County."

Dena's mouth opened without sound.

He blatantly surveyed the room, nodding in satisfaction at what he saw. "And of course we would stay here. I can't rightly invite you to live the rest of your days in my humble soddy."

Then he surveyed her. "My admiration for you, Miss Dena— in fact, the admiration of any bachelor hereabouts—can't be denied. Gottlieb"—greed shone in his eyes—"was hailed throughout three counties as a *very* lucky man."

So much for the possibility that, with his sister married, he merely needed someone to cook his meals and darn his socks.

Her skin was alive now with imaginary beasts. She could barely walk to the door. She opened it to a rush of warm wind scented with primrose. "I'm afraid I must ask you to leave, Mr. Bauer. This conversation is not appropriate at this time.

"It will not be appropriate ever," she repeated with a sniff as he grabbed his coat and walked out the front door.

He turned to her. He was reasonably tall as men went, but Dena couldn't help realizing that he could barely reach Thomas Howard's chin. "Out west here, Dena, we don't wait on fancy protocol. I'm just the first, and I say this without conceit, the best of the many who will soon be beating down your door." He raised his hat insolently as he mounted his horse and rode off.

For the first time since she discovered she was with child, Dena was sick, inelegantly so, weeping in her pain for a man who was a liar and a murderer.

Chapter Eighteen

Dena bathed before she hung the laundry on the clothesline outside, letting the sweet sunshine murmur across her skin and dry her hair.

Thomas had liked her hair long and loose across her shoulders. Shuttering her mind to the memory, she braided the long mass and tucked the plait into a serviceable coil.

Refreshed but still troubled, she sent Georg for his mother and one of Max's own cousins for Mira.

"Poor boy," she remarked out loud about Karl, the cousin who had borne an undue amount of her bad temper simply by the nature of the blood he shared.

While waiting for her friends, she brewed some horsemint tea, seriously tempted for the very first time in her life to add some of Gottlieb's whiskey.

"*Mein Gott,* Dena, I am fully expecting Bruno to have committed another murder. What in *himmel* troubles you so?"

Olga burst through the door without knocking, her hearty

face both pale with worry and flushed from exertion, her German words coming quick.

"Olga, I need to wait for Mira. I can only confide this information one time. I don't have the strength for more."

Olga's face whitened further.

"No, no, Olga, no one is sick or dead. I'm sorry to frighten you." Dena hurried to touch Olga's ample arm encouragingly.

"Well, there's a relief. But I am having a busy day."

Dena had to laugh in spite of her tribulations. "You know full well that Ida is in complete control when you are away. Your fields are starting to grow. You can relax with your friends for a few minutes."

Olga sat in the ladder-back chair, fanning her face with her large hand.

"*Ja*, I do enjoy a chance to relax, but my Wilhelm, he worries all the time. We have no extra cash to fall back on if the grasshoppers come back and we lose our crop."

Dena remembered Gottlieb's pleasantly full coffers and realized she didn't have to worry. Nonetheless, she shared her friend's anxiety.

"Olga, the worst of the damage last September was west of York. Thank God we were spared the brunt."

"*Ja*, I agree that the plague could have been worse, but that little was a huge trouble for us. As I say, we have no cash in the bank and so many *kinder*. Thank God in His wisdom, He has not thought to send us another these three years."

Olga rose from the chair then, clearly restless. Suddenly Dena was ashamed of her selfishness, dragging the busy woman from her home and her duties simply to complain about Max Bauer. To Olga, shock and tragedy were not an unwanted marriage proposal; it was worrying about another pregnancy, a swarm of locusts eating their hard work, no cash in the bank.

"*Ja*, we lost several bushels of corn, enough to make my Wilhelm feel sleepless some nights. Even now he is convinced that eggs are ripening in the ground, in the seeds, and that the grasshoppers will strike again."

"Well, I think not. And if they do, you know I can help out a little. And don't you start yammering about charity." Dena held up her hand to prevent Olga from talking further on the subject. She decided to be a good hostess and went on to discuss normal housewifely things.

"I wish I had been able to ice up the tea, it being such a warm day, but let me go get you a cup anyway." Dena went to the kitchen worktable, pouring tea in her mother's cups.

For a moment, she held the cup close to her bosom, its warmth reminding her of a cold winter day when she had used the very same cups to serve Thomas. Luke. Whatever he called himself. Whoever he was, she ached, if not for him, then for what might have been, had they met in a better time. Even in the same ladder-back chair where Olga sat once again, he had clearly been the most handsome man she had ever seen, even with his blood and the slush of snow at his feet.

But those days were gone.

By then, Mira rode up on the pretty sorrel horse her Harold had left, wearing a brown split skirt in a sturdy linsey-woolsey with a matching vest. A most sensible ensemble, Dena reasoned, and far more attractive than the made-over sacklike overalls that Olga favored when she rode her mule.

Watching Mira, Dena shook her head in wonder. Certain she recognized what men liked to see, she could not believe that the lovely widow held no interest for Jonah. Staircase Creek was not awash with attractive single women, and Mira could have rivaled any of Cape Girardeau's great beauties.

The May sunlight peeked through the curtains just at the spot at which Dena had looked out once, long ago, and watched a Pinkerton arrive on a paint horse, saw the confidence of Thomas's face, felt the comfort of his arms. She steeled herself against the onslaught of memories. At one time she had longed for moments alone with herself so she could remember him. Now she needed to forget.

Even still, Max Bauer was not the answer.

Dena poured more store-bought tea and brought a plate of cinnamon bread to the eating table. Before she sat, she spooned some apple butter into a china saucer. Both friends looked at her anxiously.

"Dena"—Mira's voice was soft but full of dread—"is it the baby? Have you lost the baby?"

Olga intoned, "When my boy dashed home in the middle of a workday, I feared some awful thing had happened to you."

"No, no," Dena rushed to reassure them. "Well, at least not dreadful in the sense you mean. I had a call from Max Bauer earlier today, and I am speechless with horror at his suggestion. His proposal!" She explained his visit in detail.

She had thought that her friends would react with the same indignation she felt. However, they sat next to her without spilling a drop of tea, Olga contentedly chewing a bite of bread slathered with apple butter for a significant amount of time.

Both women shrugged. "It might be a proposal to consider, after a proper time for mourning," Mira admitted, and Olga nodded her head with enthusiasm.

Suddenly Dena wanted to pull their hair, hide under her bed, saddle the Morgan and ride off to a world of sane people. She couldn't think of any way to respond without a scream.

"I don't believe either of you!" she exploded finally. "You, Olga, you married the man you love. Mira, you didn't. And yet you encourage me to accept Max Bauer?"

"*Ja*, I do." Olga nodded, her voice sincere. "Your babe will need a papa. And Max is a good man. He's been your friend. He is no stranger."

Dena's mouth opened almost to her shoulders.

Mira continued as though she and Olga shared the same mental thought. "You have told us many times, Dena, that you have no relations left in Missouri."

"*Ja*," Olga broke in, "and that many bad things happened to you in St. Looey. So bad you don't even tell us of them.

"You're one of us, Dena. You have no more fancy ways. You toil this land just like the rest of us." Although Olga spoke English perfectly, her German accent and phrases increased with her agitation. She shook an imperious fist against the table. The teacups rattled in their saucers.

"I think, Dena, vee in Staircase Creek are all *du habst.*"

Dena, shocked by the effect of Max's visit, barely moved as she digested their reactions. Most times in bed with Gottlieb, she had imagined him as someone else. The someone had always been faceless, but now she had Thomas Howard in her mind, her heart—her body. Might it be that simple again? To marry for prudence's sake and imagine his face in her bed on long cold nights? Was that what women did? Was that all they could expect? Was that what Mira expected?

"Mira, I've seen you with moon eyes over my brother-in-law. And I take it as a compliment. He's a fine man. Do you mean this for me? Would you marry Max Bauer if he asked?"

"Probably not," she confessed, "but I sold our place when my man died. I have a little money put away. I knew I couldn't manage a place all by myself, even with hired hands. It is a mighty difficult occupation for a woman alone.

"Maybe you could sell your place to Max. Then again . . ." Mira's voice grew pensive. A spring breeze whispered across the chokecherries and cottonwoods and brought the scent of violets and wild roses into the little house. "I miss . . . having a man sometimes." Mira's glance was careful, as though she debated how much of her physical need to reveal. "I don't mind admitting I'm lonely. I've got no place else to go, either.

"And yes, Dena, I get moon eyes about your brother-in-law. I have spent a good three years in his house, and I think I know and understand him better than anyone. I could be his help-meet. If he'd let me."

Dena appreciated Mira's candor, although she promptly dismissed the comments concerning Max Bauer.

"Well," she started, looking at Mira, "I may be able to drop some subtle hints in that regard, because I agree with you. But, my friends, I do not agree with your assessment of Max Bauer's proposal.

"I do not want him." Her words were simple. The others eyed her with sympathy.

The Outlaw's Woman

"So what is it you do want, Dena?" Olga asked guilelessly.

"I don't know." Dena got up to get more cloth napkins, something no one needed. But she did know.

A man she couldn't have. A man she shouldn't want.

Not a half hour after her guests left, Dena watched her brother-in-law ride up as her mother's clock chimed three. Mira must have passed him on the road back to town.

His visit surprised her; he rarely traveled on horseback, believing, as he did, that his buggy gave him more dignity. On a day like this, though, she figured even Jonah would appreciate the larkspur and spiderwort that were starting to thrive. The basswood trees Gottlieb had planted around the place as a windbreak were taller than ever before. Mingled with the scent of freshly turned earth was the bright melody of the meadowlark.

Oh, Jonah was handsome, she had to admit, and dressed today in a black duster without his cleric's collar and his favored derby, he looked quite distinguished, somehow out of place in this land of sod houses and rolling farmland. She saw a white handkerchief peeking from his pocket. It complemented his swarthy features, and the coat matched his black hair.

He had been stalwart in his support of her great announcement, and she wondered at his quest today. At least she was still trim and proper from her tea party, her dress with loosened seams concealing her belly. Jonah himself appeared amazingly confident.

At her door, in a very continental way and unlike any other gesture he had ever performed, he removed his hat and bowed over her hand.

The unseen animals crawled through the invisible hairs on the back of her neck again.

My God, he's courting me!

His hand, warm, touched her in a way she had never considered, in a way that somehow horrified her. Dispassionately, she tried to look at him as if for the first time.

219

The same blood as Gottlieb's ran in his veins.

He's my brother, nothing more!

Is that how it's done here, pursuing a widow without a proper mourning time? Max had said that many would be beating at my door.

Her horror grew.

"Jonah, I did not expect company. I do hope nothing's amiss."

"Bah, company! I am family. Plus I know you just had tea with Mrs. Pott and my housekeeper. Whom I trust will get back to the parsonage in ample time to prepare my supper."

Dena wasn't certain why, but she wanted to smack the words off his lips. Mira should mean more to him than a mere servant to chasten. He was smiling, though, as if he had made a big joke. Then real concern knotted his brow. "How are you, Dena?"

"As expected, Jonah. One or other of the Pott boys comes each day to help me. And I am happy that hiring Mr. Bauer's cousins has been a successful venture. And as for my condition, I feel well most times. Unlike now. Jonah, I am very, very tired. I do hope you will excuse me."

Jonah did not take the hint. He made no move to leave. She had lit the heating stove; it burned as the late afternoon air turned colder. Her manners precluded her from sending him forth without a bit of welcome.

"Please come in," she muttered, resigned. "I'll make some coffee." She doubted she would share any; her stomach still sloshed from the tea.

Her brother-in-law was never a man for much small talk. Sitting at the table, he started in at once.

"I am concerned for you, Dena. Sheriff Eilert still suspects that the James gang will storm Staircreek township and terrorize innocents."

Dena had to laugh. "You mean what's left of that gang. Jonah, that Pinkerton"—she could still see Gordon Bruce's cold, disbelieving eyes—"has assured me that the outlaw is in prison somewhere, that we innocents are safe." Without being able to stop it, the memories burst through the barriers of her mind—her grand ambition to hire a lawyer and bail Thomas Howard out of jail, tell him of their child. Bring him back somehow to be her man.

Then she saw the trim dark-haired woman holding a baby as clearly as if she stood in the room.

And a dignified one-armed woman whom she regretted not getting to know.

She wanted to comfort Jonah with what she knew. "Well, truth to tell, all I did was allow a poor vagrant a night on the straw in my barn. Gottlieb never refused a stranger. From what I hear, the Jameses take kindly to those who help them out, so I do not believe I am in any danger. And Jonah, it has been months now. I have been fine."

Jonah was still displeased. "No matter. It was a foolish decision, you all alone out here. And now expecting a . . . child . . ."

She tried to soothe him. "I am never frightened, Jonah. This is my home. Truth to tell, I am more familiar with things here than with my old life. I always lock up tight, and I sleep with Gottlieb's shotgun by my bed. And my handgun is always in my garter . . ."

The Baby Le Mat. Suddenly she wanted to burst into tears. Hadn't Mira warned her about tears and vapors?

So as not to embarrass herself, she bustled about, getting coffee, bringing Jonah some of the cinnamon bread.

"Shall I toss in some whiskey?" she asked with sudden mischief. Just in case, she brought Gottlieb's flask and set it on the table. Jonah was known to imbibe, sure as any sweaty farmer enjoyed a beer at day's end. However, he was behaving awfully prim and righteous right now.

"I can't help being worried about you, Dena, all alone out here. You and your child. Of course I know that Gottlieb trained you well."

"*Trained* me?" she bristled. "You make me sound like a dancing bear at the circus!"

221

"No, I mean, for a city girl, he . . . showed you the ways of the prairie. But I just can't . . ."

"Can't what, Jonah?"

He was silent for a full minute, both huffing out air to puff his cheeks and swallowing it anxiously. Rising suddenly, he straightened his shoulders, squirming for a moment as though his clothes didn't fit right. Ruffling his fine, white fingers through his dark hair, his eyes opened wide as if in surprise, then tightened to sly slits.

Whatever was going on would almost have made her smile if it hadn't been so strange.

All of his machinations must have given him courage, for at last he knelt and blurted, "Marry me, Dena. It's the right thing to do."

Dena had expected him to exert his manly authority as her male relative by insisting that she and her child return to civilization at Cape Girardeau, or at the very least to move to the boardinghouse in town where Mira Wuebke slept nights. Maybe even to slaughter—or at least sell—Bruno, who was certain to make a snack of her child as soon as it toddled outdoors.

She had simply not expected this. At first she laughed out loud.

"Marry you? Jonah, be serious."

He was, deathly serious. She realized it when he refused to rise, when he asked her again. This time he took her hand. She wondered if he would remark again about her missing wedding ring.

"Please, Jonah." She managed to still her laughter. "It is out of the question. Gottlieb hasn't been dead a year. And you're his *brother.*"

His eyes showed her the depths of his resolve.

Stunned now, she sank to a chair. Her second proposal in three hours.

And the man she wanted was in jail somewhere, and already had a wife and child.

"Jonah, what are you thinking?" She tried again. "You simply cannot be serious."

He had an answer. "It is the Lord's will, Dena. He says so in Deuteronomy Twenty-five that a man is to marry his brother's widow and raise his children."

She stared. "You mean that nonsense about *levirate* marriage, to prevent extinction of his line? Oh, Jonah." She tried to laugh. "Those are Old Testament orders from centuries past, from another time! I thank you for your . . . generosity, but they don't mean anything to people today!"

"No," Jonah persisted. "The gospel of Matthew affirms it."

"Yes, Jonah, the laws of centuries ago to keep property in the family." She tensed, her lips pursed. She understood him now; he was as greedy as Max had been.

Jonah, she could tell, was annoyed. Like Gottlieb, he had never cared when she demonstrated her knowledge about anything, particularly when she was right.

"That is not so. I have feelings for you. I always have, but at the time you needed a husband I didn't need a wife," Jonah admitted, almost shyly. "Now I believe I do. We can quietly promise to each other today, then wait to announce our intentions at a more appropriate time."

His words so clearly echoed Max's that she couldn't keep the farmer's face from creeping into her brain. Then she knew the reason for Jonah's improper haste, he who always acted with so much thought and decorum.

"Max Bauer visited you today, didn't he? As my 'male protector,' he asked you for my hand, didn't he?"

Jonah reddened, nodded.

"I wonder if it was before or after I refused him."

She got up, holding her hands before the Pennsylvania fireplace. Why was she cold? It was a beautiful spring afternoon. What a day. What a life. Would she ever feel warm again?

"Just as I wonder when you dreamed up this idea."

"Dena, I've thought of nothing else since you announced your . . . condition."

"No, Jonah." She refused to meet his eyes. "It is out of the question. I think you had better go soon. Please finish your coffee and show yourself out."

Jonah opened his mouth to protest, to insist, but she dramatically turned her back and walked to the room where Thomas Howard had slept. Where she had not slept since returning from Missouri.

She closed the drape that Thomas Howard had touched when he had been part of her life. Remembering the drift of his finger across her face, she lay down, burying her face in the pillow. She wanted to smell his clean scent, but it had gone long ago.

The goosedown muffled her sobs, but she knew that Jonah could hear them. She heard him slosh his brother's whiskey into the china cup of coffee.

Jonah was a miserable speck in the afternoon gloaming when she finally emerged from Thomas's room. At least everyone who ever visited her on a normal basis had already called on her that day. She could literally let her hair down and wear slovenly clothes.

She ripped the pins from her hair and unloosed the braid. It rippled like wheat in the wind across the plane of her back. And the loose dress she had copied in purple dimity with lavender stripes from *Godey's* illustration of an invalid gown let her breathe normally after she tore off the gray day dress. At least women on the prairie, practical and hearty, made no use of the bustles and endless petticoats *Godey's* prescribed as decent. At one time, in another life, she had believed it, too. Now it didn't matter. Nothing did.

The house where Thomas had lived with her tightened around her with whiskey breath and leftover tears. It might help to take comfort from her livestock, whose eyes always locked with hers as though they understood. But the barn, and the yard in front of it, were all places where she had known Thomas's caresses, the lips with the taste of sage and tea, the hefty man's part that had made her a woman. She could still feel the way her body had tightened around it, and she moistened now at the thought.

The pain never quite stopped, no matter how she tried to talk herself out of it. Never once had he tried to contact her. Why would he, when he already had a wife and child? How convenient he must have found her, a lonely widow who fell into his arms like a ripe apple after giving him warmth and food while he, a notorious outlaw, escaped a Pinkerton. Her lies and deceptions had assisted him even then.

And if the Pinkerton was right, and Thomas was convicted of murder, by now he had probably met the hangman.

Unable to stop them, she felt the tears start again.

She stumbled to the creek. Long ago, the snowdrifts had caught her feet, but he had stood at her side when she lost her footing. She'd still been a virgin then, full of hopes and dreams, believing a man who told her she was his home and that he would be back.

But the creek that should have healed her did not. Here, with nature come to life, nurtured by the melted snow, the cottonwoods and willows—some of which she had planted herself on Arbor Days—was where she would have met Thomas in a fairy-tale time when he had no wife or child and had not ridden with a band of robbers and killers. Where he might have been a simple farmer like Wilhelm Pott, who loved his wife and stayed by her side to watch their children grow.

She listened to the laughter of the water as it chased itself downstream. Around her, the rolling farmland was thriving, telling her that life continued, in spite of grasshoppers and angry bulls.

A muskrat slipped by on the current, its fur glossy and alive. In another life, she would have crooned to it, named it. A squirrel chattered.

It was impossible to believe that she had received two proposals in the space of hours from two most unsuitable men. She could not look either of them in the eye again, yet she was not the one who had instigated the awkward situations. It was the same as with the other tumultuous events of her life—she had to suffer for others' poor decisions. She had nowhere else to go.

She found the small cottonwood she and the Pott children had planted on the last Arbor Day. Someone said that Nebraska now had millions more trees, with people planting them all over on the last four Aprils. Wiping her eyes, she smiled, certain that she had done her part. Indeed, life went on.

"How do you fare, little tree? Planting good strong roots?" She placed her hand on her belly, hoping the same for her child.

"Maybe I should sell my place." Gottlieb had some accounts left, and after all, everyone believed she carried his heir. "Maybe I could go to Wyoming, where there is untouched land and women are allowed to cast a vote. It might be a good place to bring up a child, a place where people have open minds, not just open land.

"Mira seems to say neither of us has any place else to go. Well, I truly am sorry that Jonah isn't bending his knee to her, but I do not need to wait on Jonah's eyes to turn to moons when he looks at me. Let Mira wait. And Olga . . . well, if the grasshoppers strike again and they lose their place, maybe she and the rest of the Potts will come along too. They won't be the first defeated by the Nebraska prairie. And they are my family, too."

She listened again to the water tripping on its light feet. Who had told her to listen to nature, that it would heal? An author from one of those literature classes from another life. An author she had thought she would have no need to remember. But suddenly she did. William Cullen Bryant had promised his readers that nature would heal them.

The water in the stream ran against the wind.

"Someone once told me that Staircase Creek was called Rolltreppe, German for the moving staircase. But then, that same person is a widda lady who talks to trees. Who could believe her?"

The man's voice was soft, silky, a voice Dena heard at night when she was all alone with her dreams. It was the voice she had longed to hear for real in the daylight, and had decided would be her damnation if she did.

Turning, she saw Thomas Howard standing tall and straight as the cottonwood behind him.

The water waltzed now, then pirouetted, then polkaed in double time.

Dena fainted for the first time in her life on the muddy banks of Staircase Creek. Her golden hair glanced across the water as the creek raced to the Blue.

Chapter Nineteen

For the second time in his life, he had watched her from a stand of trees, knowing that somehow she wrestled with demons. He liked her better in the flowing gown of dainty purple stripes that she wore today than in the fool mourning clothes, pleased that she preferred comfort to the senseless dictates of fashion.

The first time he had imagined her eyes as blue as the summer sky, most likely because of her golden hair. He had been surprised to find them as storm-cloud gray as a winter sky. Today they shot shafts of green at him as she opened her eyes while she struggled to wake up.

Ashamed for startling her, he now ran quickly to help her to her feet. So far, she hunched up on her elbows, still watching him as if he might disappear.

"Thomas." The words were air, not sound.

"Dena, Dena, are you all right?" Hadn't she once told him that she had survived the brutal deaths of both husband and father without weak knees? He admitted that months had passed and he hadn't sent word to her, but certainly the real man was better than a dusty letter weeks old.

She sank back down into the springtime mud. He knelt at her side, lifting her long shafts of hair from the stream. Taking a kerchief from his pocket, he wrapped the damp strands in it to dry them off. Almost like an infant, Dena curled up into herself, and then he saw it, the swelling of her belly beneath the loose gown.

She was with child! How could it be possible? Hadn't she told him she was barren?

When he reconsidered, he realized she had said no such thing. He had believed it, however. After all, the only logical explanation when a married couple was childless was a barren wife, wasn't it? Her birth-bag had somehow rotted inside, or weakened, so that a baby couldn't stay put. Everyone knew that men always made more seed after using some up during the act. A barren woman had only herself to blame.

He did some mental arithmetic. Sure enough, since she wasn't barren after all, he was certain to be the father of this babe. Pride at his masculine triumph swelled his heart.

But if the townsfolk knew of her condition, how was she bearing her shame? He felt downright bad thinking he had been the only one with problems these past months.

"Thomas . . ." Almost weakly, she held out her hands to him, then suddenly recoiled.

His heart broke even in its pride. The first time he had made the dread ride from Minnesota, he had traversed snow in endless pain to find kin that no longer existed.

This second time, spring had warmed him, sung to him. His heart, soul, and even his body remembered that Dena waited for him this time. She was real. Certainly she wanted him back with her as much as he longed to return.

But from the sparks of anger in the eyes gone suddenly steely, he realized that he was wrong. She loathed him.

"Or Luke. Whatever am I supposed to call you?"

He hung his head like a naughty child "Dena, let me get you

back to the house. Then we can sort this all out proper.

"First off, are you all right?" He raised her to her feet and kept his arm across her shoulder. Immediately she shrugged out of it.

"Things aren't what they were, Thomas." For a second, he thought he heard disappointment in her voice, not anger. "I've got two field hands living on the place now. And as you can see"—she met his eyes dead on—"I have been blessed unbeknownst to my poor Gottlieb with his posthumous child."

Gottlieb's posthumous child.

Unsure at first how to respond, he instead tried to brush mud from her sleeve.

"Leave me alone." She rushed out irritably. "I'm not a child. I can clean up all by myself."

"Well, that must be good news, mustn't it; about your child, I mean?"

Suddenly she glared at him with empty eyes. He had never seen eyes so dead. Even the eyes of the Younger brothers hadn't shown such complete defeat with the posse coming up behind them.

Oddly, Aunt Zerelda had spoken of a young, lost soul she'd met on a train, wondering if some bastard had stolen her innocence. However, she had to disembark before getting through to the young woman that she would like to be her friend. Like Zerelda, he wished now he could help in some way. He could tell Dena that it didn't matter, that he could love and raise Gottlieb's child as his own.

"Dena, we need to talk."

"Thomas, that need ended long ago." Her voice was as dead as her eyes. "I have a new life now, something new to plan for. Something I didn't expect but now truly welcome."

They had reached the house. In the spring sunlight, it was far prettier even than when drenched in snow. Nothing the snow had hidden could displease anyone. The trees planted to shield the place were in full leaf now. Around the front porch, roses bloomed, and poppies.

"I mean it, Thomas. Luke. Whatever. I know we made some promises once, but those were made in haste."

"But Dena . . ."

"Like I say, things are different now. But please, tell me who you really are. And did you really kill that old man?"

"No, no, Dena. I told you true, I never killed anyone. I . . . was accused but acquitted."

"But you are Luke Woodlease. I saw the reward poster."

Oh, indeed, he had told her the truth just then. He hadn't killed anybody. And this next lie wasn't so terrible.

"Yes."

"Why on earth did you lie to me?" She stood at the door, as if deciding whether or not he was welcome inside.

"Dena, I fly under two flags."

She looked at him with no comprehension.

"I need an alias sometimes."

"Alias?"

"I was running from the law then, you remember. I had to protect myself. I had no way of knowing whether you would turn me in. Or that—that we would . . ."

That we would fall in love he wanted to say, but couldn't.

"Yes, I can understand that, at first. But afterwards . . . You always told me you would reveal to me whatever I needed to know. The little fact of your honest name escaped you? Which one is it, anyway?"

He watched her face crumple and he knew why. Giving herself to him had been in its way the purest form of trust, and he hadn't reciprocated in kind.

But in no way could he betray Jesse, no matter how much he loved Dena.

"I have my reasons, Dena. They are good ones. Maybe you'll be able to trust me a little longer. If not, then I respect your decision."

"So be it." Dena's cold voice reminded him of that winter, the ice in the air that had frozen his own words when he had ridden through a blizzard to return to her. But she had been there at the end of the journey to warm him. Now he reached

231

for her hand in a conciliatory way, and her fingers were as cold as her words.

"I thought things would be so different if we met again." Now she only sounded lost and sad.

"Dena, I told you I would find you! I told you I would be back!"

"I did believe you for a time, Thomas. Or Luke. But far too much has changed since then. Well, you might as well come in." She opened the door.

Once inside, she reached for her belly in a secret, gentle way that was so familiar that he knew she did it often without thinking. Without anyone else even noticing.

He turned from her and looked around the room where he had lived in his mind for the past five months, feeling hope and love surge in his soul. Then he watched her eyes blink, eyes that had gone dead again.

Dena had not counted on her dreams coming true when she couldn't let them.

Not since Kearney, with the pretty brown-haired wife holding the sweet baby, had she thought to see this man again. Nor had she thought she wanted to, after the lies and the murder, the empty months with no contact at all.

If just once, married or not, he had written or wired her, needing her like he had needed her last winter, she could at least have been his friend. Maybe helped with bail, or hiring a prominent attorney from those she had known socially in St. Louis. But nothing, nothing but empty months of false grief, empty dreams, and a fatherless baby.

And she might have even confessed to him, if he at least trusted her enough.

Then the womanly part of her came to life, the part that had both loved and loathed him all this time. She still felt shaky and wanted to brew some tea to comfort herself. The store tea tin was empty, and she tossed it angrily to the floor. She'd settle for the dandelion tea Olga made from the weeds in her garden.

Dena was not fond of it, but it would bring the comfort of her dear friend to mind.

"You might as well bring me up to date. I will set some tea brewing."

He nodded awkwardly. "Place looks good."

Dena smiled a little, noticing his look of discomfort and liking the little triumph. "Gottlieb would be pleased. Gottlieb's wheat is coming up fine. And we'll have oats, corn, and alfalfa come autumn.

"I have hired two of my neighbor's cousins from York to help me out. They were ruined by the plague last September and do not really want to return to Illinois, where their folks started out."

"Plague?"

"Obviously you were too busy robbing trains and banks to read the newspapers. The Rocky Mountain locusts made literal hay of crops, leaving lots of folks ruined and desperate."

He blushed, and once again she was glad. She normally did not have much of a mean streak, but for a perverse childish moment she was delighted at his embarrassment.

"There have been several quite severe plagues the past three years."

"Yes, I believe I do know that. Had them at Aunt Zee's place a couple years back. You in danger?"

"From grasshoppers?" she asked pointedly. "No."

He got up awkwardly from the armchair where she had imagined him, all the months of winter. In her heart, she wanted him there. In her brain, she remembered the pretty brown-haired wife holding the baby, in a trim cabin in Kearney, and wondered how he would explain them away.

The teakettle sang into the sweet spring air. She set the leaves to steeping, and into one of her mother's china cups she splashed some of Gottlieb's whiskey. Jonah had taken just a little.

"Thomas, Luke, I just expected something, all these months. A note, a telegram. I might have been able to help you in some way."

"I told you, Dena, I wouldn't do anything to set the Pinkertons down on you harder than they had been. Frank and Jesse are still at large in Tennessee. By now their families have caught up with them and they will hide out until it's safe, but I can't wish that on you. The Pinkertons are bound to think you know something, even if you don't."

"I know they found sanctuary in Tennessee. For a little, I thought you met up with them in Nashville. There was gossip about a third man. I'm a God-fearing, law-abiding woman, but I still cheered for you all." Her voice had grown shy, almost friendly. "I liked what you said about their wives."

She brought out some sweet potato pie. Until that train ride, she hadn't had any since her Cape Girardeau days, but the baby made her crave it, and she had found the recipe simple to make.

"No, that for sure wasn't me, but I heard the rumor, too. I figure it was Bob Ford, who's been hankering for some time to ride with the boys when they go out again."

"Go out again? You mean you haven't learned yet?" Dena was aghast.

"I learned, Dena." He sounded weary. "I don't plan on riding with them again. I learned my lesson. I learned so much about what's important. A farmer in Coffeyville that I counted on betrayed me for money."

Dena remembered Songbird and her trail of friends. "But Songbird . . ."

"Songbird. Without her I would have been lost during the Moon of the Snowblind. She helped me change some of my wrongful attitudes about people. I regret what I said about darkies and Indians. And another fine man, a Negro, helped me out for two days when Whisper cast a shoe."

"Whisper . . ." Dena's voice was a breath of hope.

"Safe in Kearney." He laughed a little bitterly. "Truly a loyal friend and helpmeet that at least got better food and shelter after I got caught. He was held for auction in Colbyville."

A flash of memory flickered in Dena's mind. She recalled the horse in the livery that had seemed so familiar. Now she wished she hadn't been so distraught, that she had investigated its identity. If she had, maybe the wonderful horse would be with her now.

"Aunt Zerelda's mulatto boy bought him back for me." His voice was both grateful and shy. "I'll be picking him up someday."

Dena felt better hearing that. "Even still, Thomas, there is so much I could have done. I have a little money. I could have bailed you out. I could have hired an attorney."

"No, Dena. I didn't tell anybody of my travails. There are reasons for my secrecy. You just must trust me. I didn't even go whining to any of my kin, so don't you feel insulted."

"But your aunt somehow knew?"

He spoke carefully. "She and her family have their ways."

For some reason, maybe relying on the same instincts that had guided her last winter, Dena almost did trust him again. But she had to know; she had to know right now.

"Thomas, do you have family of your own?"

He almost acted annoyed at her questions. "I already told you about those sisters of mine."

Dena waited, but he said nothing else. His words had been short and clipped, and he did not meet her eyes. She took that as a reason not to ask him further. Instead of expounding on any other relations, he tried to smile.

"You can still call me Thomas, but Luke will work right fine, too. I just told the folks at the saloon that I'm Thomas in case they read any news articles about the killer Luke Woodlease. Even though I was acquitted, folk always tend to remember the bad things."

She did not smile back. His words reminded her that she still had too much to find out before she could tell him the secrets of her own. She trusted her instincts to guide her. It was not the time. He had lied, he had not trusted her in his time of greatest need. She could certainly understand him not revealing his true identity at first, but afterward, especially after they had made love? Or even before. He couldn't even tell her his real name. She had little reason to believe him now.

Other than the fact that she carried his child and they had shared love once.

If that was enough, only time would tell.

She couldn't resist hurting him a little more.

"Mr. Bauer has supplied excellent advice for my spring planting."

He was suddenly shy. "Well, I figured I might stay on and help. I owe you for the half eagles. Thought I could work off the sum."

"Well, I don't know. Mr. Bauer has my best interests at heart. In fact, he has asked for my hand in marriage."

Dena hadn't seen the whites of his eyes since she'd held a gun on him. In fact, truth to tell, she could see that her words were darn near as powerful now as her Baby Le Mat had been.

The tea warmed her, and the day was certainly fine, but Dena felt chilled somehow.

Maybe it was the fainting, practically in the water itself. Here she was with the man of her dreams caught in an impossible tangle of lies, Dena herself having announced to the world that she expected Gottlieb's child. And Thomas—or Luke—had a wife and name he wouldn't positively reveal.

Her chest hurt, not with an illness, but with the pain of a heart in turmoil. She really didn't want him to leave, but she knew full well she couldn't allow him to stay, not in the way he had stayed with her last winter.

Suddenly she stood and carried the teacup to the worktable in the kitchen. Turning to face him, she wished life had dealt them a different hand. She should be throwing herself into his arms, telling him about the baby. Announcing to both Max Bauer and Jonah that she was marrying someone else.

"Thomas." It was the easiest name to use, for Thomas was the man with whom she had made love in the snow.

"Thomas," she said again, liking the name as it left her tongue. She almost found herself softening a little, for he belonged here with her in this room. But it was impossible.

The weeks in jail had kept him pale, but his skin was deeper in hue than Max Bauer's even still. He wore his hair long, and for a moment she held her fingers tight together to keep from running them through it. In his eyes, she saw a sadness so ineffable that she wanted to soothe his grief, even knowing she was the cause of it.

He looked up at her expectantly, preparing to rise from the chair where she had imagined him sitting every night for the past five months.

"You're welcome to stay on and help with the planting, I reckon. I can't promise you anything beyond that." She was amazed at the businesslike tone of her voice. She watched his face fall like a child's after his cookie has dropped into the mud. "I pay Karl and Erik two dollars a day including Saturdays—maybe a little more if the crop is good—and I'll cook for you. Work out those figures with your pay back. That's all I have to say for now. Let me take you to meet my other hands."

He followed her to the barn, where Karl and Erik were rubbing down the plowhorse, and introduced them all.

Max's cousins watched Thomas warily. Dena sighed, having already figured out the animosity between men about the same age, particularly when a woman was present. Gottlieb had never seemed to compete with Jonah; they were too many years apart in age, and Jonah's book learning stood between them. But she recognized that even Jonah saw Max as an antagonist rather than a friend. Now the two farmhands viewed Thomas in the same way.

Furthermore, she suspected that her being a young female had a great deal to do with it, and she was plain disgusted.

"Karl and Erik, this is . . . Luke." It was difficult to speak the unfamiliar name, and he looked at her in surprise, having requested she use the other name.

He spoke up, shaking his head. "No, I'm Thomas." He held out his hand for a shake.

Dena ignored him and continued. "He will be working here for a week or two. I thank you for welcoming him and showing him our routine." She knew she didn't sound at all thankful for anything. Thomas glowered at her, his handsome face dark and resentful.

Dena wanted to smack him. Was she supposed to feel gratitude that he had deigned to return?

Karl finally spoke into the uncomfortable silence.

"We're grateful for . . . any he'p, Miz Clayter."

Dena heard the confusion in his voice and knew he didn't mean it.

"I'll bring a blanket out later on," Dena told Thomas. "You can bunk in the loft with Karl and Erik. I'll make supper at sundown."

"I'll help." Thomas came to life suddenly. She met his eyes, realizing that he, too, had been dreaming of the barn in better times, when it had been laced with snow and lashed by north winds, the two of them warmed by straw and each other, and the kindly breath of the animals. The other men tossed Thomas strange looks, clearly understanding the division between men and women's work.

"In your condition and all," Thomas amended, reddening. Max's cousins colored as well, for this was not a subject men mentioned around ladies, particularly the one with child.

"No need," Dena replied pompously. "I am as healthy as a horse. Which reminds me; have you stabled yours?"

Thomas shook his head meekly, leaving the barn to bring in the horse that he had tethered by the watering trough.

Karl and Erik watched Thomas with proprietary eyes, as though Dena were already married to their cousin and needed their protection. She felt a sudden inexplicable need to defend Thomas.

"Thomas just needs a helping hand, like I said, for a week or two, gentlemen. He's . . . a friend from Missouri. I'll thank you kindly for taking him in."

She rushed back to the side door, unable to avoid Thomas as he walked a decent buttermilk gelding to the barn to feed and rub it down. Its fair color reminded her fleetingly of Whisper. Right now, she refused to ask the new animal's name.

"Dena," he started, but she ignored him and flounced out of the barn.

God's mercy, she missed Whisper.

Chapter Twenty

"Dena, dear, how are you going?" Mira Wuebke's words were sincere, but her face wore worried wrinkles around the eyes and mouth. Although Mira was still a young woman herself, she had, since Gottlieb's death, tended to treat Dena like an orphaned child. The two of them paused at the church steps before making their way into the front pew on Sunday.

"I am tired, Mira, but otherwise well." Dena liked Mira, she really did, and she doubted that her friend would declare her a whore if she found out the truth. However, prudence seemed to be far wiser these days.

One day soon she really needed to ride out to Songbird's and speak her mind about the events of her life. Songbird was good about keeping secrets and dispensing advice that healed both body and soul.

If she ever had time to take an afternoon off. She'd almost rather be plowing the fields and sowing seed than cooking and cleaning for three grown men. After his first offer to help with the domestic chores, Thomas—Luke—had never offered again, not willing to lose face with the other men.

And it wasn't really the physical work getting to her. Dena had eagerly embraced prairie life after the disasters of her previous one. It was simply doing the chores and tasks she and Luke had once done, when he was called Thomas, that caused memories and dreams to catapult restlessly in her brain.

Dena suddenly realized what caused Mira's worries. She obviously knew about Jonah's proposal and already considered herself defeated.

"Mira, I have no intentions of remarrying. Anyone. Case closed."

Nonetheless Jonah delivered an impassioned sermon that morning on the sanctity of levirate marriage. He never mentioned her directly, but she received more incredulous glances from the congregation today than she had when Gottlieb's posthumous child had been made known.

For more than half an hour, Jonah cited the requisite verses from Scripture, reading them directly, then interpreting them in his own words. The length of the oration was unusual, but even more alarming was the frequency of his fists pounding on the pulpit.

Dena had not seen him since the day he had proposed; she wondered if he would be able to meet her eyes. Obviously the noisy sermon was his way of reminding her that he was not about to relent.

The baby kicked madly, almost in time with its uncle's rants.

The worshipers certainly were abuzz afterward. She wanted to slip quietly away in her buggy, but Emil Chrismon impeded her progress.

"Now, Miz Dena, that was sure a fire-and-brimstone sermon. Is that a hint about you and the reverend?"

"Emil, absolutely not. Reverend Clayter is merely sharing with you all a little-known tradition from long ago."

" 'Twern't a bad concept, ma'am, now that I think on it." Emil's face tied itself into a knot of concentration. "I deliberated over it during the last hymn. I'd allow Gottlieb wouldn't mind a bit you all becoming a family, now that he's gone to live with His Maker."

Dena just shook her head and tried to move on without being rude. She had difficulty understanding Jonah's familial concerns right now.

"Oh, Emil," his wife chided him, something she was good at, "such a notion is entirely improper. Miz Dena's like his sister."

Dena was perfectly aware of the stares she received as she hustled back to her buggy. Avoiding Jonah right now was paramount. Noticing her farmhands, she waved, then regretted it. They were standing in conversation with Max Bauer, all of them watching her with interest. And now Thomas was part of the group. It was so much easier calling him that. She hadn't realized that he had gone to church. The past few days working in the fields had colored his skin and taken away the pallor of prison.

Dena wanted to spit on them all. She was not, as she had insisted to Thomas, a helpless child. They all would be advised to realize that.

Max was at her side faster than a greased pig at the Fourth of July picnic. "Good morning, Miz Dena," he whispered into her ear. "Have you reconsidered my . . . suggestion?"

With others about, she understood his circumspection but was nonetheless surprised that he brought up his proposal.

"Mr. Bauer, it is simply not possible." She tried to move as he placed his hand on her arm in a proprietary way.

Beyond him, Thomas's face darkened with displeasure. She felt glad about it, even though seeing him took her breath away now, as it always did.

Max leaned down to her ear again. "Quite a Bible lesson from our preacherman. Sounds like I may have some competition." His hand tightened on her arm. "Now, what's this about a new hand? My kin not taking good enough care of you? Hmmm?"

She wasn't sure how or why he made the words sound so intimate. "Mr. Bauer, I do not intend to marry anybody. Please believe me. And I hired a new hand for a little while. He's an old friend from Missouri who needs a chance."

The nightmare was continuing. Jonah was bearing down on her after shaking a suitable number of hands on the church porch. True, she ate dinner with him most Sundays, but today was not going to be one of them. She waved briskly at him, noticing his red cheeks and agitated hand gestures. His black robe flapped about his knees like crows' wings. His lips fluttered in the breeze as well, as though he thought she could hear him.

Let him figure she was off to her place to prepare dinner for her hands. She wasn't, though. At breakfast she had told them over warm strudel and fresh milk that they could fend for themselves this day.

She deserved a day off.

Thomas was at her side to help her into the buggy. For some reason, his action pleased her, although Jonah doing so always annoyed her. She figured he, too, was disturbed about the theme of Jonah's fiery sermon. However, all she thought about now was the warmth of his hands. She remembered the cold snow surrounding them, that one time, and him apologizing for his cold fingers.

He must have remembered, too. As he looked into her eyes, his were nearly black with intensity, and they didn't blink.

"Thomas. Luke." Once again she spoke almost without sound.

"As I told you, I'm answering to Thomas, but Luke is my real name." He settled her on the buggy seat carefully, as if she might break. She had told him true, she was as healthy as a horse, but most times around him, she felt like she was near to shattering into bits. For some reason, she remembered the lovely porcelain-headed doll she had received one Christmas as a child. She had treasured it as if it were the Crown Jewels. One day she had knocked it to the floor. It had landed on her mother's Oriental carpet but had survived. Not long after, the doll's head had gently touched a needlepoint sofa pillow and exploded into pearl-like shards. No rhyme or reason.

She couldn't help herself. She laid her hand on his, almost expecting some sort of explosion at the touch, but pulled it away almost immediately.

His face reddened as he turned away. "I'll be getting a meal at Mrs. Rausch's boardinghouse. I'll be back in time to plant some melons in your garden and pull some weeds."

"No hurry." She shrugged, trying to be casual. "Stay in town and enjoy yourself."

"That was a powerful sermon from your brother-in-law." His eyes were troubled. "He must miss his brother in a terrible way. As you do, too, I'm sure." He looked at her belly first, then into her eyes.

She watched him carefully, not breathing, the old feelings swirling in her mind and heart. Maybe he did love her. Then she remembered that there might be a wife and child. Her resolve hardened. "I was quite surprised to hear him preach so ardently on such a subject, although I must confess that he has proposed such a marriage to me."

Thomas's face blanched and he shook visibly. Dena didn't enjoy this little triumph very much, however. Maybe he had suffered enough.

But she didn't have to relent just yet.

Olga Pott was agog over Jonah's sermon. She managed to keep her entire wagonload silent and seated as she jumped out at Dena's door to speak her mind.

She called out a boisterous hello and burst through the front door without knocking.

"*Mein Gott,* Dena, the reverend preached a sensible sermon this day. I am stopping by just for a moment to give you my opinion."

Dena had been busy unhitching her horse, and currying him a bit. Once inside, she had hung up the jacket to her dark skirt and shaken the pins out of her hair. It flooded across her shoulders like rainwater down a mountain. She actually felt comfortable in the clothes she had recently made, stylish but larger.

"Olga, Jonah . . . the reverend was speaking his mind on a

little-known biblical tradition. At a time when women had little means of their own, a man taking care of his brother's widow made perfect sense. It's no longer the way things are done. This is the United States of America."

"Hrmmph." Olga walked around the house with no invitation, and Dena suspected she would like to stay for a quick snack, the fact that her family waited for her outside not crossing her mind at all.

But Dena was not in the mood to discuss Jonah. She was tired of having the lead role in Staircase Creek's gossip. At least after she had become notorious in her St. Louis social circle she had been able to escape to the Nebraska prairie, absolutely certain that no one would find her. Now, however, she had no place else to go and wanted to be left alone.

"Now, Olga, you need to get all those children along home." Dena bustled Olga to the door, feeling comfortable enough to know her friend would take no offense.

Before the door opened, however, Olga moved close to Dena's face and whispered conspiratorially, "Now, Dena, it is a sensible idea. But I do understand why you have to pretend to protest."

"Protest? Pretend? Olga, what are you talking about?"

"Dena, I have not shared your secret with a soul, not even Wilhelm, and I never will."

The blood drained from Dena's face, yet it managed to pound in her brain. Secret? What on earth was Olga talking about?

"Secret? Olga, what do you mean?"

"Like I said, I won't say a word, it having been so soon after Gottlieb's death, and you with the babe on your mind. There will be time later on, I am convinced."

By now, Dena was impatient, dusty and hot from the drive from church. Sometimes she wondered why she bothered to wake up each morning. She was miserable wanting Thomas Howard all day long when she could watch him lurk outside fixing things, tending her fields, and sleeping in her barn. At least when she was asleep, she could dream about him undisturbed.

"Olga, I am confused. I do not know what you are talking about."

"Why, Dena"—Olga's voice was coy—"I saw you that day, walking with Jonah in the snow. Just before the big blizzard. My mule had cast a shoe, and I was walking him slow."

Dena closed her eyes for a moment. Honestly weary, she also needed to reconstruct the events of those days.

Olga assisted her. "You recollect, Dena, when the two of you walked by the creek in the snow, and he took your hand. The reverend is a good match for you, Dena. He is a gentler man than his brother, and a learned man also."

Dena forced her face to remain impassive while she tried to understand just what Olga meant. She had walked in the snow by the creek with just one man—Thomas Howard.

The shock that they had been witnessed tightened her throat so that no words could come out. Of course; the day Olga had stopped by to check in on her, the day Dena had worried so because Olga was sure to remember something amiss. Well, Dena's dire prediction had come true.

Why had Olga presumed Dena's companion was Jonah? Obviously because of the height and hair color, and Staircase Creek's persistent shortage of handsome young men. Dena forced her brain to think fast, to concoct yet another wad of lies.

Later she would try to sort out the reasons that she had sunk to this sinful level of perfidy. Right now she had to assuage any suspicion that a man other than Gottlieb had been near her last winter. She could cast no doubt on the paternity of her child.

She sighed heavily. "Olga, Jonah has had just as rough a time with Gottlieb's death as I have had. One day we both sought comfort in a walk along God's beautiful earth." Something else glistened in her memory, "I think he was recovering from an ague and wanted a breath of fresh air. He was weak and tearful, and I know he would not want anyone else to have seen him in such a state. I think it would be a kindness to forget having seen him so troubled. After all, I am his sister in a sense, family." She stressed the last few words purposefully, so that Olga would realize the inappropriateness of Jonah's intentions.

Olga listened and nodded but persisted in her line of thinking. "I do share agreement with your sentiments, but on that day I do not think the reverend seemed perturbed. I will abide by your suggestion, though." Then she turned coy again. "By the by, I do think such a match would not be wrong."

"Of course you think that." Dena was impatient now. "You are my friend, and with Gottlieb gone, you feel an extra need to check up on me that my having a husband would alleviate. But Olga, I do not have any mind to wed. Not now, not ever."

"Tsk, tsk. You are far too young to think of living a life alone."

"Olga, let's speak of other things." Dena pretended grief to end the conversation, but in her mind and heart, she agreed. Only it was living a life alone, without Thomas Howard, that made her eyes fill with tears.

"Ach, let us not upset you in your condition."

"Olga, I am not an invalid. You have been through this condition many times. Now, let's get you back outside to the fruits of your labors. Have a blessed Sunday."

Glumly, Dena watched the happy Pott family ride away. It had already started, this life of loneliness. And all Thomas Howard had done was spend a half day in town.

But someday he would go back to his wife and child. Dena Clayter would not be responsible for causing a family to part ways.

The sunshine of the May Monday touched her face as gently as Thomas's hand had, in a better albeit colder time. Dena drove the buckboard to the west forty, bearing a basket lunch for the workers.

On a little rise that was home to a tall cottonwood with a clutch of seedlings at its base, she paused, looking at the scene of industry before her. Max's cousins faded unnoticed into the dust dancing lightly on the breeze, decent but unremarkable men.

She sighed. Her life would certainly be made easier if she could fall for one of them, or accept the offer of their cousin. But when she had imagined herself in bed with a fictional faceless man, she knew she could never be with anyone else without wishing it were Thomas. Another marriage of convenience was unthinkable.

Thomas paused behind the plow, pulling his shirt over his head to wipe his face. His days working hard in the warm sun had helped him regain his strength and carved his muscles into a bronze sculpture. As it had other times, seeing his beauty now, her breath caught airlessly in her throat for so long that she wondered if she harmed the child.

As if he sensed her presence, he looked up, hesitated for a moment, then waved. His motion caught the eye of Karl and Erik, who watched him warily. The cousins had been disappointed this morning when Dena had told them that since planting was done she wouldn't need them anymore.

She tore her stare from Thomas and called out to the men. "I've brought your lunch. Sliced ham, hard-boiled eggs, and fresh-baked bread."

Thomas beat the others to her side. He greeted her respectfully, but she could see worry in his eyes. "Dena—Mrs. Clayter—you've no need to wait on us all the time. We can ride back up to the house."

"Nonsense." She smiled, wishing she could explain to him that caring for him reminded her of other times, those days they had spent together once upon a dream. That doing so today let her imagine that she cared for him for real, that he was hers.

"I'm merely doing my duty. I always brought meals to Gottlieb and Willie, when he wasn't helping out at home. It's my pleasure."

She didn't get out of the wagon but handed him the gingham-covered basket. As he had the last few days, he would return it in the evening with the cloth neatly folded.

He thanked her once again, remarking idly, "The planting will be finished this afternoon. There's just a bit of alfalfa to go."

She heard the question in his statement. He wanted to know if she would let him stay.

She tried to be cheerful, wondering herself what excuse she could use to keep Thomas around now that the planting was done. "Well, I'll certainly need help at harvest, and if the summer's a dry one, you might help me irrigate from the creek and the spring. Good day, gentlemen."

Thomas handed the basket to Erik and hung back a little.

"I'll be here if you need me, Dena. Somehow." Once again, his gaze drifted to her midsection. She knew he realized that the birth and harvest time would likely coincide. The care and concern in his eyes seemed genuine. Did he suspect?

"Why, thank you, Thomas . . . Luke," was all she could think to say. She tried to laugh lightly. "It'll take me a while to get that one right. "Folks hereabout are sure to wonder why I mix the names up so much."

Still he stood by her side. "Dena. Ah, Dena."

She wasn't at all sure what she wanted him to say, but she leaned toward him.

"Dena, I missed you so. Just thinking about you got me through the snow, and prison, and the trial." He tried to speak softly and stifle the intensity of his words, with Karl and Erik not so far away.

Dena didn't care. She placed her hand on his shoulder. The sweat of it cool against her own heated hand. His wounds had healed nicely.

"I'm sure of that. Thomas . . ." The time was nearly right. However, she couldn't reveal her own secrets in a plowed field with strangers nearby. "I think we both have things to say. We can . . . visit after supper."

He laid his hand atop hers, then took it quickly away. "Sorry. I'm full of grit and grime. A visit after supper, Dena. That sounds about right."

His smile lit up his face like dawn after a storm-filled night.

For months she had longed to see that smile, and it was even more beautiful than her imagination.

Dena needed to talk to Songbird. It was hard all alone on the prairie with no one to confide in. As much as Olga loved her, she would never countenance an illicit affair with a stranger.

May sparkled around her. The wheat stood close to four inches high. Gottlieb would have been pleased. As she steered the buggy as quickly as she dared down the rutted path through the Kraft place, she listened for the sounds she had grown to love. Birdsong, of course, the meadowlarks. The water gurgling down the stream bed, Songbird's own dog yapping as it chased rabbits.

May. For a second she remembered the maypoles of her childhood. For some reason, she was reminded of the ghoulish Sundance Songbird had once told her about.

No, not ghoulish, she chided herself. Different.

Songbird sat by the door of her dugout wearing a poncholike garment of deer skin. The chair had been made for her from bent willow branches by a homesteader grateful for her advice.

"He's come back," Dena wailed, not caring that she might be disturbing her friend. She charged out of the buggy, the breeze tossing her hair and the skirts of her sprigged chintz dress in the air. "Why can't he just leave me—us—alone? And why must I love him? He may even have a wife and child."

"Then you must ask. And you must tell." Songbird's wise face broke into a smile as she gestured toward Dena's belly.

She rose and gestured for Dena to sit in the crude chair. "Let me bring you some water." After doing so, Songbird expertly unhitched Dena's horse and led him to the creek to drink.

"Songbird, it is not that easy." Dena wanted to laugh as a prairie dog bobbed his head up and down from his hole in the bluestem grass, looking her straight in the eye as he did so, but the moment was far too serious. "He has lied to me, but I have lied to him, too."

"All the more reason to speak the truth." The eyes behind

the pocked lids were intense but beautiful. "My people and I suffered much from those who spoke through both sides of their mouths. I see no sense in keeping secrets and making pretense."

"I know you speak the truth, but it is so much harder to do than give the advice." Dena's teeth chewed lightly on the cup in her consternation.

"You came here today for my advice. Now follow it. You and I are not friends merely to share tea like your people do." Songbird smiled, nodding. "You cannot listen to just part of what I say. You must hear it all."

Chapter Twenty-one

Songbird always knew best.

Knowing she would have to face Thomas Howard sooner or later, Dena drove all the way to town to avoid him.

The gossip and stares were worse than the melee and remarks after Gottlieb's death.

After two minutes, she regretted stopping at all. Obviously the citizens of Staircase Creek had taken Jonah's sermon as the fifth gospel, and herself the hussy that had corrupted him.

Two schoolboys pointed at her with their right hands while swinging their lunch buckets with their left. Dena wasn't in a good enough mood to wave back innocently, and she quite remembered some meaningful gestures from her life in the city that she had better not display. A farmer who should have known better bared his snuff-stained teeth in a downright leer.

Mrs. Thostenson compounded it when Dena stopped by the mercantile to buy some beans. Dena was no skinflint, but it was draining her, this storing up foodstuff and then cooking it for three hired men whose stomachs had no bottom. Beans were cheap and easy.

"Now, Dena, that was certainly an interesting sermon the reverend preached yesterday." The shopkeeper's voice pitched upward in a questioning way. And of course everyone else in the store heard her.

"Yes, he is definitely a biblical scholar," Dena acknowledged with a smile. Innocence would work well here. She didn't have many supporters in town other than Mira and Olga, since she had been such a young newcomer with fancy ways. Few gave her the credit she felt she deserved for adapting to a new life quickly and taking her new responsibilities to heart. However, Mrs. Thostenson was usually considerate.

"Now, you know sure well that isn't what I mean, dear." The shopkeeper's eyes, normally kind, were bright today with the hope of gossip. "May we suspect that an announcement will be forthcoming . . . after a proper period of mourning?"

The unusual sarcasm in her voice sent the other customers tittering in the shadows of the small store. Who was that trying to hide behind an unwound bolt of yellow wool? From the backroom, Dena could hear Oskar grumble a warning at his wife.

It was time to act proper and outraged. "Mrs. Thostenson, I'll happily forget hearing such an absurd notion if you forget speaking it."

The woman persisted. "Well, it is an unusual topic to be hearing from the pulpit, especially when we are moving into the Ascension, a prettier story by far."

Another woman spoke up. "I agree. I never expected anything so hideous and outrageous to spring forth from our preacher's mouth. He is indeed a marriageable young man, but certainly he realizes that you are unsuitable."

Dena did know it and agreed with the woman but felt insulted nonetheless. "Well, indeed, Frau Thornburg, I am not exactly a bug that crawled out of a box elder tree. I do have some education, and were the situation different, you just might consider me a worthy mate for him." Realizing that this was a dangerous suggestion, she changed her track. "I have no intention of marrying Reverend Clayter. Truth to tell, I don't intend to marry anyone. Gottlieb . . ." She dropped her eyes meaningfully to her belly.

"I should think not. A proper mourning period has not passed," sniffed one of the old crones, although most of the gaggle looked at Dena sympathetically. Bearing a posthumous child was certainly every woman's nightmare.

Trying to restore some of Jonah's dignity out of family obligation, Dena announced hotly, "I do not think my brother-in-law's sermon indicated that such a situation was on his mind."

"He inferred it, right as rain," Mrs. Thornburg went on.

Mrs. Mohlman picked up the momentum. She was an elderly woman whose words were respected based on her age alone.

"Indeed, such a union would be most unholy, a brother marrying a sister." Her old voice hushed to such a state that suspense rose in the room. Every eye turned to Dena as she thought of a response.

"You've got that child to consider, however," Emil Chrismon's wife spoke up suddenly. "Perhaps it is not such an inappropriate idea after all. Your first one, and the child needing a pa."

"*Ja*, the reverend is already related, and he is more to your age than Gottlieb, God rest his soul."

"You share the same last name . . ."

To silence the others, the old woman clicked her tongue against her teeth. " 'Tis no more than a brother and sister uniting. Unthinkable, and sinful to boot."

Dena had had enough. "Ladies, *frauen*"—she reverted to the German that she and Gottlieb had long given up—"please refrain from any such speculation. I will honor Gottlieb by raising his child and maintaining his farm. I do not intend to marry his brother, or anyone. I will thank you all to still your brainless thoughts."

She turned on her heel without making her purchase, to a collective gasp of horror at her rudeness.

He sat on the front porch waiting for her. She had seen him there for about a half a mile as she drove back from town, still fuming at the gossip and sneers. Maybe she should simply pay him his wage and ask him to leave, just as she'd done with Max's cousins that morning. He'd complain, though, that he hadn't yet paid back her eagles.

The thought broke her heart again, having to live without him. And yet she couldn't be with him. He belonged to someone else.

Sometimes Dena marveled at how many times her heart could fix itself before sustaining more damage.

She left the horse and buggy at the side of the house, knowing Thomas would put everything away.

"Thomas, Luke." She stumbled over the names as she reached him. "Come on in. I'll put coffee on to brew." Before she shut the door, she asked about the other men.

"They saddled up and rode out of here. Said you told them you wouldn't need them for a little while now the planting is finished."

She heard hope in his words, realizing he had missed their togetherness, their isolation as much as she had, even with all the mysteries between them. "I let them go this morning. They will most likely be back to help harvest the corn around the Fourth of July. Right now I expect they'll go back to their folks' place in York and hope we don't get any more 'hoppers.

"Then again, if we don't get good rain hereabouts, I might ask them back to help irrigate from the creek, come August."

Come August. When the baby would arrive. She looked at Thomas with her heart in her eyes.

"Stays flowing all summer, does it?" He didn't seem to notice.

"After a good winter, yes."

Dena turned away from him, unable to bear the sweet pain of remembrance and his apparent lack of interest all those months. It had been a good winter, hadn't it? At least for her, snug and warm with her memories. An outlaw who had been imprisoned and threatened with a neck-stretching might not agree as readily.

She knew what his next question would be. What about him? Would she keep him on, and if so, how long?

Dena didn't know herself. Edgar and Allan scratched at the back door, and Thomas moved to accommodate them.

Then he looked back at her as if wondering if he had overstepped his bounds. "All right to let them in? They're probably bringing in fleas and ticks."

Dena smiled. "Then I'll wash everything down with lye. Pennyroyal works, too. I do think, though, that it's such a fine day, all good dogs should be out playing. Young ones, too, when chores are done." As if in reply, her baby stretched; she wondered if the Pott children would be able to enjoy the afternoon.

As if obeying her, Thomas petted each dog briefly, then shoved them out the door again.

"What did you tell them about me?" His words were slow, as if he were afraid of her response.

Dena busied herself preparing a light meal. She shrugged. "Just that I hadn't made up my mind yet, but I knew I couldn't afford to keep three men on, and it didn't seem fair to release just one of them."

She dallied some more. Thomas had obviously had enough of her prevarication.

"Dena, what's happened between us? All I thought of all these months is you. You're my home. I told you that, and I meant it. I wanted to get back to you more than it meant to breathe.

"On the trail, in the jailhouses, at night I stopped dreaming of Northfield. All I dreamed about was you." He stood in front of her, although she had indicated the chair where he had always sat. She had to bend her head way back to look up at him.

The late spring sunshine had darkened his skin and tossed reddish strands throughout his hair. Obviously honest work and warm fresh air had banished his months of injury. It took every ounce of her self-control to keep from tossing herself into his arms, as she had done those months ago.

As if remembering the occasions himself, he held out his arms. It caused her great pain, but she ignored him.

"If you think Gottlieb's little one will change how I feel . . . well, I can love him as my own. I always liked little ones. Best of all, he's part of you."

His words warmed her through, but before she told him the truth she needed to know more about his situation. He placed his hands on each of her cheeks, as if to draw her into his kiss.

"Thomas, not yet." Shyly, she shook her head, turning away. "I'm not saying not ever, but not yet. There are things we need to say. First I must know who you are, truly. You say you fly under two flags. Well, you aren't an outlaw anymore, so why is that necessary? How did you get out of jail?"

Now he didn't hesitate at all before speaking.

"After she found out about my conviction, my aunt Zerelda hired a fancy attorney at law, Ransom Stoddard, to help with an appeal."

Dena was stunned. The high-powered lawyer had been a staple in St. Louis society.

"I . . . would have done the same, if I had known," she breathed.

Thomas smiled. "I hoped my lady visitor was you when Aunt Zee showed up. The verdict was overturned when the real killer was found. At least they didn't build the gallows where I could see it from the jailhouse windows. I could hear the hammering, though."

Dena watched his face tense at the horror of his memories. She wanted to go to him, she truly did.

"But why did she wait until after the trial?"

"Aunt Zee has no great love for northern climes, particularly one of the places on earth where her loved ones are damned as the spawn of Satan. She believed that there wasn't enough evidence to convict me, and that I would be acquitted. That was essentially true, but she didn't count on raw emotion." His voice was ironic. "No James boy could get fair treatment at the place where they had wreaked so much havoc."

"Does anyone know how the old Swede died?"

"Definitely murdered, for the money I left him for my care. Apparently the killer saw me ride away, and after learning of the gold I'd left, robbed and killed Sweyn and then described me to the law."

"But Ransom Stoddard . . ."

"I don't know why he hired on. Maybe he enjoyed the publicity. Maybe he is like a lot of folk who admire my cousins for odd reasons. Most of all, Aunt Zerelda is hard not to like, and most folk don't say no to her. I don't know how she found him or why he agreed. But I believe her full well that she paid all the costs with cash money earned honestly by Uncle Reuben."

"But Northfield—that raid? Are you still on the run?"

"That was the true miracle. Aunt Zee produced a notarized affidavit from Frank and Jesse themselves that disavowed me as a rider on the raid and a member of the gang."

"A true miracle, I agree, but I bet you felt bad nonetheless that you aren't one of them anymore."

"For some fool reason, that is so." He hung his head.

"You don't need to explain to me about mixed emotions. Are Frank and Jesse caught? How'd she get that paper?"

Thomas spoke quietly, again with words hooded with secrets. "No one knows where they truly are, except their families, who have joined them. If Aunt Zerelda knows, she didn't allow it to me. I venture that their wives heard of my predicament somehow and did the right thing."

The right thing. Whatever that was.

Dena was struck once again by the deep feelings of love and decency exhibited by these folk who had no compunction at all about being robbers and killers. She tried to determine if she would defend and support and hide her child if he grew up to be a thief and a murderer, and she decided it was very likely. Already she had lied on its behalf in front of everyone she knew, and those she held dear. Furthermore, she had helped Thomas hide without knowing much about him other than that he looked at her like no man ever had.

"Well, Thomas, who are you, really? What flag should I really hoist over your head?" She forced a smile, although the seriousness of the situation made her want to weep.

"I am Thomas Howard when it suits the situation. But I truly am Luke Woodlease."

"Well, Luke Woodlease, it may take a while to digest all of this and call you by the right name."

Especially since it's Thomas I fell in love with.

"Either will do." He laughed, almost as if everything was right between then.

But Dena had more to ask.

"Thomas, are you married?"

He looked somewhat startled, and his brow crinkled over his eyes. "Why, no. Why do you ask?"

She hesitated a little but couldn't find the words. Instead she saw the young mother holding a baby boy.

She believed him because she wanted to so badly. That sheriff in Colbyville, after all, had told her about mistaken identities, and certainly there were folk all over the world who shared the same name. But if he were married, would he tell her the truth?

Dena had to take the chance. If he were free, unmarried, and no longer an outlaw, surely she could go back to dreaming her dreams of them spending the future together. And certainly he should know about the baby. Certainly he would understand. With him locked away and her thinking the worst, she had to take precautions to protect their baby's future and pretend that Gottlieb was the father.

"Thomas . . ." she began, holding her hand on his cheek. The skin was hot to the touch. The time was now.

"What the hell?" Not callously but obviously distracted, Thomas shoved her hand away and ran to the window.

After being insulted for a few seconds, she looked out, too. What was akin to a posse was riding up from town, clouds of dust tufting at their horses' hooves like fresh-sheared sheep wool.

*   *   *

Karl and Erik still wore their work clothes, trousers of dark wool with seats and legs reinforced with buckskin. Each had on a faded red button-up shirt and a worn woolen jacket.

Dena felt a stab of pity for their loyal mounts, which had clearly seen better days. At least their weeks at her place had allowed them good food and shelter. And for their masters as well. Not for the first time, she was aware of the privileges of her life. Even on the prairie, Gottlieb's investments had allowed them a slice of life higher on the caste system than the typical sodbuster.

She wondered if they had forgotten some of their belongings. Perhaps they would prefer a bank draft instead of the eagles she had given them, an amount higher than she had promised at hiring. She doubted that they were returning to complain about the wage.

More puzzling was the presence of Max Bauer. He, too, looked like he had barely finished his work day, but he had slicked back his hair with macassar oil and tossed on the jacket he wore to church.

But the most mysterious oddity was Jonah, riding his prim sorrel with the star on its forehead. Jonah's hat was shoved to his brow to prevent it blowing off in the spring wind. He did not wear his clerical collar, and his suit was most unsuitable for the dusty prairie afternoon.

She and Thomas stood speechless on the porch. As for Dena, it was one of those times in her life when she could not predict what would happen next but was certain that it would impact her future, most likely in a negative way.

Max had slung his long, pale body from his horse and, after a perfunctory bow of politeness, he came to stand in front of her with accusatory eyes. He ignored Thomas.

"So now you entertain this . . . upstart in your home while you cast out my cousins?"

"Mr. Bauer, please." Dena tried to placate him in a tone that had sometimes worked with Gottlieb when he raged. But with others it only poured more oil on the fire of ire. "This matter does not concern you. I hired your cousins fair and square. The planting is done, and they have received decent wages for their efforts. I explained to them that I would most likely hire them back for the corn harvest."

"Yet you keep on this stranger, someone who does not belong at Staircase Creek."

Max's white face had turned an alarming purple around the eyes. Anger puffed out his normally slack cheekbones and darkened the blue of his eyes.

His cousins dismounted, silent, but nodding their heads vigorously in agreement. Jonah looked foolish in his attempts to act paternal and imperious. Not only was he just several years older than she, but he was also better recognized for his gentle calm.

She gave Jonah a glance of disgust.

"Gentlemen, under the circumstances, I doubt that I will invite any of you into my home." Her debutante tone worked on all of them but Max. The cousins retreated like children with a strict mother, and Jonah acted confused, as if he couldn't think of a thing to say, a rarity for a man who could sermonize at will.

Max wasn't finished, however. He approached Thomas with a swagger so confident that Dena might swear he had been imbibing. She was not like others in town, though, who would be critical or judgmental is this were the case. A farmer alone on the prairie had little other pleasure.

"Where do you come from, pilgrim? Taking honest labor and wage from my kin? You have no cause to be in Staircase Creek. You are not one of us."

Jonah had come to life in full force, meekness gone. Now he looked as he had on Sunday, railing about levirate marriage. "Indeed, Dena, from whence has this man come? I noticed him at services but had no idea he was your hired man." His eyes were imperious again, and she sighed in some defeat.

"I don't count this as anyone's business but my own. However, if you must know, this man is a friend from Missouri who needs work. Last time I thought about it, this is the United

States of America, and I can hire whomever I please."

"Friend from Missouri? Who on earth might that be?" Jonah's eyes narrowed in suspicion.

Dena had had enough of him. "Reverend Clayter, I can't imagine why you think that you know all of my past acquaintances or why any of this concerns you."

"Why indeed? A pilgrim, a stranger whom I don't know a thing about, living on your premises, you, a young widow woman all alone? After I humiliate myself in front of my entire congregation explaining the basis for our marriage?"

"Our marriage? There is no such thing!" Dena howled in dismay.

Max stood stiff, then clenched his fists. "Your marriage? You and the reverend? I asked you first."

"And I said no to you both."

"What is going on?" Thomas Howard managed to yell. "Who's getting married?" He looked alternately at Max and Jonah and Dena, his head swinging in disbelief.

"And I certainly don't like no strange man horning in on my territory." Max's voice had deepened into a snarl.

Neither Thomas nor Jonah heard the warning in Max's voice, but Dena did, and she flinched, knowing full well what was about to happen.

Max's fist struck Jonah first, plumb in the abdomen, rendering the reverend shocked and airless. As Jonah hunkered to the ground strangling for air, Max next attempted to land a right uppercut to Thomas's jaw.

Just before he made contact, Thomas's left fist punched Max deep in the chest. Max exploded in a grunt of air. Thomas watched, obviously satisfied, as Max Bauer joined the reverend in the dirt.

However, Max's cousins weren't about to ignore family honor. The two young men, unaware that they were tangling with a member of the Jesse James gang, both pounced on Thomas at once and knocked him to his knees, pounding their fists into him like frustrated children in the schoolyard.

Jonah had caught his breath, although he gasped inelegantly

from time to time. He wore streaks of dirt across his once tidy suit, and his hair stuck up from his head where his fingers had grasped it frantically. Not a pugilist by any imagination, he was nonetheless a man of honor who recognized that the pilgrim was outnumbered. He stumbled over to the melee and grabbed at the Bauer cousins with flailing fingers, mostly grasping their garments.

Max was on his feet now, his nose bleeding profusely. He used the backs of his hands to staunch the blood, then surged toward the skirmish. Throwing himself into the throng, he started to bash at Thomas Howard, more often than not smacking into his relatives. After that he must have realized that the reverend was actually his rival, for he started punching Jonah's handsome face.

Thomas hurled himself to his feet, pulling Max with him, prepared to knock him to kingdom come with his open hand. The two cousins grabbed his arm, sending him sprawling.

Jonah rubbed his beleagured jaw, then flapped at the Bauer contingent. By now, Thomas was on his back in the dirt, kicking with both legs and flapping his arms at anything that moved, not unlike a turtle tipped over on its shell.

Edgar and Allan, bored with chasing rabbits at the creek, joined the fray, barking like mad dogs.

Above the canine din, Dena heard the grunts and the slaps, the kicks and the curses. Even though she cringed at the sounds, she figured she was luckier to be a listener than a participant.

She sank to the single porch step and burst into tears. Then she began to laugh, huge, rolling gut wrenchers, at the absurdity before her. At the nonsense that her life had become.

When Jonah prepared to take a swing, dainty but nonetheless a swing, at one of the cousins, she had had enough.

"Jonah! Desist! Where is your dignity? How can you, a man of God, become a mindless man of violence? Come Sunday, how are you going to stand up at the pulpit with a face like that?

"What has happened to all of you, you ruffians? I do not

want any of you on my property. Off with you, every single one. Out of my sight now. Now!"

"But Dena, I came to call!" Jonah almost wailed. "I'm not really part of this mob. I came to call. I merely met them on the road." He had never before looked so helpless. She wondered if she would ever be able to listen to him harangue on a serious subject in church ever again. Then she understood the nature of his call; he had planned to come to court her.

The cousins apologized at once and obeyed, probably not wanting to endanger their chances for future employment.

Max, too, looked mortified, having been defeated and humiliated in front of his supposed future wife. "Miss Dena . . ."

"Enough, Mr. Bauer. Enough." She turned her back. Thomas wasn't saying anything, but she noticed a smile twitching his upper lip.

Jonah had rustled up as much dignity as he could under the circumstances. Why did he, in his dishevelment, look so out of place and ridiculous, while Thomas in the same degree of dirt and blood looked manly?

She couldn't control her thoughts or her anger.

"Jonah, I don't want this scenario ever discussed. Nor the subject of levirate marriage. If you want a wife, you need look no further than Mrs. Wuebke. She is a dear, she is lovely, and she already cooks and cleans for you, so you know there are no surprises there." The three Bauers nodded approvingly at the mention of Mira.

"As for you, Karl and Erik, I told you I will need you again by the Fourth of July. Thomas, here, isn't getting any special treatment. Fact of the matter is, he'll be gone before morning." She said that on purpose, but Thomas's twitching didn't stop.

"And as for you, Mr. Bauer, if you wait just a few more years, and build yourself a nice wooden house in the meantime, Ida Pott will be all grown up and ready for a husband. Yes, you're more than twice her age, but she'll catch up. It won't matter so much then. That is, if she's fool enough to take you on, which now that I've thought about it, I will properly advise against."

With a huff from her nose and a snooty turn of her backside—actions that she had perfected at the Cape when disgruntled by foolish suitors and hadn't had the opportunity to use in years—she stomped into the house and slammed the door.

Chapter Twenty-two

"Songbird," Dena wailed, "why don't I have any normal men in my life? It's been this way for a while now. I attract oddities like a . . . buffalo carcass attracts maggots."

The morning after the fracas, she hitched up the buggy and headed for the dugout on Kraft's place. She knew perfectly well how to ride astride, and fast, but thinking of the baby, she used a cautious means of travel. Not obeying her order to leave, Thomas had tried to talk to her in the barn, but she only huffed and swirled the debutante actions for the second time in many years.

She figured Songbird would give more good advice. After all, the Oglala woman had put up with white men's lies and violence for a goodly portion of her life.

Songbird was out in front of her dugout, weaving something on a primitive loom. Dena didn't know if this was a native Oglala art or if it was a new craft Songbird had picked up from white civilization. Some other time she would inquire about it. Right now her own problems came first, as as they tended to do.

Complimenting Songbird on her efforts, she began to wail again. At least she didn't have to go inside the dank, smoky hovel.

"Even Gottlieb . . . I could have loved him if he'd let me. He was charming and even debonair at first. I had thought farmers to be grimy, with Mr. Levi's garments and hay straws in their teeth. He was clean and nice-looking, but he turned so mean . . ." She stopped herself. Complaining about the dead was not what drove her here today.

"Now, Dena, Gottlieb behaved in the only way he could. He was past the middle of his life. He longed for a ripe young wife to grow his heir before he withered and left this earth. When this did not happen—" Songbird's eyes met Dena's wisely. Dena had never explained in words that her husband had been unable to give her physical love, but the wise medicine woman already knew. "His bitterness grew like a poison jimsonweed that he could not stop eating. And that made him act without control."

Across the fields of sprouting wheat and freshly planted corn, the two women could hear the song of meadowlarks wafting in the breeze. As the creekbank undulated off toward the Little Blue, Dena looked ahead, seeing the Kraft sons gathering water from their spring. She waved. At least Songbird knew the kindness and respect of this fine family in the autumn of her life.

"And dear Jonah," Songbird's voice lifted, sometimes lilting, other times a monotone, "do not forget the affection you have for him. He has long stood beside you and been your defender. You know this. When you would weep at the slaughter of a hog, or refuse to talk to Gottlieb when he hunted the deer, and even when you gave your calves and chicks white-man names, Jonah discouraged those who laughed at you."

Dena lowered her face, knowing this to be true. She tried to shove the images of the hapless preacher, dusty and defeated, from her mind.

"He is a bookish man who is devoted to your God, but that does not mean he does not belong out here on the prairie. He brings peace and respect. He is not a man to fight and grovel in mud and blood. Do not chide him for seeming like an infant when he was attacked unprovoked.

"Remember him as dignified and strong."

Dena trained her mind on the images of which Songbird had just reminded her. She smiled, remembering Jonah often as her champion, but she couldn't just yet delegate the levirate marriage nonsense to things better left forgotten.

"But Songbird, he practically told the whole congregation that it was his duty to marry me!"

Songbird got up from her loom to offer Dena some water from the creek. "Such is the way of many tribes, Dena, that a man marries his brother's widow and takes her children as his own."

"Well, it is not that way in the white man's world!"

"Yet you say it is written in your holy scriptures." Songbird used her wise-sounding voice, the one that usually allowed no rebuttal.

Dena merely sighed, nodding almost in defeat. Instead of dwelling on the idea, she decided to follow Songbird's initial advice and remember Jonah's best qualities.

"You look strong and rested in spite of the . . . incident." Wearing its rare smile, Songbird's pocked face looked ageless and beautiful. Dena had never been able to fully imagine the horrific changes in Songbird's life.

Their eyes met again. Songbird suddenly let loose a chirp of laughter, and hearing it, Dena reprised the gut-filling mirth of the day before. Around her the scent of growing things hung on the air of this May day like her lace angels on her Christmas branch. All in all, it was turning out to be a beautiful day.

"As for Max's young kin, they have been close to losing all they hold dear. It is not evil that drives them, but fear. And most likely they felt the need to mind their cousin, him being their elder. Max, too, wishes for a wife and child to comfort him on cold winter nights as his life runs its course."

Dena drank from the tin cup Songbird handed her as she had yesterday, digesting all the wise words. "Songbird, you always make more sense than anyone I know. Someday I want you to come to my home so that I can offer you my own hospitality. You always help me, listen to me, like no one else ever has. Except perhaps my mother. She let me down, too."

Songbird cautioned her again. "Do not let your own disappointments seem to be the faults of others. When people do not act just as you think they should, it is not necessarily they who are wrong.

"I will come to you when you bear your child, but it is not seemly for me to break bread with you."

"Nonsense."

"Enough of this. I will give you one more observation. This man of yours, this Thomas—he was innocent until Max struck at him. Do not let your anger with yourself drift to him."

"Anger with myself?" Dena heard her voice rise in pitch. "Anger with myself?"

"Yes. You have not told this Thomas that you bear his child although I advised this yesterday. You chide others for lack of truth and honor, and yet you are guilty of these sins yourself."

Dena repeated her good reasons. It was far better than letting her friend think she was an obdurate brat. "Songbird, I believed him married. I had very good reasons to think so. That's why I told Jonah and everyone else that I carried Gottlieb's child."

She looked Songbird directly in the eye. "There is no one so despised in the white world as a woman bearing a child for a man not her husband.

"However, yesterday I did ask, and he did deny being married, and I knew it was time to confess about the baby. But that was just when the Bauer invasion arrived to do battle."

"That battle has been won. Or lost, depending on whose eyes you look through. Now return to your man and get the rest settled."

"I sent him away."

"He will not go far."

Indeed he hadn't. Thomas sat on the porch again, as he had the previous day, waiting for Dena.

He hadn't been hurt at all in the Bauer riot. Brawling a time or two with the Youngers had taught him a few things about self-defense, and being left-handed, he always had a few unexpected moves. What he minded most was looking foolish in Dena's eyes, and damaging the reputation he was trying to build in Staircase Creek.

At least he hadn't struck the preacherman, who had, amazingly enough, come to Thomas's own defense.

He sighed, wishing he had Whisper again to talk to. The buttermilk he rode now was a fine one, but not the companion he had had in Whisper. Somewhere on Aunt Zee's Kearney farm the horse finally had a chance to rest, to sleep in the straw of a real stall, and to eat proper fodder. Someday they would be reunited, and he figured that Whisper would recall their adventures. But that didn't help him now.

Sometimes life seemed more unfair to one person than it should. Misery should at least be portioned out equally. He'd already lived through his sisters and the farmer Darcy, and getting shot. The weeks during the Month of the Snowblind and nearly getting his neck stretched, and now Dena bearing another man's child.

For a second, he looked across the rolling prairie ahead of him, the trim fields of Clayter and Bauer showing sprouts of cereal crop, and fallow areas of bluestem. All in all a right pretty place to watch from a porch.

He remembered thinking just the same, even with the place shrouded in snow.

Certainly Dena and he deserved being a couple for real. Even in prison, he had thought of her, hoping she wouldn't be ashamed of him, wondering if she would wear black for him if he were hanged.

And watching her just weeks ago as she talked to the trees

along the creek, he had dreamed the same dream, that at Staircase Creek or somewhere else, they would have their own homestead and grow their own seed, raise their own kids.

Seeing her with child, just for the flash of a split second, he had wanted the baby to be his.

He needed to keep on telling her that he would love Gottlieb's baby just as much as he would his own.

When he saw her riding back from—he guessed—Songbird's, he decided to tell her just that.

Then it all struck him, just like the sudden burst of gunshot slamming through last September's sky into his body: He had nothing to offer her. They'd shared a fairy tale last winter, in her husband's house. And he thought he was worthy of raising her child?

He didn't even own the horse he was riding, and to make it all more horrifying, he still owed her money. He had even needed her own husband's coat to keep him from freezing during the Moon of the Snowblind. It was still stuffed in the shabby saddlebag of belongings he'd carried throughout his jail terms. He hadn't even considered how much more work time he owed her to repay the loan.

He pounded his fist on the door post. Maybe someday his world wouldn't come crashing down ten minutes after he figured something out. Maybe someday everything untethered in his life would tie together.

It just wouldn't be today.

"I thought I told you yesterday to get going," Dena groused to Thomas, not really meaning it.

"I stayed the night at Max's."

Her mouth opened in astonishment.

He came over to the buggy and helped her out in such a comfortable way that he might have been doing so for years. For a moment she wanted it to be that way for real, that he would help her from buggies for the rest of her life. He wore the creases of worry over his eyes, likely expecting her to be mad at him.

"Ah, Dena." He hung his head, almost abashed. "I was just defending myself."

"Nevertheless, I will now be the talk of the town for years to come, inciting a brawl on my front stoop."

"You're not the first pretty girl to have that happen." Thomas's voice was soft, as it had been when they made love in the snow. She met his eyes, knowing he was recalling that sweet moment just as she was. The furrows of worry above his eyebrows relaxed a little. In some way they made him seem distinguished.

She sighed. It was another of nature's unfairnesses against the female sex. Her gender spent their entire lives under sunbonnets to keep the sun from withering their skin, while Thomas just grew more handsome.

She broke the tender mood, meaning to follow Songbird's advice but wanting Thomas to sweat a bit. It was true; she would never live down that fight. Mrs. Chrismon and Mrs. Thostenson would likely defend her and feel some amusement, but she could hear the old biddies already. Mira would be furious, of course, that someone other than herself had incited Jonah to such misbehavior.

Yes, indeed, her feelings of portent had become fact. Then again, she'd survived far worse, an embezzler father who had probably helped blockade runners, and getting stood up practically at the altar by Becker Blanchard hadn't been much fun.

Thomas brought her back to the reality of Staircase Creek.

"Now, Dena, Max . . . he and I made friends right away. He has apologized profusely. He had just indulged a little too much after a long hot day and was simply not in the best of moods. Karl and Erik look big and strong, but they really aren't much more than youngsters, and he's right protective of them. Erik's not much past sixteen, and Karl barely a year older. And, well, I guess he had his sights set on sparking with you and he didn't much like seeing me here."

Dena acted prim and proper as he spoke his last words to see if he was affected by the situation. In truth he seemed more than a little troubled.

Now was the time. "Thomas, I don't want Max Bauer sparking with me or the preacherman coming to call."

"What is it you want?"

"Same as you, I think. Now come on in and sit in your chair."

His words didn't make sense to her at first. "Dena, it's not my chair. Everything here is yours. I got nothing to offer you. In fact, I still owe you for all those eagles, and I still got your husband's coat."

"Thomas, what are you worried about? Earthly things don't matter."

He did sit in the chair as she had requested, but rather than recline like a beautifully carved sculpture as he had other times, he remained tense and taut.

"That's not so, Dena. A man's got to be able to offer his woman something. He isn't much of a man otherwise."

"Oh, Thomas, that's simply untrue! A man isn't just the sum of his accounts! Didn't you read Mr. Thoreau?" She ran to him and knelt at his feet, wanting ardently to lie across his lap and have him hold her close.

Thomas shook his head, and his whole body moved with the effort. "Ah, Dena." He sighed. "I wish you were right."

Dena persisted, running her hands up and down his arms. He said he wasn't married. And he wasn't a murderer. And he had come home.

"I am so glad you did come back. Just like you promised." She watched his face, suddenly shy. This man had known her in the biblical sense, had done things to her beyond her imagination. Was there any possibility that he would consider her loose and free with her morals?

His arms wrapped around her like he would never let her go.

"Dena, I already told you. You are my home."

"Then I see no problem. This place is mine."

He shook his head. She persisted. "It is mine. Gottlieb left it to me."

For a long time they sat silent, melded together. Dena felt a contentment that she never had before. All the torments of her

273

life were made right in this man's arms. He had already promised to love Gottlieb's child. Certainly when he found out the baby was his own, their bond would be cemented forever.

She opened her mouth to speak, but he stirred suddenly.

"Rider's coming."

Indeed, Edgar and Allan began to bark fiercely, so the rider was no friend. Dena went to the window just in time to see Gordon Bruce hitch his horse to the post and stride to her front door.

What more torment could the Pinkerton inflict now?

His knock was insistent, and just as she opened the door, she saw him kick at her dogs.

"Just what do you think you're doing?" she asked him angrily, shutting the door quickly behind her to protect Thomas Howard, or Luke Woodlease, or whoever he really was. He had told her that he had been acquitted and that his cousins had disavowed his presence at Northfield, and she'd believed him, but he had not always been honest with her.

For whatever reason, the Pinkerton was obviously not done with either of them. She doubted the dour agent was here to compliment her on her garden or to congratulate her on one or the other of her supposed betrothals.

He seemed taller than before, with a confident smile on his face. "You ought to train these animals, Mrs. Clayter. It might be good practice for your parenthood."

"My animals are always considerate to those who deserve it," she retorted, the sourness of his sarcasm polluting the birdsong in the air. "What are you doing here?"

"Will you ask me in?"

"No."

"Well, now, your place looks well. Your wheat is coming up nicely." He shifted from foot to foot yet did not seem tense or awkward.

"That is thanks to my husband's efforts."

"Ah, yes, your husband. But I hear you have a hired man who is much help to you."

Oh, God. He knew. Something was going on here, and she was powerless to stop it.

She kept her voice heavy with her notorious snobbery. "I have three hired hands. I will convey your compliment to each and every one of them."

"That won't be necessary. If you don't mind, I came to speak with Thomas Howard." His mouth came as close to a smile as she figured it ever did.

She thought quickly. Of course she couldn't allow it. But Thomas had said the danger was past. He had even introduced himself with this "flag" to the folks he'd met upon returning to Staircase Creek. Was the Pinkerton now a friend, or did he remain the enemy?

"I do mind," Dena began hotly, interrupted by the door opening behind her.

"I'm Thomas Howard." He announced the name proudly, looking from her eyes to the Pinkerton's with a self-assurance that Dena thrilled to see. She remembered those troubled days of him hiding under the bed with a chamber pot and his Peacemaker. But not long ago, Thomas Howard had said he was Luke Woodlease. When he needed to be. Who on God's good earth was he right now?

The Pinkerton sagged, his triumph gone. "Why, you're not Jesse James!"

Dena almost sagged, too. The baby moved inside her belly.

"No, I am not. I am Thomas Howard. Sorry to disappoint you." Thomas's voice was dry. "And before you ask, I do not know where my cousins are."

His face screwed up in disbelief, the agent was speechless. Finally he managed a few more words. "You are Thomas Howard of Kearney, Missouri?"

"I am."

The Pinkerton looked cautiously at Dena, like he might know things she didn't.

"You're certain?" the Pinkerton asked, almost in a voice of apology.

"I swear on my stepfather's grave." Thomas spoke the words

without hesitation. In fact, he sounded downright proud. "I am truly Thomas Howard."

Dena remembered the brown-haired woman holding a baby boy. She had never felt hatred before.

Chapter Twenty-three

The month of May had nearly worn itself out getting crops to flourish. Gottlieb's wheat grew so fast she could almost hear it push up earth when the wind stopped blowing.

Tiny nubbins of fruit hung on the little grove of plum trees past Bruno's pasture, like the lace angels on her Christmas branch. She wished she could stop thinking about them. The vegetables in her garden wore top hats of green feathery sprouts that tipped in the breeze blowing across Thomas Howard's neat rows. Not long from now, Dena would be eating the early lettuce he'd planted. All alone, feeling sick most of the time, she wondered why she would even want to.

Thomas Howard was gone. She'd sent him riding off as soon as the Pinkerton left. Refusing to recall the shock of hurt surprise on his face, she nurtured her own misery, both loving and loathing the child he'd left her.

The sun poured down its warmth like a teakettle spouting steam. The dust in the barnyard burned her bare feet, but she hitched up the buggy anyway and, wearing a huge bonnet, headed for Songbird's.

She almost released her foul humor as the prairie rolled past. Neighboring places were in as full bloom as her own, and along the creek, fresh spring leaves dressed winter's bare-armed branches in a dozen shades of green. Wild grasses grew tall for grazing later on, and the poppies practically glowed along the road. Just about everywhere an eye could see, growth and green carpeted the rolling knolls of prairie and farmland.

The medicine woman immediately watered Dena's horse. "It would be wise for you to wait to travel until the heat of the day has passed. Both better for your babe and for this animal."

Without invitation, Dena sat in the willow chair by the cottonwood tree. The airless dugout was not an inviting interior in such hot weather.

"Do not chide me, Songbird," she grumbled. "I am in a vile mood."

Songbird came to sit cross-legged at her side. "I do not know why you visit me at all. You ignore all my wisdom, then complain like a spoiled child."

"Spoiled child! I am an unmarried woman bearing the child of a fugitive I bedded within three days of meeting. That, Songbird, is no child." Her voice, shrill, softened in defeat. "That, Songbird, was a fool."

"Do not attempt any self-pity with me, Dena," her friend admonished. "You did not tell him the truth."

"I started to, I really did, but then the Pinkerton came . . ."

"You sent your man away without allowing him to explain."

Dena refused to cry. It was not something she did often whether in the best or worst of times and, when necessary, she preferred to do it alone. "Songbird, he is married. He swore to being Thomas Howard. I met the man's wife! I still hear the words and the solemn expression on his face.

"Damnation! I remember *her* face, all sweetness and love."

Without thinking, Dena pulled a button from the bodice of her light gingham dress. Under it, she wore a separate skirt she had made with elastic at the waist. It expanded as her belly grew and allowed her to breathe.

"I won't be the cause of a man leaving his wife. Gottlieb doesn't know it, but he has provided for us. And I'll honor his legacy and raise a good child. I will!" Her fists clenched in her vehemence. These were the hardest words she had ever had to say, and even still, she did not want to believe any of them.

"Do not make the man a hero now. You despised him while he lived."

Frustrated because Songbird was right, Dena tossed the button into the dirt, then thought better of it. She picked up the object and dusted it off. Then she looked at Songbird.

"I have no choice."

"There are always choices, Dena. Consider that you may have made the wrong one."

Songbird rose and turned to look to the west. Perspiration filled in the pocks on her face. In today's heat she did not wear the deerskin poncho, but rather a loose calico dress. "I fear tomorrow," she said simply.

In unexplainable panic, Dena's heart began to hammer against her ribs, and the baby stretched at being disturbed. Unconsciously, she placed her hand against the movement.

"Why? What do you mean? Is it something with my child?"

The medicine woman did not turn to her, but Dena could hear her clearly. "It is the locusts. They will be back; if not tomorrow, then soon."

Almost as if the insects chewed at her own skin, Dena stood up and shook them off. "How on earth do you know that? Who can predict such a thing?"

"Songbird knows. You doubt me often these days, so believe me or not."

Dena's hands brushed against her skirt in agitation.

"What shall I tell the others?"

"They will not believe me." Serenely, Songbird raised her hands to the sky

"Some of them will. I believe you, Songbird. But how do you know this?"

"I have lived it before. It is hot and it has been dry. The babes will hatch in the ground and grown-ups will fly from the Shining Mountains."

Dena persisted in her disbelief. "But it isn't even June."

"It is hot and dry for this Moon When Chokecherries Become Ripe," Songbird said sagely.

"I must go. I must do something!"

"Then go." Songbird crossed her arms over her chest. "And do all the somethings that you must."

He waited for her on the porch as he had the other times. Maybe the two weeks he had spent with Max had calmed her down. Olga had warned him, one day dropping off Georg to help plant the vegetables, that babes in the womb caused strange moods in a woman that required patience and indulgence.

Shrugging, he tossed a stick for Edgar, who romped noisily with Allan for a while before returning it. He grimaced when he touched the slimy thing, wondering anew at Dena's moods.

Why she was irritable, he guessed he understood, her carrying such a load, all the while on her feet with chores. And then the heat starting. But danged if she didn't look just as beautiful as ever during all of it. He wanted her all the more.

But the torrent of abuse he had taken for admitting to be Thomas Howard, that he couldn't understand. He even scratched his head, considering it. He'd made it clear to her that he hoisted either flag when he needed to.

And that day he certainly had needed to be Thomas Howard. Maybe she'd give him a chance to explain. Even with her mad at him, just thinking about her seemed to make things right.

The morning was already too warm for his sensibilities. He looked idly down the road as he waited for her to wake up. Olga had also told him a woman in this condition needed a great deal of rest.

Even though she disliked smoking and he knew it, he almost rolled one then just to be ornery. Then he saw a strange, almost wonderful sight. In the distance around him, in the fields of growing things, the meadows and pastures, began to move almost as if they were carpets with feet.

The heat and the outing to Songbird's had tired her. Dena had gone to bed early, deciding to heed the medicine woman's advice in the morning. Georg had told her that Thomas was staying with Max. She would drive out to see him after breakfast.

She hadn't relented enough, however, to sleep in the bed that had been his last winter. For a while, before wakefulness fully arrived, she curled up in a light sheet, savoring the few minutes of cool air the morning offered. Nighttime had been sweaty and miserable, and she had made the dogs stay outside.

In her sleepy languor, she thought she heard Thomas's voice, but no, it was the dogs barking at their play. Then in the air, almost in tune with the rise in its temperature, she heard a new sound. A crackling sound like munching on carrots.

Then came the knock on the door.

He stood in front of her, as glorious as in any dream. His eyes bore worry and confusion, but those she had seen there before. This time she suspected she was the cause of most of it. No matter. Nothing would go wrong for them again.

"Thomas! Thomas!"

She whispered his name, unable to disguise her delight, and ran into his arms. She forgot her dishabille for a moment but doubted he would mind.

He didn't kiss her, though, nor do much more than offer a perfunctory squeeze.

"Dena, Dena," he started. Now she saw true panic in his face.

"Thomas, what is it? Are you all right? Is it . . . Max? Has something happened to Max?"

Without a word, he took her hand and led her to the roadway.

Dena gasped at the moving vista.

"My God, it's the nymphs. They are on the march," she announced both in dismay and an unexplainably delicious horror. She had heard about this terrible phenomenon for years.

It was, in fact, Max Bauer's greatest nightmare.

She shared Thomas's panic and breathed the dreadful words.

"Grasshoppers. Babies. Songbird had a premonition." Nothing could be gained trying to understand the destruction on the way, and she realized she could do nothing to prevent it. Regardless, she had to try.

"Thomas, will you help me?" Gottlieb had certainly lectured her enough on what to do in such an event, but she couldn't do it all alone and didn't remember half of what he had said. "Get some blankets to lay over the garden!" She knew he would remember the horse blankets in the barn.

"All right. You go on and get dressed. Then I'll get some straw ready."

"Straw?" she asked blankly.

He pushed at her lightly. "Just go. I'll cover as much of the wheat as I can with straw. The baby 'hoppers will crawl into it to get warm. Then we'll . . . set it afire."

She paused for a moment at his words. She had announced to Songbird just yesterday that she would protect Gottlieb's legacy and her child. Now she would watch it go up in flames.

"How do you know that?"

"Clay County had 'hoppers, too, once, while I was with Aunt Zee."

"All right, then. I'll get dressed."

It was not a day for a proper toilette. She pulled her hair back with a ribbon and tossed on her chemise and a pair of Gottlieb's overalls. All she had done to remodel them some weeks ago was hem up the legs; they were round enough in girth to fit around her middle.

Thomas was nailing dark green woolen blankets to the borders of the garden.

"Here." He handed her the hammer. "You finish here. I'll toss straw on the wheat."

"Thomas." She put her hand on his arm to stop him, just for a moment, and liked the look he gave her. "Thank you. I have some things I need to say, that I've needed to say for a long time."

"I know."

The munching sound increased, as did the urgency and the unreality of the day.

He leaned down to kiss her briefly, but a real man-to-woman kiss. She parted her lips just for a second. Then he laid his fingers lightly on her mouth before he left to hitch up the gentle farm horse.

She covered the garden as tenderly as she imagined she would cover her child. Thomas had planted much of it; she had tended it, weeded it, waited for the fruits of his labor. And she knew in her heart that the blankets wouldn't help a bit.

By ten A.M. the first of the little green monsters arrived on her place after chewing off the low shrubs and weeds along the road to town and the bluestem grass in the meadows.

By half after, they had chewed through the blankets and stripped the garden patch bare.

Soaked with sweat, her skin pinked by the sun, she spent the rest of the morning smashing insects with the flat of a spade. Tears mixed on her cheeks with the sweat and dust; her efforts hadn't mattered much at all.

Nigh on to one o'clock, Thomas returned, hot and exhausted. "Got some covered, but it's too windy to light a fire right now. The pests are everywhere. I squashed them with my feet as I walked back, they are like sands on a riverbank."

"Well, that's where they lay their eggs. These babies can't fly yet. They're content to devour what they can hop on." She pointed to the garden and burst into tears.

He slung his arm around her, a blank expression of defeat belying the hope in his words. "Well, I guess there's still the prospect of another crop if the pests stay away."

"Another crop?"

"Corn's all gone, Dena. All forty acres. Just stumps swarming, with each 'hopper fighting for the last bite. And the wheat is just a dirt pile. It's a sea of green babies—at least what I suspect a sea must be. Guess they'll march over to Max's now."

She considered the chronology for a moment. "Yes, I believe we will have time to start more corn."

"We?"

She was somewhat embarrassed, remembering his declaration that nothing here was his. "Well, all of us around here, I mean. There have been infestations around the state for the last few years. I suppose in the back of everyone's mind was the possibility that it could happen to us. We've never had much here in Staircase, until now." The last two words forced reality onto her. It was not just another bad dream.

He sat wearily on the porch step, slapping at the 'hoppers still at work on her roses.

"I remember two years ago in Clay County. Everything green aboveground was taken as fast as those things could chomp. Folk said the critters even gnawed up green laundry hanging on a clothesline."

The wind started to blow from the southwest, and they sat for a few moments, cooling their faces.

Then Dena stiffened. "Oh, God in heaven."

"What now?"

"Songbird said the wind would bring more." They shared a horrified look. She knew he trusted Songbird as much as she did.

"More?"

She nodded helplessly. "From the Shining Mountains."

Thomas drank some water. "I'm rested enough now. I'll go dig some ditches and shovel as many as I can and bury them." Thomas's words were harsh with loss and pain.

"Thomas, it won't matter."

"We have to try."

She shrugged and let him go, once more feeling helpless and without recourse.

Looking up at the sky, she apologized out loud.

"I'm so sorry, Gottlieb. There's nothing else I can do."

The words hadn't left her mouth but a minute when Karl rode up, hatless and frantic, on Max's best horse.

"Miz Dena, there's a message from town. I'm ridin' hard to

alert the neighbors, for whatever good it will do. The signal service sent a wire. Fliers been seen passing overhead continuously past York, heading east."

She wanted to hug him in comfort, for his family had already suffered much from this plague, but he moved his hand in a little wave and headed off. His desperation must be real, she decided, for she had promised to use his help for the harvests, and now all she had were empty stumps herself.

Back in the house, she sat in Thomas's chair, almost unable to feel, waiting for a disaster that she couldn't stop. At least when Gottlieb had been injured, she had helped sop his blood, assisted Dr. Burkhardt's surgical ministrations as best she could. She had held her husband's hand and prayed until the last breath.

Now there was nothing to do except listen to the sound of the wind and the crackling of the nymphs as they ate. Until two, when the roar reaching her ears became more than angry wind.

It must be a torrential storm, for the room darkened like huge clouds were obscuring the sun. Maybe the storm would bring hail and crush the nymphs.

Parting the curtains, she looked out, preparing for thunder and lightning, maybe a funnel cloud.

Instead, the air had turned black, filled with grasshoppers as far as she could see. Grasshoppers as thick as the snow from the blizzard that had brought Thomas Howard to her. The vibration of a million wings was the roar in her ears.

She opened the front door in disbelief at what she saw. Across the fields and pastures, the grasshoppers moved as one in the wind. Thomas ran from the barn, slapping the creatures from his face and body. A dozen or so of the most tenacious had clasped onto his vest, and he removed it and tossed it to the ground in disgust.

A few fluttered at Dena's feet, and she kicked at them in anger, feeling a futile triumph as she crushed them under her boots.

Thomas pushed her inside. "My God." He turned to her. "I

could barely drive the wagon back. 'Hoppers kept flying in front of the horse, hundreds of them, smacking her in the face."

"I never saw anything like this," he said, drawing her to his side, holding her firm against him. "It's like Exodus, when God punished the Egyptians." As they watched the nightmare from the window, Dena wondered what Staircase Creek had done wrong.

The noise whirled in her brain just like the crackle-snap of a cruel bullwhip. She swallowed rising hysteria. A frenzied scratching at the backdoor reminded her that she had forgotten Edgar and Allan. Thomas got to them first, and the dogs burst inside, shaking as if they were wet. Their actions were futile; dozens of the hard, dark locusts stuck to each dog's fur in furious attempts to feed.

"Oh, God, Thomas, what shall we do?"

He shrugged. "I guess pick them off one by one and toss them in the stove." The dogs finally quieted.

Then came silence. The roaring stopped. The swarm had dropped to earth, devouring her world.

Chapter Twenty-four

Sobs stabbed her heart as sure as any knife. She tried to stifle them in a throat gone raw, but he heard.

At least night blinded them to the devastation lying just outside. Not just the buds and leaves of her plum trees had been eaten, but the bark as well. Along Staircase Creek, the cottonwoods were as barren as winter.

Only a few shreds of Thomas's vest remained.

The Bauer men's terrible dream had come true. Dena had a little of Gottlieb's cash money, but the Potts were ruined. Dena's grief for her friends was as real as death.

Apparently Thomas remembered his way through her darkened house. At her bedside, he pulled her into his arms, tight, as if to take her pain.

"Dena, Dena, love. Try to sleep now. Think of the little one."

He picked her up and carried her back into the room that had always been his, and laid her in the bed, still warm from his body.

She breathed in his fragrance and hiccuped like a foolish child.

"Thomas, I . . ."

"No, say no more this day. Sleep now. The little one needs rest," he murmured low, slow, into her ear. She remembered the warmth of his breath upon her face once before, when she lay in the snow, one with him.

And as she had done with him once, long ago, he shinnied into bed beside her, pulling her backside against his front.

"But Thomas, it's happening again. My world's collapsing, and I cannot do a thing to stop it."

"Then we'll build a better world. Somehow everything will look better in the morning. And truth to tell, God's earth will spring back to life." He enclosed her in his arms.

She liked his words, that the morning would be better. Songbird's warning hadn't been able to prevent the locusts, but her advice to Dena about Thomas might prevent the shattering of a new world waiting to be lived.

"Thomas. The baby . . . Gottlieb . . ."

"Shhhh," he crooned against her hair, holding her tighter still.

The flying creatures had gone by that day's end, eager to wage Armageddon in another township. Yet Dena still heard the crunch of their mandibles. Behind her eyelids, she still saw the storm of the roaring wings. She moaned, moving restlessly.

"Hush, love." He began to sing her to sleep. The vibrations in his chest drowned out the leftover sounds of the voracious invaders. The words made no sense, but nothing else did either. She breathed easy.

Over her thin lawn nightgown, his hands tightened around her midsection between her breasts and her belly. She wouldn't have minded at all if he touched her in either place, but then she realized he probably wouldn't. She had been awfully mean to him lately, and as far as he knew, the child was the fruit of another man.

In the early dawn, she knew Thomas had wakened before her, for his breathing was different. She had slept all night in the curve of his body, her knees over his own, his arms a protective circle about her.

She marveled, having spent the night with the man of her dreams. He kept Gottlieb's old nightshirt circumspectly positioned about his lower body, but even still, she could feel his hardness against her rump. It excited her, but maybe it shouldn't, in her condition.

With the windows sealed against the intruders, the air in the house was hot and stifling against her front. Thomas was just as hot against her backside. Yet she liked his heat much better.

But now was not the time for such things. A world had come to an end outside and needed whatever fixing its inhabitants could devise.

Almost as if he couldn't prevent the motion, Thomas's hands moved to her belly. The baby greeted him with a quick kick. He laughed, and Dena laughed, too, wanting to tell him, wanting the world to be normal just for a little while.

"You have a regular pugilist in there!" Thomas chuckled.

"I think we should hire him on to teach Jonah how to box," Dena replied with a giggle. Perhaps a bit of inanity would help her get through the day.

"Now, now, he is a man of peace and learning and should not be the brunt of undue criticism. I think the preacher held his own darn well." He shifted until he lay flat on the bed. She still reclined on her side.

Thomas Howard looked at her in the morning light. The curtains were drawn tight—Dena did not have the strength yet to look out—but the thin material was not much of a barrier. She liked what she saw in Thomas's eyes.

"In spite of grasshoppers, this is a mighty fine way to wake up in the morning. Something I thought of every day for months and months."

She liked his words, too. But she had to know. The young mother in Kearney; she'd been packing up to join her man. Had Thomas failed to find her? Had she died? Did he not want her anymore? Any of the possible answers saddened Dena, though she couldn't explain why. Was he an adulterer? For that matter, wasn't she? Why would he remain with her when he could so easily leave another woman and child?

There had to be some sort of mistake.

She got up on an elbow, facing him. She knew he could see the rosy rings of her nipples through the nearly transparent nightgown, and she didn't care. The fabric lay taut over her belly; she didn't mind him seeing that, too, and hoped he liked what he saw.

The morning silence was eerie; they both knew the nymphs were far from satisfied.

"Thomas . . ."

"That was quite a day yesterday."

"Why were you here, waiting for me?"

"You and me, we got some talking to do." He raised his arms over his head and rested it in his hands. His hair was very dark against the white pillow case. The sleeves pulled up to stretch across his shoulders, and inside the armholes, she saw dark hairs sworled against his flesh. Through the button placket that had pulled open, the gentle swirls of his chest hair invited her fingers.

But she kept them still. She had to know. Maybe he had left his wife for her. But would she want a man who discarded a woman in such a way?

"Why did you swear you are Thomas Howard?"

His mouth tightened. "I already told you. I use both names. Depends on the situation."

"But what's the situation now? You've been exonerated of that killing. And you've been disavowed as a member of the Northfield raid. What do you have to hide now?"

She could see by his tense face that her questions displeased him. What she didn't know was why. Once he had told her she would know all she needed to, but she had hoped that by now he might trust her.

He sighed hard and got out of the bed, making certain none of his masculinity showed.

"Dena, I just can't answer all your questions now. I got my reasons. There are some things I can't explain and that you don't need to know. Seems like you might allow a man some privacy."

The hurt now was nearly as bad as last night, but she no longer could expect the comfort of his arms; not now, not after he repudiated her trust. Not under these conditions would she trust him again. For now, Gottlieb Clayter would remain the father of her child.

She sighed, trying to speak in a normal voice devoid of hurt and anger. "You're right. Privacy is a wonderful thing. In fact, please allow me my own so that I can properly dress. Then, I guess"—she got up and headed toward the window—"I must assess the damage." Looking out, she cried again.

After a quick morning meal, Thomas hitched the loyal old dobbin to the buggy.

"The Morgan's too high-strung to stand a flock of 'hoppers flying up in his face. And believe it or not, I think Edgar and Allan are breakfasting on the crisp corpses of those that ate too much to finish their journey."

Dena shuddered at the nature of the dogs' feast, but she couldn't stop admiring Thomas Howard in spite of his lies and flaws. He was cool-headed and strong, intelligent and gentle, and had comforted her during the evil night in a mighty fine way.

And maybe, just maybe, today would be better than yesterday, just as he had said.

They drove around her fields first, and her tears would not stop. Even Thomas sniffed and tried to wipe the sides of his eyes without her noticing. The attack upon the acres of wheat and oats, and the wild grass in the grazing pasture, was complete.

"It is winter without the snow." She shook her head, sending tears sliding down her nose. Limbs of many trees had broken from the weight of the alighting grasshoppers. Naked fingers reaching for the sky, winter-bare cottonwood branches clawed at the clouds. The glorious blue reflected in Staircase Creek, on whose banks Thomas Howard had drowned and buried a thousand nymphs.

Her eyes hurt.

Disbelief dulled Thomas's eyes as he surveyed the vacant acres. He pointed. "Not all of the younglings have trekked off. I even found a slew of them in the barn. Chewed through the horse blankets, even gnawed through the hemp ropes and one of the harnesses."

"God almighty." Thomas was clearly correct. Speckles of green—nymphs, not plants or leaves—dotted the fields and the road as the creatures continued to forage. "God in heaven."

"We'd best head for town. Jonah is likely to hold a prayer service, and I know the aldermen will be setting up a town meeting of some sort. Oh, Thomas. Oh, Thomas!"

Dena couldn't hold in the wail.

He held her as close as he could without being one with her. And the kiss, while sweet and full of comfort, revealed to her the passion that would come.

If she could trust him.

The road into Staircase outlined a land that had lost a war.

Dena and Thomas passed a wagonload of silent Potts on the way to town, and met up with Bauer's cousins just past the cemetery. A few gray piles of leftover grown-up 'hoppers struggled to bite the remnants of the desolation.

"They've chewed the bluestem to the nubs. There won't be a thing for the cows to graze," Dena observed, disconsolate.

Max, eyes hollow, reined in his horse for a sorrowful chat.

"Everything's gone." His lifeless voice broke Dena's heart. "My crops are gone. Fifty acres of corn, the same of wheat. My oats, all thirty acres. The meadow, my pastureland. Even the weeds. Everything killed."

He was close enough that Dena could touch his arm. "Max, it is still springtime. We have time to replant."

His thin shoulders moved in a hapless shrug. "There won't be enough seed for us all, not a second time around. I've no seed of my own left. I better see to Karl and Erik. I promised the family I'd take care of 'em." He rode off.

The strains of "A Mighty Fortress Is Our God" spilled

through the open door of the church. Thomas helped her from the buggy and politely held her elbow as they walked in. Even his mannerly touch sent her heart racing.

She forced herself to marvel at the townsfolk keeping faith in God at a time like this. She said her prayers to be sure, but she had a way out of this—Gottlieb's accounts. Even Jonah would take her in if need be. But many of her neighbors had nothing and no one left.

After the hymn, Jonah prayed, a wonderful petition like those for which he was respected. The bruise on his face was hardly noticeable; Dena suspected that Mira and a careful application of flour paste had something to do with that.

And then the horror stories began.

The Chrismons's small flock of sheep had had their wool chewed right off their backs.

"They ate the wood of my fence," Oskar Thostenson offered.

". . . and the roots holding our sod bricks together, and the lint stuck on the washboard."

"Last year's corn stalks that my scarecrow was wearin'."

"The side of our shed that ain't been painted yet, eaten clear through."

Mrs. Mohlman, the hard old woman who'd criticized Dena so soundly, began to sob. "My lace curtain! Eaten to shreds. It was brought from Belgium, handmade. I wore it as my wedding veil but had nothing else for my parlor window. It was from my mother, when I was a bride in Vermont."

The tales saddened Dena even more. The hard oak pew bit into her backside after the exertions of yesterday. She grimaced as she tried to get comfortable.

"Are you unwell?" Thomas asked, his dark eyes surveying her with a tenderness that took her breath away. The sound only convinced him that something was wrong.

She tried to smile. "Thomas, I'm fine. Yesterday was simply a grueling day beyond all imagining." And you, she finished silently, you confuse me, which is almost the worst of all.

Swiveling her head, she tried to stretch her stiff neck muscles without drawing attention. She gazed about the folks gathered to pray and mourn—her friends and neighbors, who sat in the wooden rows almost motionless in their distress.

Both to please Jonah and to appear staid and mature, she had worn clothes of somber dark gray and the plain bonnet trimmed in maroon. Some of the rogue grasshoppers brought in by the dogs had chewed off the fake violets.

Thomas sat close to her, far closer than necessary. She wondered if any townsfolk noticed, doubting it, what with their concern for the current disaster occurring outdoors. The scent and warmth of him delighted her, but she recalled that Thomas Howard had a wife and child. She moved away, seeing at once the dismay in his eyes.

A man she couldn't name rose, moving to the center aisle to address the gathering.

"The 'hoppers stopped the trains out of Seward. The piles of their bodies are smashed on the tracks and leave such a greasiness that the wheels can gain no traction. We may see a delay in receiving supplies. The smell is worse than death."

"This *is* death." Olga Pott's voice boomed as she stood up. Even in the face of calamity, she wore her one good dress. She approached the center of the chancel cautiously, taking to heart the dictum that women should keep silent in church. Obviously deciding that it wasn't a true worship service, she turned to the assembly.

"Nothing I see for miles is taller than an inch above the ground. I doubt that there is a sprig of clover or a blade of grass anywhere. Our hay is gone, and all our vegetables have been destroyed. Our two cows and our mule will starve with no grazing. And there is no food for my children, and no money to buy any. We will need to leave our land. It seems a cruel curse upon us from our loving God."

Dena could not bear the hopelessness in Olga's voice, or the pain etched in her face. Overnight Olga had aged, her plump face deflated like a dried plum. Rising, Dena addressed the group from where she stood.

"Olga, Wilhelm, all of my friends in Staircase Creek. All during the night I thought of nothing else other than this disaster that has befallen us, and how I might help. There is hope, I promise you. We can replant the corn and the gardens. They will have all summer to grow again. Oskar, will you ship more seed?"

The storekeeper called out an affirmative response, but added that with hundreds of others needing to replant right away, seed would be in short supply.

Dena was not about to be thwarted. "And I have a little money. Gottlieb had some . . . cash remaining from my . . . dowry. I can lend sums to you for little interest. And I have a few things left from my mother that I can sell at auction."

The moans of appreciation gladdened Dena's heart. The great tragedy had made her one of them, no longer a prissy outsider. Max Bauer, however, apparently remembered that he had sought her for himself, particularly at the mention of cash.

"Miz Bernhardena, you have no charity to parcel out like an almshouse without consulting me. You're to be my wife. We are to join farms. We will replant together, revive Gottlieb Clayter's wheat fields, and make a true home for his child."

The denizens of Staircase Creek gasped as one. The resulting tumult exceeded the one that Jonah's laborious description of marriage between in-laws had caused.

Face burning, Dena lashed out. "Mr. Bauer, I did not accept any such proposal. And I don't need your approval for anything I choose to do."

"But Dena, it makes perfect sense."

Jonah seemed unwilling to let his proposal and biblical sanctions go unnoticed. He returned to center stage, stalwart and authoritative. "Now, Dena, you are wise to turn from this man. You must understand that my brother's child deserves the family ties that I can provide as your husband."

Both Mira and Mrs. Mohlman of the lace curtains protested loudly at the same time.

During the debate, Thomas Howard sat as still as a cigar-store Indian, his expression wooden. However, his dark eyes blazed. Whether consciously or not, he reached out and took Dena's hand while two hundred eyes watched eagerly.

Something on Thomas's left hand sparkled in the streams of colored sunlight coming through the lone stained-glass window. Her wedding ring. It only fit to the first knuckle of his third finger, but seeing it, she knew she was his only woman.

She knew that now was the time. Time to build another world.

"I would like to help my friends and neighbors to the best of my ability." She continued to clasp Thomas's hand. "I am far from wealthy, but I can share what I have. It should see you through until the late harvest. We shall see who of you is brave enough to accept my charity. But you, Mr. Bauer, and you, Reverend, are both misguided in your ambitions for my offspring.

"Gottlieb Clayter is not the father of my child," she announced baldly. "I carry the child of Thomas Howard."

Before running from the church, Luke Woodlease had kissed Dena Clayter thoroughly in front of God and the entire citizenry of Staircase Creek.

Back at Clayter's place, they tried to sort things out.

"Is the baby the reason you've been so angry with me?" he asked her warily. "I know it is a selfish thing to do, leave a woman with child. But I didn't suspect. I thought you were barren."

"You and everyone else for fifty miles. Why did folks assume it was my fault? Gottlieb was unable."

He was sitting in his usual chair, but at those words, he stood up and held her close.

"You mean I really was the first?"

"Yes." For a moment she hid her blushing face in his chest, unsure what to say next. "But don't get all cocky on me. For all intents and purposes, I was a married woman. I loved you, though, almost right from the start. I was a little concerned that you would deem me loose and wanton."

"Well, that might make me mad at you, but you . . ."

"Thomas, I thought you had a wife and child." The words

came out so easily that she wondered why she had put them off.

His face creased as if he stood in the sun. "Why on earth would you think that?

"I met her. I don't know who she really is, but I met her fair and square."

His hands on her shoulders, he held her at arm's length, his eyes bright with shock. "Met her? Met who? Where?"

"In Kearney, Missouri. She was holding a little boy named Jesse. That made sense to me, you naming your son after him."

"Dena, how in the world . . ."

Once again the words came easily, probably because she had already unloaded the truth in front of everyone for twenty miles.

"When the Pinkerton harassed me again, he brought me news that you were imprisoned in Colbyville. I went there. I found an empty cell and the name Luke Woodlease. But the sheriff told me where to find you. Well, Thomas Howard, anyway."

He was quiet, lost in thought. "I made a sacred vow, Dena, but I think under the circumstances I'll be allowed to explain. If you can confess in a holy sanctuary in front of everyone you know that you are bearing a bastard child conceived out of an outlaw before your husband was truly cold, I can come clean myself.

"Mary Howard isn't my wife. That at least I told you true. I have no wife and have never been wed. Jesse lives incognito in Kearney under the name Thomas Howard. Mary is really his wife Zee.

"Only their most trusted friends know the truth. As far as I know, she has joined him in hiding in Tennessee."

Dena drew him to the table. Somehow Gottlieb's whiskey made more and more sense, but she ground some Arbuckle's beans instead.

"Well, I can understand about Jesse's deception, but why on earth did you take his fake name as your fake name?"

"I don't know if it was a stupid decision or not. I figured if

I let myself be known by that name, it would create a false trail." He stretched, almost as if he were glad to be able to relax at last.

"Well, it worked. That Pinkerton certainly expected you to be Jesse."

He tensed again. "Now that the Pinkerton knows I'm not, he'll certainly continue to go after Jesse."

She selected her next words carefully, knowing his fondness for his kin. "Thomas, he is a wanted man, a killer and a thief."

"I know you are right. It's a hard matter to resolve, that's all. I love him like a brother."

Coffee ready, she got up to bring him some. "I think I understand family loyalty. My mother stuck by my father, after all. And as for Aunt Zerelda, I think she would do just about anything. For anyone."

"Yes. Families are complicated things." He sighed, pouring cream into the cup.

"Let me make some bannocks. Songbird showed me how."

He nodded, looking up at her. "Aunt Zee made me promise to forgive my sisters. I wrote to them, and already I feel better inside.

"But enough about that. I want a family of my own." He took her hand and began to talk slowly. "I'll answer to Thomas if you prefer, but do you think you could bear being Mrs. Luke Woodlease?"

As the dream swirled in truth about her, she smiled at this last, the best, of her recent marriage proposals.

"So you intend to make an honest woman of me?"

"Dena, I married you in my heart the moment you tucked your gun away and tended my wound."

His fingers entwined with hers like the woven basket he had made. At the mere touch, her woman's body came to life, bathed as she was in honesty and trust.

Luke Woodlease's voice was rueful. "We've got some corpses to clean up."

"That will have to wait. I think we deserve a second time."

His eyes widened in surprise. "Is it permitted? Will you be all right?"

"Songbird says it is a natural thing."

"Make sure Edgar and Allan are outside."

She went to the window to check. "Thomas, come see. The meadowlarks! They're eating up any 'hoppers that are left!"

"Later. There's something else I want to do first."

In his smile, she saw her future.

Epilogue

September 1877

Reverend Jonah Clayter stooped down to scoop a handful of water from the creek. He tried to find a spot where the sun shone through the trees, as if to find the warmest water he could.

Nonetheless, the baby moaned unhappily, twisting in the firm grasp of the godmother's one good arm. At her side, young Willie and Georg Pott stood in proxy for the two god-fathers who were many miles away. The creekside had seemed the most suitable place for this christening, just as this same spot had been for the wedding of the child's parents last June.

Too many in Staircase Creek's congregation had protested the sheltering of a church roof over the marriage vows of a couple who had produced a child out of wedlock. Willie and Georg had also stood as groomsmen on the wedding day in the stead of the same two far-off gentlemen.

"I baptize thee Alexander Samuel Woodlease," Jonah intoned somberly, the preacherman who had supported the couple every step of their way.

In fervor, the child's parents clasped hands.

After the blessing, the group who had gathered at Staircase Creek to celebrate the christening broke into song.

The loudest was Zerelda Samuel, although Olga Pott kept pace with her.

As they walked back to Dena's place for a celebratory meal, Zerelda walked close to Dena, keeping the child snug against her ample bosom. "Frank, now, he always thought Alexander was a sissified name. I selected it because I find it noble."

"As I do. Besides, we didn't want two Jesses." For a moment she couldn't help but remember the dark-haired "Mary Howard," with little Jesse in her arms. Perhaps they could be friends someday. By now, word came stealthily once in a while from the family, reunited incognito in Nashville.

Dena touched Zerelda's good arm with real affection. "And Luke"—it was still hard to remember to use the name— "wanted to honor you and Uncle Reuben, too."

"Well, if I had known who you were that day on the train, and if my niece Zee had any inclination that my fool nephew was using her Jesse's fake name . . . well, I just think all this"— she met Dena's eyes meaningfully, and Dena knew she meant the wedding—"could have happened much sooner!"

Back at the house, Olga and Ida puttered around the kitchen, putting out hams, *blutwurst,* and sauerkraut, while Mira warmed up a chunky applesauce. The night before, Zerelda had made sweet potato pies as deftly as a woman with both arms; Willie now whipped up the cream.

Olga sent the five littlest Potts to the barn to play with the menagerie of half-grown cats that she had not allowed them to bring home. Knowing Dena's feelings about smoking, Max Bauer and his cousins stood outside on the porch, guiltily enjoying their tobacco.

Dena looked around contentedly at every single person there. Her family.

Luke brought their son to her. "When our boy starts to nuzzle his papa, it's time to get him to you. He wants his supper."

"That, or if he needs his britches changed!" Wilhelm guffawed loudly.

When Dena headed for their bedroom to nurse, Zerelda motioned her to the armchair Luke so loved. "Now, Dena, nurturing a child is a perfectly natural thing. Don't permit yourself to stand on ceremony."

Then Zerelda walked over to Jonah. "You are a brave man, Reverend, to stand by my nephew and his bride. God be praised. Our Lord says judge not."

Jonah smiled. Much of Dena's confession had shocked him, but he had taken to heart Zerelda's last five words. Mira looked up from placing cole slaw on the table. Her strongly worded ideas and unconditional support of Dena had helped Jonah decide to stand by his convictions that Dena was truly his sister. He and Mira shared a secret look that even Dena could see. She liked what she saw.

Jonah spoke his words from the heart. "Well, Dena's family. There's not blood, but . . ."

"Kinship is more than blood," Zerelda announced in her authoritative tone. "All you folk here today are kin to Dena in some way. And therefore, kin to me as well.

"Well, Luke, Dena . . ." Zerelda spoke again like the matriarch she was. "I may trek out to that new place you claimed in Wyoming. I'll bring all the rest, of course, when they're all home again. You and Annie will enjoy some reminiscing." Her face grew wistful.

Dena laughed. "Well, Aunt Zee, it isn't much of a place yet." Only Luke had been able to travel there to select and see it, but she trusted him. "Give us a year or two."

"By then, I expect Alexander to have a sister!"

Luke laid his arm across his aunt's shoulders. "That sounds real good to me." Dena grimaced, not having enjoyed birthing much even though Songbird had deemed her experience an easy one.

Max Bauer came in then, having stubbed out his cigarette on the front porch. Dena wrinkled her nose at the smell, but the house was his, after all. Legally, anyway, although she had lent him the money to buy it. Karl and Erik would homestead in his soddy. Max's head turned from one corner to another, as though still in disbelief at his good fortune.

"Oskar has plenty of seed ordered for spring planting, and our corn harvest next month will prevent both starvation and disaster," Max told the group, even though they knew already. Hope sang in his voice. "We will have our plains of waving grain again." Once more, he looked around, his eyes finally resting on Dena, his eyes full of gratitude.

Wilhelm Pott's brood returned through the back door, and he lined them up at the washbasin, pouring warm water over their hands from a pretty pitcher from Cape Girardeau, the last of her mother's things. Dena had sold the rest.

She went to Olga, who had bravely stood as her bridal attendant despite the gossip. Wyoming was a far piece, but surely the good Lord would let them be together again, sometime. Instead of sentiment right then—both women knowing they would cry later—Olga's eyes twinkled. She and Wilhelm were not leaving Staircase Creek and had nearly paid back Dena's loan through barter and work.

"Please say grace, Reverend. Food's ready."

"No, let's wait a little while. Songbird hasn't arrived yet," Luke said softly. "Let's pray Frau Kraft's birthing went easy and is all over now."

"Hey, I see Songbird coming up the road!" shrieked a little Pott.

"Hush, Octavia, you *teufel,* and go wash up," her mother admonished.

Dena grinned. She had finally learned the child's name, although she should have suspected. The child was Olga's last.

It was a pretty name. She might use it herself sometime.

Author's Note

The Outlaw's Woman is fiction, first and foremost. It is not intended to be either history or biography. While there is some recorded evidence of a locust attack in Nebraska in May 1877, and while Jesse and Zee James did "fly under the flag" of Tom and Mary Howard at various points during their lifetimes, the events of Dena's story are based on very liberal usage of any and all fact. I allowed my imagination to run full steam, inventing details I liked, especially those about a favorite of mine, Zerelda Cole James Samuel. Deep down, I suspect that Dena's story actually started the first time I watched *The Long Riders*, one of my favorite movies.

The Outlaw's Woman became real because of some special people in addition to my family: my Nebraska friends Harold and Edna Mohlman, who shared family lore and local color—especially Marla and Kenzie's corn bag idea; my wonderful parents, who taught me to love reading and writing; my "sisters" at the Orange County Chapter of RWA; my editor, Kate Seaver, for her patient assistance; and of course, Dorchester Publishing and *Romantic Times* for sponsoring the first-ever New Historical Voice Contest.

BENEATH A SILVER MOON
DEBORAH SCHNEIDER

Sinclair Readford clings to the third-story windowsill of a whorehouse in nothing more than her unmentionables. To escape the disreputable establishment, the lady vows to go to any length. However, when her fingers slip and she plunges into the embrace of a ruggedly handsome man, she wonders if she's been saved or damned.

Jefferson McCloud has never had a woman fall out of the sky to land in his arms before. It is enough to turn a man into a lovesick fool. He should know she'll be more trouble than the devil himself. But soon, the cowboy knows he'll ride to hell and back to earn the right to call the impertinent chatterbox his own.

EXTREME MEASURES
RENEE HALVERSON

NEW HISTORICAL VOICE CONTEST WINNER

If André DuBois were a betting man, he would lay odds that the woman in red is robbing his dealers blind. He can tell the beauty's smile disguises a quick mind and even quicker fingers. To catch her in the act, he deals himself into the game, never guessing he might lose his heart in the process.

Faith O'Malley depends on her wits to succeed at cards, and experience tells her the ante has just been raised. The new gambler's good looks are distracting enough, but his intelligent eyes promise trouble. Still, Faith will risk everything—her reputation, her virtue—to save the innocent people depending on her. It won't be until later that she'll stop to learn what she's won.

Dorchester Publishing Co., Inc.
P.O. Box 6640   __5062-5
Wayne, PA 19087-8640 $5.99 US/$7.99 CAN

Please add $2.50 for shipping and handling for the first book and $.75 for each additional book. NY and PA residents, add appropriate sales tax. No cash, stamps, or CODs. Canadian orders require $5.00 for shipping and handling and must be paid in U.S. dollars. Prices and availability subject to change. **Payment must accompany all orders.**

Name: _____

Address: _____

City: _____ State:_____ Zip: _____

E-mail: _____

I have enclosed $_____ in payment for the checked book(s).

For more information on these books, check out our website at www.dorchesterpub.com.
_____ *Please send me a free catalog.*

Sinfully Delicious

Lora Kenton

A surefire recipe for true love: In a Texas whorehouse combine the two main ingredients—a New Orleans socialite and an ex-bounty hunter. Watch Kyra Lourdes and Cliff Baldwin's emotions bubble to the surface, as old feelings are stirred up in the childhood friends. Spice the mixture with danger from Kyra's vicious fiancé and threats from Cliff's disreputable past. Sweeten the dish with baking lessons that leave the pair hungry for each other. Let the heat from the couple's attraction develop into sizzling desire, until they roll together in a steamy union. Allow the lovers to bask in the afterglow of their passion. Season with tender endearments and wedding vows. The result: Home cooking that is sinfully delicious.

CHASE
THE WIND
CINDY HOLBY

From the moment he sets eyes on Faith, Ian Duncan knows she is the only girl for him.   But her unbreakable betrothal to his employer's vicious son forces him to steal his love away on the very eve of her marriage. Faith and Ian are married clandestinely, their only possessions a magnificent horse, a family Bible, a wedding-ring quilt and their unshakable belief in each other. While their homestead waits to be carved out of the Iowa wilderness, Faith presents Ian with the most precious gift of all: a son and a daughter, born of the winter snows into the spring of their lives.   The golden years are still ahead, their dream is coming true, but this is just the beginning. . . .

Dorchester Publishing Co., Inc.
P.O. Box 6640   ___5114-1
Wayne, PA 19087-8640 $5.99 US/$7.99 CAN

Knight on the
Texas Plains
LINDA BRODAY

Duel McClain is no knight in shining armor—he is a drifter who prides himself on having no responsibilities. But a poker game thrusts him into the role of father to an abandoned baby, and then a condemned woman stumbles up to his campfire. The fugitive beauty aims to keep him at shotgun's length, but obvious maternal instincts belie her fierce demeanor. And she and the baby are clearly made for each other. Worse, the innocent infant and the alleged murderess open Duel's heart, make him long for the love of a real family. And the only way to have that will be to slay the demons of the past.

*V*IOLETS ARE *B*LUE

Ronda Thompson

Although Violet Mallory was raised by the wealthy, landowning Miles Traften, nothing can remove the stain of her birthright: She is the child of no-good outlaws, and one day St. Louis society will uncover that. No, she can never be a city gal, can never truly be happy—but she can exact revenge on the man who sired and sold her.

But being a criminal is hard. Like Gregory Kline—blackmailer, thief and the handsome rogue sent to recover her—Violet longs for something better. Gregory is intent upon reforming her, and then his kiss teaches her the difference between roguishness and villainy. She sees that beauty can grow from the muddiest soil, and Violets don't always have to be blue.